N
DUGH
THE
NEVER

D1515007

ALSO BY MELISSA E. HURST

The Edge of Forever

ON THROUGH THE NEVER

MELISSA E. HURST

Sky Pony Press
New York

Sky Pony Press books may be purchased in bulk at special discounts for sales promotion, corporate gifts, fund-raising, or educational purposes. Special editions can also be created to specifications. For details, contact the Special Sales Department, Sky Pony Press, 307 West 36th Street, 11th Floor, New York, NY 10018 or info@skyhorsepublishing.com.

Sky Pony® is a registered trademark of Skyhorse Publishing, Inc.®, a Delaware corporation.

Visit our website at www.skyponypress.com.

10 9 8 7 6 5 4 3 2 1

Library of Congress Cataloging-in-Publication Data is available on file.

Cover design by Rain Saukas
Cover image credit iStockphoto

Print ISBN: 978-1-5107-0761-0
E-book ISBN: 978-1-5107-0762-7

Printed in the United States of America

For my girls.

ON THROUGH THE NEVER

1

BRIDGER
FEBRUARY 10, 2147

Purists glare at us as we walk single file to our latest assignment. When I first started training at the Academy four years ago, it bothered me that the people who deliberately reject genetic modifications are so hostile toward cadets. But these days, I'm hollow. On time trips, I constantly remind myself to keep moving, keep following orders.

Especially today.

My new team leader, Professor Dhara Kapoor, leads us through the crowded streets of downtown Austin, Texas. She's tall, with black hair pulled back in a low ponytail. It's been hard getting used to going on missions with her. Unlike my former professor, Telfair March, she puts up with no nonsense. Like now, we can barely keep up with her rapid pace. And we're not allowed to talk to anyone—not even each other.

Today's mission is to record one of the many protests that took place just before the Second Civil War erupted. Austin didn't sustain heavy damage during the war, unlike so many other major cities. And because of that, Austin is currently home to one of the largest Purist populations in the country. That leaves us with having to dodge one person after another to get to our departure coordinates. I wish we could have shifted from an area of preserved ruins, like Old Denver.

Purists are the worst to be around on these time trips. They despise anyone with genetic modifications, especially Talents. Our black-and-gray uniforms clearly mark us as cadets at The Academy for Time Travel and Research.

"You're going straight to hell. Every single one of you!" a woman shouts as we pass by.

I can't help but roll my eyes. Behind me, my friend Zed snorts and whispers, "Having to visit this state *is* hell. Right, Bridger?"

Before my life fell apart, I would have laughed at that. Texas—along with most of the southern states—is a Purist haven. Now I shake my head and keep walking. I have bigger things on my mind than Zed's immaturity. One year ago today, my father went on a classified mission and didn't come back alive.

More than anything, I want to honor Dad's legacy. That's why I'm determined to join the military, like him. The Academy finally promoted me to Level 5 of my training last month. There are no more easy missions in relatively safe time periods. Now I get to explore times of unrest, like the Second Civil War. I have to excel at everything. I have to make the Department of Temporal Affairs believe I'm a good candidate for the military division, which I'll be eligible to join at Level 6. That means keeping a clean record. That means no misbehaving on time trips. No mistakes.

Professor Kapoor leads us to a narrow alley between two brick buildings. We pass two Nulls dressed in gray jumpsuits with shields covering their faces. Nulls are criminals that have had their minds completely wiped by Mind Redeemers. Now they're nothing more than brainless servants for the government.

The Nulls are removing garbage from a business's trash compactor. I catch a whiff of the stench, but it's not too bad. Nothing like what we'll experience once we shift to 2076.

"Backs against the wall," the professor says once we reach the midpoint of the alley. She checks her DataLink and continues, "We have six minutes until departure. Please run through your final Chronoband diagnostics."

I hold my right arm up and activate the interface on the silver band encircling my wrist. It doesn't take long to check the data. Everything was programmed by techs at the Academy. Next, I adjust the comm-set so it fits snugly against my head, making sure the ear and mouthpieces are firmly in place and the lenses over my eyes are synced to the black Data-Link wrapped around my left wrist.

Then I check the mission schematics on my DataLink one more time. We're traveling to seven p.m. on November 2, 2076—just four months after President Kathleen Foster was assassinated by an ultra-conservative zealot. After Foster's death, Alan Youngblood became the new president. He was the fool whose increasingly totalitarian tactics led the country into war.

"Hey, you didn't answer me earlier. Do you want to go out with me and Elijah tonight?" Zed whispers while I'm still checking the schematics.

I ignore him. "Come on, Bridger, lighten up. You don't have to be so serious all the time."

Professor Kapoor glares at Zed. "Silence, Ramirez, unless you want to clean trash with the Nulls."

Zed makes a face at her when she turns her back. "That woman seriously needs to get—"

"Knock it off," I hiss. Zed doesn't have to finish his sentence. I know what he was going to say. Something crude, as usual.

He fixes me with a confused expression and starts to say something, but instead rolls his eyes and looks away. I'm hit with a too-familiar feeling of guilt. I hate being like this. But I need to focus on my goal. I'm already a liability in the eyes of the DTA. Ten months ago, I completely wilded out after Dad and my girlfriend Vika died within a month of each other. It was so bad that the Department of Temporal Affairs had to step in. Can't have an unstable Time Bender roaming around, right?

I'm okay now, but I'll have to work twice as hard as everyone else to be able to join the military. Zed doesn't understand the kind of pressure I feel. He plans to become an artifact retrieval expert, like his parents.

At least Elijah understands. He wants to join the military too. I really wish he was with us now, but when Elijah was promoted to Level 5, he was assigned to Professor Holland's team. He's made new friends and started spending more time with them. I'm not surprised.

I'm still friends with Zed and Elijah. We hang out together sometimes, and we're still roommates. It's just, everything is different now. They were both promoted months before I was. And they got into a lot of trouble trying to cover for me when I wilded out last year. I don't want to hurt them any more than I already have.

What I wouldn't give for things to go back to the way they used to be.

"All right, cadets, it's time. Initiate cloaking devices and prepare to engage your Chronobands," Professor Kapoor says.

I press the gold button on the collar of my uniform, which activates my cloak. The rest of the team does the same. I glance up in time to see an overweight Purist standing at the entrance to alley watching us. Sometimes Purists will do that, if they're not hurling insults. At least they know not to interfere with our missions. That's against the law.

As we vanish, the Purist shakes his head, a look of disgust etched across his face. He might be able to see the ripples in the air that show where we're standing, if he looks hard enough. We can still see each other through our comm-set lenses.

The professor heads to the front of the line and joins us standing along the wall. She then says, "Does everyone have the date and time in their minds? Ready on my mark."

I visualize our destination date like a giant calendar. My fingers hover over the Chronoband's activation button. My breathing is even. Calm. The feeling of being utterly alone, as if I'm the only person in existence, used to be the worst part of entering the Void. But that no longer bothers me. Not after all I've been through.

"Five. Four. Three. Two. One. Go!"

The all-consuming blackness engulfs me the instant my fingers hit the switch. I hold my breath and tell myself it won't last forever. The unbearable sense of isolation will pass.

I'm blinded for the moment after we emerge from the Void. After a few seconds, everything comes into focus. Colors sharpen. Sounds become clearer. I'm hit with the smell of rotting garbage coming from a dumpster that now sits near the end of the alley.

Professor Kapoor marches past us, waving her hand. "Let's go, cadets. We have exactly ten minutes to get into position. I do *not* want the other teams beating us this time."

Our team is one of four Level 5 groups at the Academy. We traveled together by hypersonic plane from New Denver, but separated once we reached downtown Austin. Each team has been assigned to a different area to record the protest.

I glance back at Zed, but he just gives me a frosty stare. I almost apologize to him for being a jerk earlier. But maybe it's better, right now, to keep to myself.

We emerge from the alley to a view that's very different from the one we left in 2147. It's dark now, and streetlights provide the only illumination. Several storefronts have boarded-up windows. Graffiti is sprayed across them, almost all of it the same symbol: a Y, representing the totalitarian President Youngblood's initial, is inside a circle, and it's painted over with a giant X—the sign of the government's opponents. I can't help but admire the symbol. The Y and circle looks like a peace sign that's been crossed out. And then I think about how stupid many people living in this time were—the ones who supported the government's actions. They nearly destroyed the country through blind hatred and corruption.

The streets are nearly deserted as we head to our assigned coordinates. Only a few soldiers dressed in fatigues and riot gear patrol our immediate area. That number greatly increases as we near our destination—the Texas State Capitol.

Thousands of ghosts—people who lived in the past—have gathered on the grounds to protest the nationwide curfew that President Youngblood implemented a few weeks before this date. The curfew was an attempt to curtail widespread vandalism and looting in response to food rationing and massive shortages of the medicine needed to combat a new disease that was sweeping the nation. This was before genetic modifications were developed, so a lot of people died from the disease. Most everybody belonging to the opposing political parties thought President Youngblood was lying about the severity of the shortage and was hoarding food and medicine for his supporters. It turns out he wasn't exactly lying, but he *was* giving more supplies to those loyal to him than to the rest of the country.

We approach the capitol from the southern side. Already the grounds surrounding the massive building are packed with people. Chants fill the air, and large signs are held high, all denouncing Youngblood and his policies. It's loud, but I know the current chaos is nothing compared to what's about to happen.

Professor Kapoor stops in a relatively clear area before we reach the protestors to give her final instructions. Several protestors are talking nearby, but they won't hear what we say. Our cloaks mask any sounds we make.

"It's time to separate and report to your assigned positions. And of course, I'll be around to observe each one of you," Professor Kapoor says.

Immediately, each cadet moves closer to his or her partner. I'm with Zed this time.

"Remember, while you should strive to obtain the best footage possible, your safety is of utmost importance." The professor and several cadets turn to look at me. They're remembering Vika's death last year, which happened while we were partnered on a time trip. I swallow past the lump in my throat and look away. The DTA cleared me of any wrongdoing, but I still feel responsible.

After we're dismissed, Zed and I head toward our assigned area on the outer right side of the Great Walk. I catch him leering at some girls, and I grind my teeth. Some things never change with him.

Once we slip into the crowd, it's impossible to avoid touching ghosts. Thousands of them are pressed together. The sour smell of sweat is overpowering. Breathing through my mouth helps, but mostly I suppress my revulsion; I've learned to ignore it.

Zed's voice comes through my earpiece. "There's an Unknown approximately thirty-four feet ahead."

I scan ahead of us to locate the Unknown. The outline of a flashing white body appears on my lens. "Copy that," I reply as I sweep the area surrounding us. "I don't see any more right now. Let's proceed."

Unknowns are Time Benders who aren't using the same cloaking frequency as us. They could be from our past or our future. The team leaders already warned us to expect to see some today. In 2123, the DTA sent a military team here to record the worst of the violence, and to identify the specific individuals responsible.

Zed and I, along with the other cadets, keep to the fringes of the crowd. We're not supposed to venture too close to the capitol building. Most of the ghosts who will be injured will be in that area. During a previous mission, Time Benders discovered that several pro-Youngblood soldiers "accidentally" mixed a nasty, paralytic gas with the standard Devil's Breath, a form of tear gas that also smells worse than a skunk. A lot of people had adverse reactions to the paralytic gas and died. Our orders are to clear out before things turn ugly, which means we have exactly thirty-three minutes to work. Professor Kapoor observes Zed and me for eight minutes before moving on to the next pair of cadets.

After she leaves, Zed and I split up to record more footage. We're careful to stay within sight of each other. As I roam through the crowd in our assigned area, I find myself feeling sorry for some of these ghosts. The ones who are too thin from malnourishment. The ones who are too weak to stand, and are simply sitting in quiet protest. I'm also shocked at how many are here with their children. The kids' fearful faces peer out from behind their parents' legs as they cling to them. I can't help but wonder if any of the kids I'm recording now will be among the nine hundred and seventy-seven casualties.

My DataLink chimes. I've been so engrossed with recording that I didn't realize how much time had passed. We have five minutes to leave. "Ready to go?" I ask Zed through my mouthpiece.

"That would be a definitive yes. I'm starting to get nervous," he replies.

I do a quick final sweep. The tension of the crowd has been intensifying steadily, and in the past few minutes it's started to boil over. People are taunting the military and police officers. I see one officer pointing his weapon at a civilian.

Idiots, all of them.

I start to follow Zed as he heads back to where we're supposed to meet Professor Kapoor, but I spot a flash of white to my right. An Unknown is standing near the Confederate Soldiers Monument. I wonder what's going on over there.

A ghost with strawberry blond hair climbs up on the monument. The Unknown appears to be focused on her. I find myself transfixed. She screams something, then reaches into her coat pocket. She takes out a small object and lifts her arm as if she's going to throw it.

A loud shot fires, and I watch in horror as a small circle appears in the woman's forehead and a trickle of blood seeps out. She falls into the crowd.

Times slows to a crawl, and I can't breathe. I get this sudden image of Vika in my mind. A similar wound piercing her forehead. Her body lying in a pool of blood on grass. I shake my head. That's not right. That's not how Vika died. She was trampled by ghosts at the Foster Assassination.

Then I'm jolted back by screams all around me. I'm shoved hard. More gunshots are fired.

I can barely make out Zed yelling, "Bridger! Where are you?"

I can't respond. It seems like time has slowed as I push through the frantic crowd. I've got to get out of here, now. The officers have already fired their guns, and I know what's next: protestors will produce weapons of their own, and the military will quickly resort to gassing everyone.

"Ramirez and Creed, what is going on?" Professor Kapoor's voice blasts through my earpiece.

"Nothing," I manage to reply while trying to get my breathing under control. "I'm almost out."

It's a relief when I burst out of the crowd. My legs feel as if they could give out at any moment, but I force myself to keep going. Behind me, the shouts and screams intensify. I don't look back. I can't let anyone see evidence of weakness. I need to be strong.

When I catch up to Zed, he waits just long enough for me to disengage my comm-set before getting in my face. "What the hell happened back there?"

I take a step back and shrug. "I don't know what you're talking about."

"Right. You look like a ghost, yourself. Something got to you."

By that time, we've reached Professor Kapoor and the others waiting at our rendezvous point by a large tree. Her arms are crossed and she looks pissed. "I'm so happy you two finally showed up," she says in a sarcastic voice.

Turning to the rest of the group, she barks, "Head out, cadets. Single file. And try to keep up." She gives me a pointed stare before setting off, and says, "I'll deal with you later."

Twenty minutes later, we're back in 2147.

Everyone's quiet as we follow Professor Kapoor back to the Academy's hypersonic plane. I tell myself I'm okay. That I did a good job. But I can't get that image of Vika out of my head. Why did I see something that never happened? It doesn't make sense.

Along the way, we're the brunt of even more taunts from Purists; the closer we get to the terminal, the more hostile they become. Some throw trash at us. A few surge forward, yelling insults and acting like they want to intercept us. Other Purists hold them back. Despite the anger, they don't want to break the law.

It's eerie how much this reminds me of the scene we just left in the past.

This is not good.

2

My new apartment at The Academy for Time Travel and Research isn't what I expected. It's not as large as my quarters back at the DTA's Chicago facilities, and nowhere near as nice. I'd thought that my apartment here would be the same, but at least I don't have to live *there* anymore. Anything is better than that place.

I look around, taking in the almost barren space. The walls are white, and the tiled floor is the color of sand. There's a tiny living area with a gray couch, a table along the right wall, and a TeleNet screen mounted over it.

On the far side of the room, there are three doorways that I assume lead to the bedrooms. I glance back at the officer who has been my unofficial guardian/instructor/source-of-all-headaches, Lieutenant Ellen Rivera. "Which one is mine?"

"The one on the left." She pauses to read something on her DataLink, then says, "Tara Martinez will be your roommate. She was brought in a few days ago, and the report says she took the one on the right. The central bedroom will remain empty." Before I can ask why, Rivera continues, "Cadet Martinez is on a time trip at the moment, but you'll meet her later today."

I get a jittery feeling in my stomach. Lieutenant Rivera never said that I would have to share the apartment with anyone. What if my new roommate hates me? What if I hate her? More negative thoughts start to surface, but I take a breath and remind myself once again that the most important thing is that I've finally made it out of Chicago. My new roommate could be the spawn of Satan, but there's nothing I can do about that right now.

Squaring my shoulders, I cross the short distance to my door and enter what will be my bedroom for the next two or three years. It's even smaller than the living area. There's only enough room for a narrow bed and dresser set, and a small black desk with a chair. I don't care, though, because it's mine. In this apartment, I'll never have to deal with Rivera. Tossing my portacase and coat on the desk, I sink onto the bed and let out a sigh—it's surprisingly comfortable. Plus, living here means having a little more freedom that I did in Chicago. That's a win.

On the flight to New Denver, Lieutenant Rivera went on and on about how fortunate I am that the DTA was looking out for my best interests by allowing me to enroll at The Academy for Time Travel and Research now. How I should be grateful that they've been tutoring me in private for the last ten months, giving me the chance to adjust to being in civilized society. And how I should be honored that they took such good care of me—never mind that I was only allowed to see my mother twice a month.

Right. And I'm a princess who was simply swept away by a misguided madman, rather than a girl who was abducted by her psychotic father. And to make it even better, said father abandoned me shortly after kidnapping me, so I grew up not even knowing I was a Talent.

Just freaking great.

"So, what do you think? Don't you just love it?" Lieutenant Rivera asks. She's now standing in the doorway to my quarters, her navy-and-red uniform a vivid contrast to the stark white room. She raises her eyebrows like she does when she's sure I'll just go along with whatever she wants, then smoothes her hands across her hair. I wonder why she even bothers doing that. Her dark brown hair is pulled back in a bun so severe it's almost giving *me* a headache.

"It's nice. But I thought I was supposed to have my own quarters."

"Well, yes, the Academy does reserve a few suites for special requests." My mouth drops open, but before I can ask what she means by that, she continues. "But in your case, Chancellor Tyson felt it would be better if you had a student mentor. Someone to help make your transition smoother."

I wonder if that's the only reason. I mean, here I am. Surely there are more kids out there like me, kids who have to hide that they are Dual Talents.

"This really is lovely. You are *so* lucky to have just one roommate." Lieutenant Rivera grins and strides into the room, looking around like she's in the midst of a luxurious suite instead of a glorified closet. "You know, I had to share my quarters with two roommates when I was here. It was just awful!" Her overly made-up face takes on an almost tragic expression, as if the memory is too terrible for her to tolerate.

I stifle a snort. What's really lucky is that I won't have to listen to her anymore. Out of the three private instructors I had in Chicago, Rivera is my least favorite. She's too perky, and she always talks to me like I'm a toddler. *You're doing great, Alora! I want you to shift one more time for me . . . you can do it!* I mean, who can be like that all the time?

The truth is, I'm terrified of sharing this apartment with a stranger. Sure, I've been by myself for the last ten months and I get lonely, but I'd rather stay this way than have to dodge a million questions from a roommate. Ever since I found out I was finally going to the Academy, I've been wondering how I'll deal with constantly being around people I don't know. And now I'm being forced to live with one of them. I wonder if she would rather have stayed with her former roommates. I mean, what if they were really good friends and now she has to look after me? I know I would hate having to be put in that position. What if she resents me already?

A loud chime punctures the silence. Lieutenant Rivera checks her DataLink and says, "I have a call I need to take. I'll be right back." Then she steps back into the living area.

I stand and walk over to the small window next to the bed. Since I'm on the fourth floor of Watson Hall, the residence for female cadets, I have a good view of the area. The Rocky Mountains look majestic in the distance, and a few cadets are standing around the large green space between the buildings, all dressed in black-and-gray uniforms. I glance down at my plain, light-blue jumpsuit. I'm so sick of wearing jumpsuits. Blue, green, and tan—that's all I was given to wear in Chicago. You would think they would let me wear regular clothing, or at least a cadet uniform, but no. I can't wait until I can finally wear normal clothes again.

I just hope I'll like it here at the Academy. I hope I can find a way to fit in.

Since I was rescued last year, I've only been allowed to be around a few adults. I thought it was weird and unnecessary that the DTA insisted on keeping me isolated in Chicago, but they claimed that my unusual upbringing warranted limiting my exposure to the outside world so I could focus on learning everything that I'd missed while growing up in backwoods Purist country.

Anyway, the only people in my life for the last ten months have been the adults assigned to teach me about what's going on in the world, and the ones who helped me develop my ability to bend time and space. They were also the ones who taught me to conceal the fact that I'm a Dual Talent. Apparently, Dual Talents are super rare, which is why they took it upon themselves to teach me in the first place. I'm never supposed to talk to anyone about my abilities, except for professors who already know the truth about me. The DTA says that there are some people who might want to harm me because they fear my abilities. Even other countries that are trying to improve their time-bending organizations might want to capture me and study my powers. So yay—I'm not only a freak, but a freak who could be kidnapped again.

Lucky, indeed.

Sometimes I wish I could remember what my life was like before. The DTA said when I was recovered last year, I didn't know much about the outside world. They said my childhood had been traumatic, since I'd been raised by an abusive woman in a tiny Purist-controlled town in Georgia.

I can still remember little things. I lived in a large, really old house. I remember drawing, sitting by a lazy river, and running through a wooded area. And I even remember what the woman looked like. She had curly, light-brown hair and a warm smile that you wouldn't expect from such a sadistic person. But they erased everything else. They said I'd be better off without those memories. I'd be a blank slate, able to start fresh with a new life.

So why does that feel so false?

Lieutenant Rivera sweeps back in my room. "Alora, I know you'd like to settle in, but Chancellor Tyson has asked me to give you a quick tour of the Academy. Then we're to meet him at his office."

I close my eyes. Is she kidding me? I thought she would be going right back to Chicago after she dropped me off. What I really want to do is see if my mom is going to visit me today. Despite the fact that we haven't been given much opportunity to really get to know each other again, I look forward to her visits. And it's been two weeks since I last saw her.

"Oh, my poor girl, I know you're tired, but this won't take too long. I promise!" Lieutenant Rivera's smile takes on a wicked glint, as if she knows how much I don't want to go with her.

An hour later, after dragging me all over the campus, Lieutenant Rivera takes me to the Academy's main building. We use the rear entrance, but I can still hear the Purists who were protesting in front of the building when we arrived earlier today. The lieutenant says a group is always at the school, but they're restricted to one area. There were some protestors back in Chicago, but I'm surprised at how many more there are here. Lieutenant Rivera told me they consider the Academy evil since they train young people to "tamper with the laws of nature."

Once we're finished with a whirlwind tour of the medical offices, the museum, and the research facilities within the main building, Lieutenant Rivera finally leads me down a long hallway on the first floor, where we check in with a turquoise-blue-haired receptionist.

Fixing us with a sour stare, the receptionist says, "Chancellor Tyson's office hours were over at oh-five-hundred hours. That was twenty minutes ago, so he's been waiting on you for *quite* a while. You need to see him *immediately.*"

I wonder if the chancellor is as irritated with us as the receptionist seems to be.

The black door behind the receptionist's desk slides open to reveal a lavish office. It has rich burgundy carpet that cushions my feet, the walls are covered with paintings that I'm sure are worth a fortune, and it features an antique desk and chairs. Artifacts are nestled in clear display cases all around the room.

A tall man wearing a black uniform with gold stripes down the sleeves stands behind the desk. Gray streaks his black hair, and only a few wrinkles crease his dark skin. He smiles and says, "Welcome to New Denver, Alora. I'm so pleased that you will be attending classes at The Academy for Time Travel and Research."

And suddenly I get this weird fluttery feeling in my stomach. I'm standing in front of a man I've seen dozens of times over DataNet feeds. He's the head of the Academy and a very high-ranking official with the DTA. I've even seen him on the TeleNet at conferences with the North American Federation's president. The power that comes with that kind of authority radiates off him like heat from a fire. "Thank you, sir," I reply, forcing false happiness into my voice. "I'm glad to be here."

"Ah, I see that you still have a bit of that accent," he says, reminding me of where I grew up. The Mind Redeemers can't erase speech patterns, but I've been working hard to make it less noticeable.

The chancellor walks around his desk and places his hand on my shoulder. I fight the instinct to flinch because he's making me so nervous.

"I hope your accommodations are to your liking. If there is anything you need, don't be afraid to ask. I want your transition to be as smooth as possible. Do you have any questions?"

I pause for a second. Sure, he asked if I have any questions, but I don't want to seem so pushy, not when I've only just arrived. "Yes, sir. When will I be able to see my mom?"

"We haven't heard from her yet, but I'm sure she will be in contact soon."

I let out a small sigh before I can stop myself. "Oh, okay."

Chancellor Tyson pats my shoulder again. "Don't worry. I'm sure she will be in touch sometime today. She does have her duties at work." He exchanges a glance with Lieutenant Rivera and clasps his hands. "Now, since that's settled, I thought I'd see firsthand what you've learned so far."

Alarmed, I glance at Lieutenant Rivera. Her eyes widen slightly, but she keeps that perfectly plastic smile glued on. "And what do you have in mind, sir?" she asks.

"I have a little test for Miss Mason," he replies.

It's weird hearing him refer to my last name as Mason. The DTA took my horrible memories, but I still know what my identity used to be. In my former life, I went by Walker, my father's last name. Even though the government allowed the DTA to take physical custody of me, my mom had final say over what name I was going to go by, so now I have her last name.

But then what he said hits me. He wants to test me. Right here, right now. I wasn't prepared for that. My heart begins to race. My mind starts racing with memories of all the ridiculous things my tutors had me do back in Chicago: Shift to the kitchen to fetch a drink for them. Shift while cloaked to listen in on conversations. Shift back in time to follow officers around and spy on them. All things that I absolutely hated doing, but that they insisted I needed to know how to do.

Well, I don't want to have to do anything like that today. I'm exhausted, and I want to be anywhere but here. I think longingly of my new room, with the lovely view from the window.

And suddenly I'm there.

Oh. My. God. I'm not supposed to do that. I've been instructed again and again never to shift without prior approval. I break out in a cold sweat. I illegally shifted right in front of the head of the Academy.

Kill me now.

I take several deep breaths. Okay, I can do this. I can fix it. All I need to do is shift back to Chancellor Tyson's office. I squeeze my eyes shut.

And nothing.

I look down at the sand-colored floor and remember what my instructors told me. It's harder for Space Benders to use their gifts when they're under stress. The trick is to focus on specific details of your intended destination. I close my eyes again and picture Chancellor Tyson's office. The burgundy carpet and portrait-lined walls.

And I'm there again. I let out a relieved sigh.

Harsh voices fill the air. But when the chancellor and Rivera see me appear, they greet me with silence.

Lieutenant Rivera is the first to speak. "Where did you go?"

I try to swallow, but my mouth is too dry. "I . . . I just went to my quarters. I didn't mean to do it. I swear!"

I want to hide under a table or something, but I make myself look at Chancellor Tyson. Instead of looking furious, he seems somewhat amused.

"I must say, you do know how to make a spectacular entrance."

That was not what I was expecting, so I offer a tentative smile. "I'm really sorry, sir. I've never done that before. I guess I'm overwhelmed. It's been a long day."

Chancellor Tyson glances at Lieutenant Rivera, and she nods. "That is true," she says. "And Alora has been an exceptional pupil so far. I really think she needs to avoid stress for a few days."

Before I can stop myself, I blurt out, "Maybe I can just go home with my mom for the weekend."

That's the one thing I've wanted most since I was first taken to Chicago, but all the officials felt I needed to get a handle on my abilities before spending time outside of their facility. They said I needed to learn what was going on in the world and to get acquainted with modern technology before I'd be safe in an uncontrolled environment—even with my own mother. I thought for a while that she would fight them—that she would force them to let me go home with her at least some of the time—but she never did.

Chancellor Tyson shakes his head. "I don't think that would be wise."

I'm stunned when Lieutenant Rivera responds, "Respectfully, Doran, I disagree. She's in a high-risk, transitional period. It might be good to allow her time to bond with her mother before she starts classes. With all she has to do to catch up to the cadets her age, she's not going to get many breaks."

After what seems like an eternity, Chancellor Tyson folds his arms across his chest. "I suppose it won't hurt to let her go. But perhaps it would be a good idea to have her wear an Inhibitor."

Rivera smiles. "That won't be a problem."

Unfortunately, I don't agree. I had to wear an Inhibitor a lot in the first few months after I was rescued, and while it didn't hurt me, it made me feel like a criminal.

Before I can object, the chancellor's office door opens and the receptionist enters, his face ashen.

"What is it now?" Chancellor Tyson snaps.

"I'm sorry, sir. We have a problem."

3

BRIDGER
FEBRUARY 10, 2147

Once we're aboard the hypersonic plane and we've turned in our comm-sets and Chronobands, everyone starts talking in frantic tones. Even the four professors are huddled together in the front.

I look through the already crowded plane for Elijah. It's easy to spot him—he's the tallest, and most muscular, black cadet in our group. Elijah and his partner, Tara Martinez, are sitting close to each other, whispering. They've saved two spots for Zed and me, and as soon as we sit in the plush green seats, Elijah leans forward and asks, "Did the Purists seem like they wanted to attack you on the way back here?"

"Yeah. It was almost like we were still at that protest in '76, minus the hideous clothing," Zed says. "What do you think happened?"

Around us, a lot of the cadets are checking the DataNet feed, and several gasp. I activate my DataLink and do a quick scan through the holographic menu that hovers over it. Instantly I see what's pissed off the Purists. The feds have passed the Responsible Citizen Act—a new law that basically punishes Purists for being "a drain on society."

"Damn," Zed drawls out. I glance up to find that he's checking the DataNet feed, too.

"Well, that explains everything," Tara says. She runs her hands over her black curls, then down the sides of her face. "Can you imagine what it'll be like back at the Academy?" She groans. "You guys, I forgot my new roommate is supposed to arrive today. They couldn't have picked a worse day to pass this stupid law. I bet she is wilding out right now."

There are almost always a dozen or so Purists protesting outside the main building at the Academy, but I'm willing to bet that number is going to be way bigger today. I sigh heavily and scroll through the feed some more. Across the whole North American Federation, Purists have taken to the streets. I find out that several particularly nasty demonstrations are taking place outside the DTA headquarters in Chicago, New York, Mexico City, Ottawa, and, of course, New Denver. What I wouldn't give to be a Space Bender right now so I could just shift straight to my quarters instead of going through them.

"I don't like this. Not at all," Elijah says, looking up from his Data-Link. "I get why they're mad and all that, but do they really think these protests are going to accomplish anything?"

I think back to the protest we just witnessed in 2076 and suppress a shudder. What I just saw on the DataNet was like an eerie echo of things that happened prior to the Second Civil War.

"I don't feel sorry for them one bit. It's their own fault for refusing modifications. They're furing crazy *not* to have them," Zed says.

Elijah shrugs. "That's true, man, but to punish them for that choice? That's not fair either."

"Oh, come on! You can't really feel sorry for them. They're insane!" Zed snaps, then looks at me. "Don't you agree, Bridger?"

I don't say anything for a moment. I'm no fan of Purists. I hate their hostility toward Gen Mods. And it doesn't make sense that they choose to live without genetic modifications. They could enjoy nearly perfect health. The ability to heal rapidly, greater intelligence, and increased memory. The ability to withstand harsh environments and survive without food for longer periods of time. Things like that. The Purists' logic states that it's fundamentally wrong to tamper with humanity's natural abilities.

But on the other hand, what were the politicians thinking? You don't just hit a hornet's nest and expect not to be stung.

Before I can reply, Professor Kapoor yells, "Attention cadets!" We fall silent immediately. "Please strap in and prepare for takeoff."

After we've latched our harnesses into place, Zed asks me again, "So? What do you think about all this?"

"It doesn't really matter what I think," I say. "What matters is not getting caught up in this mess. Nothing good can come out of it."

Elijah slaps me on the knee. "Man, that's the most sense you've made in a long time."

I get this flash of irritation. What's that supposed to mean? I know we haven't been as close as before, but nothing I've done lately has been stupid. I've followed the rules. I'm taking my meds every day. I'm doing everything I can to be a model cadet. How could that not make sense?

The plane begins to take flight. As we soar into the air and circle the city, I glance down at the ground below. It looks so peaceful and calm. So unlike the chaos we witnessed earlier.

Then I catch sight of the Texas State Capitol. There's a large crowd gathering on the green area surrounding the building.

Things are about to get ugly again.

A little while later, we land in New Denver, then take a transport shuttle back to the Academy. As soon as we're back in the air, Professor Holland gets up. His head nearly brushes the top of the shuttle, so when he stands, everybody notices.

"Attention cadets," he begins in his deep voice. "We've been informed that, due to a larger than normal crowd of protestors at the Academy, you're to disembark from the shuttle and stay with your team leader. We will escort you around the back of the main building and in through the med facilities."

It's so quiet that I swear I can hear my own heartbeat. A cadet near the front of the shuttle raises his hand.

"Yes?" the professor asks.

"Sir, how bad is it?" he asks. He sounds worried. Just like everyone else.

Professor Holland glances back at the other team leaders, and Professor Kapoor nods slightly.

He clears his throat before continuing, "I'm not going to lie; it's intense right now. But you should be perfectly safe. Chancellor Tyson has arranged for extra security. You shouldn't have to face much more than a lot of extra noise."

"Will we be able to go home this weekend?" Tara asks.

"At this time, I'm not positive. I'll let you know as soon as I find out. Now, are there any more questions?"

Nobody says anything. Out the front window, we've all spotted the massive Academy for Time Travel and Research main building. Beyond it are the Rockies. It all looks deceptively calm and normal.

And then we see the crowd. Holy fure, it's huge. It looks like several hundred Purists, at least, are waiting for us.

This is not going to be fun.

Once the shuttle has landed, the first thing we hear is what sounds like a dull roar. Definitely not good. If the Purists are that loud, they must have worked themselves up into a furious mob.

Professor Holland speaks again. "I've just received word that we will be escorted into the main building by DTA soldiers."

I can't help but notice how pale he looks. Almost everybody looks sick and scared. Except for Zed—he is fired up.

"I bet I could kick any of those Purists' asses," he says with a sneer.

"Oh, grow up, Zed," Tara snaps. "I'd like to see you try to take on all of them."

I feel like all my energy has suddenly evaporated, hearing Tara say that. It's so similar to something Vika would have said to Zed. I remember how Vika called him out on whistling at some ghosts when we traveled back in time to record President Foster's assassination last year. The very day that she died.

My stomach sinks, remembering. I shouldn't have left her alone that day. I should have stayed with her.

After a few minutes, the professors stand. Each one summons their assigned cadets and they exit the shuttle together. I raise my eyebrows a bit as I see Elijah take Tara's hand as she leans in closer to him. I wonder if they're dating now. He never said anything to me.

But then I turn my attention back to the window and my palms begin to sweat. The first team is surrounded by four soldiers dressed in dark-gray uniforms. Space Benders. They quickly march toward the grassy area behind the main building, instead of going in the front entrance like we usually do.

Finally, Professor Kapoor says, "My team, let's go."

My legs feel weak when I stand. I tell myself to man up. We have armed escorts. Nothing will happen to us.

But the instant we step off the shuttle, it's clear how bad the situation is. The transport lot is adjacent to the main building, so we have a close-up view of the protestors. This gathering is way smaller than the protest in 2076, but the noise level is still intense. These Purists are seriously unhappy. Dad used to say that angry people made rash decisions—decisions that could harm other people.

Another thing we notice is the string of soldiers standing between the protestors and the campus, all wearing riot gear and carrying weapons. My mouth goes desert dry. This isn't right. We're supposed to travel to the past to witness stuff like this. We shouldn't be living it.

Our escorts surround us, and we begin the trek to the back side of the building. My heart thuds as fast as my footsteps. Zed mutters something under his breath. I glance around. Normally at this time of the day, there would be cadets all over the campus. Hanging out with their friends. But nobody is outside now.

As we round the corner of the building, we hear a familiar noise—like a gunshot.

"Run!" one of the soldiers yells.

Somebody screams. I don't know who. It could have been another cadet. It could have been me. All I can do is move. One foot in front of another. Keep moving. Keep running.

Once we're inside the building, I almost collapse. It's too hot in here. Too many people pressed against me. Too hard to breathe.

Then I see her. Vika. Standing with a dark-haired woman on the other side of the lobby. No, it can't be her. Not here. She's dead. I see that image of her again, the one where she's lying on a grassy ground with a gunshot wound in her forehead.

Oh no. No. No. No. I can't be losing my mind again. I gasp for air.

Vaguely, I hear Zed yelling for Professor Kapoor. Then there's a slight sting at my neck. Then nothing.

4

"Did you hear that?" I ask, my head snapping to the left, where Lieutenant Rivera is standing. She barely nods. For once, she's speechless. I don't blame her; I can't believe what I'm witnessing myself.

After Chancellor Tyson was informed about the deteriorating situation outside, he ordered the Academy to lock down. Now we're waiting in the lobby of the Academy's main building, along with dozens of other people—including a team of cadets that just returned from a time trip—watching the protest taking place through the outer glass wall. Nobody is talking or moving because it sounds like a gun was just fired outside.

The scene in front of me looks like something out of the many Sims I've experienced over the past several months, while learning about the recent history of the North American Federation. Protestors screaming, some openly attacking the soldiers assigned to keep the peace. And in return, a few soldiers have started tossing canisters into the crowd. Soon a thick fog encases everyone, making it more difficult to see them and forcing them to flee the noxious fumes. The soldiers, all wearing masks, move through the crowd to arrest anyone not dispersing.

I feel like I could puke. This shouldn't be happening. Not in the present. I worry about protestors somehow getting in here, or a stray bullet piercing the glass, but I remember how Lieutenant Rivera said on my tour earlier that the glass in all DTA buildings is bulletproof. Nothing can destroy it, short of an explosion.

Someone touches my right shoulder. I recoil from the contact and pivot around to find a dark-haired woman in an emerald green and khaki uniform standing behind me. It's my mother. I'm so shocked that I can't speak.

Mom inhales sharply and says in a wavering voice, "Oh sweet heavens, you're safe. I thought you had been caught up in one of the protests somewhere." She folds me into a warm hug that envelops me with a familiar scent—lavender.

I want to feel safe in her arms, want to pretend I'm a little girl again and she can make everything better. But that's just a fairy tale for me. I pull away from her, a frown tugging my lips down. "Where have you been? I arrived hours ago."

A sour look crosses Mom's face. "I've been here for several hours already. I took off work early because I knew you were arriving today. The chancellor let me wait in a private waiting room, so I could be more comfortable until you arrived. I had no idea you were already here."

I whirl around to face Lieutenant Rivera. "Did you know my mom was being kept waiting?"

She shakes her head, eyes wide. "I promise, I didn't know. I apologize, Ms. Mason."

"Well, at least I'm with my daughter now," Mom replies, putting an arm around me again.

"When do you think we'll be able to leave?" I ask Lieutenant Rivera.

Glancing back to the protestors in front of the building, the lieutenant slowly shakes her head. "I don't know. Probably not anytime soon." Her eyes flick momentarily to me. "I can't believe how quickly things have spiraled of control. It was just a few hours ago that I heard that the RCA had been approved—and now this."

"I can believe it," Mom says. "Humanity will always make the same mistakes. You would think that being able to travel to the past and learn from it would cure of us of that, but it hasn't."

"Oh, absolutely. Purists haven't learned anything," Rivera says. She continues to rant about how they're going to destroy the country again if the government doesn't do something about them. I want to ask what the RCA is, and why it's ignited so much anger among the Purists in such a short time, but I can't get a word in. That's so typical of her. When she thinks she's right, there is no shutting her up.

I take a few steps away from Mom and Rivera, activate my DataLink, and search for information about the RCA, promptly finding out more than I want to know. Because of the RCA, Purists will now have to pay higher taxes, have higher medical costs, and be charged more for goods and services. All because they're now considered a "drain on society." Wow, talk about discrimination. Honestly, I really don't blame the Purists for being so pissed.

It takes the sound of shouting behind us to silence Lieutenant Rivera. I whirl around. On the other side of the lobby, several people are kneeling, staring down at someone sprawled out on the floor. I stand on my tiptoes to get a better view. And since I'm cursed with being so short, I can't see what's going on. My first thought is that someone was injured outside—maybe even shot.

"I'll find out what's going on," the lieutenant says before she slips through the crowd in direction of the injured person. I watch her and try to tune out the anxious chatter that's now sweeping the area.

Mom, still close to me, wraps her fingers around my right hand and squeezes gently. "It'll be okay. I'm sure it's nothing major. Lots of people panic when there's a stressful situation."

While I'm happy to be with Mom, what I really want right now is to be alone. That's always been my default when I'm under stress. I can remember running through a densely packed forest in my old life, and how it made me feel less tense. I wonder where I can go here to get the same sense of freedom. The temptation to shift somewhere private is overwhelming, but I force myself to forget about it. At least Chancellor Tyson forgot to shackle me with an Inhibitor once the receptionist told him about the escalating tensions outside.

A few minutes later, Lieutenant Rivera returns, appearing a bit more animated that she was before. "Turns out it's nothing. One of the cadets couldn't handle all the excitement and had a panic attack. His professor administered a large dose of Calmer."

"Calmer shouldn't make someone completely pass out," Mom replies, frowning.

And I want to add that there's nothing exciting about all of this. Nothing at all.

"Maybe so, but under the circumstances I'd rather have him unconscious than creating havoc in here. Wouldn't you agree?" she asks.

"I suppose so," Mom says with a heavy sigh.

Mom and Rivera might think that's okay, but I don't. That could have easily been me, a few months ago. I had my fair share of Calmer forced on me when I was first rescued, and I didn't like it. Even now, I have to take it occasionally. Thankfully that doesn't happen often. Though I wonder if a dose would help me right now. Maybe going zombie for a little while would make all of this a little more bearable.

A doc from the med facilities upstairs arrives. She directs two medics to pick up the cadet and place him on a stretcher. They begin pushing their way through the crowd, heading to the elevators next to us.

When they reach us, I get a good look at the boy and get a weird, fluttery sensation in my stomach, almost like déjà vu. I've never seen him before, but I feel like I should know him. He has dark brown hair and his skin is almost as pale as mine. I wonder what color his eyes are and suddenly think brown. They're brown.

"Mom, do you know him?" I ask after the medics step into the nearest elevator and the door slides shut.

"No," she says in a tight voice. "I've never seen him before."

Two hours later, Mom and I finally board one of the last shuttles scheduled to transport people from the Academy to New Denver. I search the small interior and spot two empty seats near the back. It's filled with both adults and cadets. One of them, a girl with curly black hair and brown skin, stares at me in surprise. I quickly look away and focus on getting to my seat.

Chancellor Tyson wouldn't let any cadets leave without one of their parents or guardians to accompany them. A lot of cadets were furious that they had to wait at the Academy until someone came for them.

Once the protestors had been cleared out, Chancellor Tyson ended the lockdown. I was thrilled to finally get away from Lieutenant Rivera, but I admit that leaving the safety of the main building was terrifying. As I headed to my quarters to retrieve my portacase and coat, I kept thinking, what if some protestors were hiding in the shadows, waiting to ambush us? Which was ridiculous because the soldiers had searched the campus before we were allowed to leave.

Once we're finally seated and the shuttle is in the air, I look around again. Everyone on the shuttle is subdued, even Mom. She's scrolling through the news feed on her DataLink, like most everyone else around us. Suddenly she frowns.

"What's wrong?" I ask.

"The governor just announced a statewide curfew. We have to be home by eleven o'clock." She pauses and pats my hand. "Are you okay?"

"Yeah, I just can't believe this is happening."

"Me either, sweetheart. Me either."

I check the time on my DataLink. It's a little after nine-thirty right now. Mom told me earlier that the ride to New Denver only takes fifteen minutes and her apartment is a few blocks from the terminal, so we should have more than enough time to get there. Still, I can't shake the discomfort clinging to me. I've never experienced anything like this—the violent protests, the curfew. This whole situation is so messed up. Coming to the Academy was supposed to be my first step toward freedom. And yet, a tiny part of me wishes I could go back to my life in Chicago. It was boring and suffocating, but at least it was safe.

I know that's ridiculous. There were protests in Chicago today, too.

A soft chime sounds, then the pilot begins speaking through the intercom. "Attention passengers, we will arrive at the terminal in five minutes. I've been instructed to inform you that upon arrival in New Denver, everyone will be searched by law enforcement officials. No exceptions."

"What? That's ridiculous!" someone in front of me shouts. My stomach clenches. Why would they do that? Surely they realize that everyone on board is coming in from the Academy. What would we have to hide?

The shuttle begins its descent. I glance out my window and catch a glimpse of New Denver. I wish I could have seen it for the first time in daylight, but the nighttime view is still pretty spectacular. The skyline sparkles as if inlaid with neon jewels. It looks so welcoming.

Upon landing, everyone is ushered off the shuttle and directed to the white, two-story terminal building. This terminal is supposed to look pleasant and welcoming—it has chocolate-brown carpet, large digigraphs of exotic places dotting the walls, and potted plants located throughout the lobby. But it's anything but inviting. Police in two-piece, steel-blue uniforms and black helmets, all carrying stunners, are stationed throughout the building. Attendants lead us to three long lines set up to our left.

Before we get in line, the dark-haired girl from shuttle catches up to me and Mom. A distressed-looking woman in a navy-blue uniform follows close behind her. "Excuse me," the girl says. "Are you Alora Mason?"

"Yes," I answer in a cautious voice. "Why do you want to know?"

The girl's face lights up in a warm grin. "I'm Tara Martinez. I'm your new roommate at the Academy. We were supposed to be introduced this afternoon, but then everything went to hell."

Despite the tense atmosphere here, I find myself laughing. "That's the truth." We introduce our parents, then I ask, "How did you know who I am?"

Tara's mouth parts as if she wants to say one thing, but changes her mind. "I was given your profile when I was reassigned to room with you, so I already knew what you looked like. We also have . . . certain things in common."

Tara's mother gives her a sharp look. "That's enough for now, Tara." She shakes my hand and then Mom's, saying, "It was so nice meeting the two of you. I wish it were under better circumstances. But we have to report to line one now."

Before they depart, Tara says she'll be in touch soon and promises to show me around campus. A part of me is thrilled. I might actually make friends. But a part of me is skeptical. What if she's working with the DTA to spy on me? That wouldn't surprise me at all.

Mom and I join our assigned line, and nearly an hour passes before we're finally searched. I break out in a sweat as I step into the body scanner, then turn over my portacase so an officer can look through it. He tosses all my belongings on a table, scans everything with a gray handheld device, then carelessly shoves everything back inside. For some reason, that really pisses me off. I don't have anything to hide, and I haven't done anything wrong. I shouldn't have to be subjected to this kind of treatment.

"It's ten-thirty. We need to hurry," Mom says when we finally leave the terminal. We set out at a brisk pace and try to ignore the military Space Benders and police that are on patrol. It's unnerving seeing so many. After walking only one block, I count five of them.

The closer we get to Mom's apartment, the more I find myself scowling at everything. This is my first time going home with her. My first visit to New Denver. I wish I could enjoy the scenery. Some of the Jumbotrons on the tall buildings are flashing reminders of the curfew, while others broadcast scenes from various protests that took place today, especially the ones that turned violent. We keep seeing reports of an officer in Seattle who shot and killed a Purist who was acting suspicions. Apparently, the Purist was wearing a device that allowed explosives in his portacase to detonate if his heart stopped beating. After the officers shot him, the case exploded and severely injured four bystanders. That terrifies me. Why would anyone want to use a weapon like that, much less one that could still inflict damage even after their own death? That's horrifying. They'd have no way of knowing whether or not innocent people might be harmed. Do they honestly think that will make the government officials change their minds?

Mom and I are both breathing hard by the time we reach her fifth-floor apartment, just ten minutes before curfew. We had to speed-walk to make it on time. She pauses in front of the retinal scanner, then enters the room once the door slides open. I stop in the doorway and stare, all thoughts of the protests fading away for the moment.

I'm *finally* home.

Mom looks back at me, worry etched into her features. She swallows, looking down for a second, then forces a smile. "Do you remember living here?"

I nod slowly and step inside, taking in everything. There are some differences, like the furniture and walls. The walls used to be a buttery yellow, but now they're light blue. The floors are still covered with tan-and-white tile. Feeling like I'm in a dream, I walk over to a black table next to the couch and pick up a small digigraph. It shows me when I was little, laughing and hugging my father in one of the city's Green Zones. I run one of my fingers along the side of the frame. We look so much alike. Same blond hair, same blue eyes, same smile.

I set down the digigraph, overwhelmed with sadness. This is the father I can remember: the one who loved me and tried to spend time with me, not the one who kidnapped me. It doesn't make sense.

"Do you want me to get anything for you? Something to eat or drink?" Mom asks, gesturing toward a doorway leading to what I remember being a very tiny kitchen. I haven't had anything since lunch, but I'm not hungry.

"No, ma'am."

"Are you sure? I can make a sandwich, or something else if you like. It's no trouble."

"I'm sure," I say, looking down the short hallway to my right, which leads to my old bedroom. I get a flash of memory: standing there when I was six, the very night that Dad kidnapped me. I remember all the shouting. I remember being terrified.

Fixating back on the digigraph, I try and fail to make thoughts of Dad disappear. "What was he really like?" I ask in a voice that sounds hollow, even to me. "The truth, not the same stuff I heard back in Chicago."

Mom seems so weary as she crosses over to the couch and sits. She starts to talk, then hesitates as if she's trying to find the right words. "He loved you with every ounce of his being. And I loved him, at one point. I wanted to spend the rest of my life with him, but then . . ." she trails off, tears filling her eyes.

I take the seat next to her and place my hands on hers. "It's okay, we can talk about it another time." I let out a mirthless laugh. "I mean, the world is going insane tonight. That's more important than rehashing painful memories."

Mom's lips draw into a thin line, then she says, "There's always something bad happening in the world, sweetheart." She clasps her hands together, curling her fingers together several times before she speaks again. "The life that I wanted to build with your father may not have happened, but he gave me my greatest joy, and that's you, even though that joy was gone all those years you were away. I hated him for that. But then I learned that he *was* a clone, and they're too unstable."

She doesn't have to say more about that. Part of my lessons involved going back to witness firsthand how, at the turn of this century, newly minted clones slowly descended into madness. It makes me wonder why the government felt the need to clone my father in the first place. Sure, he was the first known Time *and* Space Bender, which led to me, but they took a huge risk bringing him back, knowing that he would ultimately self-destruct.

"What happened to him? Did you ever find out why he took me and then dumped me in Georgia, of all places?"

Mom stiffens, her eyes shifting away from me. In a careful voice, she says, "I guess he thought he was trying to save you. The DTA was trying to take you away. But in the end, he lost himself. I was told that he was killed, but I don't know for sure. I just hope that wherever he is now, he's finally at peace."

"Yeah, I guess I feel the same way," I reply, hating how shaky my voice sounds. Deep down, I feel cheated. I wanted my father's actions to mean something, but it sounds like his good intentions were outweighed by his insanity.

Mom stands, drawing me up with her. "I know you've had a rough day, so I won't keep you up. But if you need anything at all, don't be afraid to ask. Even if it's in the middle of the night, I'm here for you."

She hugs me tight. I freeze at first, then wrap my arms around her, inhaling the lavender scent that clings to her. I remember this. It reminds me of home. For the first time today, I feel truly safe. I just wish I had been allowed to come here before now. I wish she had pushed harder for that right.

But instead of voicing those not-so-nice thoughts, I whisper, "Thank you."

Pulling back, she blinks rapidly. "I'll let you get some sleep now. Do you remember where your bedroom is?" I nod, and she continues,

"Okay. Everything is exactly the way you left it. If you want, we can redecorate."

She wasn't kidding, I think when I step into my bedroom. It's like stepping directly into my past. The walls are the bright blue I loved as a child. The bed is covered with a blue-and-white flowered quilt, with several throw pillows on it. An antique white chest stands at the foot of the bed.

I take off my coat and toss it and my portacase on the bed, then walk over to a white dresser on the opposite side of the bed and open the drawers. The upper ones are full of too-small clothes that I can't remember wearing, but the bottom two are filled with different items. I find a large, deep-blue notebook with stars painted on the front and flip through it. Even as a child, I loved drawing. I glance back at my portacase, where my current sketchbook and drawing supplies are stored.

Near the back of one drawer, I find a polished wooden box. I open it, and it begins to play a haunting melody. The box holds several pieces of jewelry, all lying on a bed of midnight-blue velvet. I pick up a shiny silver bracelet with an infinity symbol pendant. My dad gave it to me on my fifth birthday. I remember him telling me that the symbol represented his love for me. I bite my lip and set it back down. How am I supposed to feel about him? He's been painted as such a monster, but that's not the man I remember.

I almost set the box back in the drawer, but a folded piece of paper catches my eye. I pick it up, noticing that it's lying on top of a small, black, circular object. My eyes widen. It's a Mind Redeemer, an object that I know the DTA uses to erase memories.

It's also used to restore memories.

I wonder what it's doing in my room. Who put it in here?

My first thought is that I should go and get Mom. I can't have this in my possession. Only DTA officials are allowed to hold or use them. Then I remember the paper, which appears to be torn from my old notebook. I unfold it, then my hand begins trembling. A short message is scrawled on the page, in my handwriting, along with instructions on how to operate the Mind Redeemer:

If you can't remember Aunt Grace or Bridger, then use this to restore your memories!

5

BRIDGER
FEBRUARY 11, 2147

"Hello, Mr. Creed," a chipper voice says, while a hand pats the side of my cheek.

My eyelids don't want to open. I pry them apart, and instantly squeeze them shut again. Bright sunlight pours in the windows. And the room is all white and filled with an antiseptic scent. I'm in the med center at the Academy. After every mission, each cadet is required to have a checkup to make sure we haven't suffered any ill effects from time traveling, or picked up any type of disease from the past. Why does it have to be so bright?

"Oh, no you don't. You've been sleeping all night. Time to wake up!"

Wait . . . sleeping all night? My eyes fly open. I'm lying in a bed, dressed in a flimsy tan medical robe. Next to me is a man with bright orange hair, dressed in a white uniform with a large blue stripe across the chest and down the sleeves. He must be a new nurse. I've never seen him before.

I start to ask him why I'm here, then the memories return with a jolt. The protests yesterday. Seeing the girl I thought was Vika. The panic attack—the first I've had in over five months. Of course they would toss me in the med center overnight. I groan and cover my face with my hands. This is not good. I bet Chancellor Tyson is regretting his decision to promote me. I wonder if he's ready to demote me back to Professor March's group.

"You look like you might vomit, Mr. Creed. Do you need a nausea patch?" the nurse asks.

"No, I'll be fine," I say, forcing myself to inhale slowly. I have no idea what kind of meds I've been given since yesterday. Plenty of Calmer, for sure. But I don't need anything else. What I need is to get out of here.

The nurse shrugs. He takes my vitals and punches the information in on his DataPad. Before he leaves, he points to the tiny closet in the corner

of the room. "Your uniform is in there. Once the doc comes in to officially clear you for release, you can get dressed."

I can't wait that long. My head swims a little as I push up from the
narrow bed to stand and stretch. Cold air creeps through the paper-thin
robe, and my skin erupts in goosebumps. I wonder how much Calmer I
was given. Clearly enough to knock me out in the middle of all that chaos.

Oh fure. What will my mother say about this? Over the past year,
she's tried to play the part of "nice and supportive parent" more, but her
usual witchlike nature claws its way to the surface when I don't perform
to her expectations. At least I don't have to hear from her right away. A
few days ago she left for New Orleans. She's one of the artifact retrieval
experts on a mission to salvage artifacts from the Hurricane Katrina disaster in 2005. She's scheduled to return this Tuesday.

I cross the small room and open the narrow closet. Inside, I find my
uniform, freshly laundered. I'm sliding on my boots when the door to my
room opens. "Will I be able to leave soon?" I ask, thinking it's the nurse
or doc.

"Well, I don't know, but I really hope so."

I turn around to find Zed standing in the doorway. He stands there
looking all awkward. "So, are you going to invite me in, or just stare at me?"

I can't help but laugh and wave him in. "Sure thing." Once Zed is
seated at the chair by the bed, I ask, "What are you doing here? This place
has to be cramping your style."

Instead of cracking a smart retort, Zed claps his hands together and
stares at the floor. "Look, I just wanted to apologize for the way I acted
yesterday. I know you've had it rough since last year, and I've been pushing you to be the same old Bridger. And that was wrong. I guess it took
me seeing you wild out yesterday for it to really click with me. So . . . I'm
sorry."

His face is bright red, even to the tips of his ears. I don't know what
to say. I've never seen Zed act like this before. Zed, who's super confident
and always joking around. Zed, who thinks being serious is overrated.

I clear my throat. The air feels thick in the room all of a sudden.
Awkward. "Look, man, don't worry about anything. We're good. We've
been friends for a long time now, so I know you don't mean half of what
you say."

"Yeah, I guess. I just . . . I just thought I needed to apologize to you.
And I promise I won't be such a dick anymore. Elijah and I had a long

talk before he went home, and we both agreed that we need to give you whatever time you need to get better. But we also don't want to abandon you. So, whatever you want from us, just ask."

A warm feeling engulfs my whole body. I'm grateful that someone, especially Zed, is reaching out to me. "Thanks. I really appreciate it."

Zed seems like he wants to say something else, but then a familiar, deep voice fills the room. "Well, well. What is going on in here?"

My head snaps up. Standing in the doorway are two men. Chancellor Tyson, in his ever-present black uniform, and a tall man with pale skin and gray hair, dressed in dark-brown pants and a plain white button-up shirt. It's Dad's old boss, General Thomas Anderson. I'm shocked. I haven't seen him since I wilded out last year.

Why are they both here now?

I straighten as the two men cross the room. Chancellor Tyson asks Zed to give us privacy. After Zed makes a hasty exit, the chancellor sits on the chair next to the bed, while General Anderson comes up to me and extends his hand. I stare at it for a few seconds, wondering if I should shake it. He was always pleasant to me when Dad was still alive. But after Dad's death, the general became secretive and wouldn't tell us what happened to him. Said it was classified. I didn't believe him then, and I still don't.

Now, my feelings go beyond mere annoyance. I feel a sudden surge of *loathing*. But that's irrational. Probably nothing more than a side effect of everything that happened yesterday. I square my shoulders, then reach out and give his hand a firm shake.

"It's nice to see you, sir," I say, trying to inject some warmth into my voice, despite the chill I feel.

The general smiles. More wrinkles appear around his eyes and mouth than I remember. Maybe the conflicts with the Purists are taking their toll on him, too. "It's good to see you too, son."

Something tries to crawl to the surface of my memories when he says this. Son. Something about that doesn't sit well with me. But why? General Anderson hasn't done anything to me, other than keeping the truth about Dad's death from my family.

"So, I guess you're wondering what we're doing here," he says, his eyes flicking momentarily over to Chancellor Tyson.

"Yes, sir, I kind of was," I reply, sitting on the edge of the bed. I wish they would leave. Something about their visit feels off.

Chancellor Tyson leans forward and clasps his hands. "Mr. Creed, you don't have to worry about anything. I simply wanted to check in on you this morning, since you had to stay here overnight. Thomas was visiting the campus this morning and decided to tag along. That's all."

General Anderson nods. "After the protests yesterday, I felt it would be a good idea to see for myself what kind of damage was done, and determine whether there are places where we can beef up security." His expression turns dark. "I don't see these kinds of Purist scare tactics going away anytime soon."

His words make sense. Yet somehow, they don't ring completely true. I wonder if he's not telling me something. Why would General Anderson even care about me? I'm just the son of his deceased employee. Other than the fact that he'll one day be my boss—if I'm accepted into the military, that is—he has no reason to be interested in me.

The door to my room slides open again. The chancellor and general look behind them, and I follow their gaze to the person standing in the doorway.

It's a woman of medium build in a navy-blue military uniform, her iron-gray hair cut shorter than mine. My dad's mom, Brigadier General Judith Creed. I sit up a bit straighter, surprised to see her. Growing up, my brother Shan and I usually only saw her a few times a year since she was frequently reassigned to different DTA military bases around the Federation. But in January, she transferred to New Denver to be closer to us. She said we needed a positive influence in our lives since Dad wasn't here for us anymore. That may be true, but I suspect that her move had more to do with me wilding out last year.

On a good day, Grandma looks like she could cut you with her eyes. Today she's positively livid. She marches in the room and stops just before the general and chancellor, fixing each of them with a stare that makes me feel nervous for them.

"What the hell are you two doing in here with my grandson?" she asks in a low voice.

Chancellor Tyson begins, "Now, don't get upset, Judith. We're just here to check on Bridger."

"The hell you are. Is this some sort of interrogation? Because if this is, I should have been informed, in his mother's absence. In fact, I should have been informed last night that he was put in here. But no, I had to find out this morning when one of your incompetent privates finally told me the truth." By the time Grandma finishes, her cheeks are flushed. I haven't seen her this mad in a long time. What could have possibly made her this angry?

"Well, under the circumstances, I'm sure you understand why we couldn't contact extended family members," Chancellor Tyson snaps.

Grandma looks at him like he's lost his capacity for rational thought. "I'm well aware of what happened yesterday. And I'm also aware that parents were allowed to retrieve their children, so I don't see why I wasn't informed about my grandchild's location. I could have picked up Shan and Bridger last night."

When I hear my brother's name mentioned, I feel a slight sense of shame. I hadn't even thought to ask about him. "Where's Shan now?"

"He's in his quarters, along with all the other cadets who were not released to a parent or permanent guardian," Chancellor Tyson says.

Grandma lets out a huff. "I'm their grandmother, and you know perfectly well that I'm qualified to take care of my grandsons while their mother is away."

"Well, we don't have her permission to release them to you."

"Are you seriously going to play this game with me, Doran? Because we can take this to DTA headquarters if you like."

Chancellor Tyson starts to stand, but General Anderson holds up a hand. "I think, given the circumstances, it would be fine for Judith to take the boys. What could it hurt?"

Nobody says anything for the longest few seconds of my life. I just sit there, hoping the chancellor will listen to reason. I need to get out of here.

Chancellor Tyson pinches the bridge of his nose and exhales slowly. "Fine, you can take them with you, but only under the condition that you do not let them out of your sight. The last thing I want to deal with is an angry Morgan Creed when she returns."

Grandma waves a dismissive hand and snorts. "Morgan is always angry. Let me deal with her."

"Now that's something I'd like to see," General Anderson says with a smirk.

Grandma's head whips around and she gives him a death glare. "My business is not for your amusement . . . *sir.*"

I'm gaping at them, open-mouthed, by this point. Even though Grandma is also a general, Anderson still outranks her. But she's obviously not afraid of him.

General Anderson's eyes narrow for a moment, then he lets out a laugh. "I've missed having you around here, Judith. Never a dull moment."

Grandma shakes her head and comes over to my side. She sits awkwardly on the bed, careful not to touch me. "How are you feeling? Are you dizzy or anything?"

Before I can answer, Chancellor Tyson says, "I talked to his doc earlier and he assured me that Bridger is fine. He was only overwhelmed because of the protests. The doc feels that was understandable, considering the time trip that Bridger just returned from. And as a matter of fact, several more of his teammates had to visit the med center yesterday thanks to the upset."

Unsettled that I feel so much better after hearing that, I focus on the white-tiled floor. "Did anybody else have to be sedated in front of everybody?"

"Well, no. But you have nothing to be ashamed about, Bridger. That is, unless there's anything else you want to tell me?" Chancellor Tyson is still smiling, but that last question betrays the real reason for his visit. He's trying to figure out if I'm about to lose my mind again.

I close my eyes. I think about how scared leaving the shuttle made me, the fear that nearly froze me in place upon hearing the gunshot. Then the complete shock at seeing someone who looked so much like Vika. It nearly did me in.

I can't let them know that. Not any of them.

"Is that question really necessary?" Grandma snaps.

I glance at her and say, "It's all right. I don't mind answering." Turning my attention to the chancellor and general, I continue, "I'm fine. It was like you said, just the shock of coming from a violent protest in the past to one in the present. Things like that shouldn't be happening now."

The chancellor and general both murmur in agreement. Chancellor Tyson checks his DataLink, stands, and says to the general, "I have a meeting in an hour, so we should go now."

"Of course," General Anderson replies.

"Take it easy for the rest of the weekend, Mr. Creed. I expect you back at the Academy Monday morning, ready to resume your studies," the chancellor says.

He exits the room before Grandma can say anything else. The general starts to follow. Before he leaves, he pats me on the shoulder. "I think you're doing just fine, Bridger. I'm sure your father would be proud of you."

I get an unexpected lump in my throat. I'd give anything for my dad to be here now. Grandma holds her gaze steady on the general, but I see her swallow a few times.

"If you need anything, feel free to contact me," the general says. "I always look out for my own."

Then he pivots and quickly exits the room.

And I'm left wondering what he means by that. Could that be his way of saying I will be accepted into the DTA's military division? If only I knew that were true.

Grandma breaks the silence. "Well, that was complete bullshit. But at least I can take you and Shan home with me for a few days."

6

It's almost seven o'clock in the morning when a low chime sounds, right before my bedroom door slides open. I barely have time to shove the Mind Redeemer under my pillow before Mom walks in. "I'm sorry," she says in a rush. "I didn't realize you were already awake. I just wanted to check on you."

"Yeah, I'm awake," I say while trying to stifle a yawn. I don't tell her that I didn't sleep much last night. How could I, when I have an illegal device in my possession with a note in my handwriting telling me to use it?

In fact, I've been sitting on my bed for over an hour, alternating between drawing in my sketch pad and trying to work up the nerve to use the Mind Redeemer. Every time I start to activate it, a little voice inside hisses at me to stop because it's wrong.

But what if it *isn't* wrong? I keep thinking, what if I'm *supposed* to use the Mind Redeemer? I've spent so much time wondering about all those years I can't remember. Sure, I remember where I lived, and the appearance of the woman who kept me, but nothing about my actual life. Did I have friends? A boyfriend? Where did I go to school? What were my hopes and dreams? Then that stupid voice reminds me that there's a good reason I can't remember those things. Hello, traumatic childhood.

Mom pauses before gingerly perching on the edge of my bed. "Are you okay? You don't look like you've slept much."

Just great. I must look like utter crap this morning for her to say that. I'm still wearing the same blue jumpsuit I had on yesterday, only now it's wrinkled. But at least I brushed my hair. That was a beast of a chore. Tossing and turning most of the night leaves more tangles than I care to deal with, especially since my hair reaches halfway down my back now.

"I'll be all right. I guess it's just weird, finally being here." Not exactly the truth, but not exactly a lie either. I really can't believe I'm in New

Denver, back where I truly belong. But while it may have been my home once, it doesn't feel that way anymore. How can I get that feeling back?

For a few uncomfortable moments, Mom doesn't say anything. Then she spots my bright purple sketch pad on the bed next to me.

"Can I look?" she asks.

I shrug my shoulders. "Sure, but there's nothing special in there."

While she flips through the pages, I try not to cringe. I really hate letting anyone look at my art, but privacy was nonexistent while I was being rehabilitated in Chicago. If I wanted to draw, which was one of the few things that made me feel better, I had to let Lieutenant Rivera inspect my book. Because under no circumstances was I allowed to recreate any of the few memories that I still had from my captivity in Georgia.

Which is why, after dozens of pages of generic drawings from places I visited in Chicago, Mom stops on one page near the middle of the book—the sketch I was working on last night.

"Is this the house where you grew up?" she asks.

Cursing myself for being so stupid, I consider lying. But what's the point? Mom knows everything about where I lived during my childhood. I'm not a great artist, but I'm pretty decent. "Yes," I finally admit. "But please don't worry. I can't remember anything specific, only what it looks like from the outside."

A crease appears between her eyebrows, then she sets the sketch pad back on the bed. "It's a good drawing, Alora. All of them are really good. You should be proud of yourself."

I'm not sure what I expected her to say, but that isn't it. A light feeling engulfs me, and I find myself smiling.

Mom starts to say something, but then stops, as if she doesn't know what to talk about now. Finally, she asks, "Are you hungry? I can fix you something to eat."

My stomach growls as if on cue, and we both laugh. She leads me to the kitchen, and while I sit at the tiny black table, she sets about cooking. The kitchen is exactly like I remember it. Light green walls, gray countertops, black and silver appliances, and the table with three chairs resting in the corner. I wonder how lonely it's been for Mom all these years, eating at that sad little table by herself, with only those two empty chairs for company.

Mom rummages through cabinets that appear to be stocked mostly with cans and sealed silver packages that contain Ready Meals. I would rather not eat any of those. They're supposedly super-nutritious foods approved by the government, and they take just a minute to heat up, but they're so bland.

Mumbling under her breath, she then checks the refrigerator. "I have a few eggs and some bacon left. Do you like those?"

"Yes, but I can have something else," I blurt out. While I often ate fresh foods back in Chicago—a special privilege because I'm a Talent—most people don't eat them except on special occasions. Prices for those items are outrageous, so only the wealthy individuals, people working in high-level positions for powerful government agencies, or Talents can afford to eat them on a regular basis.

"Nope, you get the good stuff today," she replies.

A part of me wants to insist she just give me a meal bar or something, but I keep quiet. I've eaten several varieties of those, and they're all disgusting. I guess I'd better get used to them. Just not right now.

A short while later, she sets a plate in front of me, along with a glass of dark-red juice. I immediately start shoveling the food into my mouth, even though the eggs and bacon are slightly burned. The eggs are edible, but the juice tastes bitter. I spit it back into the glass before I can stop myself.

"Oh, sweetheart, I'm so sorry. I didn't realize you didn't like pomegranate juice. That's all I could get this month," Mom says in a rush, frowning slightly while looking back in the direction of the refrigerator. "I have water, and I think there may be some green tea left."

"It's okay," I say. "This is fine." Honestly, I'd rather dump this stuff down the drain, but I know how much it must have cost her. On one of her visits to Chicago, she confessed that her salary was slashed when she could no longer perform her Time Bending duties and had to transfer to programming Sim Games.

Her DataLink emits two long beeps. She checks it and shakes her head. "Great. You'd think my boss would leave me alone this weekend."

"What's wrong?"

"I have to finish a project today. I thought I had until Monday, but he wants it by this afternoon. The History Alive rep wants to view it tomorrow." Mom pinches the bridge of her nose. "I can't believe it. Of all weekends to have to work."

"It's okay, Mom. I'll be fine."

"Are you sure? If I start now, I should be finished by early afternoon. Then I can take you out and show you around, maybe get you some new clothes. That is, if you want to."

I offer her a genuine smile. "That sounds good. And I'll try to take a nap, since I'm still kind of tired."

After Mom retreats to her study to work, I clean up the kitchen, then head back to my room, where I immediately pull the Mind Redeemer out again and flop down on the bed. I keep turning it over in my hands. Should I use it? Should I put it away? Or should I tell Mom about it?

The note is definitely in my handwriting. I even copied the sentence myself, just to make sure. The swoops and swirls of each letter were identical. So, when did I write the note? And why did I put it in here?

I lie on the bed for a few more minutes, debating what to do, but I'm only wasting time. There's only one way to find out for sure.

I turn the Mind Redeemer on. It lets out a low hum as I follow the prompts to set it for memory retrieval, then hold it in front of my forehead. My hand trembles as I look up at the bright green light. I could stop now and pretend I never found this device. I mean, it could seriously damage my brain, maybe even kill me. It would be smart to just get rid of it.

But then I'd always wonder about what was erased. The DTA said they just took traumatic memories of my tortured childhood. But what if that's a lie? What if there's more?

Before I can change my mind, I press the button that will restore my past. Burning pain shoots through my skull, and sweat beads on my face and neck. The pain lasts for a few seconds that feel like they last forever. And then it's gone.

My arm feels like rubber as I lower the Mind Redeemer. It only takes a moment before the stolen memories start to surface. Slowly at first, like little ripples, then all at once. I remember Aunt Grace. She wasn't a psychotic Purist; she was my father's sister. We lived together in an old plantation house that she and her late husband had converted into a bed and breakfast inn. That was in a small town in Georgia. And it wasn't in the present; it was in the early twenty-first century. She raised me from the time Dad saved me from being taken by the DTA and left me with her, in the twenty-first century. She loved me and wanted to protect me.

I also remember Bridger, the young Time Bender who came back to prevent what was supposed to be my murder. He was the unconscious boy I saw back at the Academy yesterday, during the protest.

And then there is Vika, the half-sister I never knew. As a clone, she started to destabilize and wound up trying to murder me in 2013, but instead was killed by Bridger. We burned her body in order to fake my death in that time period so I could return here. Then there's the fact that before she died, she told me her mother made our father pay for what he did. I have no idea what that means.

And there are others. Trevor. Sela. Kate. Naomi and Mr. Palmer. I close my eyes and press my fists against them. Oh my God, what he did to Naomi, and almost did to me. I curl up on the bed, feeling so sick. The memories are coming so fast now, I want them to stop. But I need to know more.

There was a cloned version of Bridger's father, Leithan, who told us to take his body back to New Denver. How Bridger and I shifted together and brought the original Leithan's body back to 2146. Even though he wasn't a Space Bender, Bridger managed to coach me through shifting to the ruins of New Denver. I had to take the body there first, then shift to my bedroom, a place I knew I would visit at some point in the future, so I could stash the Mind Redeemer, all because Bridger was positive that the DTA would remove my memories. For some reason, he thought he would be executed or Nulled, but he wanted to make sure I would have a way to remember the truth.

I'm shivering and sweating by the time all my memories have returned. Because the very last thing I remember is what happened when I shifted back to Bridger. I had to leave him in Georgia since he can't shift through space like me. We turned ourselves over to the DTA, hoping they would show mercy on us. But no, they separated us and took my memories. And just before they wiped my mind, they allowed me to see Mom. I shake my head in disbelief. Mom was crying. But she did *nothing* to stop the DTA.

"Don't fight them, my love. It'll be over soon, and then we can forget about everything that's happened. We can start over."

I'm gasping for air, and my hands and feet are tingling. I force myself to breath slowly. Inhale through my nose, exhale through my mouth. But I can't stop thinking, *How could Mom do that to me?* She should have done *something* to help me, instead of just sitting back and letting the DTA rip my childhood away from me. They stole my memories of Aunt Grace and my dad, people I love dearly.

Or does she even remember, herself? What if the DTA took her memories, too? I don't know what to think anymore.

My first instinct is to shift back in time to see Aunt Grace. I've never felt such an ache, like a bandage has been ripped from my soul, leaving this black hole sucking the life out of me. I need to see her and let her know that I'm okay. The problem is, I don't have a Chronoband to help me shift to the date I want, and there's no way I can get one. The DTA has all of them. I could always free shift like Bridger did when he came back to help me in 2013, but there's no guarantee I'll make it to my target date.

And Bridger . . . I have no idea what happened to him after I saw him passed out yesterday. He could be anywhere. But I need his help. He's the person in this time who I can really trust. Since I can't go back to Aunt Grace right now, I have to find him. Today.

1

BRIDGER
FEBRUARY 11, 2147

Two hours after Grandma busts me out of the clinic, Shan and I follow her into what used to be Dad's apartment. Since Shan and I now own it, we agreed to let her stay here when she moved back to New Denver from her last assignment in Chicago. Mom didn't like that at all. She said we barely knew Grandma. Of course, that's ridiculous, because we visited her once or twice a year while growing up. And even though we were never *that* close, she's here for us now, at least. I can't remember the last time I saw Mom's parents. They're too busy traveling the globe on assignments for the DTA.

I toss my portacase on the nearest chair. Grandma immediately heads to her bedroom, calling over her shoulder, "I have a splitting headache, boys. I'm going to take something for it and shower, and I'll be out in a little while."

Shan and I stand awkwardly in the living room, not saying anything. This is only the second time I've been here since Grandma moved in. I'm pretty sure this is Shan's first time since right after Dad died. The apartment still looks the same as when he was still alive. White walls; black overstuffed couch and chairs; antiques from past time trips; and family digigraphs displayed on the walls. Even the large digigraphs playing scenes from Dad's favorite old films still hang across from the couch. I find myself smiling at the one showing scenes from an ancient movie called *Blade Runner*. The futuristic city looks so cheesy, but Dad loved it. The only thing that's changed since Grandma moved in is that she's added a few digigraphs of her own.

Shan glances around the room and closes his eyes for a few moments. I wonder if he's feeling Dad's loss as much as I am. Especially since we've reached the first anniversary of his death.

Three sharp beeps emit from the TeleNet Screen. That's the signal for an incoming house-comm. A feminine voice announces that it's from Professor Telfair March.

I give the command to accept the comm. Professor March's upper body appears on the screen. To say he looks worried is an understatement.

"Bridger! How are you feeling? I just found out about your accident," he says in a rush. He rubs his right hand across his buzzed hair, like he always does when he's nervous. I've learned a lot of his habits over the years. Not only was he my former professor, he was also Dad's best friend, ever since their days at the Academy. Dad used to joke that the professor was closer to him than he was to his own sister, Olivia March.

"I'm okay. It was . . ." I trail off, not wanting to talk about it in front of Shan.

But Shan blurts out, "He completely wilded out after his time trip. Everyone thinks he might go insane again."

"Really, Shan? Did you have to say it like *that*? And how do you even know that?" I ask, my face feeling way too hot.

Shan glares at me. "What's the big deal? Everybody knows what happened. Did you think I wouldn't find out? I'm not a baby, you know."

A string of insults flies through my mind, but before I can let loose, Professor March says, "Okay, that's enough boys."

"But I didn't do anything. I just told the truth," Shan says.

Any thought of lashing out at Shan evaporates when he says those words. So everybody thinks I'm going to wild out again. What if they're right? What if the DTA decides to take even more of my memories to keep me under control? Soon I'll be no better than a Null. I lower my eyes, focusing on my hands. Unconsciously, I've started rubbing a fist into the palm of my other hand.

"Bridger, look at me," the professor commands, this time in a softer voice. I slowly lift my head and make eye contact with him. For a moment, he places his fingers over his mouth. The bright gold of his antique watch stands out against his dark brown skin. Finally, he says, "It's true, we all know what happened to you yesterday. But nobody is holding anything against you. We were on the cusp of a major crisis. With all that stress, I completely understand why it would be overwhelming for you."

All I can feel is shame. My eyes drift away from the screen. I catch Shan staring at me with his arms wrapped tightly against his chest. It's almost like he's worried.

Professor March continues, "I didn't mean to upset you. I just wanted to check in myself, to see if you're all right. Well, I wanted to make sure *both* of you are fine. Things are pretty scary now."

"I'm fine," Shan says. "I'm just happy that Grandma was able to get us. I didn't want to have to stay at the Academy all weekend.

"You're lucky. I'm on Warden Duty, so I can't go anywhere," Professor March answers with a grin. Focusing on me again, he says, "I really wanted to visit you in the med center earlier, but I couldn't leave the remaining cadets unattended."

"It's fine, sir. Really. And besides, Chancellor Tyson and General Anderson visited me. I had plenty of company."

Professor March arches one eyebrow. "Oh really? I bet that was a . . . nice surprise."

"It wasn't, until Grandma showed up and bullied them into letting her take Shan and me with her," I say with a smirk.

"That sounds like the Judith Creed I know," he replies, laughing. "Anyway, I have some chocolate bars that I retrieved on my last time trip. I'll give them to you when you get back to school. You know, a little pick-me-up."

"Oh wow, thanks, Professor," Shan gushes. We rarely get to have chocolate.

"Professor, you really didn't have to do that," I say.

He shrugs, grinning. "Of course I did. I promised Leithan I'd look out for you two, and I reserve the right to spoil you when I can. Now, I've got to go, but if either of you need me for anything, please send a comm. You know I'll do whatever I can to help you boys."

After the comm ends, Shan's happiness quickly deflates. He tells me he's going to his room and starts to walk away. But he hesitates just before reaching the short hallway leading to our bedrooms. Turning back to face me, he says, "I'm sorry, Bridger. I really didn't mean anything back there."

He bites the inside of his cheek like he does when he's nervous. I want to say something in return, but all I can think about is how he's starting to look more and more like Dad. Especially since he turned fourteen and hit another growth spurt. He's now about the same height as Dad, and he has the same hazel eyes and light brown hair. But he seems thinner and paler than usual. Sure, I see him on campus sometimes, and at Mom's apartment almost every weekend, but he usually keeps to himself. He's always been absorbed in his Sim Games, or out with other Level 1 cadets. The few times he's tried to talk to me, I've had other plans.

"Don't worry about it, we're solid." Something about the way he's looking at me seems kind of off. "Are you all right?"

"Yeah. I'm just worn out. Yesterday was wild, right?"

I offer a tentative smile. "Yeah, it was intense."

Shan returns the smile, but it's tinged with sadness. He seems like he wants to say something else, but he just turns and goes on to his room. I get an urge to follow. Something definitely isn't right with him. But I stop myself. What would I say? It's not like we've ever been close. He's always been a complete mama's boy. Her favorite. I'm not sure he would really listen to me, even if I knew what to say.

Not really wanting to be confined to my room just yet, I wander over to the closest table with digigraphs resting atop it. I scan them, particularly paying attention to the new ones that belong to Grandma. One really stands out, and I pick up the delicate crystal frame. The scene on loop is from the day Mom and Dad brought Shan home after he was born. Thanks to those genetic modifications that allow us to retain more memories than Purists, I remember that day, even though I was only four. Looking at the digigraph brings back a flood of memories.

I'm waiting in the apartment with Grandma, bouncing with excitement. She came to New Denver to stay with me while Mom and Dad were at the med center. "When are they gonna get here?" I ask over and over.

"Soon. They're on the way home."

Then the door opens and Dad sweeps in, looking so happy and alive. Mom follows, clutching baby Shan close to her chest. He's wrapped in a soft green blanket. Immediately, Grandma gets up and leads me over to them. I'm not thrilled about meeting this tiny person who's taking all the attention from me, but Dad picks me up and holds me just as close as Mom holds the new baby. His familiar, woodsy scent calms my anxiety.

"Son, you're a big brother now. You have a big responsibility to protect the baby. He's going to need you, whether he knows it or not. Do you think you can always protect him?"

Of course, being four years old, I agree. "Yes, Daddy. I'll keep him safe for you and Mommy."

Dad ruffles my hair, grinning. "That's my brave boy."

And then they let me hold Shan, who promptly starts screaming. But that doesn't matter, because we're all together. A whole, happy family.

For a short while, anyway.

As I replace the digigraph, Grandma comes back in the room. She's changed into some regs—a shiny gray shirt and pants suit with a wide silver belt. It's strange seeing her out of uniform.

"Where's Shan?" she asks.

"He's in his room. Said he was tired."

Grandma pauses as if she's unsure what to say next. That surprises me. Grandma is one of those people who always has a take-charge attitude. I guess us being here is strange for her, too. This is the first time she's been responsible for Shan and me on her own in years.

"How did you get away from headquarters to check on us?" I ask.

"When you get to be in my position, you can delegate tasks," she says with a smile. I believe her. Since her transfer back to New Denver, she's been promoted and is now third in command at the DTA's military division. She only has two bosses: Brigadier General Rashida March, and the one at the very top, General Anderson.

"Besides, Anderson may be an ass most of the time, but I do have to admit that he has everything under control for now. He's coordinated with the city's civilian police and Space Benders from the Department of Teleportation to keep patrol units on the ground twenty-four hours a day. Let's just hope the Purists realize all their protesting isn't going to change anything, and knock it off."

"I hope so," I say, not feeling convinced. Purists have always been vocal about how much they dislike anything to do with genetic modifications, and their anger seems to increase each year. And now that the RCA has passed, it'll only get worse.

Grandma rubs her temples, frowning. "You know what? I'm starving. Let's get out of here."

"Are you sure?" I ask. "There were a lot of police out patrolling this morning."

"What are we going to do, hide in our homes all the time now? And besides, I'm dying for a burger."

Thirty minutes later, we're sitting at a booth in a replica 1950s-style diner a block from Grandma's apartment building. This one has gone all out, with a black-and-white-checked floor, light blue walls, and red plastic booths and bar stools. Retro businesses from the twentieth century are popular all over the NAF now, since Time Bending missions have moved into that era.

The place is packed despite all the protests yesterday, but there aren't many servers. It takes a while before a harried waitress dressed in a red skirt with a ridiculous poodle on it takes our order. "What will it be for you guys?" she asks.

"Three burgers and fries for us," Grandma replies. "And make it the real stuff. I can't abide by that synthetic crap."

The waitress's eyebrows shoot up. "That'll cost you quite a few credits."

An irritated expression flashes across Grandma's face. "I assure you, I can pay for it. Now, can you please tell me what's going on? We've been waiting nearly ten minutes just to order."

"I'm sorry," the woman replies, sounding a little out of breath. "Two of our servers didn't show up this morning. Purists, of course."

Grandma offers a slight smile to her. "Of course. I apologize. Hopefully things will get better soon."

"Maybe so," the woman replies, glancing toward the front of the store. Through the glass, we can see two police officers walking by. On the way here, we saw several more on patrol. But at least there were no Purists out starting crap with anyone. In fact, most people seemed content to go about their business as if nothing happened yesterday. I guess they have more faith in the government than I do.

Grandma puts on a too-bright smile as she turns her attention back to us. "So, what have you boys been learning at the Academy? Anything interesting?"

"Not much," Shan mutters with a shrug. He goes back to gazing out the window next to us, staring at people passing by.

Grandma steeples her fingers. "Okay, I see. And how about you, Bridger? Have your studies been more exciting since your big promotion?"

I try to share what I've been up to lately, but I really wish I could get away with just zoning out like Shan. Besides, I can't stop thinking about what happened to me yesterday, or the conversation between me, Shan, and Professor March.

After we eat, Grandma sends Shan up to the counter to order dessert even though we both insist that we're not hungry. In fact, we both barely touched our burgers or fries. It's hard to focus on eating when you keep wondering if you're about to wild out again.

"What do you think is wrong with him?" I ask.

Grandma cocks her head and raises an eyebrow. "Bridger, I'm a little disappointed in you. It's obvious. He's depressed."

"Why? What would he have to be depressed about?"

"Really?" Grandma asks, looking dumbstruck. "Yesterday was the anniversary of Leithan's death and you don't know why your brother is depressed? And I bet you didn't know he's on Calmer now. It happened a few weeks ago when Morgan was on a time trip, and the med center at the Academy contacted me for permission to start him on it. Apparently, he recently started having anxiety attacks."

I feel like I've been dunked in ice water. It never occurred to me that Shan cared that much about Dad's death. You know, mama's boy and all that. He never really wanted to spend time with Dad, even when he was alive. But the fact that he's displaying the same symptoms I went through last year is surprising. It's just weird that he's only now displaying them.

"Don't look so shocked," Grandma says. "I can tell something is bothering you too."

"Why would you say that?" I say, feeling suddenly defensive.

"Bridger, you may not look much like Leithan, but you act just like him. I could always tell when something was bothering him, and you're the same. Save us both the time and stop making excuses. I want the truth."

My stomach churns. So Grandma's no-nonsense attitude is back. I remember how Dad used to tell me that she always knew when he was up to something when he was younger. The question is, do I keep denying it, or just come clean?

From Grandma's steely gaze, I figure it's safest to just tell the truth. Or at least part of it. "Okay. So, yesterday when I got back to the Academy, I was scared just like everyone else. But after hearing that gunshot and running inside, I saw this girl. She looked almost exactly like Vika. You know, my girlfriend who died last year? And we had just come from a time trip with a major protest going on. So, I don't know." I pause and look down at my hands in my lap. I've clenched one into a fist and started rubbing it with the other hand. "I don't want to lose control again. I can't. I need to stay sane so I can join the military."

"Just like Leithan." Grandma checks to make sure that Shan isn't coming back yet. He's next in line to order. Then she leans closer to me. "I already knew about your episode. I shouldn't tell you this, but I think I should under the circumstances. That girl wasn't Vika. The girl you saw is a new student. She was kidnapped by her father when she was little and was raised by a lunatic Purist, completely isolated from modern society.

The poor girl had to have her memories erased so she could even function. She's at the Academy now because her instructors felt she was finally ready to be around more people her own age."

I sit up straighter, trying to keep the surprise off my face. I remember hearing about a girl being kidnapped when I was little. I just didn't realize she had been found. I guess that was around the same time I wilded out. "How do you know all of that?"

"Remember how I was just stationed at headquarters in Chicago? That's where she was, too. I saw what that girl went through, Bridger. She had to relearn everything about living in modern society. It was a huge learning curve for her."

"Why are you telling me this?"

Grandma gets a look on her face that almost looks like pity. "This girl may have an uncanny resemblance to Vika, but she is most definitely not the same person. She's extremely fragile. Possibly a bit unstable. I really think it's best that you stay away from her."

"But why?" I ask. "We're both going to be at the Academy. I'm sure I'll have to talk to her at *some* point."

"Just promise me that you won't get involved with her," Grandma says. "You don't need to get wrapped up in the drama surrounding her life. You need to look out for yourself, especially if you're serious about becoming a soldier."

I want to ask Grandma more, but a loud voice booms through the already noisy diner.

"Furing freak. Your kind shouldn't exist. You're ruining the lives of decent, hardworking people!"

Grandma and I search for the source of the yelling, and when our eyes land on it, I'm horrified to see a middle-aged man with a receding hairline has cornered Shan near the counter. My brother's back is pressed against the dessert case, and he's pale and shaking. I wonder why the man is targeting him for a second before it hits me. Like me, Shan is still wearing his Academy uniform.

Grandma takes off. She gets up in the man's face, pointing her finger and speaking in a low, stern voice. "If you know what's good for you, you will get the hell out of here this instant and leave my grandson alone."

"And what are you going to do about it," the man sneers.

Holding up her wrist, Grandma activates her DataLink, pulling up her identification. "I'm Brigadier General Creed of the Department of

Temporal Affairs. You will leave immediately or I will have your ass tossed in The Black Hole for so long that your family won't even remember who you are when you get out. Hell, I may even have you Nulled."

"You can't do that," the man says, looking uncertain.

"Try me," Grandma says.

By now, everyone in the diner is now focused on the two of them. Shan is still as a stone at the counter. My heart is pounding. I want to do something to help, but I don't know what.

Finally the man backs away. Pointing a shaking finger at Grandma, he says, "You'll be sorry. All of you will. Jode Lincoln says he's got something planned for all of you freaks. You just wait."

The man pushes his way past other customers, grumbling the whole time. Once he leaves, everyone resumes what they were doing. Chatter gradually fills the diner again.

Grandma quickly pays the bill and leads us out of the diner. Shan leans against the window by the door, breathing hard. I stand next to him, feeling angry and powerless. I wish I had done something—anything other than sitting stunned, not doing a damn thing to help my brother.

"Who's Jode Lincoln?" I ask.

"I have no idea," Grandma replies. She places a hand on Shan's shoulder. "Do you need some Calmer? I have some back at the apartment."

He nods.

"Okay, let's go get it."

She ushers him away, and I start to follow, but I'm too agitated. I need to be by myself for a while. To clear my head. I don't want to run and hide in Dad's apartment just because some idiotic Purist tried to start something with Shan.

"Bridger, come on," Grandma says, looking back at me.

"Can I stay out for a little while?" I ask.

"I don't think that's a good idea," she says, her eyes flicking back to Shan.

"Please. I really need to just be alone. I'll go to the closest Green Zone. It's only two blocks away. And you can track me," I say, holding up my wrist so she can see that I'm wearing my DataLink. "Besides, police are everywhere. Nothing's going to happen to me."

She frowns, then lets out a heavy sigh. "Fine. But be home in an hour. You do *not* want me having to look for you today."

8

Mom enters the living room from her office at exactly 1:07 in the afternoon, cocking an eyebrow at me and flashing a half-amused smile. "I didn't realize you were that anxious to leave."

For the past half-hour—the last time I asked her if she was almost finished working—I've been pacing in the living room. I've already taken a steam shower, changed into a clean green jumpsuit, and even managed to detangle my hair and pull it back in a loose braid. Unconsciously, I touch the slight bulge in my pocket, where I put the Mind Redeemer. I hope I won't have to use it on Bridger, but I'm betting they stole his memories, like they did mine.

"I don't really have anything else to do," I say, forcing myself to speak in a calm voice. A part of me is angry with her, but she may not know the full truth either. I have to remember that.

I check my DataLink again. It took me most of the morning to figure out how to track Bridger through it. He arrived at a small restaurant several blocks away a few minutes ago. If we leave now, I can convince Mom that I'm starving, even though the last thing I want is to eat. I need to talk to him—in person, since I can't risk sending a message. But how can I do that without Mom seeing me? If she does know the truth about my past, then she has to know that Bridger was the one who brought me back from 2013. Unless I want to risk her blabbing to the DTA, I can't let her see me talking to him. Then I could kiss my memories goodbye again.

By the time we make it outside, I could practically crawl out of my skin. I pat the Mind Redeemer in my pocket again, just to make sure it's still there.

"Are you all right?" Mom asks, giving me that concerned, parental look as we exit the apartment building. Aunt Grace used to do that to me all the time. If I don't start acting more normal, Mom might realize that I'm up to something.

I roll my shoulders and neck and attempt an excited-looking smile. "I'm fine. I guess I'm just a little nervous. You know, this is my first time out in New Denver since I was little."

Mom bites her lip. "Yes, that makes sense. It's just . . . I wish everything wasn't so tense." Our eyes immediately cut to a pair of officers approaching us. They're in riot gear, as if they expect another protest to take place any minute, and they're not alone. Across the street, another pair of officers are patrolling. The whole effect just makes me even more anxious. I clench my fists and try to ignore the jittery feeling spreading throughout my body.

The one good thing I can say is that there don't seem to be many Purists out, if any. Most everybody appears to be Gen Mods—their lean bodies are a giveaway. Some are wearing sleek, fitted suits in bright shades and asymmetrical tops that randomly change color. From what I've learned, they're super popular now. Others wear clothes retrieved from different periods of time in the past. Like, right now I see a woman wearing a shiny white coat and a short orange and yellow dress with yellow tights that appears to be straight from the 1960s. She's walking with a man dressed in plaid bell-bottom pants, a navy-blue turtleneck shirt, and a brown blazer. I cringe. Even today, people still make questionable fashion choices.

"So, are you still hungry? Or would you rather get some new clothes first?" Mom asks, eyeing my jumpsuit and plain black coat that's a size too big for me.

I seriously can't blame her; the few clothes that I have are hideous. But as much as I'd like to ditch them, I need to talk to Bridger while I know where he is.

"Let's eat first. I'm starving," I lie again, still way too nervous to eat.

"Well, there's a row of replica twentieth century restaurants just around the corner," Mom says. "I'm sure we can find something you'd like there."

"No! I have something else in mind," I say a bit too quickly.

Mom side-eyes me. "Really? And what would that be?"

I give her the directions to the diner where Bridger is right now. Mom sighs. "That's nearly five blocks from here. Are you sure about that?"

"Yep. Positively. I've been dying to eat there ever since I heard about it." My mind races, trying to figure out a legitimate way I could have heard about the restaurant. "One of my tutors back in Chicago talked about it all the time." I almost feel guilty lying to her, but I push the feeling away, remembering that she's been lying to me for the past ten months.

I'm torn between constantly checking my DataLink and trying not to gawk at the scenery around me while walking through downtown New Denver. Sure, I've been out in Chicago some with my tutors, and I've seen countless vids showing what other cities are like in this time, but now that I have my memories back, comparing the cities of today to what I grew up with is so freaking weird.

I can't stop noticing how different things look from the time I grew up in. Nulls are everywhere, performing maintenance and cleaning services—doing jobs that nobody wants. There are no cars, only shuttles whizzing past over the tops of the buildings. Pods, which are smaller white shuttles that can carry just a few people at a time, glide overhead much closer to the ground than regular transport shuttles. Pods function like taxis, but only some people can afford them, since they're so expensive. The government tries to encourage people to walk or take a Maglev while traveling within the city.

We're a block away from the restaurant when I check my DataLink again. My stomach clenches into a heavy knot: Bridger isn't there anymore. My steps slow and Mom turns to me.

"What's wrong?" she asks.

I lower my arm quickly and look up at her, my mind searching for an excuse to bail on the restaurant now. "Um, I don't feel so good."

She places her hand on my forehead, her brow crinkling. "You're a little warm. Do you need to sit down?"

I nod. She leads me to a short bench reserved for people who are waiting for a Pod to pick them up. That's another difference between this time and the past; their streets are nothing more than wide paved areas, just big enough for a small shuttle or Pod to land on.

"Can I have something to drink?" I ask. My mouth is dry, but it's from fear that I won't be able to talk to Bridger, not from being sick.

"Of course," Mom says. "Stay here and I'll be right back." She hurries away to a nearby vendor selling bottles of water. I take the opportunity to track Bridger again. The blinking red dot indicating his location is moving at a rapid pace. I look up at Mom. She has the water bottle in hand and is handing over payment. She'll be back any minute now.

I watch the dot. Please stop. Please.

And it finally does, just a block from here. I check the location and find that's it's a nearby Green Zone. Now to convince Mom I need to go there. This should be interesting.

But fortunately, she buys my story that I'm just exhausted from all the excitement of moving and experiencing the protests yesterday, and I need a walk to relax. We make it to the Green Zone within five minutes. I search for Bridger and my legs almost give out when I see him sitting on a bench under a large tree.

"Mom, I'm kind of hungry again. Do you think you could get me a little something to munch on?" I ask.

She takes a deep breath and stares at me hard. "Are you sure? I thought you wanted to try out that restaurant."

"I feel weak, so I kind of want to stay outside for a while," I say, then I remember a memory from my childhood. "I used to love coming to Green Zones, right? I feel comfortable here right now. Not so anxious."

"Okay, then. I can't argue with that. I'll just grab some sandwiches at that shop over there," she says while pointing to a small bistro behind us. It has a flashing a sign over the door advertising its menu. "Stay right here, got it?"

"Yes, of course."

I wait long enough for her to get out of sight, then turn and make myself walk to Bridger—even though I want to run to him. I wonder how he's going to react. What he will say.

I'm nearly ten feet away when he suddenly looks up from his Data-Link. His mouth opens and shuts a few times, and he turns so pale that I wonder if he's going to pass out.

Oh, dear God, please don't let him faint. I won't have enough time to talk to him.

Or even worse, what if he refuses to talk to me?

9

BRIDGER
FEBRUARY 11, 2147

*I*t's not Vika. *It's not Vika,* I tell myself as the girl I saw at the Academy strides toward me. The same girl Grandma just warned me to stay away from. It's like I'm looking at a living ghost. Same blond hair. I bet their smiles would be similar, but I have no idea. But then, I'm starting to notice differences, too; her eyes are a lighter shade of blue, and her face is a little rounder. This girl has a determined expression on her face as she stares at me.

But why is she here? What does she want with me? I should just get up and leave. Nothing good can come from talking with her.

But I stay in place.

When she reaches me, she glances over her shoulder for a moment then joins me on the bench. "I know you're wondering why I'm here. But before we get into that, I need to know if you remember me."

I try not to look too much like an idiot, but I have no idea what she's talking about. "I've heard stories about you, but other than that, no. I've never met you before in my life."

The girl heaves a sigh. "I swear, I'm beginning to hate the DTA. Do you even know my name?"

I shake my head.

"That figures. It's Alora."

She slides her hand into her pocket and extracts something small, then flips her hand over so I can see it. I blink a few times to make sure I'm not hallucinating. It's a Mind Redeemer. How did she get one of those? Only DTA operatives can have them, and only while on assignment to erase the short-term memories of ghosts in the past who have accidentally witnessed a Time Bender.

"What are you doing with that?" I ask, looking around us to make sure nobody else can see the Mind Redeemer. There aren't many people close to us. Just an elderly couple two benches away from us talking to each other, a few people jogging, and several Nulls picking up trash off the ground. I shudder looking at them.

I never want that to happen to me.

The girl—Alora—stares down at the Mind Redeemer clasped in her palm. "I found it in my bedroom with a note telling me to use it on myself if I couldn't remember my Aunt Grace. Or . . . you."

I look sharply at her. "Me? Why would it say that? We've never met."

She reaches across and takes my hand. Her hand feels nice against my skin. "But we have met. I'd tell you everything, but I think it would be better if I let you remember for yourself."

She holds up the Mind Redeemer, but I panic and scoot away, glancing at the Nulls again. "No, I can't do this."

Her brow crinkles, and I'm reminded of Vika. "Why not? The DTA has been lying to both of us. Don't you want to know the truth?"

A huge part of me does. After all, I lost several weeks of my life when they took my memories after I went temporarily insane. But according to this girl, I met her and something else happened. It must be really important if she's risking her own safety to come to me.

But I don't know if I can handle remembering the truth. Maybe it's better that I don't know. I've finally been promoted at the Academy. I have a good chance of being able to join the military, just like my father. Even General Anderson said he'd look out for me, so that has to mean something. I don't want to jeopardize all that I've worked for.

"I don't think this is such a good idea. I think you should just go," I reply. But even as I say those words, I wish I could take them back. The look on her face is hard to bear. It's as if I've punched her.

For a moment, I think she's about to stand, then her hand whips up in front of my forehead and she whispers, "I'm sorry." Then I'm hit with a pain that's like someone shooting a stunner right into my skull.

I close my eyes and grit my teeth to keep from screaming. It seems like the pain will never end. But it slowly recedes, and the memories begin to return.

And they all center on Dad. How he sent me back to the year 2013 to save Alora from being murdered. Discovering that both he and Vika were cloned, and that he's still alive. Realizing that I didn't wild out last year at all, like everyone said.

The DTA lied. My mother lied. Everyone lied.

I bend over and rest my head between my knees. Alora rubs her hand across my back. "I'm so sorry. I had the same reaction."

I can't do anything for a while but gasp for air. Feelings of rage and betrayal consume me. The DTA did this. General Anderson was somehow behind all of it. Last year, after I illegally shifted to 2013 and returned to this time, he was determined to capture and then Null me, while Professor March pretended to help me to escape. But then Dad warned me not to trust the professor again. I feel sick. Professor March's comm from earlier today echoes in my mind. He's been acting all concerned, checking in on me and Shan at school since last year. But he's never even mentioned his part in orchestrating my "escape" from being Nulled—the plot that Anderson apparently engineered. Why did they do that? Why did they cover it up?

When I finally feel well enough to sit back up, Alora is biting her lip and looking at me with concern. I remember how I was starting to develop feelings for her when we found out that she's Vika's half-sister. Oh man, that's *so* messed up. But Alora is here now, and I'm overwhelmed to realize how much I've missed her. I lean over and throw my arms around her. God, she smells so good. Like lavender. Her arms tighten around me, too. I wish we could just stay this way: two people trying to make sense of a world that unjustly tore us apart.

She pulls back suddenly, looking back over her shoulder again. "I can't stay much longer. My mom will be here any minute now, and she can't see us together. I don't know if I can trust her."

"I know exactly what you mean," I say, hating how bitter I sound. "I don't really know who we can trust, either."

"What are we going to do? Your father is still out there somewhere, and I don't know what happened to my dad. We have to find them."

"I know, but I don't think we should do anything right now. We can't let anyone else know that we remember the truth."

Alora crosses her arms, frowning. "I've been living in this century for the past ten months. How much longer do I have to wait before I can find my father? I promised Aunt Grace I would before I left."

"Look, I get it. I really do. I . . . I just need some time to think. We can't do anything to make the DTA suspicious."

"But Bridger—" Suddenly Alora turns to look behind her, then whips her head back around, her eyes wide. "I've got to go. My mom is on the way. Please stay in touch, okay? I need some answers soon."

"I'll find you at school on Monday. Just stay out of trouble until then."

She looks like she wants to say something else, but just nods and begins walking toward the dark-haired woman standing on the other side of the Green Zone. The woman looks so relieved when she spots Alora. I remember her: Adalyn Mason, the woman who broke my father's heart when she refused to marry him so many years ago. The woman who originally asked him to retrieve Alora from the past. She's partially responsible for my dad's death before he was cloned—along with the cloned version of Vika.

I should hate them, and I do, a little, but mostly I'm furious at the DTA. Specifically, General Anderson. He covered up what Dad did before, and I suspect he covered what I did, too. But *why*? Were we about to expose a secret that he wants to keep hidden? If I have to guess, I bet it's something to do with the fact that Dad, Vika, and Alora's father were all cloned, which is illegal now. Or maybe it's because Vika and Alora's father—and even Professor March—are Dual Talents. At the Academy, we're taught those don't exist.

As I leave the park to go back to Grandma's apartment, I promise myself that though I may not be able to do anything right now, I *will* find out the truth, no matter what.

And then I almost run smack into someone. I try to brush past the person, but he grabs my upper arm.

Alarmed, I glance up and immediately my heart begins to race. The man standing there, still holding my arm, is my father. Here. Still very much still alive.

10

BRIDGER
FEBRUARY 11, 2147

After a moment, I realize I must look like an idiot. My jaw is slack, and I can't speak. Dad is really here. Or at least, the cloned version of him. Still, it's my dad, wearing the standard navy Time Bender uniform.

"Son, are you all right? You look like you're about to pass out," he says, with a trace of amusement in his voice.

The only thing I can do is nod.

Dad scopes out our surroundings, then inclines his head to the left. "I only have six minutes before I have to leave. Walk with me to my shift point."

Still feeling numb, I manage to shuffle along beside him as we walk through the Green Zone. I can't stop staring at him.

"You need to quit doing that," Dad says. "We don't want to draw unwanted attention."

"I don't understand. Where have you been? Why are you here now?"

Dad looks at me as if I've grown a third eye or something. "I've missed talking to you. I miss being with you and your brother. It's been hell, having to stay away from the both of you."

I think for a moment. From my perspective, it's been over ten months since I last saw him. But I don't know at what point in the timeline Dad is from. He refused to share the year with me when I last saw him, which was the night that Alora was almost killed in 2013. After I was forced to kill the cloned version of Vika because she had just murdered Dad—and was trying to do the same to Alora—Dad's clone appeared to us. He stayed long enough to let me know that he—not my real dad—was the one responsible for sending me back to save Alora in the first place. "How long has it been for you?"

Dad lets out a light laugh. "Nice try, son. I can't disclose that information."

"I don't get it. Why all the secrecy?"

Dad grows quiet as we pass two military Space Benders in dark gray uniforms, patrolling as we leave the Green Zone and set off down the street. Once they're past us, he says, "I'm not supposed to exist, for starters. Technically, you shouldn't even know about me. Your memories were wiped, so you're supposed to think I'm dead, remember?" He leans close to me and lowers his voice. "But if you still thought I was dead, you would have wilded out when you first saw me a few minutes ago. So it seems you've got your memories back."

Regret sinks inside me like a stone. I'm an idiot. How could I let that slip, having a conversation with him about things I shouldn't even know? I know I can trust Dad, but I didn't even think about what I was doing before I told him those things. I can't make mistakes like that if I'm going to make it in the military. I need to be sharp at all times. Not like this.

"It's okay. I already knew you had restored your memories." His face hardens. "I saw what that girl did to you."

"You saw that? If you didn't think she should restore them, why didn't you stop it?"

"Because from my point of view it's already happened. I can't change it."

I stop walking. "Wait. Exactly what time are you from?"

"I can't tell you that, son. You know it could influence your actions, and I have to let things play out like they're supposed to."

"They why bother coming back to see me at all?"

"This is the only way I can check in on you. The DTA monitors my whereabouts when they send me on missions in the present, but they can't when I'm on assignment in the past. This is a detour for me. In fact, it's my second one. Right after the protests, I checked in on you at the med center. You were sedated, so you never saw me."

I feel detached, as if I've stepped out of my body. "I just . . . this is too much to take in," I manage to say. "Am I in trouble? You know, for getting my memories back?"

Dad laughs. "Of course not. I'm not telling anybody. Honestly, I'm glad you have them back, even though I don't approve of you spending time with that girl. Just to make it clear, I wasn't around when Anderson gave the order to have you erased. Maybe I could have talked him out of it. You're old enough to handle the truth."

With those words, the tension in my body begins to ease. "So, what exactly *can* you tell me? Why are you talking to me now? Aren't you putting the timeline at risk by doing that?"

"No. In fact, I'm helping you. It's important that you continue to act like you don't remember anything." Dad turns down an empty alley between two skyscrapers. "Don't try to look for me. Don't help that girl. Don't tell anybody you saw me. Not your friends, not my mother, not even your brother—he tells your mother everything. Your objective is to maintain the status quo, so you can stay safe."

I follow Dad halfway down the alley. He stops and rests his back against the wall of one of the buildings, then lifts his left arm to check his Chronoband.

"Wait, you have to leave now?" I ask. My pulse begins to race. "You just got here."

"It's time for me to go. If I'm late, General Anderson could send someone back to check on my whereabouts."

"So Anderson *is* behind everything," I say, not even bothering to hide the bitterness I'm feeling. "What's his end game?"

"Can't talk about that now, son. Just know that he's one of the good guys. I'll be in touch soon. And remember, stay away from that girl—and from Telfair."

Before I can say anything else, he activates his cloak and vanishes.

II

I. Can't. Sleep.

After spending most of the night staring at the ceiling in my bedroom, or sketching scenes of my life with Aunt Grace, I finally sit up. According to my DataLink, it's almost four o'clock in the morning. I lean across the bed and swipe my finger across a sensor on the bottom of my window, which deactivates the night screen and allows me to see outside. It's still dark. The only flashes of light are from a few shuttles flying overhead and from some nearby Jumbotrons, which cast faint shadows across my walls. A few lights are on in different buildings, but most of them are dark, their inhabitants more than likely lost in their dreams.

I let out a sigh and lie back on the bed. The only thing I can think about is my conversation with Bridger. I keep replaying what he said in my head, wondering if he will decide to help me. I thought once I'd restored his memories, he'd be completely on my side, but it seems like he's unsure. It hurts me, but I guess I can understand. He's lived his life separate from me since we returned to this time—ten long months where we both made the best of our respective situations. I can see how he wouldn't want to jeopardize what he's spent that time working for.

But still, I need answers. I need to find my father, and figure out why he was cloned and brought to this era after his death in the military in 1994. I need answers as to why he never came back for me. Why did he rob me of a life with him in it?

The DTA is hiding something from me—and Bridger—and we need to find out what that is.

But at the same time, I miss Aunt Grace so much. The ache is stronger than it was yesterday when I finally remembered her, and all I want to do is go to her right now. I have to know that she's okay, that nobody from the DTA hurt her. I know I shouldn't; it's illegal to time travel without the DTA's permission. But I'm not exactly feeling warm and fuzzy toward the DTA at the moment.

I need to see her.

Before I can change my mind, I jump out of bed, strip out of my new pajamas, and dig through my closet. Mom went a little overboard buying me clothes. I barely remember the shopping trip—I just went along with a lot of what she chose. I find a pair of jeans and a plain blue T-shirt with labels stating that they were retrieved from 2004, along with a pair of white-and-gray sneakers. This'll have to do.

Once I'm dressed, I remember to retrieve the Mind Redeemer from its hiding place in my dresser and stuff it in my pocket, just in case someone from the DTA went back and took Aunt Grace's memories, too. I hope they wouldn't be that cruel to her.

Then I close my eyes and picture the forest behind the former plantation house that was our home. I think of the path where I used to jog to the river every day, picture where the path ended and the yard began. That's where I need to appear, since I don't know if I'll be able to free shift to my target date. My last day with Aunt Grace was July 4, 2013—the day I "officially" died at the hands of the homicidal man who was a guest at Aunt Grace's inn, Dave Palmer. I'll try to return two weeks later, on July 18. That gives her enough time to deal with the immediate aftermath of what happened and get past my fake funeral.

Entering the Void sucks. I hate this part of traveling through time more than anything; it feels like I don't exist. But at least it's over quickly. Warm air wraps around my skin like a welcoming blanket as soon as I emerge. I breathe in deeply, relishing the scent of pine and earth. This is what home feels like. Kind of ironic how much I wanted to get away from Willow Creek when I lived here.

And for once, I'm so thankful that I'm a Dual Talent. If I were only a Time Bender, I'd have to travel to what's left of Willow Creek and shift to the past from there, which I could never do right now.

Upon opening my eyes, I find that I'm standing a little way down the path to the river. The opening in the trees that I know leads to the inn's yard is visible, but not the house itself. I'm surprised to hear a lot of voices and laughter, like a party or something.

What could Aunt Grace be doing right now? From the slant of the sunlight streaming through the trees, I can tell that it's late afternoon.

Normally she would be preparing for supper, but I'm not so sure now. Before our lives were turned upside down, she had decided to sell the inn to her evil former sister-in-law. If I landed on a later date than I meant to, Aunt Grace could already have sold the house and moved.

Before I do anything else, I set a timer on my DataLink to alert me when two hours have passed. That way I won't be tempted to stay too long. For every hour I spend in the past, the same amount of time passes in my own time.

I move toward the opening and peer out. What I see hits me like a punch to the face. The backyard is full of people dressed in formal clothes, all standing around talking and laughing. Underneath a huge white tent, round tables are set up, covered with white linens. Rows of white chairs are lined up before a flower covered arch.

Oh my God, this is a wedding. That must mean that Aunt Grace has already sold the inn. She's gone. I want to sink to my knees, but I force myself to keep standing. So, I obviously missed my target date. Go me. I'll just have to try again and hope that I don't mess up.

But before I can shift again, a familiar figure appears in the crowd. It's Aunt Grace, dressed in a royal-blue sleeveless dress. Her light brown curls are pinned up on her head, and she's laughing and talking with several people. An electric feeling pulses through me. When I left Aunt Grace, she had been shot in her shoulder. She appears to be completely healed now. I must have really been off on my target date.

I want to race across the yard and fling myself into her arms, but of course that's a stupid idea under the circumstances. If I want to talk to her, I'll have to find a way to blend in until I can get close. I glance down at jeans and T-shirt. I can't just waltz up to a wedding like this. And I need to hide my identity, since I'm supposed to be dead. Hopefully my bedroom is still intact.

I take a deep breath and picture my bedroom, focusing on the purple walls and fluffy comforter on my bed. I picture myself standing there, and before I can even open my eyes, I'm overwhelmed with the scent of lavender. The voices from the wedding outside are now muffled.

Then I'm hit with a wave of dizziness. Just great; I'm having a reaction to shifting so many times in such a short period of time. This usually happens when I shift more than four or five times in one day, but I guess that's only when I'm bending space, not space and time together. My tutors in Chicago preferred to keep my space-bending and time bending-lessons separate.

I manage to make it to my bed and lie down, closing my eyes. After a few minutes, I'm able to sit up, though I feel slightly weak. I wish I could stay in here. Just being in this room brings back so many memories. When I was little, Aunt Grace used to tuck me in every night and read stories to me. And I would spend hours in here, drawing in my sketch book. I even remember Bridger being in here with me on the day I tracked down a man who knew my father in hopes of learning more about my past. I remember how close Bridger and I came to kissing.

And I remember how we *did* kiss at the river.

Heat rushes to my face. That's the last thing I need to think about right now. Forcing myself to stand, I march over to my closet, search through my clothes—thankfully, Aunt Grace kept everything—and pull out a long, light-green sundress and a pair of silver sandals.

It feels heavenly to slip on the dress. I'm not really a dress-wearing kind of girl, but it's so nice to wear something that actually belongs to me, not some clothes that Time Benders scavenged.

I check myself in the mirror. My hair hangs in loose waves down my back. That's way too eye-catching. I need to hide it, but with what? Maybe a hat would work.

Five minutes later, I check the mirror again. My hair is pinned up under an oversized cream-colored beanie that I found in my dresser, and I'm wearing a pair of sunglasses.

Not the best disguise, but it'll have to do.

Downstairs, I hear voices and realize that the house isn't empty. My stomach knots when I spot some guests sitting in the front parlor, sipping champagne, and caterers in the kitchen prepping food. One of them looks up at me, quizzically. I lower my gaze and head out the back door.

Outside, I'm overwhelmed at the sheer number of people here. I get a few curious looks as I walk through the crowd. Way to go, Alora. At least I don't recognize anyone so far.

It takes a little while, but I finally find Aunt Grace under the white tent, talking to the bride and groom. But I can't just walk up to her; she would probably freak out. Instead, I search for one of the caterers and walk up to her. "Excuse me. Grace Evans is needed in the kitchen, but I don't know who she is. Could you please give her the message?"

The lady looks skeptical, but she nods and sets out in Aunt Grace's direction.

Feeling a bit smug, I turn around to go into the house, but I smack straight into a man behind me. I freeze, looking up at him. He's tall, with brown hair and glasses. My first thought is Palmer, but no. This man is younger, maybe in his late twenties. Still, my heart is racing.

"Do I know you?" he asks, squinting at me. "You seem familiar."

I just shake my head and push past him. I don't allow myself to relax until I'm back inside the house. I go halfway down the hall and try to open the door to Aunt Grace's study, but of course it's locked.

The back door opens, and I whirl around. It's Aunt Grace. She immediately locks eyes with me. and her mouth drops open as the blood drains from her face. "Oh my God," she whispers, leaning against the wall. "You . . . you're dead," she says in a hoarse whisper.

Stupid, stupid DTA. They *did* take her memories.

I rush over to her and wrap my arms around her. She's limp at first, then hugs me back, so tight that I can't breathe. And there are tears. So many tears.

Behind us, I spot one of the caterers poking his head out of the kitchen. "Is everything all right?" he asks.

Aunt Grace glances at him, wiping her eyes. "Oh, yes, everything is perfectly fine."

He raises an eyebrow. "Okay, ma'am. Let me know if you need anything," he replies before retreating.

"Let's go upstairs. I'm feeling a little faint," Aunt Grace says.

Wrapping my arm around her back to support her, I help her climb the stairs to the second floor. I try to ignore the lingering guests and savor the sight of the inn as we walk down the hallway, past the front parlor, and up the stairs.

In my bedroom, I pull off the beanie and sunglasses and toss them on my dresser. Aunt Grace locks the door then leans her back against it, staring at me for a few moments. Then she crosses the room to fold me in another hug. "I've missed you so much. This past year has been so lonely without you." She pulls back to look at me again. "I can't believe you're alive!"

I pull back from her, stunned. "Year? What's the date?"

"It's July 19, 2014. Why? You didn't know that?"

"No," I say, running a hand over my face. "I'm way off target."

"Oh, sweetie, I can't get over this! God, your body was found burned in that old shack in the woods! I had to bury you!" She holds her hand over her mouth for a second, trying to hold back a sob. "What happened? Is this something like what happened with Nate? Something with the government?"

My heart aches for her, knowing that she's suffered for over a year, thinking I was dead. "I have something with me that will explain everything," I say as I cross the room to retrieve the Mind Redeemer out of my pants pocket.

It doesn't take nearly as long to restore her memories as it did mine. Apparently whoever wiped her mind only erased the few hours surrounding my "death." How freaking kind of them.

Once she remembers everything, I catch her up on my life in my new time, and when I'm finished, she's as mad as I am.

"I can't believe that DT . . . whatever treated you like that! What did they expect to gain by erasing your memories and lying to you? Did they think you'd run away to see me all the time?" She pauses and holds up a hand. "Wait, scratch that last statement. You obviously did that, but that doesn't mean you would've done it any other time without a good excuse, right?"

"Yes, ma'am. I've been following the rules. It's just that I was so upset when I found out the truth. And I found Bridger and gave his memories back because I thought he'd help me, but I'm not sure if he will. He was just as mad as me, but he was also scared." I pause and dig my fingers into the comforter. "I swear, Aunt Grace, if they had only trusted me with my own memories, I would've understood. I would've listened to them. But now . . . I don't trust anybody from the DTA."

Even as those words slip past my lips, I know they're a lie. Sure, I don't really belong in this time, but that doesn't change the fact that I have a history here, and a relative I adore. Of course I'd have wanted to come see her, no matter what.

Aunt Grace purses her lips. "Maybe that's the whole reason. I know you like I know myself. And there's no way you would've agreed to never see me again. Maybe they took your memories to keep you from coming back here and messing with things. Remember how Bridger said the timeline had to be preserved, no matter what?"

"That's ridiculous," I reply. "I wouldn't do anything to jeopardize the timeline. I don't see how just visiting you would hurt."

"Sweetie, maybe that's just too big of a risk for them take. Even with you."

I want to tell her she's wrong, but I can't. What she said makes sense. It doesn't excuse the DTA's decisions, but I can kind of see it from their point of view. I shrug my shoulders. "Maybe you're right."

"Of course I am. And as much as I love seeing you, you need to go back. I wish you could stay forever. But if your mom reports you missing, you're going to find yourself in some serious hot water. And you need to do whatever it takes to convince Bridger to help you find Nate and his own father."

"I just got here, Aunt Grace. It won't hurt to stay a little longer. Besides, I don't know what's going on with you. Has that psychopath, Palmer, come back? I'm worried about you." I reach over and clasp her hand.

She squeezes back. "You don't have to worry about me. I doubt he'll come around here again, what with all the media attention. And with my new businesses, he wouldn't dare show his face."

I perk up. "I suppose that has something to do with the wedding?"

Aunt Grace's expression turns devious, and she laughs. "Oh, yes. After what happened with you, I decided it didn't make sense for me to sell the house. We had so many memories here. So I kept the inn open, started a catering business, and I also rent out the grounds for weddings and parties."

I find myself grinning. "I'm so happy for you. But how did Celeste react when you backed out of the deal?"

"It wasn't pretty, but I really don't care. Life's too short."

We talk for a few more minutes about the people in town, and then the timer on my DataLink beeps. My stomach sinks.

"What's that?" Aunt Grace asks.

"I forgot that I had set my alarm. I need to go now." I stand up and grab my jeans and T-shirt off the floor, along with the sneakers. "Do you mind if I just keep the dress?"

"You can take whatever you want."

I glance around the room, wishing I could take everything with me. Impossible, but I still want to. Instead, I decide to take just one more thing that was important to me while I was here. I search through my backpack, which is still propped against my desk, and extract my old purple sketch pad, the one that I left behind. Clutching it to my chest, I turn to face Aunt Grace. "Okay, I guess I'm ready to go."

Then the dam that's been building inside me since I first arrived bursts, and tears flow down my face. Aunt Grace envelops me in a smothering hug.

When I pull away, sniffling, she says, "It's okay to go. I don't want you to get into trouble."

"I'm scared, Aunt Grace. What if the DTA finds out that I know about my past now and erases my memories again?"

"Then you just have to make sure that they don't find out. I'm also counting on you to find Nate. And when you do, promise me that you both will come see me, at least once. I know you're not supposed to mess with the past, but Nate used to visit me on my birthday and I don't think that hurt anything. Okay?"

I nod. "I promise."

I take a few steps away from her and give her a sad smile. "I love you, Aunt Grace."

She wipes at her eyes and forces a smile. "Love you too. See you soon."

Reluctantly, I close my eyes, clutching my sketch pad, my lifeline to the past. I think of the date I need to return to, and of my other bedroom that doesn't feel like my bedroom. I barely notice entering the Void this time—I'm already numb. When I open my eyes again, I'm standing in my bedroom in New Denver.

And my mom is sitting on the bed, staring at me with a horrified expression. "Where have you been?" she asks in panicky voice. "And where did you get that dress?"

Oh my God, what is she doing in here? I was only gone two hours; she should have been asleep the whole time. I need an excuse—I don't know if I can trust her with the truth. But all I can do is stand there like a Null, my brain completely empty.

"I thought someone from the DTA had taken you again," she says, swiping tears from her eyes. "I came in here to check in on you and I couldn't find you!"

I stare down at the floor, at the stupid silver sandals that I should have left behind, along with this stupid dress. Sure, I thought that Mom would sleep the whole time, but I should have considered the fact that she might not. I don't know much about her. I don't know if she likes to wake up early or if she prefers to stay up late. I don't know her favorite color or her favorite food or what she likes to do for fun. What I do know is that she lost me once and when she learned I was living in the past, she was desperate enough to send Bridger's father back to find me. Now I feel horrible for hurting her, for selfishly not thinking about how she would feel if she suddenly couldn't find me. I cross the room and lean down to hug her.

"I'm so sorry," I whisper. "I just . . . I just had to do something." Despite my guilt, I can't make myself tell her that I went to see Aunt Grace. I have no idea how she would react to that. "I couldn't sleep again and I remembered that . . . that I had left this notebook and outfit at my quarters back at the Academy. They were going-away presents from my professors."

It's surprising how the lie came out of nowhere, how easily it slipped past my lips.

Mom stares at me for a few seconds. "I have no idea if that's the truth, but I'm going to choose to believe you because I *can't* lose you again. I just can't, Alora." She takes both of my hands in her own. "Please promise me that you won't illegally shift again. You were supposed to have an Inhibitor on this weekend, and if the DTA so much as suspects that you've been shifting, I'm afraid they won't let you come home with me anymore. Or even worse."

At her words, my chests tightens and it feels as if someone has sucked all the air out of the room. I can't let that happen, not if I'm going to search for Dad. From what she just said, I don't think she would report me to the DTA if she knew that I've regained my memories. But I'm also sure she would do whatever it takes to keep me from searching for my father.

So I lie to her again.

12

BRIDGER
FEBRUARY 12, 2147

Sunday morning, Grandma takes Shan and me out for breakfast. Neither of us eat very much. We don't talk much, either. I guess Shan is still too depressed, or whatever is wrong with him. I'm too angry about my memories being stolen, and I'm torn over Dad's too-brief reappearance. It's all I can do to keep pretending that everything is fine while I'm around Grandma. The only thing I really want is to punch something.

Then we head straight back to the apartment. More Purists are out today. Many gave hateful looks to us and other Gen Mods, and one idiotic Purist tries to start a fight with a Gen Mod just ahead of us. At least there are still plenty of police officers out patrolling; they immediately take control. Still, the whole time we're outside, I can't help but wonder how long it will be until another protest takes place. The Purists are still angry.

As soon as we get back to the apartment, Shan makes for his bedroom. That's where he's been all weekend, just playing one Sim Game after another.

"Hey, come back in here," Grandma calls out to him.

He glances back, raising an eyebrow. "What? You want to talk to me?"

"I want to talk to both of you," Grandma replies, her steely gaze cutting between the two of us. "Both of you, on the couch. Now."

Shan give me a what-does-she-want look. I just shrug and sit down. He slumps on the opposite side from me, the leather creaking as he settles in.

Grandma takes a seat across from us, but she doesn't say a word. I start to squirm. Shan looks down at his hands, his lips pinched together in a sour expression. I can see how Grandma rose to such a high rank in the military—she can be intimidating when she wants to be. That happens to be pretty much all the time.

"I've noticed you two aren't very happy," she says.

"That's not true," I begin, but Grandma holds up a hand.

"That's complete bull. Shan has been moping around here all weekend. And *you* weren't too bad until yesterday, when you came back from the Green Zone." She takes a deep breath. "So I've decided to do something about that. I think we need to go camping for a few days."

Shan's head snaps up, his mouth forming a little "o" shape. And me? I'm not sure what to say. I used to love camping. Dad took us a lot when we were little. I carried on the tradition with Zed and Elijah. In fact, last year we used a camping trip as my cover story while I traveled to Georgia so I could illegally shift back to 2013 to find out why Dad wanted me to save Alora.

"Isn't it too cold? And what if it snows?" Shan asks.

"It's not *that* cold. And there is no snow in the forecast. I've already reserved our campsite, and I'm not taking no for an answer," she says, gesturing in the direction of our bedrooms. "So go pack. We'll head into the mountains tonight and come back Tuesday morning."

"But what about school?" Shan asks.

"They're not going to kick you out for missing a few days. With everything that's happened lately, I'm sure Chancellor Tyson would agree that it's best for you two to get away. The fresh air will be good for you."

Shan glances at me, then back at Grandma. "What about Mom? Does she know?"

Grandma sighs. "Your mom would be perfectly happy letting you go."

I snort. Grandma winks at me, then orders us to get cracking.

I'm nearly finished when I hear loud voices coming from the living room. Shan is standing in the hallway with the guiltiest expression I've ever seen on his face

"What did you do?" I ask as I walk down the hall. Shan follows me.

We stop at threshold of the hallway. I immediately spot Grandma, standing in front of the TeleNet on the far side of the living room. Mom is on the screen, her dark hair pulled back in a ponytail, and she's in her royal-blue and black field uniform. Even with dark circles under her eyes, she still looks furious.

I glare at Shan and whisper, "You just had to tattle, didn't you?"

Shan argues back, in a quiet voice. "I thought she should know. Mom's in Louisiana, and I didn't even know if she knew we were here.

And now Grandma wants to drag us camping without even asking her? I didn't think that was right."

I rake my fingers through my hair, to stop myself from wrapping them around his throat. "Shan, you can be such a furing idiot sometimes. All Grandma wanted to do was get us out of town for a few days. In case you haven't noticed, things aren't great around here."

"Yeah, but . . ."

"But nothing, Shan. She was just trying to help us. And you had to go and call Mom." I storm away from him. "It's time you grew up."

Shan recoils. "You think I'm stupid and that I'm babied by Mom, but maybe you're the one who doesn't get it. Maybe Grandma is doing something that isn't good for us. Maybe *I* needed to look out for us."

"Yeah, right. You don't know how to look out for anybody but yourself."

I join Grandma in the living room, where she and Mom have escalated to shouting at each other.

"I never gave my consent for them to stay with you, Judith, and I'm certainly not going to give my consent for them to go camping. It's too dangerous. There could be Purists hiding in the woods."

Grandma rolls her eyes. "If you believe that, then you're a bigger fool than I thought. The mountains just might be the safest place I can take them."

Mom notices me. "Bridger, I absolutely forbid you and your brother to go with her. I want you two to return to the Academy immediately."

Grandma's face flushes. "I've heard enough of this nonsense. I have every right to visit with my grandsons. And I'd love to see you try to stop me from seeing them."

Mom's lips flatten to a tight line, then she says, "Judith, those boys are my world. I don't want anything to happen to them. Please, don't do this."

"I would never put them in danger, Morgan. They're all I have left of my son." Grandma says in a much quieter voice.

Then she deactivates the screen and turns to face me. "Well, that went well."

I don't know what to think of that. Mom said *we're* her whole world. Not just Shan. Touching, but not really accurate.

I look back at Shan. He's still standing in the hallway, looking like he could faint. Like I said before, he's a total mama's boy. I turn my attention back to Grandma. "So, does that mean we're staying here?" I ask.

"Of course not. I'm not about to let her tell me what to do. Let's go, boys!"

It takes us a little over two hours to rent a mobile camping shuttle, travel to the campsite in the Rockies, and set up everything up. I kind of wish we could have used Dad's old army-green tent and thermal sleeping bags. He used to say camping that way made him feel more connected to the ghosts we visited on each time trip because it allowed us to experience life the way it was for some people in the past. But since it's still cold, Grandma figured the mobile shelter would be best. I've never used one before. It's a rounded, silver vehicle about the same size as a small transport shuttle, but it has beds, indoor plumbing, and a tiny kitchen area. This one cost a small fortune to rent. But if anyone can afford it, she can.

"Well, that's done," Grandma says when we're finished setting up the camp. She steps back and admires the view. It's gorgeous. Nothing but mountains and pines and crisp air. "It's been too long since I've been out here. Leithan and I used to come out here a lot when he was little."

Shan does a weird double take at her. "You used to camp with Dad?"

"Seriously? Dad used to tell us stories about his trips with Grandma all the time," I snap. How could he not remember? It was just Grandma and Dad. He didn't grow up with a father figure, since Grandma never married, instead using a sperm donation from an anonymous Time Bender to have a child. Dad said that she claimed the military took the place of a demanding spouse.

Shan manages to look a bit sheepish. "I don't remember a lot from back then."

"Or maybe you weren't paying attention," I snap.

Before Shan can reply, Grandma interrupts. "You know what? I have something to show the two of you."

While she steps inside the camper, Shan spits out, "I wish you'd stop being such a jerk. I really don't remember things Dad talked about. I just remember having fun, so give me a break. I was a little kid when we did all of that."

A few moments later, Grandma emerges holding her DataPad. "You might not remember this, but sometimes Leithan would record the two of you out here with him, and he would send the vids to me. It let me keep up with you from afar, since I couldn't be here all the time."

Shan and I stand next to her while she taps on the pad a few times and retrieves one of the messages. The time stamp reads August 22, 2137, when I was eight and Shan was four. The message starts with Dad's face filling the screen, and then he starts speaking. Just hearing his voice makes me miss him even more, even though I know the cloned version of him is still here.

"Hi, Mom. I thought I'd show you what you're missing since you couldn't get away from work," he says, his eyebrows raising in the way that always showed he was being slightly sarcastic. Then he pans his camera around to show the view. "Bet you're kicking yourself in the pants now, huh?" He grins, then points the camera to his left, where Shan and I are wading in a creek. We're laughing and splashing each other.

Then the scene cuts away several times, showing us doing different things. Toasting gooey white globs called marshmallows, which were a rare treat for us since they're no longer made in this time. Occasionally, Dad found some on time trips and brought them back for us.

Then we see scenes that include hiking and fishing. The final scene shows me catching a fish, yelling in glee because I was helping Dad with our supper. Shan is standing next to me, pouting. He looks back at Dad and says, "No fair! I want one too!"

Then it cuts away again, this time showing Shan reeling in a small fish. The look on his face is one of pure delight. "Daddy, I did it!" he screams while holding it up.

I'm standing next to Shan, grinning and yelling along with him. I remember that moment. I was so happy for him. He had been trying for hours—he wanted to be just like Dad and me.

Dad's voice cuts in over our excitement. "Good job, boys! I'm proud of you!"

Shan suddenly jerks away from us. I look up from the DataPad in confusion as he rushes into the camper.

Grandma swipes her finger across the DataPad, ending the message. A huge ache fills me. I miss those days. I miss being little and not having to worry about anything. I miss actually getting along with Shan, even if it was sporadic.

"Do you think I should talk to him?" I ask. "He's really not acting right."

Grandma shakes her head sadly. "No, I think I should talk to him. I get the feeling that he might open up more if he's alone with me. But you know, watching that old vid has me craving fish right now. Why don't you go see if you can catch some for supper?"

"Do you have a back-up plan in case they aren't biting?" I ask. It's been a while since I've even tried to fish. I could have luck, but more than likely I'll come back empty-handed.

"I have Ready Meals. We won't starve," she says with a wink.

"I'll try extra hard, then," I reply. We get enough Ready Meals at the Academy. I can do without having to choke down one of those tasteless things.

The stream is about a mile away, down a path leading from our campsite. I find myself relaxing more the farther I get from camp. Maybe this is what I need: just to be by myself for a while.

I'm almost to the stream when I suddenly get this overwhelming feeling that I'm not alone. I hear a crackling in the forest, as if someone is following me. I spin around, but there's no one on the path, or in bushes. I set out again, feeling foolish. I tell myself that it's just my nerves. That's to be expected after everything that's happened to me. Right?

13

ELLIS
OCTOBER 22, 2155

It's late afternoon when Ellis looks out the window of the abandoned house he slept in during the day. All he can see is piles of rubble surrounding the few residences that are even partially intact. This neighborhood, once home to some of the wealthier citizens of New Denver, was demolished in the early stages of what everyone now calls The Last War.

He searches through his satchel and takes out one of his Ready Meals. It's supposed to be a type of protein pie, but it's rock hard and stale. He eats it anyway. Being choosy about a meal is a luxury he hasn't experienced in years.

After hoisting his air tank onto his back, Ellis straps its accompanying mask around his neck. The air is safe to breathe in most places, but he frequently stumbles upon areas in which enemy soldiers have used Death Bombs, which render the air toxic for hours after detonation.

Before he leaves the house, Ellis checks through his satchel one more time to make sure he hasn't accidentally left anything behind. Fifteen Ready Meals, three bottles of water, a digigraph of his family, and the comm-set that he stole—along with a Chronoband—from the military bunker he lived in up until a year ago. He also pats his pocket, feeling for the DataDisk he always keeps in there, and makes sure his stunner is secured at his waist.

It's because of the stolen Chronoband that he has to keep moving. He'll never be forgiven for taking it, since so few remain in existence. The regional commander issued a reward for his capture—extra rations and a secure post within the bunker at all times. That's the last alert he was able to receive on his DataLink.

He takes out the comm-set and fits it over his head. Not only does it help him look for cloaked enemies, it also still functions as a recorder.

And Ellis has been recording a lot of his surroundings—he needs proof of what life is like in this time.

Because Ellis has decided that he's had enough of living this life. A life in which he, along with the rest of the country, has lost everything. The only way out is to prevent the war from even happening—which means traveling to 2147.

But in order to preserve the timeline up until the devastating act that led to the destruction of the North American Federation, Ellis first has to retrieve four items from the past.

Ellis presses the stone on a necklace he's wearing. It's a Jewill that belonged to someone he knew as a child. Once he's cloaked, Ellis leaves the house and begins recording, adding to his existing material. No one looking at this footage will be able to deny that this future is real and devastating, he thinks as he hurries through the near-silent neighborhood.

As he nears the heart of what used to be downtown New Denver, Ellis becomes more cautious. He passes some civilians wandering aimlessly, including a few children. A small part of him aches for them, grieving the world that they never knew. It would be smart for them to stay out of sight, but so many have given up hope.

Several times, he has to duck into partially destroyed buildings or hide behind downed shuttles when he spots someone in the distance. It's hard to tell if they're foreign soldiers or local ones, and it doesn't matter. They're all wearing comm-sets, which would alert them to his presence, and they would either kill or try to capture him.

After miles of passing nothing but desperate survivors and decomposing bodies, hiding intermittently, Ellis leaves the boundary of the city limits and arrives at his destination—the remains of The Academy for Time Travel and Research. This is one of the few places that kept Chronobands and comm-sets on site. His mission is to shift back to the day that the Academy was bombed and retrieve two Chronobands and comm-sets before they are destroyed.

The buildings that made up the Academy were completely demolished by a steady stream of bombs launched by the European Coalition. Inspecting the coordinates on his DataLink, Ellis locates an area close to the main building. He then checks the date that he programmed into his Chronoband several days ago. It's September 2, 2147, at 11:05 in the morning. That's five minutes before the attacks began, targeting the Academy and New Denver. The European Coalition, upon realizing that the outbreak unleashed by the bioweapon on April 5, 2147, was spreading to other countries, decided to take out population centers with huge numbers of infected people.

Closing his eyes, Ellis shifts. It takes him a few seconds to adjust to being in his past, but soon his vision and hearing clear. Around him, the grounds of the Academy are nearly abandoned. There are several people walking through the grassy expanse between the Academy's buildings. Soldiers are posted at every entrance.

Ellis stands close to the wall on the rear side of the main building, waiting until the first bombs begin their descent. At first there's only the distinct sound of approaching aircraft. That captures the soldiers' attention. Everyone looks in the direction of the noise, laser rifles raised.

While the soldiers are on alert, Ellis takes off running, heading toward the closest entrance. He knows he has less than five minutes to find what he's looking for, so he's got to make every second count.

The soldier guarding that entrance is wearing a comm-set. Normally he would see the cloaked figure advancing in his direction, but he's occupied with looking in the opposite direction, trying to find the source of sounds Ellis knows are coming from an approaching stealth bomber. Ellis shoves the soldier hard, then pivots to his right and enters the building.

Still running, Ellis has barely reached the desk where a young cadet is sitting when the first bomb strikes the academic building. The resulting blast shakes the immediate area. People dash out of offices, staring at each other in confusion. Then another bomb hits the boys' residence hall.

Ellis runs faster.

With people rushing past him, screaming, the only thing he concentrates on is getting to the vault room, located next to the chancellor's office. At least he doesn't have to worry about encountering him. Chancellor Doran Tyson died in the initial outbreak in April, and in the resulting chaos no permanent replacement was assigned.

A retinal scanner is required to open the vault. Ellis taps instructions on his DataLink, which brings up a stored scan of the former chancellor's eye on his comm-set's left eye lens. That does the trick, and the door slides open, revealing a dark interior. As soon as he steps inside the small room, lights blink on. Ellis rushes to the nearest wall. It's lined with dozens of metallic drawers. He reaches drawer three, yanks it open, and extracts two comm-sets. Then he tugs drawer eleven open and grabs two Chronobands.

A loud boom reverberates overhead. A bomb has hit the main building. Ellis races out of the vault. Time seems to have stopped for him. His whole world is reduced to the sound of his pulse throbbing in his head, his footsteps pounding along the floor, and another detonation hitting the building. Debris falls from above; chunks of ceiling crash down around him. He passes a man stretched across the ground with a large pillar pinning him in place. A part of him wishes he could help, but it's useless. The man is long dead to him. A ghost.

Outside, Ellis keeps running until he's clear of the immediate blast zone. In the final moments before he shifts, he sees another bomb fall and take out the rest of the main building.

With his heart pounding, Ellis allows himself a moment to sit once he shifts back to his time—but only a moment. He pulls a small black bag out of a pocket in his pants and gently places the stolen items inside, then tucks the bag into his satchel. After taking a swig of water, Ellis stands and starts his journey toward a campsite in the Rocky Mountains, where he will finally deliver his message to Bridger Creed. It'll take several days to get there, but Ellis has plenty of time.

That's all he has anymore.

14

BRIDGER
FEBRUARY 12, 2147

'm almost to the stream when I notice a faint shimmering in front of me. Someone is there, cloaked. I grip the fishing pole tighter, holding it up like a weapon.

The shimmer disappears as the cloak is disengaged, and I'm left staring at someone slightly taller than me, with greasy brown hair that's a little longer than mine. He's dressed in faded brown pants and a dull leather jacket. Some kind of breathing device rests on his collarbone, with tubes running over both of his shoulders. A large, patched satchel is slung over his shoulder, and a stunner is sheathed at his hip. A low chuckle comes from the dirty gray cloth wrapped around the lower part of his face. He looks like someone straight from a war zone.

"I wish you could see yourself. This is wild," he says in a raspy voice. His eyes crinkle in a way that lets me know he's really enjoying this.

But I'm not. "Who the hell are you?" I ask, taking a step closer and holding my fishing pole higher. I could probably do some damage with it, if I needed to.

"Come on, Bridger, put that down. I'm not going to hurt you." He spreads his arms wide, his palms facing up. "I came a long way to talk to you."

The muscles in my arm tighten as I grip the fishing pole harder. "How do you know my name? And why are you hiding your face?"

"That's not important," he replies. "What's important is that I need to talk to you. It's urgent."

"I'm not saying a thing until you tell me who you are and if you're alone," I snarl.

"You don't need to know my real name—at least not yet—but for now you can call me The Prophet. And I promise I'm by myself."

I laugh. "The Prophet? Are you serious?"

He stands a little straighter, like he's offended. "I am. Considering that I'm from your future and I have information you need." Then he laughs. "Okay, I'll admit that is kind of lame. You can call me Ellis."

I stare at him for a few moments. Whoever this guy is, he has to be lying. He should know that the DTA forbids Time Benders from interacting with anyone when they travel to the past. "You're from *my* future. How do you expect me to believe that? If that's the case, then you wouldn't be talking to me at all. You'd know that that could contaminate your timeline, even get you arrested."

"That's true now, but in my time there is no more DTA, and people with Talents are long dead. I'm from 2155 and, as you can tell," he says, gesturing to his clothes, "things aren't so great."

I don't know how to respond. How am I supposed to believe his claims? As far as I know, he could be a Purist who's stolen a Jewel of Illusion, which is illegal tech that would allow him to conceal himself without using a government-issued cloak that's part of our uniforms.

I lower my fishing pole. "Okay, I'll play along. Let's say I believe you. What do you want with me?"

His eyes narrow. "In my time, we're in the middle of a world war. A war that begins with the detonation of a bioweapon that will be unleashed soon in New Denver. It'll kill every Talent once the disease spreads, and over half of the Gen Mod population. The only Talents who *do* survive are the few who were in underground bunkers during the detonation. What I want to do is stop that bomb from being detonated. But in case I'm unsuccessful, I still need you, your family, and your friend Alora to live through this. That must happen, no matter what."

I shake my head in disbelief. "How do you know about Alora? And how do you expect me to believe this? That sounds completely ridiculous."

"It was ridiculous to risk my life to come back here to warn you, but I did it anyway. Bridger, it's important that you live through this. You're an important part of the future."

I let out a harsh laugh. "Okay, this really has to be some kind of joke."

Ellis pushes up his sleeve, and I'm shocked to see that he's wearing a Chronoband. "I was almost shot for stealing this." Then he holds his hand over the pocket of his coat and says, "I have some information that I know you've been looking for. I'll give it to you, but only if you promise that you'll come with me when I return for you and the others. I'll take all of you to a secure location."

He reaches into the pocket and extracts something. Opening his fist, he steps closer to me and reveals the items. In his palm are two round DataDisks—a silver one for data storage, and a bronze Sim Game program.

"These are for you. One contains information that will help you and Alora find some of the answers you seek. The other is a little taste of what's to come if I'm not able to stop that bioweapon."

"You didn't answer my question. How you know about Alora? And what about my father? Do you know where he is?"

"I know everything about you, Bridger. Everything."

"Then tell me what's going on with him. I need to know."

"I would, but you would never believe me. This is something you have to discover for yourself."

Suddenly I want to punch this guy, but I tell myself to calm down. Just because he claims that he's from the future and knows about Dad doesn't mean he's telling the truth. But, still, the fact that he has a Chronoband makes me wonder.

I reach out to accept the DataDisks and shove them in my pocket. "If what you say is true, then when will the bioweapon detonate?"

"I can't tell you that yet. I need to preserve this timeline as much as possible before the bombing. But a few days before it happens, I'll come back and warn you. That should give you enough time to prepare your family and then I'll get you to safety," Ellis says.

I have so many more questions. If he's from the future, why does he want to alter his timeline? I know he said there's a world war, but there's no telling what changing his past could do to him or the rest of the world. And why does he want me, Alora, and my family in particular to survive? It doesn't make sense.

Before I can ask anything, Ellis says, "Look, I've got to go now. I've already been here too long. Just . . . try to stay safe and out of trouble. And here's one more thing you're going to need." He extracts a black, plastic-looking bag from his satchel and tosses it to me. "Take care of those. You have no idea what I went through to get them."

Then he shifts, leaving me alone once more. I open the bag and nearly drop it when I realize what's inside—two Chronobands, and two comm-sets.

15

So far, my second day at The Academy for Time Travel and Research has been a little better than my first. I mean, at least I sort of know what to expect. Yesterday, Lieutenant Rivera escorted me to each of my classes: basics like math, science, and language arts in the morning, with afternoons reserved for my new team leader, Professor Telfair March, who is responsible for my history lessons and actual time travel training. In between all that Mom kept checking in to make sure I was doing okay.

Maybe it wouldn't have been so bad if I didn't have Lieutenant Rivera here. At least she's leaving tomorrow. I can't wait.

"Come along, Alora. No time for dawdling," Rivera says over her shoulder as we leave the cafeteria located in the bottom floor of the main academic building.

I want to snap that I'm not dawdling; I'm just feeling a bit sick after eating that horrible excuse for a lunch. Some kind of protein pie made with the synthetic meat that's common in this era, and a side of very bland mixed vegetables. Absolutely no dessert. What I wouldn't give for Aunt Grace's cooking, especially a huge slice of her chocolate cake. But I certainly can't say that out loud. At least I was allowed to eat with my new roommate, Tara. She seems nice, though she was really cautious around Rivera. Can't say that I blame her.

We pass a security guard, one of dozens that have been stationed all over campus for our safety, and a lot of cadets who are openly watching us and whispering. The same thing happens as we make our way through the building to the nearest elevator. I want to roll my eyes. Some things never change, no matter what time you live in. I always felt like a freak when I lived in Willow Creek, and I still do now. I was stupid to think wearing the Academy's uniform would help me blend in. The fact that I'm a new cadet, with a scandalous history, no less, and that I look so much like Vika—well, of course that makes me gossip material.

I try to ignore Rivera's idle chatter while she leads me to Professor March's class. Everywhere I go, I've been looking for Bridger, and I haven't seen him. I'm too afraid to search for him using my DataLink. There's no telling if everything I search for is being monitored, especially while I'm here. I wonder if he's tried to look for me. He wasn't exactly thrilled after I restored his memories. Maybe he just wants things to stay the same.

On the third floor, we exit the elevator and walk down a long, white-tiled hallway, passing many rooms with closed doors, until we get to room number 327. We're early. Professor March is at his desk, but the only other student is a girl with bright pink hair seated in the back corner. I remember seeing her yesterday, but I didn't speak to her.

"Hello, Miss Mason," Professor March calls out with a grin.

I can't help but smiling in return and wave at him. But then I quickly lower my hand, sure I look like an awkward dork doing that. I liked him immediately when I first saw him yesterday. He's a tall, lanky black man, and something about him reminds me so much of one of my favorite actors from when I lived with Aunt Grace.

Lieutenant Rivera notices the girl in the room, and her eyes flick between her and the professor. "Telfair, may I have a word with you in private?"

Professor March looks at Rivera as if she's a bothersome insect. I smile even more. "Of course, Ellen."

Lieutenant Rivera calls out to me, "I'll be back at the end of this session to escort you to your next class, Alora."

I look sharply at her. "Next class? I thought this was the last one for the day?"

"I can take her," Professor March interrupts, giving me a reassuring smile

Lieutenant Rivera purses her lips like she's been sucking on a lemon. "We'll see," she finally says.

Once they're both in the hallway, I immediately set down my DataPad down on the nearest desk and sit, trying to hear what they're saying. Most of their words don't make sense, but I do hear Professor March saying something like "It would be better coming from me." I have no idea what that means. I just want to find out what this extra class is supposed to be.

"So, you're the new girl. Brilliant."

I'm startled hearing the prim, accented voice coming from the other side of the room. It sounds vaguely English, or at least what was English when I lived with Aunt Grace. I'd nearly forgotten that I'm not alone in here. The pink-haired girl comes over and takes the seat next to me.

"Yeah, I suppose I am," I snap, wishing she would leave me alone so I can hear what's going on out in the hallway.

"I'm Everly Darville, by the way."

I honestly wish I could just ignore the girl, but Aunt Grace always told me to not be rude. I force myself to smile and say, "I'm Alora."

Everly props her elbow on her desk, cupping her jaw in the palm of her hand. "Oh, I know. Everybody has been talking about you. Something about you looking similar to a cadet who died here last year. It must be a bit odd wearing a dead girl's face."

Wow, she's not subtle at all. But from the sound of it, she's not familiar with what happened. I decide to see what exactly she knows. "That's what I've heard too. What do you know?"

"Not a lot. Until you arrived, I was the new kid on campus."

"Okay," I drawl.

She flashes a wicked grin. "Oh, the others were right. You don't know much of anything, do you?"

"What's that supposed to mean?" I ask, scowling at her. Jeez, and *I* was worried about appearing rude.

Her smile fades and she bites her lip. "I'm sorry. I'm a little blunt sometimes. Anyway, I didn't mean you're dumb or anything, I just meant that you're kind of naïve. It's because you were kidnapped, right?"

It's weird; I knew that everyone was talking about me, but it's strange having that confirmed by Everly. And though I wouldn't have thought it was possible after the terrible lunch, my stomach sours even more. I manage to nod. "Yeah, that's right."

A few cadets begin to trickle into the room. As soon as they see us, they stop talking and tiptoe to their seats like the floor is covered with glass. They don't sit near me, or Everly.

"Well, as you can see," she says, indicating their valiant efforts to ignore us, "I haven't had too much luck making friends. I'm an international transfer cadet, and the blokes over here don't like *foreigners*," she says, using air quotes for the last word. "I've only been here since last August."

"Sorry to hear that," I mumble. I get it; she's probably lonely. But I don't know a thing about her, and I really need to focus on finding out what happened to my father, and to Bridger's—not making new friends. At least, not right now.

By the time Professor March reenters the room, the entire group is already seated—eleven cadets in total. He takes one look at me and leans down to whisper, "I know things are tough for you right now, but I promise I'll do everything in my power to help you succeed here. I know exactly what you're feeling."

His words are comforting, and I really wish I could believe him. Before we left 2013, Bridger told me that Professor March was the one who helped him escape when he was captured while trying to help me. Now that I've been around the professor, I feel like I could trust him, especially since Bridger told me that he's also a Dual Talent. But I can't let him know that I know the extent of his abilities.

Still, there's another thing that's troubling me—Bridger's father warned him to never trust Professor March again. When Mr. Creed spoke, he seemed so calm and rational, and yet that version was a clone. And from what I've learned since living here, clones were outlawed because they always went insane, just like Vika did.

So what am I supposed to believe?

My second day in Professor March's class is similar to what I experienced with my private tutors. Even though I didn't really care for the way my tutors treated me, I did enjoy my history lessons. They were a million times better than any of my high school classes from the time I lived with Aunt Grace. Instead of sitting in a history class where the teacher yaps at you or makes you read from a textbook, I was able to experience actual events recorded by Time Benders through Virtual Lenses.

Today, after Professor March distributed the lenses, we're led through a complex "city" underneath what used to be the Denver International Airport—currently, downtown New Denver. The city is used for historical tours now, but during the Second Civil War, once Washington, DC, was pretty much destroyed, the government was evacuated there. This is where President Youngblood continued to direct the nation's military, even though large parts of Denver were destroyed, too. It's surreal moving though the different levels with the lenses, watching military officials making decisions that impacted millions of lives, and witnessing whole areas where citizens of Denver were evacuated during airstrikes. It's the regular people who get to me: actually seeing their fear, hearing children cry, feeling the atmosphere of utter hopelessness.

I hope I never have to experience that in real life.

At the end of Professor March's class, he annoys the entire class by announcing that all time trips have been cancelled for the next week until the situation with the Purists settles down.

While the others file out, I stay in my seat and try my best to ignore them—easy enough, when nobody acts like they want to speak to me.

"Good luck," Everly says as she stands, grabbing her DataPad. "Let me know if you need anything, or just want to chat. I forgot to mention that I'm two doors down from you in the residence hall."

I feel a little guilty. I hadn't even noticed that she lives so close to me, and she's trying so hard to be nice. But I can't forget about my goal. I don't need any distractions now. "Yeah, maybe we can talk sometime."

Once Everly leaves, Professor March clasps his hands. "So, are you ready for your next class?"

"I suppose so," I say, feeling a bit annoyed because I'm anxious to find Bridger so I can talk to him. "But what is it? I don't remember having another one listed on my schedule."

"That's because this isn't an official class. You're one of very few Dual Talents here, Alora. The Academy's sole focus is to train Time Benders, but we also want you to develop your second Talent. So for you and the other cadets like yourself, we bring in professors from the other schools to continue your training. Unfortunately, that means this training has to be done off the record."

I blink a few times in shock before I can speak. "Are you serious? I'm not the only one here?"

Professor March laughs. "No, you're not. In fact, now that you're here, we have a grand total of eight Dual Talents. Your new roommate is one, too. That's why we assigned her to stay with you. She's the closest to your age, and she can act as a kind of mentor to you. And if it makes you feel any better, I'm also a Dual Talent; a Mind and Time Bender."

I'm dumbfounded. Nobody in Chicago told me that there would be others here like me. They made it sound like Dual Talents are super rare. And not only are there others—Tara is one too. I'm even more surprised that Professor March admitted that he's one as well.

"So . . . I'm not the only Space and Time Bender?" I ask. Since Vika was also like me, I've always wondered if there are any others. That would be wonderful, not feeling like the star of a freak-show.

"Well, yes, *you* are. The others on campus are Mind and Time Benders. And there are Mind and Space Benders at the other schools, as well as some Mind and Time Benders at the school for the telepathic Talents. But there are no others like you."

And just like that, my hope deflates. So I'm still alone. Awesome. But then I wonder, does that mean I'm the only one like that still in school? Are there others who are grown? Vika was like me, and so was our dad. There have to be more than just the three of us. I want to ask Professor March, but I'm not sure if I should.

I fall silent as Professor March shares that my tutor is a professor from The School of Teleportation and Research, and that he will meet us in a room in the Main Building. Apparently, I can't tell anybody the truth about this class, except for Tara. She's to act as my confidante. If any other student asks, I'm just getting extra tutoring twice a week to help me "catch up" with everybody else.

"Hello, Sebastian," Professor March says to the surly, blue-haired receptionist I met on my first day here. "Is the room ready for Miss Mason?"

"Of course it is," he snaps. "Chancellor Tyson and the others have been waiting for nearly ten minutes."

Oh just freaking great. Why does Chancellor Tyson have to be there? And if he's there, I'm sure Lieutenant Rivera will be, as well.

Professor March gives the receptionist a tight-lipped smile before leading me down a short hallway that branches off behind the receptionist's desk to the right. He stops before a door and says, "Don't worry, Alora. You'll be fine."

Inside, I find Chancellor Tyson, the ever-present Lieutenant Rivera, and another man wearing a red-and-gray uniform seated at a long conference table. They stand as I enter. The man is the one who catches my attention, and not in a good way. He's tall, has brown hair, and looks like he's in his late thirties. He somehow reminds me of Mr. Palmer. Chills cover my body. I tell myself to get a grip. Palmer is long dead, and this guy doesn't even look exactly like him; they just happen to share similar features. I have to force myself to stop staring at the man, who is obviously my new tutor.

"Thank you for delivering Miss Mason to us," Chancellor Tyson says to Professor March.

"Would you like me to stay since I'm her team leader?" Professor March asks. "I think it would be beneficial for me to be here for this part of her training, so I can see what she's capable of doing. After all, her abilities are extremely rare."

The chancellor strokes his chin for a moment. "I hadn't considered that, but it's a good idea. Have a seat, Telfair."

I feel a little lighter, knowing that Professor March will be here with me. He's a Dual Talent, too, so he should be on my side, at least. As for the others, I don't know. I get the feeling that I'm just a tool for them to use, something to advance their agenda.

As I start to take my place at the table, I hesitate for a few seconds, a little voice inside reminding me again that Bridger's father warned us not to trust Professor March. But then again, he was a clone. I've learned that they aren't exactly reliable. I shake off the thoughts and quickly sit in the chair next to the professor.

Once we're all seated, Chancellor Tyson gives me a warm smile. "It's good to see that you're settling in, Miss Mason. I've talked to both your mother and Lieutenant Rivera, and they've assured me that you are adjusting nicely to your new environment. Now, I'd like to introduce you to your tutor." He extends his hand to the man. "This is Professor Dan Jackson. He will be responsible for furthering your Space Bending education."

I shift my attention to Professor Jackson.

"Hello, Alora," he says. "I look forward to getting to know you better."

Yeah, he still creeps me out. I need to get over this right now.

"Now that you two have been introduced, let's see what you can do," Lieutenant Rivera chirps.

I'm definitely glad that Professor March is staying. I thought it would just be me and my new Space Bending tutor, but until I get over my ridiculous aversion to him, maybe it's best that someone stays with us. And I'm not sure I'd feel so comfortable with just the chancellor and Rivera.

Even so, an hour later I'm ready to scream. I need to find Bridger, and Professor Jackson has sent me all over the freaking campus to retrieve small cubes that Lieutenant Rivera placed throughout the day, without using my cloak. It's exactly the same sort of exercise my private instructors loved to put me through.

Professor March calls for a quick break, then comes over to me. "You're doing great, Alora. I know this must seem pointless to you, but Professor Jackson has to see what you're capable of doing before he can put you through more advanced maneuvers."

He's right, but I still feel an intense irritation. This all feels like a complete waste of time.

Professor Jackson joins us, placing his hand on my shoulder, and I shudder under his touch. "One last shift, and then you're free to go for today. I have to admit, I'm impressed with your skills. So, for your final task, I want you to shift to the museum and retrieve a golden cube that's hidden on one of the shelves."

Okay, I can do this. I step away from the two professors to prepare for my last shift of the day. Hopefully it won't take too long. Lieutenant Rivera loves hiding those stupid boxes so I have to search for them, which wastes even more time. What I should be doing right now is looking for Bridger. I close my eyes, picturing his face. The dark brown eyes, the dimples that appear when he smiles. I *need* to find him.

"Holy fure, Alora, what are you doing here?"

My eyes fly open and I let out a horrified gasp. I'm no longer in the conference room in the Main Building. I'm now standing in an unfamiliar bedroom.

And Bridger is right in front of me.

16

BRIDGER
FEBRUARY 14, 2147

lora blinks a few times, then looks around the room. "Where am I?"

"You're in my quarters at the Academy," I reply. "I don't understand. How did you get here without knowing where you were going?"

"I . . . I don't know. I don't know how I got here." Her cheeks turn pink. "Oh my God, I'm gonna be in so much trouble."

"Why? Where were you?"

She shakes my head. "No time to explain. I've got to get to the museum."

"Okay . . . but wait a second. Do you think you can come back later so we can talk?"

"I don't know. I'll try."

I quickly check my DataLink. "Okay, it's nearly five-thirty now. Come back after supper, around seven-thirty."

Her breath is coming in short gasps now. I wish there was something I could do to help her, but I have no idea what kind of trouble she's in. All I can do is watch while she looks around the room again, probably trying to make sure she'll remember how it looks. Then she closes her eyes and tries to concentrate on shifting back to wherever she came from.

When she disappears, I run my hand over my forehead, wondering how on Earth she got here. Space Benders shift by visualizing exactly *where* they want to go, but Alora has never seen my room before. And from her reaction, she doesn't know how she got here, either. How is that even possible? Could this be a new kind of space-bending ability that even the DTA doesn't know about?

"Man, we need a night out on the town. I feel like my parents have had me on a leash ever since that law was passed," Elijah says.

"Sounds good to me," Zed chirps. He turns to me and pretends to look all serious. "That is, if Mr. Creed over there decides to honor us with his divine presence."

Elijah snort-laughs. I glare at both of them. Of all the nights, they just *had* to stay in here with me tonight. Usually they prefer to do other things. Elijah is really into lifting weights, while Zed spends a lot of time in the common room or the Virtual Reality room.

Why didn't I tell Alora to come later, when I'm sure they'll both be asleep?

Elijah and Zed are reclining on the black couch in the living room of our quarters, while I can't stand still. Ever since I got back from the cafeteria, I've been too nervous to sit anywhere for long. I even straightened up my bedroom and finished unpacking from my trip with Grandma and Shan.

A quick peek at my DataLink reveals that it's now 7:15. Ten minutes after the last time I checked. Alora should be here in fifteen more minutes. I'd rather be in my room right now. But knowing Zed and Elijah, if I don't socialize with them for a while, they'll keep aggravating me until I come out.

So social time it is.

"We've never gone to The Silver Lining," Zed says. "Now that we're all eighteen, we can get in. I vote for that."

"Works for me," Elijah says with a grin. "I'm sure Tara wouldn't mind meeting me there."

"I knew there was something going on between you two," Zed squawks. "Details, my man. Details."

A chime sounds throughout our quarters, and I turn to face the door as it slides open. My mother strides in without waiting for a welcome. I groan. Not *now*. I can't deal with her, too—especially knowing how she's been lying to me.

"Is that any way to greet your mother, Bridger?" she asks, crossing her arms. She's still in her field uniform, so she must have come straight here when she got back from Louisiana.

I reply, through gritted teeth, "I have a headache."

"That's your standard response for everything lately, isn't it?" she says, taking in the area. All of our coats are tossed on the small table in the corner of our kitchenette. Food containers litter the countertop, some empty, some half-full. "I see that you three haven't learned how to keep the place clean yet."

While her back is turned, Zed holds his fingers over his head to make devil horns. Elijah has to smother a laugh. A part of me wants to smile, too, but I'm too damn pissed.

"So . . . Mother . . . what brings you here?" I ask.

She turns to face me again. Her features relax into something like a look of caring. "Really? Purists are wilding out all over the country and you want to know why I'm checking in on you?"

I start to tell her exactly what I'm thinking, but I bite back the words. Maybe I should give her the benefit of the doubt. "Okay, fine. I'm sorry. But you could have just commed me."

"You know, your brother was more than happy to see me. He told me all about your trip with Judith this weekend. I can't believe the nerve of that woman, taking both of you out there! It isn't safe to do things like that anymore."

And just like that, any semi-warm feelings evaporate. The more she gripes, the more my blood pressure rises. I begin to breathe harder. My pulse pounds a furious rhythm. No, this can't happen now. I try to talk myself down. Tell myself that I'll be fine. But I can't make the weight on my chest go away. I can't make my heart stop racing.

I vaguely hear Mom calling my name. As I pass them, Elijah and Zed stare at me like I might shatter into a million pieces. Maybe I will. It certainly feels like it.

I somehow make it to my bedroom. Inside the top drawer of my dresser, I paw through my skivvies until I find the wooden box that contains my Calmer. My fingers are shaking as I grab a vial of the golden liquid and inject it into my neck.

Immediately, my breathing slows and the pressure on my chest eases up. I lay my palms against the dresser and lean my head down, waiting for my muscles to fully relax.

"Are you all right?" Mom asks from the doorway to my bedroom. She looks a little shaken. I guess no one would want to have their son wild out.

I almost snap at her, but I remember Alora will be here soon. I check my DataLink and nearly choke. It's almost seven-thirty.

I have to get rid of my mom, and now.

"I'm sorry, Mom. I've just been under a lot of pressure lately with my workload, then all this crap with the Purists and the protests. I guess it's making me a little irritable."

For a moment, I think she's not going to buy the lie. She frowns and purses her lips. "Honestly, I really don't blame you. I'd forgotten how intense this level at school can be. But try not to be so antagonistic toward me all the time. I'm your mother, not your enemy."

It sure seems that way sometimes, but there's no point saying that to her unless I want a fight. I stand up straight and paste on a smile. "You know, I am feeling better now." I brush past Mom and reenter the living room. Zed is still sitting on the couch, looking like the irritation might kill him.

"Where's Elijah?" I ask.

"In his room. He had a call from a certain lady friend," Zed says with a wolfish smirk. He starts to say something else, then his eyes flick to where Mom is standing.

I whirl around, terrified that Alora may have appeared behind her. But it's just Mom.

And I need to get her away from my bedroom.

My mind is a jumble of thoughts. What can I say to get her to leave— or at least to get away from the room where Alora's about to appear? Think, Bridger, think.

"You guys, I'm burning up. Do you want to go outside with me?" I blurt out. It's the first thing that comes to mind, and strangely enough, it's the truth. I feel as if I'm on fire.

Mom's hurries over to me and places her hand on my forehead. It's strange, having her act so maternal. Reminds me of my childhood, when she liked me a hell of a lot more than she does now.

"You're a little warm. But that's to be expected with the Calmer," she says as she lowers her hand. "Maybe you should sit for a while."

"Yeah, Creed," Zed says, "It's way too cold outside right now. I have no idea how you survived camping the past few days."

Mom's expression darkens again. My fists clench as I mouth "You're an idiot" to Zed. He just shrugs.

Elijah emerges from his bedroom. "So, what's going on?"

"Don't ask," I say, still glaring daggers at Zed.

"Eh, sounds like I didn't miss much," Elijah says. I glance back at him. He's smiling as he walks past the doorway to my bedroom, but then something inside seems to catch his attention. He does a double take and his jaw drops.

My pulse begins to race.

Alora must have just appeared.

17

ALORA
FEBRUARY 14, 2147

The instant I materialize in Bridger's bedroom, I wonder if I made a mistake. I wonder if I'm even in the same room—it has the same green blanket on the bed, the same white walls, the same furniture that looks similar to my own. But what if all the rooms in the boys' hall look like this? And if I *am* in the right room, then where's Bridger? I thought he would be in here to meet me.

The sour feeling I've had in my stomach for most of the day intensifies. I shouldn't have done this. What if I'm caught by whatever professor is on Warden Duty over here? Or what if Bridger's roommates see me? How are we going to explain my being in here?

I close my eyes for a moment and tell myself to relax. My space-bending skills are strong, so I'm certain I'm in the same room I materialized in earlier today, even though I have no idea how I did that just by thinking about Bridger. I still can't get over it. Like, I've been taught Space Benders can only bend by visualizing *where* they want to go, not *who* they want to go to.

Voices filter in from the outside the open door. I'm trying to decide if I should stay put or peek out to see who's talking when an unfamiliar boy walks past the doorway. I stand still, hoping he doesn't notice me, but I have absolutely zero luck today so of course he does.

It's almost comical how his expression morphs from irritation to shock in a few seconds, his mouth parting in surprise. He glances over his shoulder and calls out, "Hey, Bridger, can I borrow your new blue shirt? I . . . think I might have a date this weekend."

Crap, no, he can't come in here. I close my eyes, trying frantically to get a clear mental image of my bedroom so I can shift back.

But before I can, he's by my side, whispering, "It's okay. I won't say anything. But you might want to hide again so we can get rid of Bridger's mother."

Hide *again*? Jeez, he must think I came in here earlier and have been hiding this whole time. I don't know why I get the urge to laugh. This is insane, getting myself into this mess. I smother the laugh, because I'm sure it would make me look irrational, and just nod. The boy waves me over to a tiny closet in the corner, where I squeeze in between the hanging clothes. Before leaving, he gives me an incredulous look. "I can't *wait* to hear why you're here."

At first, all I can think about is how stupid it is for me to stay put in Bridger's closet. There's no telling how long it will take for him and his friends to convince his mother to leave. But oddly enough, something about being surrounded by Bridger's clothing comforts me. It smells like him: sort of like being outdoors. It reminds me of the time we spent together back in Willow Creek. Of how close we got, in such a short time.

I wonder if we'll ever be that close again.

The voices start to get louder, and then I hear footsteps crossing the room. I try to shrink back as far as I can.

"Alora, are you still in there?" Bridger calls in a soft voice.

Relief floods through me as I push my way out of the closet and stumble right into him. His arms immediately wrap around me, pulling me into a strong embrace. Instinctively, I hug him back. It feels good to be here—it feels right, somehow.

"How did you get your mom to leave?" I say.

"My roommates helped with that. They told her that we have a huge exam tomorrow and that we all needed to study."

"Well, well, isn't this a surprise."

Bridger and I jump apart as if struck by an electrical current. Two boys are standing in the doorway to Bridger's bedroom—the tall boy who hid me and a shorter, wiry guy with spiky black hair.

"So, are you going to introduce us?" the taller one asks.

Bridger's face flushes. "Don't mind those two clowns. They'll leave us alone."

The shorter one—the one who spoke the first time—places his hands across his heart and says, "Aw, man, Bridger, you're killing me." He focuses his attention on me. "And since Bridger is clearly going to be rude, I'll make the intros. I'm Zed Ramirez, and he's Elijah Beckett," he says, gesturing to the tall guy. "We're the roommates."

"I think she gets that," Bridger mutters, running his hands through his hair. "Would you two mind giving us some privacy?"

"Oh, no, you're not getting rid of us that easily," Zed replies. He saunters into Bridger's room and plops down on the bed. "I have some questions. And the first one is, why the hell are you hiding a chick in here who looks exactly like Vika? Don't you think that's . . . weird, to put it mildly?"

Bridger blows out a few puffs of air and stares hard at Zed, then at Elijah, as if that will make them go away. Then his shoulders slump and he shakes his head slowly. "This is so furing messed up." His eyes seek out mine, looking so defeated. "Do you have the Mind Redeemer with you?"

"Wait, what?" Elijah asks. "You have a Mind Redeemer? How is that possible?"

"It's a long story," Bridger says.

"Bridger, what are you doing?" I ask, my voice high-pitched.

"It's okay, we can trust them," he replies.

Heat flares in my face and spreads through my body. Trust them? Bridger wants me trust two boys that I don't even know? I grab his arm and pull him to a corner of the room. "Have you lost your mind? Why did you bring up the Mind Redeemer in front of them?"

He quickly explains that Zed and Elijah knew everything about his plans to save my life last year and even assisted in his escape when he was captured by the DTA. And now, while they know my name and my official story, they obviously don't know the whole truth.

So they've had their memories wiped, too. God, I'm hating the DTA more and more every day that I'm here.

I glance over at Zed and Elijah, who both seeming to enjoy being in the spotlight. "I'm sorry I flew off the handle like that."

"It's fine," Elijah says. "We're strangers to you. But it doesn't have to be that way."

"Same here," Zed chimes in. "We can all hang out and raise hell together."

I find myself smiling, despite my reservations. Maybe I can learn to trust them. These guys seem loyal. Not like my last so-called friend, Sela. The one who ditched me to raise her social status at school.

"So . . . do you have the Mind Redeemer here or not?" Bridger asks me.

"No, it's hidden in the same place," I reply. "But it won't take me long to get it."

By the time I shift to my bedroom at Mom's apartment and return, only a few minutes have passed, but I'm sweating. While I was at Mom's house, I overheard her talking to someone on her DataLink, which reminded me that she'll be checking in with me close to my curfew time.

It takes five minutes to restore Zed and Elijah's memories. The process is painful for them, but doesn't take as long because apparently the DTA only erased their memories of helping Bridger escape and taking him to Georgia. They'd been told that Bridger officially had his nervous breakdown just prior to the camping trip in which they had covered for him.

To say that Zed and Elijah are furious at the DTA is a huge understatement. Elijah scowls and lets out a string of swear words.

"I just . . . I feel so violated." Zed slams his fist against the mattress. "I'm sorry for acting like such a dick to you, Bridger. I didn't know."

Bridger shrugs. "None of us did," he says. "Whoever is behind cloning our fathers and Vika did this to us. They need to pay for it."

"How are we supposed to do that?" Elijah asks. "You know, a cover up of something like that would have to come from the top of the DTA. We're not talking about some lowly peon." ,

Bridger goes to his closet, extracts his portacase, and takes it over to the bed, where he extracts two DataDisks. "Okay, this is going to sound weird, but I met a guy while I was on the camping trip with Grandma and Shan. And he told me some wild stuff. Like, that the world is about to end."

Zed leans close to Bridger, making like he wants to feel his forehead. "You feeling okay? 'Cause that sounds completely bonkers."

Bridger knocks his hand away. "I'm not joking, you guys."

"I don't know, man, I have to agree with Zed on that one," Elijah says.

A part of me agrees with Zed and Elijah, but with everything that's happened to me in the past year, who can say what's crazy and what isn't?

Scowling, Bridger says, "If you two would shut up, I could explain. So, I was going fishing and this guy just appeared in front of me in the woods. His clothes were really worn, he had a breathing apparatus, and here's the kicker—he said he was from *our* future, and a bioweapon is going to detonate here sometime soon. It's going to be bad." Bridger looks down, his face growing pale.

After a few seconds, Elijah asks, "Exactly how bad?"

Bridger lets out a shaky breath. "It's going to kill the majority of Talents and a huge chunk of the Gen Mod population. Worldwide."

My stomach gets a sinking sensation. That can't be true. I didn't survive a murder attempt just to die in a bioweapon attack. I try to laugh it off. "Are you serious? Was it somebody just pulling a prank?"

"He was cloaked, guys."

"So what?" Zed pipes up. "Lots of people have Jewills even though they're not supposed to. That guy could have had one. Hell, he could have been a Purist just messing with you."

"I thought the same thing at first," Bridger says. "But then I saw the information on the DataDisks. And he kept saying he was going to try to stop it from happening, and just in case he couldn't, he wanted my family and Alora to go to a secure location."

"Hey, what about us?" Zed says in an irritated voice.

"I dunno. That's just what he told me. But I don't like it at all."

Even though my stomach is still in knots, I'm not sure what to think. "How do you know he's telling the truth?" I ask. "Something about that seems kind of off, don't you think?"

Elijah plucks the bronze DataDisk out of Bridger's hand and examines it. "I agree with Alora, man. That's crazy. Did you at least check these out?"

"Of course I did." Bridger reaches in the portacase again, this time taking out a pair of Virtual Lenses. "I had to take these from Shan when he was asleep. If I'd asked to borrow them, the little tyrant would have demanded credits."

"You didn't have to take his. I have a pair here," Zed says.

"Yeah, well, I didn't know for sure if you still had them," Bridger replies.

Zed rolls his eyes. "That's because you haven't wanted to be around us much lately. Ring any bells?"

Bridger looks down for a moment before handing the lenses to me. "I think you should see this first, since Ellis mentioned wanting to save you, too. And trust me, it's really disturbing."

I take the bronze DataDisk from Elijah and insert it into the slot on the left side of the lenses. I'm familiar with these because my tutors in Chicago used Virtual Lenses to introduce me to modern society while keeping me safely enclosed behind DTA walls.

I slip the lenses over my head, pausing to insert the ear buds, and then activate them. Bridger's room disappears, and I'm dropped into the middle of what looks like a war zone. I'm walking down a sidewalk in a city, surrounded by destruction. Damaged skyscrapers and other build-ings, many peppered with faint graffiti that looks like blue flames. Rubble everywhere, Jumbotrons full of holes or hanging askew. A few people are walking around aimlessly, looking shell-shocked. Some are crying, some are pawing through the rubble, searching for who knows what.

The worst part is the bodies. They're everywhere. Mostly soldiers, but there are some who are clearly civilian, even children. I can't stand it. My mind screams for me to run, to get away from the madness. I rip off the lenses, my breath coming in great gasps.

"What the hell?" Zed asks, his eyes huge as saucers.

Bridger tosses the lenses to him. "Take a look for yourself. Apparently that's what the future is going to be like, unless this Ellis fellow can stop that bioweapon from going off."

While Zed views the apocalyptic scene, Bridger inserts the other disk into his DataLink and pulls up the contents. Elijah and I flank him to see what's on the holographic screen, which hovers over his wrist.

It's a simple document with instructions:

I'm sure you checked out the Virtual Scene I gave you before reading this. It's not pretty. But knowing you, Bridger, in the back of your mind you're still doubting my sincerity. So here's how to get the piece of the puzzle that you're trying to figure out. You and Alora need to shift to the military division at the DTA building on August 10, 2126. Arrive at approximately oh-nine-hundred hours at room number 2505. I would tell you what happens there, but you need to witness this for yourself to fully believe that it's real. And one more thing. Do NOT share this information with any authority figures. I can't risk them doing anything to change the timeline. Good luck.

I back away from Bridger, stunned. This is it. This could help us fig-ure out what the DTA is really up to—why they went through so much trouble erasing all of our memories, why they've been illegally cloning people.

Vaguely, I see a stunned Zed passing the Virtual Lenses to Elijah. After he views the message, he places his hand across his mouth before running it down the side of his jaw. "This is so furing insane. What have we gotten ourselves into?"

"We haven't gotten ourselves into anything," Bridger replies, his eyes narrowing. "All of this started with my Dad's death. I'm going to do whatever it takes to find out what happened to him and who cloned him. The same goes for Alora's father, too. The DTA needs to learn that they can't just come in and mess with our lives like they've been doing. And they can't keep breaking the law and cloning people."

"So what are we going to do?" I ask. "We have a place to start, but how on Earth are we going to get into the military division of the DTA building? I mean, that place will be heavily guarded. And how are we going to get to that exact date? Free shifting is out of the question," I say, thinking of how far off I was when I tried to visit Aunt Grace. "If we're going to do this, there can be no room for error. So that means we have to have Chronobands."

Elijah tears off the Virtual Lenses, his mouth curled in horror. It's not every day that you get to see a part of your own future, especially one that's so desolate. "That was definitely New Denver, and it has definitely never looked like that," he says, glancing at the lenses.

"I know," Bridger replies.

"What if it's a fake?" Zed says.

"It could be, but that doesn't make sense. Why would Ellis bother giving me fake information? Or these, for that matter?" He reaches back in his portacase and pulls out two Chronobands and two comm-sets.

"Hey," Zed says, scowling. "He just gave you just two sets?"

Bridger nods.

"Fine, but don't expect us to just sit here twiddling our thumbs. We're going to help however we can. Right, Elijah?"

"You can count on me, man," he says, placing his hand on Bridger's shoulder. "I've missed being around you these past few months. I thought we were broken, you know? But it wasn't us. It was whoever's been pulling the strings. We've been puppets to them."

"And it's time for us to cut the strings," I say, feeling a little better about Bridger's decision to tell Elijah and Zed the truth. "So, what's next?"

A slow smile spreads across Bridger's face. "My grandmother is in the military, and her office is at DTA headquarters. I think it's time we visit her at work."

18

BRIDGER
FEBRUARY 18, 2147

Mom arches her eyebrows as I walk into the kitchen. "Why are you wearing your uniform?"

Shan is at the counter, attacking a tall stack of pancakes, already dressed in jeans and a white T-shirt with the red, blue, and green triple rings of the North American Federation's flag on it. He glances up, then shoves a forkful into his mouth and goes back to scrolling though the DataNet feed.

I grab a plate and pile several pancakes on it. I'm still kind of in shock that Mom felt like cooking breakfast for us this morning. "I told you last night. Grandma is giving Elijah, Zed, and me a tour, since Zed is thinking about joining the military."

Of course, that's just the cover story that we came up with to convince Grandma to let us see the building. She had to submit an official reason for the request, but it worked. Our appointment is at ten o'clock. I have exactly an hour to get there. Then we'll take the tour, which hopefully won't last too long.

And then Alora and I will meet up after we're finished and shift to 2126.

"Well, I'm not so sure that's a good idea," Mom says. She takes a sip of her juice and continues, "What if another protest forms while you're inside? You could be trapped."

I tell myself to keep calm. The last thing I need to do is start an argument with Mom and have her forbid me to leave the apartment. Of course, I could leave anyway, but then she would report me to the DTA, and I do *not* need that on my record. "I'll be with Grandma. At the DTA headquarters. If something were to happen, that's a pretty safe place to be."

Mom closes her eyes for a moment before she says, "I know you think I'm trying to hold you back, but I'm not. I want what's best for you. For all of us," she says, her eyes straying to Shan.

Of course she has to look at him. That's who she's really concerned for, not me.

"Mom, I'll be fine. I'm not a child. And if you want to, just track me through my DataLink. I'm meeting everyone at headquarters, and as soon as we're finished, we're going to Elijah's house. That's all."

That's the truth. Or at least most of it. I just omit the whole part about shifting illegally.

Mom's DataLink chimes. She checks it and sighs. "I have to take this. I'll be right back."

I finish my breakfast in silence, totally surprised that it tastes decent—not like the synthetic junk we usually have. When I get up to leave, Shan stops me. "Hey Bridger, have you finished using my Virtual Lenses yet?"

My cheeks grow hot. I was going to sneak them back into his quarters after Alora, Zed, and Elijah had viewed Ellis's Sim. But I've been so pre-occupied with school and wondering what we'll discover when we shift to 2126. I just forgot. I think about denying that I have them, but it's no use. He knows.

"Um, yeah," I stammer. "I . . . how did you know I took them?"

"I saw you."

My brow furrows. I thought he was asleep. The little sneak. I'm impressed and a little embarrassed.

"Why didn't you stop me?" I ask.

He looks away and shrugs. "I dunno. I guess I figured you've wanted to borrow them for a little while, since Dad gave them to me."

With those words, the dark, empty space in my chest pulses, reminding me of what I'm missing. Of what Shan and Grandma are missing. That Dad's still out there, somewhere in our future, alive. And I can't tell them. At least, not yet. Hopefully I'll have some answers soon.

But right now, I have to get out of here. I'm too ashamed to be around Shan right now. I mumble an apology and promise to give them back Monday, then grab my portacase and leave before Mom can come back to start any crap with me.

I gaze up at the Department of Temporal Affairs building as I approach it. Built in the early part of this century, it's an oval-shaped, sixty-story-tall building composed of glass walls. The base starts out wide and tapers to a narrow rooftop. Dad used to bring me here sometimes, when I was little. I didn't have to request an appointment for that.

My eyes still on the sky, I almost bump into a Purist woman. "You people think you own everything," she snarls at me.

I want to hurl an insult back at her. But it's not worth it. Instead, I incline my head to the officers on duty just ahead of us. These appear to be regular police. But down the street I spot a few military Space Benders and I grin.

The woman scowls and hurries away.

"You're late," Grandma says when I finally arrive in the small court-yard outside the DTA building. She's already sitting on a stone bench with Zed and Elijah. Behind them is the massive memorial wall bearing the name of every Time Bender who's died.

They're not happy with me. When Grandma glances toward the entrance, Zed holds up both hands, his fingers curled in like he wants to choke me. Elijah is giving me a major stink eye. I check my DataLink again. Our appointment is in ten minutes. But Grandma is one of those people who's always early.

"I'm sorry," I say for the second time today. "I got held up at the Maglev station."

I don't bother telling her why I got held up there. Two Purists decided to pick a fight with a couple of the military Space Benders on patrol, and that led to a few more Purists coming to their defense. They claimed the Space Benders had insulted them. I doubt that's what happened. What would the Space Benders gain from doing something that juvenile? But Purists picking a fight, now that's something I believe would happen.

Grandma stands, smooths out her uniform, and motions for us to follow her. "Let's go, boys. You're only cleared to be in here for an hour and a half."

Elijah and Zed flank me, and we fall into step behind Grandma.

"Your grandmother practically interrogated me," Zed complains. "She wanted to know what made me change my mind about joining the military, and all sorts of fun stuff. I even had to tell her about my dads and where they live now." He pauses to heave a sigh. "You owe us big time."

Elijah agrees with him. "Man, I vote that you take us out to eat some-where expensive and pay for it."

The plan is that, after the tour ends, we'll exit the building and meet Alora in the alley around the corner. She'll give me my Chronoband and comm-set, since I can't smuggle them past the DTA's scanners. I'll leave my DataLink with Elijah and Zed. From there, Alora and I will activate our cloaks, sneak back into the lobby of the DTA building, and shift to 2126 from there. Elijah and Zed will go back to Elijah's house to wait for us.

We pass two soldiers stationed outside the entrance. Once we're inside, we sign in with a retinal scanner and walk through another scanner that searches for weapons or explosives. Then we meet up with a short woman with shoulder-length black hair and deep brown skin, dressed in a navy-blue uniform. Even though I haven't seen her in several years, I recognize her as Professor March's younger sister. Dad told me once that they were never close because the professor was so much older than her, so she was always annoying him. I can totally relate to that.

"I'm Captain Olivia March, and I'll be your guide today," she says in a clipped voice.

"Hey, are you related to Professor Telfair March?" Zed asks.

The captain's back straightens. "I am. He's my older brother."

And because Zed has no shame, he says, "Huh, that's weird. He's never said anything about having a sister."

I want to sink through the floor. Elijah looks like he wants to do the same thing.

Grandma snaps, "That will be all, Ramirez. We're here because you're considering joining the military yourself. Please act accordingly."

Zed blushes. "I'm sorry. That won't happen again."

"Apology accepted," the captain says. "Now, if you will follow me, we'll begin the tour."

It takes exactly an hour to complete the tour. In that time, we make a brief pass through the DTA's civilian sector, which takes up the top thirty floors. The lower thirty floors house the military division. The difference between the two sectors is stark. The civilian portion of the building is decorated in a kaleidoscope of styles from the various points in time that have been visited so far. The military section is much starker, painted in varying shades of gray.

And for the military sector, we're only allowed to tour the Operations Center on the fifth floor, several artifact recovery rooms, and Grandma's office as a special favor. But floors twenty through thirty are off-limits. I'm exceedingly annoyed. I didn't know that. I had hoped we'd be able to check out the room we were instructed to visit before shifting. If I can't get there now, will Alora and I be able to once we shift to 2126? What if we need some kind of key or biometric scan to access it?

Captain March deposits us back in the lobby at precisely eleven o'clock. "I hope the tour was beneficial to you. Please do not hesitate to contact me if you have any questions, Cadet Ramirez. I sincerely hope that you decide to join us in the military. The work is quite rewarding."

"Charming lady," Grandma says as soon as she departs. "Well, can I interest you boys in lunch? My treat."

Zed looks like he wants to accept so badly. But of course, he has to decline along with the rest of us.

"We're supposed to eat lunch with my parents," Elijah says quickly. I could kiss him for coming up with a good reason not to go with her.

"Oh well. I'll grab something in the cafeteria then. I'll see you later," she says. She casts a glance back at us. It seems so longing—almost like she's lonely and really wants us to go with her.

I wish I could. I really do. The way she looked just then reminded me so much of Dad. I can't wait to find proof that he's been cloned and tell her that he's alive. That's better than nothing. But I certainly can't make those claims right now.

We have to check out before we're allowed to leave the building. That's to be expected, but it doesn't leave us a lot of good options for shifting to the past. Once Alora and I go back inside, we'll have to stay in the lobby.

"Are you sure about this?" Elijah asks once we're past the soldiers on guard. "You can always change your mind. We won't judge you, right, Zed?"

"You speak the truth, Elijah," Zed replies. "I admire you for wanting to do this, but it's dangerous. What if you and Alora get caught?"

"We won't. We have the Chronobands. We'll be fine."

"I hope so," Elijah murmurs. "I really do."

"Let's just hope your mother doesn't send one of her space-bending buddies over to my house to check in on you. I don't know how I'll explain having your DataLink," Elijah says.

"I hope it won't come to that," I reply.

By this time, we've reached sidewalk. We turn left and hurry to the thin sliver of space between the DTA building and the neighboring sky-scraper. Halfway down the pristine alley, we find Alora already waiting in the shadows. She's standing really still, with her back against the wall and her arms folded tightly against her chest. Her face lights up when she sees us. I find myself grinning.

Elijah elbows me in the ribs. "You have a thing for her now?"

"No, of course not," I snap.

He snorts. "Right, man. I hear you."

I clench my jaw. Alora and I are just friends. I like her a lot, but I can't be distracted with a relationship. And besides, the DTA can't know that we've been spending time together. They might suspect that we both remember the truth of what happened to us in 2013.

"I'm so glad you're here now," she says when we reach her.

"How long have you been waiting?" I ask.

"I'm not sure. Maybe fifteen or twenty minutes," she says.

Zed looks at her in disbelief. "You knew what time we said we'd be here. Why didn't you just pop in from your apartment?"

Alora gives him a withering look. "Because I've never seen this alley before. And besides, the only way I could convince my mom to let me out by myself was to tell her I was going to the museum today. So I went there first and hid my DataLink in some bushes so she could track me. And then I had to run into the restroom to change into my uniform."

"Oh, sorry," Zed mumbles. "I didn't realize your mom is like Bridger's. We have to take his DataLink with us, too."

"Which reminds me," I interrupt while I remove my DataLink and hand it to Elijah. He puts it in his pocket.

Alora reaches into her portacase and pulls out my Chronoband and comm-set. I slip the comm-set over my head first, then fasten the Chronoband on my wrist. I won't be able to record anything since it's not joined with my DataLink. That's fine. I just need it to see Alora, once we're cloaked, plus any Unknowns we may encounter.

I look at Elijah and Zed and say, "See you two soon."

"Good luck," Elijah whispers.

"And don't get caught," Zed adds.

Alora and I lean against the side of building, exchange a quick look, then press the gold buttons on our uniform collars to activate our cloaks.

Elijah and Zed head out of the alley in the opposite direction. Alora and I walk in silence until we arrive at the entrance of the DTA building.

Alora's steps slow when she spots the two guards outside the entrance. "You're sure they won't be able to see us, right?"

"I'm positive," I say. "They're not wearing comm-sets. We'll be fine."

MELISSA E. HURST 111

Alora reaches out and grabs my hand. "Okay. Let's get this over with."

We stand next to the entrance for a few more minutes until an officer enters the building. As soon as he opens the doors using the biometric scanner, we fall in behind him. Then we turn left and stand with our backs against the wall.

I've already programmed the date and time into my Chronoband, and Alora should have done the same. "Are you ready?" I ask.

"More than you know."

Over the last few days, we studied an old set of floor plans for the DTA building that I downloaded from the DataNet. The plan is to make our way to the staircase on the western side of the building, the one closest to our destination. The elevators are a no-go; they ask for a code to get to the ten floors that are for personnel with special clearance.

"Ready on my mark. Remember, we need to arrive fifteen minutes early to give us time to reach our target. I'm picturing the date and time in my mind." I pause to let her do the same, while I think the same date over and over. August 10, 2126. 8:45 a.m. "And go on three. Two. One."

I press the button on my Chronoband and enter the Void. I wish I'd taken Alora's hand again before entering. That would have made this a little more bearable. But at least I don't hate this part as much as I used to. Living as a shell of a person makes you not care so much about feeling like one for a minute.

The past materializes as a swirl of senses. Colors. Smells. Noises. All faint, until everything crystallizes at once.

I look to my right again.

Alora isn't there.

19

ALORA
AUGUST 10, 2126

A knot forms in my stomach as soon as I emerge from the Void. Bridger isn't with me, and I'm no longer in the lobby.

The room I'm in is stark white, with what looks like medical equipment scattered around it, and a woman in a white uniform is attending to someone strapped to a bed. My legs grow weak when I take a few steps closer to the bed and get a glimpse of her patient.

It's my dad.

Tears spring up in my eyes. I was thinking of him as Bridger and I shifted—thinking of how he looked in all the pictures I've seen of him, both in the past with Aunt Grace, and now, with Mom. My professors in Chicago were training me to shift back in time and through space simultaneously, but I hadn't mastered the skill yet when I came here. Of course, it had to work this time—when I *have* to stay with Bridger.

But strangely . . . I'm glad. This is the first time I've seen Dad in person since I was little. It's so surreal, watching him as he sleeps. He's so still, so lifeless. He appears to be in his in his early twenties, with no wrinkles. This must be sometime soon after he was cloned. Buy why is he strapped down if he's only sleeping? He's obviously been sedated, but for what reason? And where are we?

Taking a few steps closer, I whisper into my comm-set's mouthpiece. "Bridger, can you hear me? I accidentally shifted to my dad."

I expect him to reply, but I only receive silence. I try to call him a few more times, but still nothing.

I should shift back to Bridger right now because he's probably freaking out, but I get the overwhelming urge to hold Dad's hand for a moment before I go. I hurry to the opposite side of the bed, wondering why the woman is attaching so many electrodes to his head and bare torso. He's already hooked up to a machine monitoring his vital signs. A screen built into the wall behind him displays the stats.

My fingers tremble as I reach out and touch his hand. It's freezing. Then I place my hand against his forehead, and it's just as cold. I frown. That's odd, since the room is warm. It's as if he's been kept in a refrigerator.

I wish I could stay with him longer, but I know I can't. This version of my father belongs to 2126, and he can't know about me yet. I have to keep looking for the one that exists in 2147, wherever he may be.

And that means getting back to Bridger immediately.

I lean over to kiss Dad's cheek and whisper, "I'll keep looking for you. I promise."

Just then, a screeching siren pierces the silence. The woman across from me looks around the room in alarm. Her DataLink, a slightly clunkier model than mine, beeps. She checks it and a man's voice barks, "We just performed a security scan. There's an Unknown in the room with you. Secure the specimen."

"Understood," she answers in a curt tone. She reaches under her tunic and withdraws what looks like a small gun from a holster. The woman's eyes dart back and forth and she takes a few steps away from the bed. "Whoever you are, show yourself," she commands.

My heart is beating so hard that I feel lightheaded. I have to get out now. I squeeze my eyes and concentrate on Bridger's face.

Please work. Please.

A few moments later, I appear just behind him. We're standing in a stairway, and he's looking through a narrow window in a metal door. The stupid siren is still blasting. "Alora, can you hear me? Please respond."

I lean over to grasp my knees, taking deep breaths. "Oh my God, I made it."

Bridger whirls around with a panicky look on his face, then his shoulders sag when he realizes it's me. "Where have you been? I've been trying to reach you for almost five minutes. And now something's triggered an alarm." He takes a long look at me, realization dawning on his face. "It was you, wasn't it?"

I lower my eyes, realizing I shouldn't have lingered so long. "I'm sorry. It's just that I appeared in the same room with my father, and I tried to reach you but couldn't. And then for some reason they performed a security scan while I was in there."

Bridger places his hands on his hips. "That's not good. We need to get to our target right now."

"Are we at least on the correct floor?"

"Yep, but we're stuck in here," he says, pointing to the biometric scanner next to the door. "I need you to shift to the other side and see if you can open it."

He moves aside so I can peek through the window, since I need a specific location to focus on when I shift. I'm looking at a grim hallway, with dark-gray carpet and light-gray walls. I concentrate on the area just ahead of me, picturing it in my mind, then close my eyes and shift.

Bridger waves at me through the window, then points at the sides of the door. I check and, seeing that there are no scanners or anything else, quickly open the door. Bridger sprints out, and we start to advance down the hallway. We make it past several doors before six soldiers emerge from a room about halfway down the hall, all of them holding some sort of device that I'm not familiar with. The one in front speaks into his Data-Link. "Project Firebird room is clear."

One of the soldiers takes up a post outside the double doors. The others turn left and head down the hall, then enter the next room. Then the elevator opens and two women dressed in navy-blue officers' uniforms exit. The soldier outside the door salutes to them as they enter.

Bridger cringes. "That's the room we need to get into."

"We're still cloaked. We can just walk right by them."

"No, we can't. Those things they're holding are a type of scanner that will reveal our cloaks. It's similar to the tech in our comm-sets."

I groan. "Jeez, we can't catch a break. So how do we get inside?"

Bridger thinks for a moment, his forehead scrunched up, then stands up straighter. "We can't, but if I can draw that soldier away, you can get inside."

Fear floods through me. "No! You can't leave me. We have to do this together."

"I wish we could, but there's no way we're both getting into that room. You can't shift in because you don't know what it looks like, so you'll have to go in through the doors. And you can't do that with the soldier scanning the doorway."

I want to argue with him, but he's right. And we're running out of time. Ellis's note said to be in the room at nine o'clock. It's now 8:55.

"Okay, I'll do it. But how will you get out?" I ask.

"Don't worry about me. I'm going down the stairs. All I need to do is get back to the lobby, and then I can shift. Easy enough." He tries to laugh, but it sounds hollow.

I give him a hug and whisper, "Thank you. I'll shift back to the alley and meet you there soon."

He pulls away and bangs his fist against the metal stairway door before opening it and slipping through. Instantly, the soldier stationed outside the door takes off running toward the stairway, yelling into his DataLink that he's in pursuit of an Unknown. A few seconds later, three of the soldiers in the next room rush out and follow the first.

I press my back against the wall to let them pass before hurrying toward the now unguarded room. I manage to make it inside just before another soldier takes up post outside the door.

Trying to slow my breathing, I duck into a back corner and scope out my surroundings. It's a large conference room, nearly twice the size of the one back at the Academy. A long, white-topped table with silver legs stretches down the center of the room, surrounded by twenty comfortable-looking black chairs. Three of the walls are white, while the wall opposite me is made entirely of glass. Outside, the New Denver skyline stretches below us, while the sky overhead is a clear blue. It looks so serene, so unlike what I'm experiencing in here.

Twenty men and women, all in navy-blue uniforms, are seated around the table, chatting in animated tones. I guess it's not every day that a security break happens here.

Several minutes pass, then the lights overhead dim, while at the same time the glass wall darkens until it's a smoky gray. The silver-haired woman sitting at the head of the table stands and walks to a narrow white podium.

"Welcome, members of the Project Firebird Oversight Committee," she says into a sliver of a microphone. "I want to apologize for the delay. I've been assured that the Unknown is no longer on the premises."

Some of my tension drains away when she says that. At least Bridger is safe.

The woman continues, "Today I have the honor and privilege of presenting to you someone who will become a *very* important part of our future. In the days since our scientists stumbled upon the creation of the Talents as a by-product of genetic modification, we've always wondered if, somehow, multiple Talents could be merged into one person to produce a Dual Talent. But so far, scientists have failed to create such a person on their own. And after one of our earliest trips into the past revealed a natural-born Mind and Time Bender who died in the year 2022, we developed Project Firebird with the goal of finding more Dual Talents in the past, relocating them to our time upon their deaths, and introducing their unique genetic sequences into our population."

Many of the audience members nod, as if this is old news, but several, who I presume are the new members, look astonished. I know how they feel—my mind is reeling. So this is why they cloned my father. My instructors taught me that cloning was outlawed because clones always become unstable, but the DTA chose to risk it in order to create more Dual Talents in this time.

"So far, we've collected three natural-born Mind and Time Benders and two Mind and Space Benders. Today, I'm delighted to share that we have finally, after *many* years of searching, located a man who was a natural-born Time Bender and Space Bender."

The room explodes in excited chatter.

"What year is he from, General Carter?" one man shouts.

"Has he been cloned yet?" someone else asks.

Suddenly, one of the members shoots to his feet. I stare at him in shock. Even though he appears to be in his early forties, I recognize him as the same man who ordered my memories to be wiped. He was even in the room with me when it happened. I'll never forget his condescending smile, his reassurances that it was for the best.

General Carter gazes at him with a distasteful expression. "Major Anderson, take your seat immediately."

He stands a few seconds before he complies, but then he says, "I object to this. I've already stated in prior meetings that introducing Dual Talents into our society could be disastrous. And creating Space and Time Benders would be a thousand times worse. With their skills, they could become a danger to society."

Another committee member sighs heavily. "And why would you think that, Thomas?"

"Are you not using your brain?" he asks. "Think of all the power that such individuals could wield over the general population—hell, even over the rest of us!"

"You're fear-mongering again, Thomas," General Carter snaps.

"Am I, ma'am?" he asks in a voice dripping with disdain. "I've already explained how a Dual Talent Space and Time Bender from a foreign government could shift to any time period from *any* location, while now we're all forced to travel to our target location before shifting to the past. Imagine what intel they could steal from us. Their agents could shift straight into our secure buildings without ever leaving their home countries. Think how easy it would be for rogue Dual Talents to take over our own government, from the inside. It would be a disaster!" A few other committee members nod when he says that. "I move that we terminate this subject. There are too many unknown variables at this time, and frankly it's too much of a security risk."

General Carter stands up straighter and narrows her eyes at the major. "Motion denied. Now, I want to turn the meeting over to Colonel Rashida March, who will be responsible for training and integrating the subject into the ranks of our military."

The general gestures to a woman sitting across from her empty chair. She has to be Professor March's mother—even though she's a lot shorter, they have the exact same smile.

Once the colonel takes General Carter's place at the podium, she presses a button on the DataPad she's placed on its surface. A round glass tube suspended from the ceiling lights up, and then an image is projected over the table. It's a hologram of my father in his old army uniform.

"Our subject is Nathaniel Walker, a private first class in the former United States Army," the colonel says while focusing on the image. "He was killed in action while serving in Iraq in 1994, which is where we sent our operatives to retrieve his DNA sample and upload his consciousness."

The image of Dad is replaced by a holographic video. My heart starts to race. I should look away, but I can't. The Time Bender recording this, along with a second Time Bender, is standing a safe distance away from a military convoy as it drives through a desert terrain. The first truck suddenly explodes. The operatives immediately break into a run and head to an area just outside the truck. Shouts come from the others in the convoy.

And then they find what's left of my father.

Oh God, no. *No.* I squeeze my eyes shut, bile rising in my throat. I wish I hadn't seen that, but it's seared into my memory now.

"Moving on to the next part," the colonel says, as if she hadn't just watched someone die.

I peek through my lashes, terrified of what I'll see. The hologram is showing a live feed of the room I was in earlier. Dad is still lying on the bed, unmoving. More medical personnel are in the room now, some checking various machines, others working directly around him. The feed zooms in, and I'm shocked that I recognize one of the people working on him. She's younger, but it's definitely the blond woman who tried to take me away from Mom when I was six years old. The one who Bridger later told me was Vika's mother.

"This will be quite exciting for you," Colonel March says. "We retrieved Mr. Walker a few months ago, and his cloned body just finished its growth cycle last night. So today, my friends, we will witness the resurrection of Nathaniel Walker!"

Applause breaks out among the committee members who seem to support the project, while Major Anderson and his allies sit in stony silence. I want to scream. That was why Dad was so cold and still. It was just his cloned body lying there, not *him*. How could they do this? It's bad enough to know he was mistreated by the DTA, but to know that he went through this . . . this is degrading. It's almost as if they don't even consider him human.

The colonel presses a button on the podium and says, "Dr. Liu, are you ready to proceed?"

A woman with black hair streaked with bright red is checking the equipment next to Dad's bed. She glances up at the camera. "Affirmative, Colonel March. We're ready."

She smiles. "Excellent. Let's begin."

A part of me thinks I should leave now. I've already learned why my father was brought back to life. I don't need to see it happening. But another part tells me I need to stay; I owe it to him to witness what his rebirth was like.

I focus on the video feed above the table again. Everyone in the room with Dad is now surrounding his bed, watching him.

Dr. Liu checks a few of the electrodes on his head, then taps the screen of her DataPad before saying, "Here we go."

Small blue dots light up on all the electrodes. I half expect Dad's body to surge up in the same way I've seen people being revived in movies, but he remains still. Nearly a full minute passes this way, and I allow myself to almost relax. Maybe this won't be so bad.

But then Dad's eyes fly open and he screams. It's not the scream of someone who's scared; it's the scream of someone in agony. Someone in overwhelming pain. He begins to writhe and fight against the restraints. I want to close my eyes again, but I make myself to keep them open. I *have* to see what he went though.

One of the nurses says, "His blood pressure is spiking."

Dr. Liu checks her DataPad again. "It's fine. He's almost finished downloading into the body."

And then it's done. His screams stop and his body sags back onto the mattress. Tears flow from his eyes as he searches the faces staring at him. "Please, somebody help me."

I can't do this anymore. I've seen all I can take. I adjust the date on my Chronoband, close my eyes, and shift back to 2147.

20

BRIDGER
AUGUST 10, 2126

My adrenaline kicks into high gear as I race down the stairway. I have to hang on to the railing as I run to keep from falling down. I'm just passing the twenty-third floor when the door I went through crashes open and footsteps pound on the steps. The soldier shouts, "Stop where you are!"

Yeah, like I'm going to do that. I've got to get out of this building so I can shift back to my time.

My whole world revolves around trying not to trip over my feet as I fly down the stairway. But then a noise from below brings me to a screeching halt. More soldiers have entered the stairway from the floor beneath me. Fure, I can't catch a break.

I don't have a choice. Closing my eyes, I try to block out the footsteps getting dangerously close to me, and concentrate on my present. February 18, 2147.

I've never been so relieved to enter the Void. But a thought occurs to me while I'm in there—as soon as I emerge in my time, my cloak will set off an alarm in the DTA building. Around the year 2133, they finally developed the tech to the point where sensors could be placed throughout the building to constantly monitor for cloaked individuals.

I'm not sure if I can deactivate my cloak in the Void. As far as I know, it's never been done before. But I've got to try. I reach up and press the button on my collar.

As soon as I'm out of the Void, I hold perfectly still until reality sharpens again. It's weird how the stairway looks almost exactly the same now as it did in 2126. All gloomy gray. Still, I'm too afraid to move. I could be in a sector of the stairway that is invisible to the sensors. Or I could be uncloaked. I don't know. Well, it's not like I can just stand here. I have to find out, one way or another.

Breathing deeply to calm myself, I take a few tentative steps. Then a few more. Then I walk down to the level below me.

Relief floods though me. I did it.

But the relief doesn't last. I'm not supposed to be in the building at all. How the hell am I going to explain that? And I'm still wearing my illegal comm-set. I take it off, fold the ear- and mouthpieces against the lenses, and slip it into my pocket.

I pass a few people on the stairway. Nobody recognizes me. And then I see Captain March. I lower my gaze, hoping she won't recognize me.

But I apparently have no luck today.

"What are you doing here?" she asks, her brows drawn together in disbelief. "The tour ended over an hour ago."

Think, Creed, *think*. "I'm going back to my grandmother's office. I think I left my portacase in there."

"And why aren't you with her?"

Okay, now she's just being nosy. "She's at lunch, waiting for me to get back," I lie, hoping that she won't comm Grandma to see if that's the truth.

A pressure begins to build in my head, gradually increasing. I try to keep surprise from registering in my eyes. Evidently Captain March is a dual Time and Mind Bender, like her brother. Thinking fast, I throw up a mental block, like Dad taught me. When she realizes she can't get past the barrier, her eyes narrow to slits.

"You need to come with me. Immediately."

I must look like an idiot, with my mouth hanging open. I have to play this cool, make her think she's being unreasonable. Time to pull out some of my Grandma's tactics.

"I haven't done anything wrong. I told you all I was doing was look-ing for my portacase. And I know that you just tried to do a mind probe on me." I pause and cross my arms. "Can you tell me how that's possible? You're a Time Bender. You shouldn't be able to do that."

The annoyance on her face fades into a controlled, blank expression. She looks back over her shoulder, then back at me. "I don't know what you're talking about. I most certainly did *not* try to probe your mind."

"Well, then, if that's the case, why don't you let me go? I need to check my grandmother's office, and I don't think she will be happy with you reporting me for something minor."

She thinks for a long moment, looking at me like she wishes I would burst into flames. "You remind me a lot of your father and your grandmother. That'll be an asset to you if you work here in the future. In the meantime, I don't *ever* want to catch you in here unattended again. Is that clear?"

I salute her. "Yes, ma'am. I can promise you that."

My uniform feels positively drenched in sweat, and I'm sure I smell as bad as a Purist by the time I get to the floor with Grandma's office on it. I glance up the stairway to see if Captain March has followed me, but it doesn't appear that she did. From here, I could follow my original plan. Or I could actually go to Grandma's office. She should be out for a while, and I might be able to slip in and access the DTA's network using her office TeleNet. It's a golden opportunity to see if there are any records about what my dad is doing now, or where Alora's father may be.

It doesn't take long to reach Grandma's office again. I glance around, checking through the partial glass walls that indicate entrances to other offices. Most are empty, but in I see an officer sitting at his desk. At least his back is to me—but if he turns around he'll see me.

Heart pounding, I stand in front of the retinal scanner. Earlier, when we visited Grandma's office on the tour, we had to have our eyes scanned before we could gain entrance. I cross my fingers, hoping like hell that my pattern is still in the system. Otherwise, I'm screwed.

The longest three seconds of my life pass before the light on the scanner changes from red to green. The door slides open and I rush inside. Without knowing exactly how long Grandma will be away, I need to work fast.

Once I get the TeleNet out of sleep mode, I whisper, "Search for last known information relating to Colonel Leithan Creed."

The results only show reports about his death and subsequent burial. The official cause of death is listed as a gunshot wound from an unknown assailant while on a mission. Nothing else. My fingers curl into fists. I give several more commands, looking for any information about General Anderson's connection to Dad, my dad's trip to 2013, or even my involvement. Nothing is available. I even search for Vika's last known whereabouts, but all that I find is the report about her death last year.

Absolutely no mention of her or Dad being cloned.

I want to slam my fists on the desk. Break something. I'm in the furing DTA's mainframe and still can't find information about what happened last year. General Anderson is definitely hiding all of this. And I want to know why.

Before I leave, I say, "Search for last known information about Nathaniel Walker."

Fully expecting nothing to show, I'm shocked when the screen displays dozens of documents about him. I quickly search through them, wishing I had time to read everything. One document, dated May 20, 2136, stands out because that's the date Alora was kidnapped and taken to the past by her father.

I get a surge of adrenaline when I realize I'm reading a report of the events leading to his death. I wasn't expecting to see that. I glance over at the door again before I scan over the contents, slowing down to read the passage detailing how he died:

Walker returned to Mason's apartment an hour after kidnapping their daughter in order to abduct her as well. Officers from the Department of Temporal Affairs and the Department of Teleportation, already on the scene due to the earlier kidnapping, were able to arrest Walker and fit him with an Inhibitor to prevent him from fleeing the premises. While en route to DTA headquarters, Walker's transport shuttle was destroyed in an explosion. Efforts to determine the cause of the explosion have been unsuccessful due to the dangerous nature of bending into the shuttle mid-flight. The deceased included Captain Mary Baker, pilot, Lieutenant Jonas Lake, arresting officer, and Walker.

I take a few steps back from Grandma's desk. I wasn't expecting to discover this. I really thought Nate was being held somewhere, or that he had been Nulled. The thought of having to tell Alora fills me with dread.

I check the time on the TeleNet. Fure, I've been here way too long— I need to get out now. By the time I make it down the stairs and to the lobby, I'm out of breath. I'm just glad that nobody else tried to stop me. Maybe being the grandson of one of the superior officers here is a good thing. Still, I'm not supposed to be here anymore, and the guard knows that. I wait until he's distracted before I slip behind him and out the door.

Now to get to the alley. Hopefully Alora is waiting for me there.

Half an hour later, I'm pacing in the alley. Alora hasn't showed up yet, and I can't comm her. My mind keeps conjuring one disaster scenario after another. I'm almost certain she was caught in 2126 and interrogated. That could contaminate the timeline. But if that had happened, wouldn't things be screwed up here? Wouldn't reality already have been destroyed?

"I'm back."

I whirl around. Alora has appeared behind me for the second time today. This time, I rush over to her and fold her in a hug. She clings to me—starts sobbing. I want to look her in the eye, to ask her what's wrong, but I can't bring myself to let her go. I never want to let her go.

Finally, she pulls away from me, wiping her eyes. "I'm so sorry. I shouldn't have done that."

I place my hands on her shoulders. "You don't have to apologize. I can't imagine what you saw."

She closes her eyes for a moment. "It was awful."

She shares what she learned. How the DTA created Project Firebird to find natural-born Dual Talents and clone them. How the clones were used to create Dual Talent children in our time. And how she had to witness the moment just before her father's death—and his resurrection.

I don't know what to say. I know I should tell her what I discovered about Nate, but one look at her face makes me forget about it for the moment and pull her into a hug. She stays in my arms for a long time. Then she pulls back, tilting her face up to me. Her eyes are so blue. So beautiful. I'm overwhelmed by the urge to kiss her.

And then I tell myself to stop being so selfish. She's hurting. The last thing she needs is for me to try to kiss her. Especially since I'm about to break her heart with what I know.

"Thank you," she says.

"For what?"

"Do you really have to ask? For being here. For listening to me, and shifting back in time with me to day. Suddenly her face lights up. "I forgot to tell you. I also saw some people I recognized."

"Who?"

"One was the man who wiped my memories. His name was Thomas Anderson, and he wasn't happy about my dad being cloned. He argued that Space and Time Benders like me would be too powerful and dangerous, and he wasn't crazy about having other Dual Talents either."

I stare at her incredulously. "Wait, you mean General Anderson was there?"

"General Anderson?" she asks, frowning a little, then dawning lights up her face. "Crap, that's the guy who was after you when you went back for me. Right?"

"Yep. He's now the head of the DTA's military division."

"Jeez, that's just great. The head of the DTA doesn't like Dual Talents. But then . . . why does he allow us to be trained? Something isn't adding up." She shakes her head. "Anyway, there was also a woman who was in the room when Dad was revived—Vika's mother. Oh, and the person heading up the project was Professor March's mother."

Her words hit me like an icy wind, numbing me to the core. Somehow, I *knew* it. I knew that Halla Fairbanks was involved with the cloning. And I'm honestly not surprised to hear that Professor March's mom was involved, as well. Not since both of her children are Dual Talents.

But what I still don't understand is why my dad was cloned. He's definitely not a Dual Talent.

Alora's eyes widen. "I feel so stupid."

"Why?"

"Because when we went into the Void, I thought about my father and ended up in the same room with him. I could just do that now and see where he is."

She looks so hopeful and trusting. I wish I could keep what I learned to myself, but that wouldn't solve anything. I'd be lying to Alora, and I can't do that to her. We've both been told too many lies. I have to let her know the truth.

Reaching out both hands and placing the on her shoulders, I take a deep breath. "I'm so sorry, but I have to tell you something."

21

Everything that happens after I part ways with Bridger feels surreal. After retrieving my DataLink at the museum, I make my way to Tara's apartment. I don't remember much of the trip—flashes of color as people passed by me, sounds blasting from Jumbotrons, and the glint of shuttles passing overhead.

The directions on my DataLink lead me to an unfamiliar apartment building. I immediately take the elevator to the fourteenth floor and search for Tara's apartment. It's amazing how similar this building looks to Mom's, even though it's six blocks away.

Once I've located her apartment, I press my thumb on the sensor beside the door that visitors use. It takes a few moments to read my print, then the door slides open. Tara is standing just on the other side. "Good grief, you look terrible," she says while pulling me in.

A man and a woman are in the living area, watching the TeleNet screen.

"Are you going to introduce us?" asks her mom. She looks like an older version of Tara, with medium-brown skin and curly black hair. Her father's skin is slightly lighter than Tara's, but his hair is dyed an electric shade of blue. He smiles warmly at me and tugs at his collar of his orange button-up that looks like something straight from the 1960s. "Do you think this shirt clashes with my hair?"

I try to smile back, but I'm sure I look like I'm cringing.

"Alora, these are my parents, Salina and Tannis Martinez," she says, then glares at her father. "Of course it clashes. It's hideous."

"Well, I don't care. I dig it," he replies.

"Yep, it's groovy," her mom says, and they both cackle like it's the funniest thing they've ever said.

Tara rolls her eyes. "You two are so beyond embarrassing."

We do the small talk thing for a minute or so. They want to know about my parents. I nearly choke up when I say my father is missing, since that's the official story—the only thing I'm supposed to know. They murmur condolences about my terrible childhood, and then, thankfully, Tara ushers me into her room, where she leads me to an overstuffed green-and-white polka-dot chair and orders me to sit.

Once she's seated, cross-legged, on her bed, Tara asks, "Is there anything I can do? Do you want anything to eat?"

I shake my head no. My stomach is in knots, so I don't even want to think about food right now.

When Bridger told me that my dad was dead, I didn't want to believe him. But just seeing how heartbroken he was on my behalf was enough to convince me. I couldn't stop crying. I managed to get myself together enough to part with him, since he had to go to Elijah's house to pick up his DataLink. I couldn't face Mom just yet, so I commed Tara to see if I could stay with her for a while. But I didn't tell her why. I just said I needed somewhere to go.

"Your parents are nice," I say in a rush.

"They're all right," she says with a shrug. "So, are you going to tell me what's wrong?"

"I just found out that my father is dead," I blurt out.

Her jaw goes kind of slack. "Oh shit, Alora, I'm so sorry. I didn't know."

"It's okay," I murmur, looking down at my hands. They're shaking in my lap. *Don't cry, don't cry, don't cry*, I tell myself over and over.

It doesn't work. Tears fall fresh down my cheeks. Tara hops off the bed and a few moments later hands me a soft tissue.

When I manage to compose myself, Tara perches on the edge of her bed and says, "Do you want to talk about it?"

What can I tell her? She has no idea that I restored my and Bridger's memories. She has no idea what we did today. I wonder if I can trust her, but then I remember that she's dating Elijah. If Bridger trusts Elijah and Elijah trusts her, then I'm sure I can too.

It takes me nearly half an hour to share the craziness that's been my life for the past ten months.

Tara is gaping at me by the time I'm finished. "That's so wild. But what are you going to do next?"

My DataLink chimes. It's my mom. I sigh and accept the comm. Immediately, her image hovers over my wrist. I was expecting her to be angry, but instead she lets out a huge sigh of relief. "Oh my God, Alora, where are you?"

"It's okay," I say in a flat voice. "I'm visiting my roommate, Tara. Remember I told you about her?"

"Yes, but you told me you were only going to the museum. You nearly gave me heart failure when I saw that you weren't there."

A flash of annoyance fills me. I really don't want to be suffocated by her, especially since she was in on lying to me. "You don't have to worry about me. I'll be okay."

She seems stung by my words. "Of course I worry. Especially now that I have you back."

My anger evaporates. I just don't have it in me anymore. Mom suffered all those years while I was living with Aunt Grace.

"I'm sorry. I'm on the way home," I say.

"Please be careful," she says. A deep crease has formed between her brows. I recognize it. Perpetual worry. Aunt Grace wore that look a lot, too, when her financial troubles started.

Tara walks me to the door. "Are you really okay? I can walk with you."

"I'm fine," I hear myself saying. It's funny how hollow I sound. "I think I need to be alone for a bit, anyway."

She nods. "I totally get it. Is there anything I can do?"

I cast a longing glance in the direction of the kitchen, where her parents are happily preparing the evening meal. "Just don't take them for granted."

I'm nearly home when I make up my mind—I need to see my father. One last time. Not in a digigraph, but in person.

I need to say goodbye.

When I'm close to Mom's apartment building, I step out of the crowd and into an alley. A Null, dressed in a drab gray jumpsuit, is picking up litter. I retreat immediately, waiting along the outer wall until the Null leaves. My tutors taught me that the shielded helmets Nulls wear contain recording devices and can detect cloaked people. I don't want any record of me using my cloak outside of school.

Once I'm back in the alley, I program the target date into my Chronoband—May 19, 2136. That's the day before Dad took me from this era and delivered me to Aunt Grace. I remember that day clearly, because that's the last happy memory I have of him from my childhood. Mom had let him spend that afternoon with me after he begged to see me for weeks. He took me to the New Denver Zoo, and then we got ice cream cones and spent our last hour together at the Green Zone near Mom's apartment. That will be my destination.

After activating the cloak on my uniform, I picture the date and my destination and shift back to 2136, emerging from the Void in a daze. I almost drop the cloak, then notice two Nulls cleaning trash near the entrance to the alley along with a supervisor. My pulse races—I'm not sure if the Nulls in this year have recording devices. I stay still as a statue until they finish their job and move on.

The Green Zone is mostly filled with parents and their children, as well as a few couples. It doesn't take me long to find Dad and the younger version of me. When I was little, I always wanted to stay at the playground when we visited this spot.

As soon as I find them, though, I get a weird sensation. I feel happy and sad at the same time, watching myself giggling at something Dad says. I almost wish I could join them, be a part of the fun they're having, but that's ridiculous. I was there—I just wish I was experiencing it now instead of sitting on a bench and watching.

And the longer I sit, the more the doubts creep in. What if I screw something up? Could I really destroy the timeline just by being here?

By the time the younger version of Mom shows up to get me, I've convinced myself not to talk to Dad. But I can't make myself leave. I watch as my younger self flails against Mom, reaching for Dad. I witness how Dad starts to follow them, then turns away when Mom threatens to call the authorities if he doesn't back off. Anger shoots through me. How could she be so cold toward him? I know her story—that he was erratic and had a temper that scared her. But I just spent the past hour watching him, and his love for me was so obvious. He would never have hurt me.

And I know he's about to die.

Before I can stop myself, I follow him across the Green Zone. He seeks out an empty bench and slumps down onto it, looking as if he could cry at any moment. My heart breaks for him.

Maybe I can just talk to him for a few minutes, without letting him know who I am. That shouldn't hurt anything.

But as soon as I sit beside him on the bench, he glances up at me and his eyes widen. "It can't be," he whispers.

My spine stiffens. "What do you mean?"

"You look like somebody I know," he says, still staring at me. "So similar to my sister." His eyes zero in on my uniform, and then he peers into my eyes. "Oh, God. Is it you, Alora?"

Some people say that when you're caught off guard, you can feel the blood rush from your face. I never really understood that, but I think I do now because I'm lightheaded. I close my eyes for a few seconds, trying to decide if I should lie or tell him the truth.

And when I look at him again, he looks so hopeful, so happy. I can't lie, not when I know what's going to happen to him tomorrow. "Yes," I say, hating how my voice cracks.

Dad covers his mouth with both hands before slowly lowering them to his lap. Then he reaches out and draws me into an embrace. My whole body begins to shake. I'm here with him and he knows it's me, and suddenly I know I was right to come here.

When he pulls away, he says, "I have so many questions. But first I have to know how old you are."

"I'll be seventeen in two days," I say, smiling.

He shakes his head as if in disbelief. "I can't believe it's you. You're so beautiful and grown-up, but you still look the same. I'd know you anywhere." He reaches for my hands and wraps his fingers around mine. His hands feel warm and rough against my skin. "I'm so happy that you're here. But why did you come? You should be living in . . . a different time."

My smile fades. I'm not sure how to answer, but he's staring at me expectantly. If I tell him the truth, then he could do something differently tomorrow and destroy the timeline. But I don't want to lie to him either. What can I say?

Finally, I decide to compromise and give him a bare bones version of the truth. "I know you want some answers, but I can't tell you everything. You know, the timeline is sacred, right?"

His expression darkens. "You're at the Academy now?"

Oh crap, no. How could I let that slip? I need to fix this, now. "Dad, I know you want to know all about my life, but I really can't share everything with you. What I can say is that I grew up in the time you wanted. Aunt Grace was a huge part of my life and I'm so grateful for that."

Dad blows out a long puff of air. "You don't know how relieved I am to hear that. I've been preparing for some time to save you and your mother. It hasn't been easy sneaking off from my unit to get fake identifications for the two of you."

So that's how Aunt Grace had a birth certificate and other legal documentation for me, things that I found in her safe when Bridger and I broke into it to look for answers about my past. That's also where I found my Jewill.

"But you never answered my question. Why are you here now? Is something wrong?" he asks.

I bite my lip, wondering what to reveal. "I really can't tell you too much. I *can* say that Mom and I are both fine. I just wanted to come back and relive this day, that's all."

He doesn't say anything for a while. The muscles in his jaw flex, as if he's not sure what to say next. "You said Mom and I. That doesn't include me, does it?"

And now my throat goes dry. For a clone—and one who's supposed to be unstable—he's extremely sharp.

"You don't have to say anything else. I think I get the picture." He runs his right hand over the top of his head, then reaches into his pocket and pulls out a small box. "I've been wanting to give this to your mom for years, but first the government denied our application to get married, then she decided that we weren't a good fit anymore. I was hoping once we shifted to 2003 that she would change her mind, but . . ."

As his voice trails off, he hands me the box. I lift the lid and find a plain gold band inside, inlaid with a purple stone. My eyes fill with tears, knowing what it is.

"People in this time aren't big on wedding rings, but I was raised differently. I wanted to give that to her, but I guess I never will, now. So . . . I'd like for you to have it."

"I can't take this," I whisper, my voice cracking.

"You can," he says firmly. "It would've been yours one day, anyway."

I slide the ring onto my right hand. "I don't know how to thank you."

He pats my hand. "Just be happy, sweetheart. That's all I've ever wanted. That, and for you to be safe."

I wish could warn him about what will happen when he tries to rescue Mom tomorrow. It's killing me, knowing that this is the last time I'll ever be able to talk to him.

It takes all my strength to say, "I've got to go now."

"I know. I wish you could stay longer, but I understand."

I fling my arms around him again, never wanting to let him go. "Bye, Daddy."

"Bye, my beautiful girl. I'll see you again one day."

Tears are flowing freely down my face now. He thinks it's goodbye for now. But I know it's goodbye forever.

22

BRIDGER
FEBRUARY 19, 2147

It's barely ten o'clock in the morning, and already adrenaline is coursing through my body. The time trip I took with Alora yesterday just raised even more questions. Today I'm going to try to find some answers. I'm going to Halla Fairbanks's house to talk to her in person, since Alora said she worked on the project that revived her father. And since Vika's consciousness was uploaded at the same time my dad's was, back in 2013, maybe she'll have some answers for us. After that, I'm going to meet Zed, Elijah, Tara, and Alora at the museum so we can figure out what to do next. Since I couldn't comm Alora myself, I asked Tara to get in touch with her and tell her of our plans.

The only problem is my brother.

"Will you hurry up?" I snap at Shan while I stop to let him to catch up. He's walking about ten paces behind me on the sidewalk, talking to someone on his DataLink. There are too many people out for us to get separated without me worrying about losing him in the crowd. We've already passed one small group of Purists chanting in front of city hall. I really hope things aren't about to turn sour again.

Shan signs off just before reaching me.

"Who were you talking to?" I ask, thinking it was probably Mom.

"One of my friends," he says. "Not that you care."

I glance at him out of the corner of my eyes. His sullenness around me has only increased in the past week. The camping trip with Grandma was the turning point. But when I told Mom I needed to go out this morning, she made me take Shan. She said she would be busy working on a project all day and that he needed to get out more. Personally, I think she just wanted the apartment to herself for a few hours. Either way, it sucks because I'm stuck with someone who clearly has issues with me.

But I decide to try to reason with the little tyrant. "Who says I don't care? It's good that you have friends. Maybe you should bring them around the apartment more."

Shan snorts. "Um, no thanks. Mom would embarrass me. I'll just stick to seeing them at school."

It's all I can do to keep a straight face. "I thought you loved Mom. You're clearly her favorite."

"No, I'm not," he spits out. "She's just nicer to me because I don't openly hate her, like you do. You and Dad were always so close. There was no room left for me. Or for Mom."

I want to scoff at him, but what if he's right? It's true that Dad and I spent a lot of time together, but that's because we had so many things in common. Camping, of course, but we also loved watching old baseball games together and sometimes playing hockey or soccer with Zed and Elijah. Shan never really liked any of those things, except for camping, but even that was only when he was little. The older he grew, the less he wanted to join us.

"Well, maybe if you hadn't been playing Sim Games all the time, you could've done more things with us."

Shan stops in his tracks. "Did it ever occur to you that one of the reasons I played those games so much was so I could get a head start on other cadets at school? With Dad and you being so good at everything, I didn't stand a chance. Those games were the only way I had to train. And besides, that's not all I like to do."

"That's all I ever see you doing," I reply, trying not to sound like a condescending ass.

"That's because you're never around me, Bridger! I go rock climbing with my friends when we're at the Academy. I read a lot of books. I even watch some those old cheesy movies Dad used to like."

"I like doing those things, too," I mutter in disbelief. "You could always have asked if I wanted to do anything with you."

"Would you really have done them with me, though? Because I don't think so. Remember, I'm just a whiny little mama's boy." He pauses for a moment to take a few deep breaths, his fists clenched. "And you know what's really sad? You think so little of me, but I would do anything for you. I've *always* looked up to you." With those words, he stalks off ahead of me.

My face is on fire. Somehow, he must have overheard me saying that about him.

Maybe he's not as brainwashed by Mom as I thought.

By this time, we've reached the Maglev. We have to wait a little longer than normal to board. Apparently, some Purists decided to throw some graffiti bombs—we arrive just in time to see them get arrested.

The Maglev trip across town to where Halla Fairbanks lives takes a little less than ten minutes. Shan doesn't say another word to me. And honestly, I can't be mad about it. Maybe I *have* been too judgmental of him. I should try to work on that more.

When we reach Colonel Fairbanks's house, which is in a not quite wealthy, but definitely upper-class neighborhood, we're stunned to find Professor March already there. He's sitting in a swing on the small porch of the Fairbanks's brick cottage.

"It's about time you two showed up," he says, leaning forward in the swing. "I was beginning to think I guessed wrong. But with your trajectory, I figured you were coming here."

Shan sputters, "What—*why* are you tracking us?"

"Because I promised your father that I would always look after you two. And I have a bad feeling that you're getting yourselves into something you can't handle." He looks pointedly in my direction.

"Where's the colonel?" I ask. I try to peer into one of the front windows, but it's impossible to see inside. The night screens are activated.

"She's gone," Professor March says. "When she retired eight months ago, she moved. I never heard where she went."

"Why didn't I hear about that?" I ask, stunned. Colonel Fairbanks had a cushy job with the DTA, and as far as I know she's nowhere near retirement age.

Professor March shrugs. "I have no idea." He turns to Shan, "Listen, buddy, I need to speak to Bridger in private for a few moments."

"Sure, I'll just go over there and do *nothing*." Shan shoves his hands in the pockets of his jeans and glares at me before he walks over to the Green Zone across the street. While I'm glad Professor March sent Shan away, a small part of me feels guilty. Especially after what he said to me on the way over here.

"Now, let's get to the important stuff. You're clearly up to something. I want to know what you think you're doing," March says.

"What are you talking about?" I ask.

"Don't play dumb with me. Why are you really here?"

"Why do you want to know?"

"Well, I received a disturbing comm last night from my sister. She said you were acting strange at headquarters yesterday."

"I didn't realize you two talked so much, sir."

"Really, Bridger? She's my sister." Professor March heaves a sigh and continues. "Anyway, she did some digging and discovered that you accessed the DTA network yesterday in your grandmother's office."

My pulse spikes. "She what? Did she . . . did she report me?"

"Fortunately for you, she didn't. She knows the relationship I have with you and Shan, so she decided to let me know first, to see what I thought about the situation. You owe her big time."

My legs feel weak. I sag onto the top step of the porch. I wish I could deny everything, but he's got me. "Yeah, I logged onto the system. That was my only way of finding out what happened to Dad."

Professor March cocks his head to one side. "What happened to Leithan? Why would you want to do that?"

My pulse quickens and I begin to rub my left hand. I just don't know what I should do. Dad told me not to trust Professor March anymore. He *had* to have a good reason for doing that. But Professor March and his sister could have reported me for breaking into the DTA network, and they didn't. I wonder why. Maybe I can give him just enough information to learn something from him.

I share how Alora and I regained our memories, but omit everything about Ellis and our time trip to the day Nate Walker was revived. When I'm finished, I point a finger at him. "It's your turn now. Why did you help me escape last year? Why did you lie to me about the DTA not knowing about the existence of Dual Talents? What are you and General Anderson hiding?"

The professor's eyes widen. "You both have your memories back and have kept that a secret from everyone. I have to admit, I'm impressed. You're definitely Leithan's son."

I want to trust him. I remember all the time he spent with our family while I was growing up. But I can't forget Dad's warning. "You didn't answer my question."

Professor March holds up both hands. "I'm not doing anything with Anderson. He approached me and said that you and your father were caught doing something illegal, but he refused to elaborate. He said Leithan covered his tracks too well, and the only way to figure out what year he'd gone to was to stage your capture and then see what you did when you escaped. It was also to protect you once you went rogue."

"Yeah, but he threatened to have me Nulled!" I shout. "He had my Mom thinking I was a goner."

"Bridger, I went along with it because I had no choice. I never said I agreed with it. The whole thing was shady. But when a powerful official from the DTA tells you to do something, you do it."

"So you didn't know that Vika and Dad had been cloned?"

"They *what*?"

"Wait a second . . . General Anderson didn't tell you what happened to us in 2013?"

Professor March places both hands on the top of his head, his face a mask of disbelief. "I wasn't allowed access to the final report. It was classified."

I fill him in on everything that took place between Vika, Alora, Alora's aunt, and my dad. Professor March looks completely aghast.

"I don't know what to think anymore," he says. "I swear, Anderson just said he needed my help because he felt I was the only person who could get you to cooperate. His objective was to get you to shift to the exact date your father went to, so he could determine why Leithan went there. He could have extracted the knowledge from you, but he didn't want to risk hurting you."

That does make sense. Submitting to Extractors—Mind Benders who forcibly take information from people's brains—usually ends up giving the person permanent brain damage, or even kills them.

I don't know what to believe. Professor March seems sincere, but Dad wouldn't have told me to stay away from him for no reason. The fact that he helped Anderson trick me is still pissing me off. But I need more answers from him. "I'm just trying to figure out what's going on," I say in an exasperated voice. "My dad and Vika are still out there somewhere. I want to know why they were cloned and what Anderson's end game is."

"I do, too. But I don't think it's a good idea for you or Alora to keep poking into things yourselves. It's too dangerous."

I decide to change tactics. I let my shoulders droop and look away from him as if in defeat. "Yeah, I guess you're right. I don't want to put my family, or Alora, at risk. We both know what the DTA is capable of."

For the first time, Professor March smiles. "I think that's best, Bridger. Maybe I can get my sister to look into things, but for now you and Alora need to stop playing detective."

"Okay. But promise me that you won't report that we both have our memories back. We deserve to keep those."

"All right," he says. "It's the least I can do."

I glance at my DataLink. The others should be on the way to the museum now. "I have to go," I say in a rush. "I promised to take Shan to the museum this afternoon. I can't go back on that, or he'll pout all day."

"Then you'd better keep that promise." Professor March stands and starts walking down the porch steps. He looks back when he reaches the sidewalk. "Please, comm me if you need anything. I promised your father I'd always be here for you."

I want to believe him. But I can't forget Dad's message. Then a wave of sickness slams into me.

What if Professor March is still reporting to Anderson?

What have I done?

23

om comes into my bedroom while I'm braiding my hair on Sunday morning. She sits on my bed, eyeing my clothes. "You look nice."

She has to be kidding. I'm only wearing a plain gray tunic with a pair of black leggings: colors to match my mood. Both pieces are lined with a soft fabric designed to keep me warm, but I'm still freezing. That's probably because I can't stop thinking about everything that happened yesterday. I still can't believe that Dad is really dead. In the back of my mind, I figured he was hiding out somewhere, or maybe even captured. Glancing at the mirror over my dresser, I flinch at my appearance. My eyes are puffy from crying so much.

I'm hurt and angry and beyond frustrated. As far as I'm concerned, the DTA is responsible for Dad's death. But I want to learn who or what caused his shuttle to explode. I owe it to him to find out.

"What's the occasion?" she asks.

And here we go. I take a deep breath, steeling myself for another argument. Yesterday she didn't want to let me leave the apartment by myself, so I ended up yelling at her, saying that I had been coddled and sheltered for the past ten months, and I needed to be alone for once. She flinched as though I'd slapped her, but reluctantly agreed to let me go. I felt horrible, but I had to do whatever it took to meet Bridger, Zed, and Elijah at the DTA headquarters.

And today I have more plans.

"I've made some more friends at school, and they invited me to spend the day with them."

It's not exactly a lie, but it's not the entire truth either. Since I can't officially be around Bridger one-on-one without raising suspicion, Tara commed me earlier to let me know that Bridger wants to meet with all of us today. He'd reached out to her because he's worried that his comms are being monitored by his father. After he talks to Vika's mother, we're all supposed to meet at the museum. Tara, Zed, and Elijah are coming over to meet Mom and pick me up. They should be here any minute.

"Honey, no. Since it's your birthday tomorrow, I thought we could spend today together."

And now I feel like the worst daughter ever. I had no idea she wanted to do that. Why didn't she say anything about it last night? I just figured she was too upset with me because of our fight, and because I went to Tara's apartment without letting her know first.

"It'll just be for a few hours, then I'll come back and we can spend the rest of the day together. Or we can go out for supper. Whatever you want."

She tilts her chin down slightly, shaking her head. She looks like she wants to argue more, but a chime reverberates through the apartment. "I take it that's your friends?"

"Yes, ma'am. I didn't think you would mind."

"I really wish you'd asked me first," she says, following me to the living room.

I answer the door and invite Zed, Elijah, and Tara inside. They stand awkwardly side by side while I introduce them to Mom.

"It's lovely to meet you," Mom says. She directs her attention to Tara. "Thank you for befriending Alora. It means a lot to both of us."

"No problem, Ms. Mason. Alora is one of the nicest people I've ever met."

Elijah looks sharply at her in fake shock. "Hey, now, what about me?"

"You come in a distant second," Tara says with a smirk.

Then Zed pipes up. "Don't even look at me. I know I'm not even on your chart."

Mom laughs, then turns to me. "Can I talk to you in private for a moment?"

Kill me now.

Twin flames burn my cheeks. I mumble an apology and follow her to the kitchen.

"What's wrong?" I ask.

"Are you really sure you want to go out with them? You were gone all day yesterday, and I saw on the DataNet that Purists are starting protests again in some cities. I'm worried something will happen today."

I try not to snap at her, but I'm really getting tired of her being so overprotective. "Will you please stop treating me like a child? I'm almost seventeen! I can take care of myself."

Mom starts to speak, then pauses as if she's deciding exactly what to say. After a long few seconds, she says in a soft voice. "I'm sure you can. But I lived all these years without you, Alora. I don't ever want risk losing you again."

Guilt gnaws at me. What am I doing? She's my only surviving family member. I need to stop being such a brat to her. I wrap my arms around her and whisper, "I'm sorry. But I've got to go. I promised to spend the afternoon with them. We're just going to the museum, that's all."

Mom leans back slightly, with a weird look on her face. "You sure do like that museum, don't you?"

"I guess," I reply. "After all, I did miss out on so much of this life."

We rejoin the others in the living room. I pull on my coat, and as I open the door to leave, Mom calls out, "Don't forget, we're celebrating your birthday tonight. Don't be too late."

As soon as we're out of the apartment, Elijah says, "So, it's your birthday today?"

"It's tomorrow, but Mom wants to do something special for me tonight since I'll be at the Academy tomorrow." I don't add that I'd rather not do anything. But all I can think about is the fact that my own father will never be able to celebrate with me. I touch the ring that he gave me, the one intended for Mom. At least I have this to remember him by.

Zed gives me a pitying look. "So, you have to celebrate your birthday with an overprotective parental unit. That should be fun."

I sigh. "I know, but at least I got out. So shut it."

Zed clutches his chest. "I'm hurt. Your words are like daggers in my heart."

Tara stares at Zed in disbelief. "Are you always so melodramatic?"

"Unfortunately, he is," Elijah says.

"Unfortunately?" Zed asks in mock anguish. "You're killing me."

We all start laughing. It weird being part of a group, to feel like I'm starting to belong, but I like it. I never had that back in Willow Creek. My only friend, Sela, ditched me for a more "popular" crowd. Even now, the memory still stings.

"So, have any of you heard from Bridger?" I ask once we're outside. A cold wind is blowing and I shiver even though I'm wearing my coat.

"Not since earlier this morning," Elijah says. "He wasn't happy. He said his mom forced him to bring Shan along because they needed to spend more time together. That's why he wanted to meet with us at the museum. Shan can entertain himself without getting into our business."

"Oh, he was more than unhappy. He was furious," Zed says.

"Well, I don't get why he hates being around his brother so much. I've seen Shan around campus and he seems nice. A little on the quiet side, but nice," Tara replies.

When we get to the Maglev station, it takes us a little longer than usual to board. Earlier in the day, someone threw graffiti bombs showing the NFA's triple rings encased in blue flames on two of the station's walls. Nulls are busy deleting the images from the walls, and we all have to submit to a security check.

I'm relieved that I left my illegal tech back in my apartment. This time I hid it all separately, in pockets of several of the outfits hanging in my closet, just in case Mom decides to search my room.

We find four open seats in the last compartment. Once we're seated, I ask. "What's that all about? I've never seen that kind of graffiti before."

Zed checks out the people seating around us to see if there are any eavesdroppers. "You haven't checked your DataFeed?"

"No. Should I have?"

"Yep," Tara says. "Lots of crap going on now with the Purists again. Rumor is they have a leader who's stirring them up. And that graffiti we saw back there popped up in certain NAF cities last night."

"I hope that's all they're going to do," I say, suddenly feeling queasy. I don't want anybody to get hurt, but I also want Bridger to be able talk to Vika's mom as soon as possible. And we can't do that if all hell breaks loose in the city.

We find Bridger and his brother just inside the front entrance of the museum. He comes over to me immediately and gives me a hug. "How are you feeling today?"

"A little better, I guess." I want to tell him that I went back to visit my dad, but I'd rather do it in private. Somehow, I'm positive Bridger would understand, but I'm not sure how the others would react.

"So, how did it go with Colonel Fairbanks?" I ask.

Bridger's expression turns grim. "Get this: she's retired now, and she moved out of the city months ago."

"How did you find that out?" Elijah asks.

"Professor March followed me there. He had some interesting things to tell me." Glancing around the crowded main hall, Bridger says, "Let's go to one of the quieter exhibits. Too many people around here."

He's right. The front part of museum is designed to draw people in with a variety of exhibits showcasing renowned pieces from the past. Original paintings by Picasso, Van Gogh, Rembrandt, and many other legendary artists. Ancient statues. Personal belongings of famous people from the twentieth and twenty-first centuries, all retrieved at the times they were supposed to be destroyed. I wish we had more time to explore them. Maybe I could get Mom to bring me back here later tonight.

To our left is a long hallway labeled Sim Rooms. We turn to our right, which is labeled Original Documents. Bridger finally stops at a large room filled with rows and rows of books. Actual, physical books. I inhale deeply. God, how I've missed the smell of them. That's something I never really thought about in 2013, but almost everything is digital now. I never thought I'd have to go to a museum to find a real book. Aunt Grace would be appalled.

We find an isolated table in the back and sit. When Bridger notices Shan is still with us, he scowls and says, "Look, I know you're still mad at me, but we have a lot of important stuff to discuss that doesn't involve you. Can you go somewhere else for a while?"

Shan's face turns bright red. "Seriously, Bridger? First you and Professor March refuse to talk around me, and now this?"

The rest of us sit looking at each other. The tension is palpable.

"It has nothing to do with you," Bridger says. "So can you give us some privacy?"

"Fine. I'll leave so I won't be such a furing *burden* to you," Shan says. "But you know, maybe I could help if you'd just trust me."

"Just go, Shan," Bridger says through gritted teeth.

After he storms out, I tell Bridger, "Do you think that's such a good idea? He's really upset."

Bridger shrugs off my words. "He'll be all right. I'm willing to bet he'll head straight to the Prohibition Era Sim Room. That's the newest one."

Zed lets out a laugh. "That figures. I've never seen someone so obsessed with those things. I'd love to hitch a ride when he finally gets to shift to an event with a little excitement. I bet he'll shit himself."

"I swear, Zed, you are an idiot sometimes," Bridger mutters.

"But I'm a lovable idiot," Zed says.

Elijah snickers and retorts, "That's questionable, man. Really questionable."

The whole exchange doesn't sit well with me. "Bridger, I think you're being too mean to Shan. Would it really hurt to let him stay? I mean, who knows? Maybe he could help."

Bridger lets out a harsh laugh. "Trust me, I can't let Shan know what's going on. He'd run straight back to Mom and blab everything to her."

"What's to say he won't tell her that you talked to Professor March and that we're all meeting in here?" I reply. His attitude toward Shan is infuriating. If I had a sibling who I'd actually grown up with, I'd do just about anything to be close to them.

"I can come up with something if he tattles again. She always believes the worst about me, anyway. But more than likely I can just give him some credits. That usually works."

Awkward silence follows, until Tara speaks up. "Before we get started, there's something I think you all need to know."

Running one of her hands down the back of her dark curls, she focuses on Elijah. I wonder what she's doing when his face morphs from confusion to something that appears to be shock.

"Holy fure, babe, you can read minds? Why didn't you tell me before?"

"Well, I am now," she says with a sly grin. She leans over and kisses him on the cheek.

I'm shocked. I can't believe Tara just outed herself to everyone, especially since we've been instructed not to let the regular Talents know. Then I feel like a total hypocrite because Elijah and Zed already know about me.

Her eyes cut to the rest of us. "So, now you know my secret. That's why I was assigned to room with Alora. But I'm not alone—there are several more of us at the Academy."

Zed blinks. "Wait, what? We've been told our entire lives that Dual Talents can't exist, and suddenly I'm finding out you guys are everywhere. What the hell is going on here?"

"That's what I want to know." Bridger leans back in his chair and crosses his arms, frowning. "The DTA, and specifically General Anderson, are up to something. And I want to know what it is."

"But first I want to know why Professor March followed you," Elijah says.

"That's because of his sister," Bridger says. Then he shares what happened with Captain March yesterday back at the DTA headquarters, and what he learned upon sneaking into his grandma's office.

"Wow. That's so messed up," Zed says in amazement.

Elijah, sitting next to me, pats me on the shoulder. "I'm sorry about your dad, Alora."

Allowing myself a glance at Elijah, I say, "Thank you." Then I lower my head and close my eyes for a moment. *Don't cry,* I tell myself sharply.

"So what are we going to do now?" Tara asks. "I doubt you'll be able to sneak into your grandma's office again, since Captain March knows what you did. Even if she did choose not to snitch on you."

"I've been thinking," Bridger says. "What we need to do is find Colonel Fairbanks. She was there when Alora's dad was first revived, and when he was killed. She's Vika's mother. And Vika and my dad both had their consciousness uploaded by an Unknown back in 2013. She's the common thread. I'm willing to bet she has answers."

"Well, genius, how are you going to find her? The good professor said he didn't even know where she went." Zed taps his chin, his eyes cutting to Bridger. "That is, if you believe him."

"I'm thinking the same thing," Bridger replies. "Dad warned me not to trust him."

"I don't know, man. He went out of his way to help you last year." Elijah leans forward and rests his forearms on the table. "Maybe you should trust him. I mean, your dad may have said that, but he was a clone. You know they're not stable."

Bridger's face flushes. "You weren't there. He seemed completely sane. Didn't he, Alora?"

All eyes shift in my direction, making me uncomfortable. I don't know how to respond to that question. The cloned version of his father did seem normal. But then again, I had just been through a traumatic experience with Dave Palmer kidnapping me and a cloned version of my own half-sister trying to murder me. I finally say, "Well, compared to the clone of Vika, he did seem rational."

Tara speaks up next. "I sort of agree with Bridger. I think finding Colonel Fairbanks is what we should concentrate on now. Maybe she'll even know where Bridger's father is."

Bridger starts to speak, but before he can all of our DataLinks begin to buzz loudly and the touch screen flashes red, indicating an emergency alert from the government.

We activate our DataFeed, but instead of a message from the government, an unfamiliar man stares out at us. He's bald, with tanned skin and a muscular build, and he's dressed in a blue, button-up shirt. His eyes are a piercing hazel, but that's all I can see of his face. His nose and mouth are covered by a black mask.

Something is off about him.

"Greetings, fellow NAF citizens. I wish I didn't have to hack into the news feed, but it's become clear to me that it's necessary. You see, as someone classified as a Purist, I frequently experience discrimination. It's something I, and millions of others like me, have put up with for too many years. But that's going to change. Since the government has decided to unfairly punish us for our right to choose how we want to live, we have decided to take matters into our own hands. Knowing that most of us work jobs that barely provide a living wage, the government still decided to punish us further by forcing us to pay more for basic goods and services that everyone should have equal access to. Now, our families are forced to forego health care, and some are starving because of your actions."

He glances down, his expression anguished, before continuing. "My own son is suffering because of this. He has a rare form of cancer, and I can no longer afford his treatments. And without them, he will soon die. We've tried protesting, which was our right, but the government even took that away from us—we can no longer demonstrate peacefully without being arrested. So I, and some like-minded people, banded together to stop this tyranny. Our demands are simple. The government *will* repeal the Responsible Citizen Act, or there will be severe consequences." He pauses and looks to the side for a moment. "And now, unfortunately, I will leave you now with a little taste of what's to come if our demands aren't met. Citizens of Seattle, New York, Mexico City, and New Denver, beware." He holds up both of his fists and cries out, "We will have justice!"

The feed cuts off, leaving an image of blue flames surrounding the NFA flag. The same image that was on the graffiti at the Maglev station. We sit in stunned silence.

And then we hear it. It's faint because we're in the back of the book room but unmistakable—gunfire. Terrified screams follow.

Bridger jumps up from the table, his face drained of blood. "Shan!"

He takes off running, and we all follow. Elijah shouts for Bridger to wait for us, but he doesn't listen. We skid to a halt at the end of the original documents hall. A pale man, dressed head to toe in black, right down to the black mask like that of the man from the vid, is standing twenty feet in front of us. He's slowly rotating clockwise, firing what looks like an antique semiautomatic rifle at anybody who's moving. Each shot sounds like an explosion, echoing through the cavernous area.

A bullet whizzes past Zed's ear, and he drops to the floor, clutching his arms over his head. We all do the same. Except for Bridger. He starts to move away from us.

"Get down!" Zed screams at him.

Then someone pushes Bridger down just as more bullets hit the wall where he was standing. They lie still for seconds that stretch into eternity. Were they hit?

Finally, the man on top of Bridger rolls to the side. It's Professor March. Bridger stares at him in apparent shock, then shakes his head and begins to belly-crawl toward the Sim Game rooms. The gunfire suddenly stops, and I look back up. The gunman is staring at me. I freeze, afraid he might shoot me next. But instead, he vanishes. I can barely comprehend what I just saw—the man was a Space Bender. But why would a Space Bender attack innocent people? I stare helplessly at the chaos surrounding us. People sprawl on the floor, unmoving. Others hide behind smashed displays. How could someone do this to so many innocent people?

Cries of terror snap me out of my daze. I check on Zed first. "Are you all right?" I ask.

His eyes are wide and he's breathing hard, but he manages to nod. "Where's Bridger?" he asks in a shaky voice.

Elijah sits up and looks in the direction Bridger was headed in. Then he lets out a whimper. "Oh, no. Please no."

I whirl around. Bridger is kneeling next to someone stretched out on the floor. Professor March is leaning over that person, feeling for a pulse in his neck. I run over and look down, horrified.

It's Bridger's brother. And he's been shot.

24

BRIDGER
FEBRUARY 19, 2147

Mom and I are about to enter Shan's hospital room. We had to wait over an hour while the doc on duty patched him up before we could see him. But Shan was lucky. One bullet hit him in the fleshy part of his upper left arm, and another grazed his left cheek. He's going to be fine.

I can't help but think about what would have happened if Professor March hadn't followed Shan and me to the museum. He saved my life. Now I'm even more torn, and I'm feel guilty for ever doubting Professor March. I don't understand why Dad doesn't want me to trust him, but I also know now that the professor wouldn't hurt me. Hell, he put his own life on the line just to save mine. What if Dad is wrong about him? I just wish I knew what Professor March did to make Dad feel the way he does.

The moment we see Shan, Mom goes to pieces. He looks so helpless, lying in his bed sedated. She sits at the side of his bed and sobs again.

The door slides open and a nurse enters the room, dressed in the hospital's blue med uniform. "Are you Leithan's mother?"

Mom glances up at her, wiping her eyes. "He goes by his middle name, Shan. Leithan is his first name."

"I see," the nurse replies. "I need to ask you a few questions, if you don't mind."

While Mom talks to the nurse, I stare at Shan, completely gutted. His wounds have been cleaned and bandaged. Thanks to the genetic modifications the Purists hate so much, he should be completely healed within a day or two. Except for scars. Shan will have to deal with those forever, whether he likes it or not.

But he shouldn't have to. He shouldn't have been shot. If I hadn't made him leave the book room, he would have been fine.

Shortly after the nurse leaves, Grandma enters the room. She looks like she's aged a decade. "I got here as soon as I could. How is he?" she asks, joining Mom by his bed.

In a hollow voice, Mom says, "He'll live."

Grandma starts to take a seat on the other side of the bed, but Mom says, "Judith, now isn't a good time for you to be here. I'd prefer to be here alone with my children."

I sit up a little straighter. Wow, even under these circumstances, Mom still acts completely selfish.

Grandma sits in the chair anyway and reaches out to hold Shan's hand. In a quiet but firm tone, she says, "You have a lot of nerve telling me to leave. This is my grandson. My flesh and blood. I will be here for him if I damn well please." Her eyes flick to Mom for a moment. "Besides, I don't see your parents. At least *I'm* here."

Under different circumstances, Mom's expression would be comical. Her mouth opens and shuts several times and she practically sputters. But Grandma is right. Mom was furious earlier when she found out that her own parents decided not to come see Shan. They're part of a team of DTA field agents who collaborate with international versions of our time-bending organization. And since they're in the middle of a six-month work trip in China, they said they would just come visit once their assignment is finished. All because Shan's injuries aren't life-threatening. But I don't expect them to even show up then. They didn't even bother returning for Dad's memorial ceremony last year. The last time we saw them was three years ago.

Mom closes her eyes and slides her hands slowly over her face, then looks back at Grandma. "You're right. I'm sorry. It's just . . ." she trails off, her eyes drifting to Shan. "I've never been through something like this. It's terrifying."

"It is. I've been where you are. Only things didn't work out so well."

A thick silence follows. I know they're thinking of Dad. We were devastated when his body was discovered last year, especially Grandma, but she forced herself to keep going. She said she had to be strong for Shan and me.

Suddenly I wish I could just tell them the truth about him. That he's still alive. That someone has figured out how to stabilize clones, and he's totally sane. But I can't. They'd think I was having another breakdown.

A little while later, my DataLink chimes. It's Elijah. "I'll go to the waiting room," I tell Mom.

"Come right back when you're finished," she says.

It's weird. As I walk out of the room, something in the corner by the door catches my eyes. The air appears to shimmer for a moment. My heart begins to race. Could it be somebody cloaked? Maybe Dad? Or was it just my imagination. I stare at the spot for a few seconds, but I don't see the shimmer anymore. I just shake my head. With everything that's happened today, I must be seeing things. After all, I did have a large dose of Calmer right after the shooting, and hallucinations are sometimes a side effect.

In a quiet corner of the waiting room, I accept the comm. Elijah and Zed's worried faces appear together. Since Zed's fathers live out of state, he usually stays with Elijah when he goes off campus on the weekends. But sometimes he flies out to California to visit them and his eleven-year-old sister, Alycia.

"How's Shan doing?" Zed asks. For once, he's completely serious.

"Okay. Thankfully his injuries weren't serious."

Elijah sighs in relief. "That's the best news I've heard all day. But how are you doing? You could have been seriously hurt, man."

"Yeah, I'm relieved that Professor March followed you again," Zed adds. "I don't even want to think about what could have happened if he hadn't."

I think back to the immediate aftermath of the shooting. Space-bending medics arrived within minutes. After Shan and the other wounded people were taken to the hospital, Professor March stayed with me while I answered the investigators' questions, then he accompanied me to the hospital to meet Mom. He didn't go in with me, though. He said his presence would probably agitate Mom. Before he left, I asked him why he followed us to the museum, and he said he'd had a gut feeling that he should watch out for us a little longer. I'm glad he did.

Elijah leans in closer and says, "You know what's really scary? The DataFeed is reporting that the shooting here wasn't as bad as in the other cities that Purist psycho mentioned. Nineteen dead in Mexico City, fifteen in Seattle, twenty-eight in New York, and ten here. All in museums that house artifacts brought back by Time Benders. That is one sick bastard to order something like that."

"I know. I just don't understand. What was he thinking? The government will never go along with what he wants," I say. "And now everyone is going to be too damn afraid to do anything."

"Yep, and to think all the gunmen were Space Benders. Furing traitors," Zed says with a sneer.

That's something I still can't wrap my mind around. Why in the hell would Space Benders agree to commit murder for those Purist scum? In the attacks today, which all occurred simultaneously, the gunmen entered the museums, shot as many people as possible, then vanished before authorities could arrive. Time-bending agents who were sent back to investigate the crimes had no way to know where they went when they shifted.

Meaning it could happen again.

"You're right, man. I've never been so scared in my entire life," Elijah says.

"Yeah. I thought we were all going to die," Zed says next.

"Same here. I never want to go through anything like that again." I pause for a moment. "How are Tara and Alora? I don't even remember seeing them after Shan was shot."

"They're fine. Tara's parents picked her up, and Alora's mom came for her right after that. My dad wouldn't leave them alone at the museum," Elijah says. "Let me tell you, Alora's mom was freaked. I heard her saying she was never letting Alora out of her sight again."

Zed nods. "I bet she's having the worst birthday ever tonight."

"It's her birthday?" I ask.

"It will be tomorrow," Zed replies. "But her mom was oh-so-insistent earlier that she come back home to celebrate with her."

I feel awful for her now. I had no idea.

Grandma waves to me from the doorway. "I've got to go," I say. "I'll see you tomorrow at school."

The moment I get back to Shan's room, Mom says, "I'm going to let you go with Judith tonight. You'll be more comfortable with her."

"Really?" I ask, looking from her to Grandma. Mom has never liked me going to Grandma's, and with the camping trip last weekend, I figured she would try to force me to stay away.

"We've come to an understanding," Grandma says.

"You stay with her and don't go anywhere else tonight. Understood?" Mom asks. "I'm not taking any chances of you getting hurt too. Not until those fanatics are found and Nulled."

Then she gets up and hugs me. "I love you, Bridger." Then she says to Grandma, "Please take care of him."

"Always," she replies.

I look away. I can't remember the last time Mom said that she loved me. I can't remember the last time Mom and Grandma were civil to each other. I blink a few times because my stupid eyes are filling up with tears. I tell myself to man up. Dad would never act like this.

It's early in the evening by the time we get to Grandma's place. She orders some food to be delivered to the apartment. Neither of us want to be out in public right now.

And apparently nobody else does, either. On the way here, the area was practically deserted. Except for the police and military Space Benders. There were even more of them out on patrol.

Grandma and I eat mostly in silence. She asks a few questions about what happened at the museum, but she already knows most of it. Investigators already questioned the survivors who weren't injured. I still can't believe that it happened. Mass shootings were common in the past, but things like that shouldn't happen now.

All because of a few furing Purists. They're so insistent on sticking with their backward way of thinking. If they paid attention to the past, they would know that violence like that doesn't solve anything. If anything, the government will punish them even more. They'll punish *all* of them, not just the Purists who were involved in the shootings.

"I'm exhausted. I'm going to take a shower and go to bed. Do *not* leave this apartment," Grandma says.

"Don't worry," I say. "I'm not going anywhere."

Feeling restless, I activate the TeleNet and scroll through the DataFeed, but there's nothing but news about the shooting, which I don't want to relive. It's seared into my brain. All the bodies scattered around the museum. I remember what Shan looked like when I got to him. He was lying on the ground, clutching his hand over the gunshot wound in his arm. And the blood. There was so much of it. On his clothes, on his face, on the floor. His face was so pale and ghostlike. He was in total shock. He couldn't focus on anything. And he kept asking if he was going to die. I'm thankful Professor March was there to reassure him. I was a complete wreck.

I press my fists against my eyes. We used to be so close, but lately I've viewed him as nothing but a nuisance. If I'd just let him stay with us today, he wouldn't have been hurt. I need to change—spend more time with him, like I used to when we were little.

I switch off the TeleNet, my thoughts drifting to Alora. I wish I could let her know that Shan's going to be okay. But sending her a comm is off limits. I wonder what she's doing tonight, how she's reacting to everything. And then I remember what Elijah and Zed said. It's her birthday tomorrow. I feel a pang of regret for not getting a present for her. I know, it's ridiculous to care about that with the shooting and Shan getting hurt. But I do. I don't know why, but I do.

Then I remember something. Last year, I stole the Jewill that her father had given her when she was a child. That's because at the time I didn't know that she really belonged in this century and thought it was a bad idea to leave future tech in the past. When I returned to this time period to find a Mind Redeemer, I stashed the Jewill in one of the hidden compartments in Dad's desk.

I rush into his bedroom, which Grandma uses now. It still looks the same as when Dad lived here, only his scent—something kind of woodsy—is long gone. In the bathroom, I hear Grandma getting out of the shower. My fingers fly, opening the middle desk drawer of Dad's antique desk, and seeking out the hidden compartment. I snatch out the Jewill and barely have enough time to stuff it in my pocket and get out of the room. A few moments later, she emerges in the living room, dressed in dark green pajamas.

"I thought you were going to bed," I say.

She sits on the couch next to me and pats me on the knee. "I wanted to see how you were doing first. Are you okay?"

I shrug. "I suppose so, under the circumstances." I look away for a moment, thinking of the warning we received right before the shooting. "Do you know if there're any leads on finding the man in the vid?"

"I checked in at headquarters a little while ago. They did manage to identify him. His name is Jode Lincoln, and he was an Information Tech specialist who was fired ten years ago for hacking into his company's system to steal money from wealthier Gen Mods who controlled the company. He served several years in prison for that, but since his release, he's been living off the grid. We have no idea where he is now. We also haven't had any success in identifying the shooters. It's impossible to track Space Benders when they shift. But I can promise you that if they're ever found, they will be charged with first-degree murder and Nulled. It's beyond inexcusable that they would kill their own kind," she says with a look of disgust. "I'm so frustrated. We haven't been able to trace the origin of the broadcast, so that means Lincoln has professional-level tech help on his end. But we're not giving up. We'll find them, one way or another. People like that always make mistakes."

She has to be right, but still, it's hard to hear that the investigators don't have any other leads. Since the threat was made to the government and all Gen Mods, the feds will be involved in trying to stop them. That means local police will be working with military Space, Time, and Mind Benders. Hopefully it won't take too long to catch the shooters. I can't imagine what it'll be like otherwise.

And that makes me think of Ellis and the Sim of our war-torn future. These rogue Purists have to be responsible for the bioweapon he told me about. But how would they have access to that kind of tech? I understand how they could learn to hack into the DataNet. That's something any-body can learn to do, with enough patience. But creating a weapon that specifically targets Gen Mods is something only a geneticist would be able to do. Purists aren't allowed to enter fields like that anymore. So that means there must be even more traitors working for them than just the Space Benders.

I'm so tempted to mention it to Grandma, but Ellis's warning not to talk to authority figures makes me wait. He was adamant about preserv-ing the timeline until the bioweapon attack. I understand that. I mean, I've had that drilled in my head by Dad since I was little.

But Ellis could have warned me about Shan being shot. I could have kept him safe.

"I'm turning in now. Goodnight." Grandma stands and arches an eye-brow at me. "Remember, no going out tonight."

"Trust me," I say. "I don't want to. Not with psychotic Purists out there."

An hour later, I exit the apartment building. My eyes are fixed on the cloudy night sky, and I suck in great gulps of the cold air. It makes me feel better, being out here. But I also feel guilty for breaking my promise to Grandma. I tried to go to sleep, but my mind wouldn't stop playing back the scene at the museum, freaking out about what could have happened to Shan. About what could have happened to me, if Professor March hadn't pushed me down. My throat was tight, and my chest felt like a shuttle was parked on it. Since the Calmer I'd taken earlier had worn off and I couldn't find any more in the apartment, I had to get out. My body felt like it would explode if I didn't.

Right now, it's only a little after nine. There's still an eleven o'clock curfew, thanks to the protests. I'm not sure where I'm going. I just need to be outside for a while. To feel like I'm still free, even though it's feeling more and more like I'm not. How can you be free when you're constantly worried that you could be hurt at any moment?

I don't pass many civilians as I walk down the sidewalk. But there are plenty of law enforcement officers, both police and military. They stare at everyone who passes them. I force myself not to look away. No reason to make them suspicious of me, especially since I haven't done anything.

"It's a nice night for a stroll, isn't it?" someone asks from behind me.

I whirl around, instantly recognizing the voice. It's my dad, and he's staring at me with such a sad expression.

I don't know what to say at first. It's still weird seeing him like this—Dad was forty-four when he died, but the cloned version of him appears to be a decade or so younger. Probably not old enough to have an eighteen-year-old son, anyway.

I have a million questions. Instead of asking anything, I cross the short distance between us and hug him. His folds his arms around me, and suddenly I feel like I'm a kid again. I feel safe.

"I'm so glad you're here," I say.

"There isn't anywhere else I want to be right now. I just wish your brother were here too."

I pull away from him. "Do you know what happened?"

"Of course. I got to the hospital soon after he arrived."

So it wasn't my imagination—that shimmer I saw in the corner was Dad checking in. I feel bad for him, not being able to interact with us. Not being able to talk to his own mom. I can't imagine how lonely that would be.

"Can you believe Mom and Grandma actually got along?" I ask.

Dad runs a hand over the top of his hair, his eyebrows raised. "That was wild. I thought hell would freeze over before that would ever happen."

"How's Shan doing now? Did you get to see him when he was awake?"

"I did. He was . . . doing as well as can be expected. He's not in any pain, but he's terrified."

My fists clench. I've never experienced blind hatred for anyone, not even General Anderson when he was such an ass to me last year. But if Jode Lincoln or one of his followers were directly in front of me, I wouldn't hesitate to shoot them.

"Maybe he'll be able to go home tomorrow," I manage to say.

"That's the plan. The doc came in right before I left and said as much." Dad pats me on my shoulder. "So you can stop worrying. He'll be fine."

"But it was my fault."

"Don't blame yourself. If anything, I wish I'd been here to stop it. But I can't change what's already happened."

"I know," I say, lowering my gaze. "It's just, if I had let him stay in the room with me today . . ."

"But you didn't. It happened, and there's nothing you can do about it now. What do you want to do? Keep second guessing yourself? That path leads to fear, and you can't do that for the rest of your life. None of us can. We need to take action and get rid of people like those terrorists. They're a threat to our security and freedom."

Two military Space Benders are heading our way. They scope us out and politely nod to Dad as they pass since he's wearing his uniform. For the first time, I notice that his insignia indicates that he's a colonel now. At the time of his death, he was a lieutenant colonel. So not only was he cloned, he's also been promoted.

I point to the badge. "So how did that come about?"

Dad gives me a weary-looking smile. "It's part of my new identity for when I have to go out in public, since I'm officially deceased. I hope at some point I can rejoin the DTA using my real name. That is, if the latest drug they're using to stabilize me, Clonitin, works permanently. It's tedious being sent on solo assignments all the time."

I've been wondering about that. The whole reason cloning was outlawed at the turn of the century was because they always ended up going insane. And according to Adalyn when I talked to her last year, the same thing happened to Alora's father.

"So if this new drug works, do you think the government might legalize cloning again?"

"Possibly. I don't know for sure. I'm just happy to be alive."

"But how do you keep it a secret? Everyone at the DTA knows you."

Something like sorrow crosses his face. "I'm not allowed to be around the people who used to know me. All of my assignments are out in the field, and they're given to me through my DataLink by my superior officer."

"You mean General Anderson?" I ask.

Dad ignores my question and leads me to a nearby café with outdoor tables. We sit at a table near the entrance and he orders two lemonades for us when the waiter approaches. When we're alone again, Dad leans back in his chair and studies me for a moment.

"Look, I'm going to just be blunt here. I know you've still been seeing Alora. Son, I told you to stay away from her for a reason. She isn't good for you."

"Why do you keep saying that?"

The waiter returns with our drinks, glancing around nervously as Dad pays him.

After the waiter scurries back inside the café, Dad takes a sip and grimaces. "That's a little bitter, but I suppose it'll have to do. Now, to answer your question. There are two reasons you can't trust her. First of all, she's a Dual Talent. Don't you remember before how I told you to not trust Telfair anymore? Same reason. Telfair and I were best friends from the time we entered the Academy, and yet he never told me that he was a Dual Talent. It was only after I was revived that I learned the truth, and learned about all the deceitful things he did over the years. That's the way it is with those people. They're power hungry and will put themselves first. Every time."

"How could you believe that? The DTA has been training Dual Talents at school. Why would they do that if they're as bad as you claim?"

He sighs. "There's a split in the government. Some believe that Dual Talents are an important part of our future. Lawmakers; leaders in all three departments governing Time, Space, and Mind Benders; the owners of the History Alive Network—all of them would do anything to create even more Dual Talents. But there are others, like me, who believe they will eventually ruin everything. General Anderson is one. Even President Tremblay. With their abilities, Dual Talents could make a power grab and turn this country into a dictatorship. We can't let that happen."

"But Alora isn't like that. In fact, all she wants to do is find out who is responsible for her father's death."

Dad takes another sip of his lemonade. "I can help you with that. The DTA was behind it. He was a danger to innocent people, so they had to eliminate him permanently."

The words are like a knife in my chest. How could he say such things about Alora and other Dual Talents? And how could he sound so cold about Nate Walker? The father I remember wouldn't have been so harsh. He always tried to soften any bad news. Maybe the change in him is starting. I hope not. I don't want to lose my dad again, even if he's a clone now.

Remembering he said there was a second reason, I ask, "Okay, you think Dual Talents can't be trusted. Then why did you bother going back to save Alora in 2013 if you thought she was so awful? I thought it was because of Adalyn. You used to love her, right?"

Dad lets out a rueful laugh. "True, but that's when we were young. Adalyn did ask me to save Alora since we had remained friends, but I wasn't going to at first."

"She never said anything about that when I visited her," I say, leaning forward in my seat.

"That's because I never told her no. I asked her to let me think about it for a few days."

"But then you changed your mind. What made you decide to break our biggest rule?"

Dad closes his eyes and heaves a sigh. "Son, I had orders from General Anderson. If you think about it, it's not surprising. I had a non-regulation Chronoband when I originally went to 2013. How do you think I got it?"

"Wait, what? Why would he do that?" I ask.

"For the same reason he covered up the real cause of my death, the same reason he went through all that trouble to capture you and then allow you to escape."

Before Dad can finish, the answer hits me. General Anderson already knew what was going to happen, and he was making sure he preserved the timeline. Professor March revealed to me that the general personally investigated Dad's death after his body was found last year. He already knew I was going to go rogue. He already knew that Alora was going to live and that Vika would die. He knew Dad and Vika would be cloned.

He just made sure it would all happen, because during his investigation, he realized certain things *had* to happen to ensure the continuation of the timeline. The only thing I don't get is why he personally investigated Dad's death in the first place.

Fure, I'm going to wild out if I keep thinking about this.

I close my eyes and inhale slowly a few times. The implications for what Anderson has been doing are staggering. How much tampering has he done in order to preserve the timeline? Or has any DTA leader done? Do we really have free will, or is our fate sealed on the basis of what someone from our own future says we have to do?

"I don't know what to think," I mutter, looking away from Dad. Across the street from us, a Jumbotron flashes Jode Lincoln's face repeatedly, along with the images of the gunmen. All wore masks that completely covered their heads and faces, concealing their identities. There's a reward for any information about the location of Jode, or anyone connected to his organization. Then the feeds cycle to various news reports of protests being suppressed around the country.

Pointing a finger to the Jumbotron, Dad says, "That's what you should be concerned about, not chasing ghosts. And if you don't stop . . . well, I might be forced to alert the general that Alora knows more than she should."

My face grows hot. "That's completely unnecessary. We haven't done anything wrong."

"You should know by now that life isn't fair. So you have to do whatever it takes to protect innocent people, especially those you love. From now on, I want you to stay out of trouble. Do your work at school, go home on the weekends, and don't do anything that could put you, your brother, and my mother in jeopardy. And that means staying away from Alora, Telfair, and any other Dual Talents you might come across."

"But why? It's not like I do anything now to get in trouble. And Alora would never do anything to hurt me."

"You feel that way now, but eventually she will." He glances over his shoulder, then says, "I'm working on a way to ensure that nobody will ever get hurt by those terrorists again. I'm going to make sure that you and everyone else will always be safe."

Alarm bells go off in my head. I wonder if he's talking about the bioweapon that's supposed to detonate sometime in the future. The first thing that pops in my mind is that he could be responsible for the weapon.

But that's ridiculous. Ellis said the bioweapon was designed to kill innocent people. Dad would never do anything like that. He may not like Dual Talents, and he doesn't like what the Purists are doing, but he's not a murderer. Jode Lincoln, on the other hand, *is* a murderer. He has to be the one behind the bioweapon. After all, he hates all Gen Mods, especially Talents. So instead, I ask, "I don't understand. What exactly are you going to do to keep everyone safe?"

Dad glances at his DataLink and stands. "My time is up, but believe me, I do have something in mind. I just can't tell you right now. I can't do anything to jeopardize the plans." He leans in closer to me, lowering his voice. "I need for you to trust me on this one, and I promise that soon we'll get to be a real family again. Now it's time for you to go back home. It's getting late, and you don't want my mother to find you missing."

I don't want to leave him. I wish I could stay. I could talk to him for hours. "When can I see you again?"

"It'll be sooner than you think."

I stand and we embrace. Then I tear myself away and head back to the apartment. I turn back around to see him one more time, but he's already gone.

25

"Are you okay, Alora?" Mom asks me, her eyes drifting to my hands. I keep clasping and unclasping them, wiping the palms on my pants.

"I'll be fine." I can't look straight at her. I'm barely holding myself together, and if I make eye contact, I'm afraid I'll burst into tears.

Right now it's a little after eight o'clock on Monday morning, and we're taking a transport shuttle to the Academy. Other parents are escorting their kids back to school, too, and everyone is quiet. I guess we're all thinking the same thing: wondering if Jode Lincoln will send one of his gunmen here as his next act of protest.

My body grows tense as I remember the fear I felt at the museum. And then there's the fact that not only was I interviewed by police yesterday, Time Benders have probably already been sent back to investigate the moments before, during, and immediately after the shooting. When the DTA officials view their recordings, they'll see Bridger and me together and realize that we've regained our memories. Because what are the odds of the two of us randomly meeting up at school and becoming fast friends within a week of my arriving?

What a way to celebrate my first birthday in this century.

Mom reaches over and grasps my right hand. "I'm so sorry our plans were ruined last night. I'll make it up to you, I promise."

That's the last thing on my mind. Mom and I still had my birthday supper together, but it was really subdued. And it was hard for me to show enthusiasm when she gave me my present—a set of canvases and paints. I really love them. It's just . . . how can you feel any joy when you've just witnessed people being murdered? Adults and children. And the look on Shan's face as Bridger and Professor March tried to comfort him is seared in my mind.

As we land, the pilot's voice comes over the intercom. "May I have your attention? I've been instructed to inform you that as you disembark the shuttle, you will find armed escorts waiting for you. Please stay with them until you reach your destination."

Mom and I stare at each other in shock. So now we're going to be escorted everywhere on campus? Things must be way worse than I thought. Last week, the escorts were only for the worst of the protests.

Our escort drops me, Mom, and several others off at the entrance to Watson Hall, where we find another guard posted at the door, and several more on the first floor. It's disturbing, seeing them here. We shouldn't have to live in fear like this.

We exit the elevator on the fourth floor and promptly run into Everly and her mother coming out of her room. "Hi, Alora," she says, waving.

I really don't feel like making small talk right now, and from Mom's expression I can tell she doesn't, either. But the Darvilles approach us anyway.

While our moms introduce themselves, Everly pulls me to the side. "Have you heard anything about the shooting yesterday?" she asks. "The DataFeed isn't reporting any new information, just the same old stuff."

My stomach lurches. *Why* did she have to bring that up? The shooting is the last thing I want to talk about. But she's eyeing me so expectantly. So I take a deep breath and say, "No, I haven't. Have you?"

Everly jerks her thumb over her shoulder. "My mum has been trying to find out news from our embassy, but those bloody bureaucrats don't know anything either. Just that Time Benders have already been sent back to investigate and they will let us know if we need to evacuate."

I take a few steps away, feeling lightheaded. "I . . . I've got to go," I stammer. "I'm not feeling so good right now."

Everly's face pinches into a frown. "Oh no, I'm sorry if I upset you. I'm an idiot sometimes. You must not want to talk about all that. My mum says that some people are really sensitive to violence."

I excuse myself, rush into my room, and lie down on my bed, wondering how long it will be before someone comes to take my memories again. I don't want that to happen. I can't lose my past again. It's not fair.

Mom soon joins me and sits on the edge of the bed, rubbing my back. "Maybe I should take you back home for a few days. I don't think you're ready for this."

A part of me wants to take her up on it, escape the school. But if I do that, then the DTA will come for me there, and that will freak Mom out. She doesn't deserve that. If I'm going to have my memories wiped again, at least they can do it here, where she won't have to find out about it. And I won't have to be hurt again, knowing that Mom would let them do whatever they want.

"It's okay. I'll be fine. Tara should be here soon, so I won't be alone."

She seems skeptical and insists on staying until Tara gets here. So twenty minutes later, after Mom finally hugs me goodbye, I collapse on the couch.

"I take it she's having separation anxiety," Tara says. She sets her portacase on the floor and sits next to me.

"I know. But I understand. She has every reason to worry about me."

"Oh, I almost forgot!" Tara exclaims. She rummages in her portacase and extracts a small box. "Sorry I didn't have time to wrap it. Anyway, happy birthday!"

It takes me a few tries to swallow the lump in my throat before I can speak. "Oh God, Tara, you really didn't have to get me anything."

"Of course I did. We're friends, and friends get birthday presents for each other. By the way, mine is May twenty-seventh."

Fingers trembling, I take off the lid and find a small, lilac-colored journal with a matching pen. "It's perfect," I say, grinning. "You don't know what this means to me. Thank you."

"It's nothing. I remembered you said that you used to have a journal when you were younger. I thought you might want another. I have one and can vouch for how therapeutic they are."

My DataLink beeps, alerting me to the fact that our first classes will start in fifteen minutes. "Time to go," I say, groaning.

"Yeah, I guess we need to get the day over with," she says with a heavy sigh.

Those words fill me with dread. Because what if today is the last day I have with all my memories intact?

The rest of the day is a blur. I'm hollow, waiting for someone to come for me, but nobody ever does. Everly even surprises me in the cafeteria with a small birthday gift—a four-leaf-clover pin.

"How did you know it was my birthday?" I ask, feeling terrible for storming out on her this morning.

"Your mum mentioned it to mine. And when I saw how upset you were, I figured you could use a little cheer. This is my good-luck charm," she says, while pinning it to my uniform. "It's been good to me. It helped me survive through things I never thought I'd get through." She looks down for a moment. Then she brightens. "But Mum and I made it to the NAF, and we're just fine. So I think you could use it now."

"Thank you. I love it," I say, wondering what she meant by surviving things. I've been so wrapped up in my own problems that I forget other people have to deal with demons, too. My arms itch to hug Everly, to try to comfort her in a small way, but I don't because it would draw too much attention to us. I'd much rather remain invisible for now—but at least I'm certain I have another new friend who cares.

That counts for something.

At the end of the day, I attend my private tutoring session. If anybody had told me last year on my birthday that I'd spend part of my next birthday bending space while jumping from a moving shuttle, I would've thought they were high. Or trying to mess with me.

And yet, here I am, doing just that. Lucky me.

I'm in a small shuttle with Professors March and Jackson, complete with an armed escort who is making me extremely nervous. At least I didn't have to deal with Chancellor Tyson today. Professor March said he often leaves the city for conferences and meetings, so his absence isn't unusual.

Because I can't be seen shifting outside anywhere near campus, we take the shuttle to a small field several miles out in the country that's owned by the feds. It's used by all three schools for the Talents to train without prying eyes around. Today we have it to ourselves.

So far today, I've jumped out of the moving shuttle ten times. My goal is to shift while I'm in motion to a safe location on the other side of the field. Another of my teachers from the Academy, Professor Cayhill, waits for me. The other professors had to recruit him because we needed a third teacher here to help out with the drills. I wish they had asked any other of my teachers. Cayhill seems to be a bit of a jerk. Out of my ten attempts, I've only been successful three times. And each time I managed to get to him, Professor Cayhill had a smart comment to say. Most recently, it was a snide "It's about time you got it right, cadet. I was about to go to sleep over here."

I wanted to ask him how well *he* could bend space just to see his expression, but I kept my mouth shut. You never get anywhere fast by mouthing off to teachers. That's true in any time period.

Back when I lived with Aunt Grace, I used to watch a lot of movies where actors would leap from moving cars or whatever, and they always made it seem so easy. Clearly, that was a lie. My whole body feels like one giant bruise.

As if he can sense my weariness, Professor March looks back at me from the pilot seat and says, "I think this jump should be her last one for the day, Dan."

"I agree. We don't want to push her too hard," Professor Jackson says, giving me a sympathetic smile. I find myself smiling back. I'm starting to feel more comfortable around him. It's unfortunate that he shares features with a dead psychopath, but he's definitely nothing like Mr. Palmer. He's been super helpful and patient with me, especially today. I've really needed that to counter Professor Cayhill's attitude.

Professor March turns the shuttle and slowly guides it to the opposite end of the field again. I stand by the open door, my knees bent slightly, and close my eyes. Picturing the soft patch of grass next to Professor Cayhill and the portable chair he brought to sit in, I jump, hoping with everything in me that my attempt to shift works.

But my eyes are jolted open when I slam into the ground yet again. I groan.

Worst. Birthday. Ever.

When I get back to my room, I fully expect someone to be there, waiting to haul me away to see General Anderson, or to just erase my memories right there. But still, nobody shows up. Don't get me wrong: I'm beyond grateful, but I wonder what's going on. The DTA has to know by now that I was at the museum with Bridger, and if they sent an investigator into our room to eavesdrop, then they should know we're looking for Halla Fairbanks, too. The only thing they couldn't know is that I have a new shifting ability: the ability to shift without knowing the exact location I'm going to.

At least I know for sure I can trust Professor March. He could have told someone that Bridger and I have our memories back, but he hasn't. In fact, he went out of his way to be nice to me today.

It's late at night before I can shift to Bridger's quarters. When I get there, Bridger is stretched out on his bed, sleeping. I think about leaving him alone; he looks so peaceful, and I know that the last two days have been traumatic for his family. But I need to talk to him.

I gently touch his arm. Immediately, his eyes fly open and he bolts upright, his head swiveling back in forth in confusion. He blinks a few times when he notices me standing next to his bed.

"How are you doing?" I ask, sitting next to him.

"I'm okay, I guess." He rubs his hands over his eyes, then turns to me. "What about you? I've been looking for you all day, but I never see you anywhere."

"Our schedules are way different," I say with a shrug. That's to be expected since he's a Level 5, and I'm only a Level 4. "How is Shan? I haven't heard any news about him."

"He's going to be fine. He should be back at school in a few days. That is, if Mom will let him out of her sight."

Then he reaches over to the table next to his bed and grabs something. "Before I forget, I got you something for your birthday, and I hope you're not mad when you see what it is."

A tingling sensation starts in my belly and spreads throughout my body. I can't believe he thought to get me a gift, even with the stress over his brother getting shot—with everything that's happened, really. "Why would I be mad?"

"You'll see. Close your eyes and hold out your hands."

He sets something cool and metallic in my palms. My eyes fly open and I gasp. It's my necklace—the one I thought I'd lost in 2013. The one with the silver chain and black pendant that I found hidden in Aunt Grace's safe.

I look up to face Bridger and smile. "I figured you took it. But why?"

Holding up his hands, Bridger explains. "Because it's not just a necklace. It's a Jewel of Illusion. I couldn't let that kind of tech stay in the past. I realized that you had one when you told me about seeing yourself and you thought you were losing your mind." He takes the necklace from me and fastens it around my neck.

Understanding dawns on me. I've learned about these: they're cloaking devices, but now are considered illegal. And in 2013, they didn't exist. So *that's* why I was invisible when I shifted in the bakery at Willow Creek and scared the crap out of the past version of myself.

It should be funny to me, but instead I find myself tearing up. Then I get mad at myself for getting all weepy in front of Bridger, and that in turn makes the tears flow faster. *Jeez, Alora, stop being such a crybaby*, I tell myself.

"Are you okay?" Bridger asks. His voice sounds so worried.

I can't answer.

Then I hear a second voice right next to my ear. "Man, what did you *do* to her?" Elijah asks.

An arm drapes around my shoulders. Looking up, I find that it's Zed. "It's okay, kid. Even though you're all red-faced and snotty, you still look good to me."

That's enough to make me laugh. "I'm sorry. You must think I'm ridiculous," I say to Bridger.

"No," Bridger says. "You've been through a lot over the past year. I'm surprised you haven't wilded out before now."

I smile at that phrase. I don't think I'll ever get used to it.

Elijah leaves the room for a moment, then comes back in with a handkerchief. I wipe my eyes and thank him several times. I explain how scared I am that someone will come to erase my memories again because of the Time Benders' shooting investigation.

Bridger looks down at his lap, his face turning red. "What's up?" Zed asks. "Because clearly you know something."

Heaving a sigh, Bridger then says. "I had a visit from my dad last night."

I'm sure I have a dumbstruck look on my face. "And what did he say to you?"

"You're not going to like it," he replies. "He knows about us, and that you restored our memories. He's fine with not reporting us, but only on the condition that we break off all contact with each other."

I'm pretty sure a punch to the face would hurt less than what he just said. Why would his father want to keep us apart?

Bridger goes on to explain how his dad doesn't trust Dual Talents. Even worse, the only reason he agreed to my mom's request to save me in the first place is because of General Anderson. The general ordered him to make sure I returned to this era because he already knew it would have to happen.

So basically, we're nothing but puppets to Anderson. That pisses me off more than anything. "Don't you see, we need to fight back. We can't just follow in line and do what they tell us. Otherwise, what kind of lives are we living? We have free will. We need to be free to make our own choices, not be at the mercy of anyone in our future."

"Alora, if we continue to see each other, my dad said he would tell Anderson that you have your memories. I honestly don't know how we can get around that. Since Dad put me on notice, I'm afraid he could check in on me at any time. He's already done it twice—last night, and right after you restored my memories. Even if we tried to meet off campus like we did at the museum, I'm worried that he could follow me and find us together."

I shake my head. Bridger is the one person I trust more than anyone, other than Elijah, Zed, and Tara. I can't stop being around him. I *can't*.

"What about Colonel Fairbanks?" I ask. "Your dad doesn't know that I can still shift to her location just by thinking about her."

"No, he doesn't. But maybe that's not such a good idea," Bridger says. "It could be too dangerous right now, with everything going on with the Purists. And besides, Dad brought up something else. He says he's working on something to keep us all safe for good. I think it might have something to do with stopping the bioweapon that Ellis mentioned. Maybe we could focus on figuring out if there's a way we could help with that."

I shake my head. "Your father still doesn't want us to be together," I say bitterly. "So I think I should still find Halla and see what she knows. You know, the thing we were planning to do yesterday?"

Bridger gets real quiet. So do Elijah and Zed. They know something. "Okay, whatever it is, just tell me."

"I don't know how to say this. I mean, I was going to wait and all . . . but I guess you deserve to know now. When I talked to Dad, he said to tell you that he knows who's responsible for your father's death." Bridger reaches out and takes my hand. "Alora . . . your father was killed by the DTA. All because they saw him as a threat. If you shift to Colonel Fairbanks without having a plan, you could get caught. We don't even know where she is right now. You have no idea where you'll materialize, or whether the DTA will be watching her location. And if the DTA was willing to kill your father just because he was caught doing something they didn't like, they could decide to do the same thing to you."

I snatch my hand away. "You're seriously flaking on me like this? It's obvious the DTA killed my dad. He wasn't following their orders, and he was a clone. He was showing signs of instability. And since my father was becoming more unstable, what's to say the same thing isn't happening to yours? Should you really put so much faith in what he says?" I pause, realizing I'm almost shouting. In a lower voice, I continue. "Besides, you just said that your father doesn't like me because I'm a Dual Talent. So of course he told you that information. He'd probably say anything to get you to stop helping me."

Bridger's face flushes. He glances at Zed and Elijah, as if looking for help.

Elijah holds up both of his hands, palms facing out. "Hey, leave me out of this."

Zed, rubbing the back of his neck, says, "Same here. She does have a point."

Bridger stares at them as if they just betrayed him, eyes narrowed. Then he sighs and looks at me again. "I don't like any of this. I hate that he wants to keep us apart. Maybe, with a little time, I can convince him to change his mind."

"Are you serious? He doesn't like Dual Talents. He'll never accept me."

"I have to try," he says again, almost in a whisper. "Please, just wait a little longer. Let's find out what his plans are to keep us safe."

"I can't sit here and do nothing," I snap at him.

Before Bridger can argue with me any further, I close my eyes and shift back to my room. I don't need someone like that in my life—someone who is willing to ditch me at the first sign of trouble.

So why does my heart feel like it's been shattered into a million shards?

26

The moment I reappear in my bedroom, I know something is wrong. My bed is unmade, and the drawer on my desk, which I hid my DataLink in before shifting to Bridger's room, is open. A quick peek inside reveals my DataLink missing. Oh, God, no, this can't be happening. Not today, of all freaking days.

I speed outside my room living area. Tara is sitting on the couch. Her mouth parts when she sees me. "Where have you been? Didn't you hear today that they've imposed an earlier curfew on us? Professor Kapoor wilded out when she couldn't find you."

Adreneline kicks in. I rush out into the hallway and find Professor Kapoor, Watson Hall's warden for this week, standing to my left. She's speaking into her DataLink. I can just make out my DataLink in her other hand.

"What's going on?"

I look to my right, where Everly is peeking out from her room two doors down from mine. I whisper, "I'm in trouble."

Understanding dawns on her face. She waves me into her room. "Okay. I don't know what's going on with you, but I take it you were caught out of your room?"

I nod.

"Did you at least have the sense to leave your DataLink in there?"

Another nod from me.

"Okay, that's good. Just follow my lead." She loops her arm through mine and leads me out of her quarters, laughing loudly. I do the same, but it sounds so fake. "Hi, Professor Kapoor," Everly calls out. "Is it curfew time already?"

Professor Kapoor turns around and fixes me with an intense stare. "Cadet Mason, where have you been?"

"She's been with me," Everly says, grinning. "We have a test for Professor March in a few days, and we were studying together. I need all the help I can get."

The professor advances upon us, holding up my DataLink. "If that's the case, why did I find this in your room?"

My mouth is dry. So dry I don't think I can speak. Everly glances at me, her eyebrows raised. I look down, thinking. And then I see a large bruise on my arm from my space bending practice. "I hurt my arm today, and the DataLink was making it worse. I didn't think it would be a big deal to take it off for a while."

I hold up the injured arm so Professor Kapoor can inspect it. "That does look bad," she says. "How did you do that?"

I'm not sure who at the Academy knows that I'm a Dual Talent, so I just stick with a generic answer. "I fell on it in class. Ask Professor March; he was there."

A long few seconds follow before the professor says, "Next time you decide to visit Cadet Darville's room, take the DataLink with you. I was in the process of reporting you missing. And try to remember that curfew has been moved up to nine o'clock until further notice."

"Yes ma'am. I will."

After Professor Kapoor leaves, Everly follows me into my room. "So where were you, really?"

Tara chimes in, fixing me with a frosty stare. "Yes, Alora. I'd love to know."

Everly doesn't know I'm a Dual Talent, so I can't say that I shifted to Bridger's room. But maybe I can let her think I somehow found a way to sneak out. "I was meeting up with a friend of mine," I say. "And I missed the announcement that curfew had been changed."

She waits for me to say more—and to give her a name, I'm sure—but I really can't do that. So I feel like the ultimate jerk as I say, "I'm sorry, I can't say who it is. We're in a kind of complicated relationship right now."

Tara tries, unsuccessfully, to smother a snort.

Everly grins and claps her hands together. "Oh, is this an illicit romance? That would be brilliant."

Through the doorway, Professor Kapoor's voice drifts in. "Cadet Darville, go back to your room!"

Letting out a loud sigh, Everly starts to retreat. At the doorway, she turns back and says, "I want the full scoop if you ever get to announce the name if this mystery person."

"You got it," I say, blushing. "Thank you for helping me out. I owe you one."

She smirks. "Oh yes, you do."

As she leaves, I realize how much I'm starting to like Everly. It's amazing how quickly I've been able to trust and count on her as a friend—especially when I remember that, when I first got here, I was too afraid to be around anybody at all.

Then I frown, thinking of Bridger, Zed, and Elijah, and how I've come to count on them, too. Maybe I was being too harsh earlier. But I can't give up on our plans. Just like them, I want to find out what General Anderson is hiding. I'm not going to let fear dictate my every move anymore.

So I need to talk to the one person who could have answers for me. And it has to be tonight.

I stay up with Tara for a little while longer, filling her in on what happened with the guys. Then I excuse myself to go to bed, telling her I'm exhausted.

In my bedroom, I activate the lock on my door, hide my DataLink in my drawer again, and hope like hell that Professor Kapoor doesn't come back to check on me. The slight weight at my chest reminds me of Bridger's gift—my Jewill. This is perfect. Remembering from my tutoring lessons how Jewills are activated, I press the black stone for several seconds, only letting it go when I notice a faint shimmer around my body.

Then I close my eyes, visualizing the blonde woman I'd dreamed about all my life—Halla Fairbanks. For years, I had nightmares of her and my mother, along with my father. The scene was always the same—Halla standing over my mother, who was lying in a pool of blood in our apartment. I also dreamed of Dad, with his hands stained in blood. He was forced to leave Mom behind to take me to the past stay with Aunt Grace. The problem is, I didn't know who the two women were until Vika restored my early childhood memories with a Mind Redeemer the night she tried to murder me.

I concentrate on Halla's blue eyes, her finely chiseled features.

Before I open my eyes again, I notice a distinct chill in the air—and when I peek, it's completely dark. Then there's a sharp sound, like an alarm. A light snaps on, and I find that I'm standing in a small bedroom. Light blue walls, wooden floors, white covers on the full-sized bed—with two people in it. The person on the right is Halla. She's sitting upright, eyes darting back and forth as she searches the room. She reaches into a small table next to her bed and extracts a silver stunner from it.

"Whoever you are, show yourself immediately. The second I see so much as a hint of your cloak, I'll shoot," Halla says, holding the stunner with a shaking hand. As she says this, she scoots closer to the person on the other side of the bed and leans protectively over them.

I take a few steps closer to that person. It's Vika. Or a clone of Vika, anyway. The last time I saw her, she was completely insane and Bridger had to kill her in order to save me. But right after that someone cloaked appeared and uploaded her consciousness, along with that of Bridger's father. I have no idea what to think about this version of Vika. Is she also insane?

"I said show yourself!"

That unnerves me. She's nervous, meaning she'll fire at anything. So I call out, "I will, but please don't shoot. I think you know me. I'm Alora Mason."

Halla presses a button on a DataPad that's on the bedside table, which seems to deactivate the alarm. Then she cocks her head to the side. "Let me see."

Hoping she won't shoot, I press the black stone to deactivate the cloak. I wait for the longest few seconds of my life. I'm not sure what Halla is thinking. Her face is a blank canvas as she studies me, her icy gaze never giving any hint of emotion.

"What is it?" I ask. Her scrutiny is making me way too uncomfortable.

"I'm trying to figure out what's going on. I knew you were also a Space Bender, like Vika. But how the hell did you get here? Did General Anderson send you?" she asks with a faint trace of anger in her voice. "If he did, then he violated our agreement."

General Anderson. So he's definitely in on this—but to what extent? In 2126 he appeared to be against cloning Dual Talents from the past and using them to create more. It would make sense if he was the one responsible for cloning Bridger's father, but not Vika. So why would he help Halla?

"The general didn't send me," I say. "I'm just trying to find out what exactly happened to my dad."

Halla's face takes on a bitter expression. "He's dead."

"I know, but I'm trying to figure out how General Anderson is involved in all of this. He's been up to something behind the scenes, and I want to know what. I have the right to know. It's affected my whole life."

"Well, that's not my problem. You need to go now, before you wake Vika. It's not time for her medication yet, and I don't want to have to deal with any unpleasantness as a result."

I have no idea what she means by that, and I don't really care. "Look, I apologize for breaking in like this, but you're my last hope. And since you've gone to so much trouble to erase every trace of your existence, then you and whoever helped you must be hiding something. So either tell me what I want to know, or I can let the DTA know you're here. Because it seems obvious to me that General Anderson is the one who helped you."

I hope she can't tell that I'm bluffing, because I have no idea where we are. I step closer to the window in the bedroom to peek out, but it's still too dark.

Halla stares at me hard, then flashes a rueful smile. "You know, you remind me of Vika." She glances down at her. "The old Vika, anyway." She scoots out of bed and says, "Come with me. I don't want to wake her."

We enter a tiny, open space that doubles as a kitchenette and living area, with only a small blue couch, TeleNet screen, and a table to eat at. Halla leads me to the table.

"What do you want to know?" she asks once we're seated.

"Why don't you start with Project Firebird," I say.

Halla closes her eyes for a moment before asking, "How did you find out about that?"

"I've been looking for answers for a while."

"Right," she says, now tapping her precisely filed nails on the table. "Well, to start, I was an assistant to the doctor in charge of resurrecting the clones. While I was assigned to the project, I was a part of a team that scoured the past for any indication of natural-born Dual Talents. We had luck finding them occasionally, but they were all Mind and Time Benders or Mind and Space Benders. Nathaniel—your father—was the first Space and Time Bender. Once we uploaded his consciousness, it was also part of my duties to assist in his revival and subsequent training. The former head of the project felt it would be better for the subjects if the same people who were present with them at their revival stayed with them throughout their acclimation to our time."

I swallow a few times, trying to push the vision of Dad at the moment of his resurrection out of my mind. Trying to forget about his screams.

"Once Nathaniel was conscious, we had to erase his memories of his former life almost immediately. But we also had to let him retain enough to keep him from becoming a Null. We told him those residual memories were just dreams—that his real memories had been lost when he was in a shuttle accident."

"So you basically took his life away, and gave him a fake one."

"That's accurate." She yawns and pushes back from the table. Reaching into a cabinet behind her, she extracts a small vial filled with a blue liquid and injects it into her neck. "That's a little boost, since you woke me up early. Would you like some? You look like you're exhausted, yourself."

I *am* exhausted, but I have no idea if she's telling the truth about the liquid. "No thank you. I just need answers."

"Of course you do," she says in a flat voice as she leans against the table. "Okay, so I was at the part where we gave Nathaniel a new life. The DTA wanted to train him to join the military. Our general at the time thought it would be a seamless transition, since he was already a soldier. And it was, until the drug that was keeping him from going insane stopped working."

"Did they ever come up with some other drug to give him?"

"Oh, they tried, but by then he was already suspicious. He stole a Mind Redeemer and managed to recover his memories. That's when he became a liability."

"My mom said the same thing. That their relationship was good up until a certain point, then she called it off. I don't think that went over so well with him," I say.

"I remember. Of course, we knew when you were born that you had the genetic markers for being a Space and Time Bender. My superiors decided it would be in your best interest for us to leave you alone while you were a baby and toddler, but when you were six they felt it was time to examine you and run a few tests. That's why I was ordered to bring you in. However, Nathaniel found out, took it the wrong way, and kidnapped you."

"And we both know the rest," I say bitterly. "But what about you and my father? Were you two involved before he met my mother?" I feel my face growing hot. I mean, who wants to talk about their own father having a child with another woman?

Halla sits again, now looking amused. "Oh, no. That's not how it worked. One of Nathaniel's roles was to provide his genetic material. The DTA wanted a Time Bender within the organization to carry the first child from his gene pool, so I volunteered." Halla gets a faraway look, smiling. "When Vika was born, I instantly fell in love with her. And I swore I'd do anything to protect her. I knew from the beginning of the pregnancy that she would also be a Dual Talent, and therefore constantly tested and scrutinized."

"Is that why you had her cloned the first time?" I ask gently.

Halla's eyes take on a glassy sheen. "That's something nobody should have to experience. It was the worst day of my life. I knew Anderson would never allow me to go back and save Vika, so instead I cloned her. It wasn't that hard. The cloning labs are still in use, but only for people that the government wants to clone. The division that the labs operate under is classified Top Secret. All I had to do was hack into the system and input a false identity for Vika."

"Wait a minute. You're telling me that people are *still* being cloned?"

She nods. "Only certain *important* people, and the approval has to come straight from the president or the Secretary of Temporal Affairs. The same thing goes for the Departments of Telepathic Affairs and Tele-portation—if any Space Bender or Mind Bender is to be cloned, approval has to come from their direct leader."

"What about ordinary citizens?"

"I don't know about that. All I know is that for the general public, cloning is illegal."

I think for a moment, stunned by what this means. "So you're basi-cally telling me that even though General Anderson is the head of the military division, he can't decide who can be cloned?"

"That's right. After Vika stopped responding to the drugs stabilizing her and disappeared, Anderson told me he'd discovered what I'd done to Vika. Because it was illegal, he used it to blackmail me to go back to 2013. He just told me I'd be expected to clone two people who had been shot, no questions asked. I had no choice. You can imagine how shocked I was to find it was Leithan and Vika, and that you and Bridger were there. But I was under strict orders. I came back, falsified Leithan's identity at the lab so that a clone of him could be created. Anderson's end of the bargain, aside from keeping my secret, was to help me leave the country. That's why I'm in London now. Cloning is legal here, and the drug they use to stabilize clones here seems to be having a better effect on Vika, as long as it's administered on time, every time."

I sit up straighter. "Wait, General Anderson just let you leave? I thought the DTA never let Time Benders go."

"Well, in our situation, we both had information that the other wanted to keep hidden. Don't ask me why he wanted to clone Leithan, because he never told me. He just said that the events had already happened and that he just needed to find the person who was supposed to carry them out. And that person was me."

Suddenly, we hear a loud scream from the bedroom. Halla jumps to her feet. "I have to administer her meds, or she'll completely wild out on me. I can't let that happen."

Grabbing a vial from her fridge, Halla hurries into the bedroom. I follow and see Halla reach Vika just as she's sitting up, now crying. "Oh, god, oh no, no, no, please don't shoot me," she says with a low moan.

Halla gathers Vika into her arms, crooning something softly to her. With her left hand, she takes the vial of clear liquid and injects it into Vika's neck. A few seconds later, Vika relaxes and pulls away. "Hi, Mom. I had the worst nightmare."

"Hi, sweetheart," Halla says in a strained voice. "I have a guest that I need to see out. I'll be right back. Why don't you go ahead and get dressed?"

Vika pouts for a moment. "I'd rather stay in bed. But I guess I will if you say so," she says in a quiet voice. "Can we go to the park today? I really don't want to go to the lab again."

"I'll see what I can do," Halla says.

I start to follow Halla back to the kitchenette, but Vika reaches across to her nightstand and picks up a small digigraph that I hadn't noticed before. "I love you, Dad. I love you so much."

I freeze upon hearing those words. Ignoring Halla's command to leave Vika alone, I cross the distance to her bed and snatch the digigraph from her.

"Give it back! That's my dad! You can't have him!" she screeches.

But her words, along with everything else, fade away. I feel like I've been sucked into the Void. On the digigraph is a short scene: Vika sitting in the kitchenette, blowing out candles on a small, chocolate birthday cake. There's a man standing next to her, smiling just like a proud parent. He's bald, and deep burn scars cover his face and hands. But the eyes are the same deep blue.

It's my father.

Halla snatches the digigraph from me and gives it back to the sobbing Vika, then grabs my arm. I cry out in pain as she squeezes the bruises from shifting earlier today. She ignores me and pulls me out of the bedroom.

In the hallway, I manage to snatch my arm away from her. "You didn't have to do that," I snarl.

"Yes I did," she says in a low, murderous tone. "I want you to go now."

I'd like nothing more than to do that, but I'm not going anywhere without the truth. "I'll leave just as soon as you tell me why you lied to me about my dad and where I can find him. And remember, I can tell the DTA where you are if you don't."

Halla's eyes narrow to slits. "Fine, but when I do, I never want to see you again."

I follow her back to the kitchenette, where the sun is just beginning to shine through the tiny window. I can barely make out the tops of tall buildings and shuttles moving through the pink and orange sky.

"Here's what I know," she begins. "Officially, Nate was declared dead. He had been captured and the transport shuttle he was on exploded. The blast came from within the shuttle itself, but we never figured out exactly what happened. Three bodies were accounted for in the rubble, and they were declared to be those of Nate, the pilot, and the arresting officer. And life went on for Vika and me. So imagine my shock when Nate appeared here shortly after Vika and I moved in. He refused to tell me how he pulled off his escape. He would only say that he shifted just before the explosion and he's been living in exile ever since."

"Where?"

"I don't know. He refused to tell me. And no matter how many times I've told him to leave us alone, he keeps coming to visit Vika once a month. It makes her so happy, so I stopped trying to make him stay away. We have an . . . unusual relationship, to say the least."

"Have you ever tried to track him or anything? You have to have wondered where he's living," I say.

"I've told you everything I know. Now, please, go. And don't come back. I barely have Vika under control. The doctors here think it's because she was cloned more than once. Their drugs keep her more stable, but she must have the doses every six hours, exactly. *That's* the price Vika and I had to pay."

"I'm sorry, I really am," I say. Halla's as much as a victim as anybody else, just wanting to protect her only child. And I find myself wanting to know more about Vika. She's my half-sister, after all.

Maybe one day we can work something out. But only after I figure out what is going on at the DTA.

27

After a night of practically no sleep, I haul myself out of bed a half hour before my wake-up time and shower. That helps some. At least I'm awake, but I still feel nothing but guilt. I regret telling Alora that my dad wants us to stay apart, and I regret trying to get her to stop searching for Colonel Fairbanks. I can't stop thinking about how pale she got when I told her—like she would pass out. I expected her to be sad, even shocked. What I didn't expect was her anger.

Zed said I was an idiot and should have kept my big mouth shut. Elijah pretty much agreed. But at least he said that she would probably come back once she cooled off and thought things through.

But Alora didn't come back. I just hope that she didn't try to see Vika's mother. Not with all the security checks going on, and no way of knowing what kind of dangers there are wherever Halla's living.

Wrapping a towel around myself, I leave the bathroom. I'm kind of glad I got up early. Normally, Zed or Elijah are banging on the door wanting me to hurry up. Or I'm doing the same to one of them.

"Oh my God," a voice exclaims as soon as I get to the doorway of my bedroom.

I nearly drop the towel. Alora is sitting on my bed, her face a fiery red. She quickly looks down.

"I'm so sorry. I didn't know you would be like . . . that," she says.

I can't help but smile. Alora had a similar reaction when I stayed at her aunt's inn back in 2013. She peeked in my room to invite me to supper and saw me in my skivvies. She could barely look me in the face when it happened.

"I'll go so you can get dressed," she says.

"No, wait," I say in a rush. I don't want her to leave—not when she came back after being so upset with me. "Just stay here. I'll dress out here."

I grab a uniform and hurry to the living area. I keep looking down the short hallway leading to Zed and Elijah's rooms. For some reason, I don't want them to know that Alora is here. I want to talk to her in private for once.

Back in my bedroom, I sit next to her on the bed. She still doesn't speak, just fidgets with her fingers. She looks so lost and sad. It makes me angry with myself, knowing I did that to her.

"I'm sorry about what I said last night. It was stupid of me to try to tell you what to do."

"It's okay," she says in a quiet voice. But then she looks at me and flashes the biggest grin. "Besides, I have some good news. I found Colonel Fairbanks, and guess what? My father is still alive!" She's practically bouncing as she says that.

I feel my eyes go wide. "Wait, you went to see her last night?"

"Yeah. She tried to make me believe that Dad was really dead, but I found a digigraph of him with Vika that was *recent*. He's been showing up there every month to visit with her."

Without thinking, I wrap my left arm around her and draw her close. She leans her head against my shoulder. We fit perfectly together. And yet we're in the midst of a perfect mess. How can I stop seeing her, like Dad demanded? After she left last night, I felt as if a part of me had been ripped away.

Alora fills me in on everything Halla told her. By the time she finishes, adrenaline is racing through my body. I'm stunned that Vika is alive . . . but apparently a shell of the girl she used to be. I still remember how full of life she was. And she was brilliant. It's sad thinking of her being incapacitated like that, relying on drugs to keep her from permanently wilding out.

But the information about General Anderson isn't so shocking—it just confirms what I already knew. That he is the puppet master pulling all of our strings. It still doesn't explain his motive, though. Why would he risk his career to clone my father? I mean, he was smart enough to get Halla to do the actual work, but still, *he* was behind it. And why go through so much trouble to hide the fact that Dad had illegally shifted before his death, and that I illegally went back looking for him? He claims it had to happen, but I'm not buying that.

Something isn't adding up.

What Dad told me yesterday, about having a plan to stop the Purists, is really weighing on my mind now. Knowing that Dad is working for General Anderson alone makes me suspicious. I can't stop wondering when the bioweapon attack will happen. How it will happen. And how will Dad be involved? Because that has to be what his plan is about: stopping the detonation. I can't see him being an instrument of mass murder.

I want to talk more to Alora about it, but she's too giddy. "Bridger, I need to find him. Today. I need to let him know I'm okay." She pauses and frowns. "And I want to know why he's been visiting Vika, but not me." She shakes her head and takes a deep breath. "No, I'm not going to think like that. He must have a good reason for not coming to see me. It's probably because I'm in DTA territory. It would be easier for me to go to him."

She suddenly leans over and hugs me tightly again, then pulls back. Her blue eyes meet mine. Then my gaze slips down to rest on her lips. They're parted slightly.

I don't know what comes over me. I lean down and brush my lips against hers. For a moment she doesn't move, and I think I've made a horrible mistake. But then her lips part even more and she deepens the kiss. I reach over cupping her face with my hand. Her skin is so soft against my fingers. I never want to let go.

"Holy shit, I never thought I'd see action in here!"

My head snaps up and turns in the direction of the irritating voice. Of course, Zed has to be standing there with the biggest idiot grin on his face.

"Oh, don't stop just because I'm here. Pretend I'm invisible."

My entire body tenses. "Go away, Zed."

"Fine, fine, I can see that I'm unwanted here. I'll leave you two lovebirds alone in your cozy little nest." He flutters his fingers at us before heading back to his room. No—probably to Elijah's room to gleefully recount what he just saw.

I storm over to shut the door, then activate the lock.

"I'm sorry about that," I say, returning to Alora's side. "Zed has a way of turning up in the wrong place at the wrong time."

She shrugs her shoulders, smiling. "It's fine. Really."

I frown. What she said before she hugged me is bothering me. "Look. I don't have any right to tell you what to do, but I don't think it would be a good idea to shift to wherever your father is right now. There are too many unknown variables."

She rolls her eyes. "That's what you said when I wanted to get to Halla. But that worked out."

"Think about what you're saying," I plead. "Halla Fairbanks has a child she's protecting. She was working for Anderson, and he helped set up her new residence. On the other hand, your father somehow faked his death. Nobody knows where he's been hiding. He could've been living by himself all these years, or he could've been with others. My point is, there isn't any way to know for sure. It's too big of a risk."

She recoils. "How could you say that? You know what, Bridger? You're a hypocrite. It was fine for you to go looking for your father when you thought he was dead. But when all I want to do is see mine, who is very much alive, you tell me no. I wish I'd never come here."

Before I can say anything else, she closes her eyes and shifts.

I can't move. A part of me is screaming that I'm a furing idiot. How in the hell did we go from kissing to fighting so quickly?

But then something Dad said about Dual Talents surfaces in my mind: that they're just out for themselves. Is that true? Alora is behaving recklessly, going off on her own to talk to Halla, and now shifting to who knows where to speak to her father. Going to him could put me, and all of our friends, in danger.

Maybe Dad was right about her all along.

28

The alarm I set on my DataLink yanks me out of a fitful sleep at 4:45 in the morning. I get up, already dressed in black jeans and a dark purple sweater, and braid my hair. After that, I hide the DataLink in my dresser. Then I touch my Jewill, making sure it's still fastened around my neck, and check the mirror. Dark smudges line my eyes, but there's nothing I can do about that. Sleep will have to wait.

I've decided for sure that I'm going to see my father today.

It's now a little after five o'clock in the morning. I don't have to be at my first class for another three hours. That should give me time to find Dad and figure out why he's stayed away from me for the ten months I've been in his time period. He owes me an explanation, especially since he's been seeing Vika regularly.

A lump appears in my throat. I wish I could wash it down with some juice, but I don't want to go into the kitchen and risk waking Tara. More than likely, she would try to talk me out of going. And I'm done listening to other people when it comes to my own father.

Standing in front of my bed, I press the stone on my Jewill, then close my eyes and carefully picture Dad's face as it appeared in Vika's digigraph. His features were the same, but the head full of blond hair was gone, and his skin was covered in scars. Please, let me go to him. Please.

The comfortable warmth of my bedroom is replaced with a searing heat and a pungent stench. My eyes fly open and I twist around to see that I'm standing in what appears to be a small, wooden barn. The floors are packed dirt, and a rusted, old-fashioned wood-burning stove has been fitted along the far side of the wall. A rickety picnic table sits to the left side of the stove. And directly in front of it, but out of the direct path of the heat, are five dirty cots, men and women sound asleep in them. A sixth man is standing in the barn's doorway, staring up at the sky.

My heart leaps when I realize it's Dad.

I want to rush over to him, but curiosity and common sense make me wait. I need to figure out where I am and who these people are. First I study Dad. He's holding a white mug with steam coming off the top. I wonder if it's hot chocolate, because Aunt Grace told me once that Dad always hated the taste of coffee.

He's wearing dark-brown denim pants, a plain green button-up shirt, and a brown leather coat. The scars are harder to see in the dark, but I can still make them out. I ache for the pain he must have gone through, but I'm glad he made it out of the explosion alive. Surprisingly, I feel sympathy for the other two DTA officers who died. I wonder if Dad has any idea how the shuttle exploded.

Suddenly, Dad turns around, as if he senses I'm here. I hold perfectly still.

He doesn't seem to notice me. Instead, he takes a sip from his mug, then barks out, "Get up, get up! It's time to work!"

Usually, when I wake up, I allow myself a few minutes to stretch and shake off the last bits of sleep. Not these people. They spring up and are on their feet in just a few seconds, standing at the ends of their cots. They're all wearing wrinkled clothes that look like they haven't been washed in weeks. I guess that explains the smell.

"Let's go. Milt's got breakfast ready and he said not to be late if you want to eat," Dad says. He turns and saunters out of the barn, while the five people behind him follow in a line.

My brow wrinkles. What on earth is going on?

By the time I get to the entrance, they're already halfway across the yard. The sun peeks over the tops of pine trees that surround the clearing where we're located. In addition to the barn I'm standing in, I can see the clearing also holds a two-story white house with a sloping roof and wraparound porch, a chicken coop, a field of cattle behind the house, two old sheds. Most surprisingly, there are also two small silver shuttles about the size of compact cars from Aunt Grace's time, and one shuttle that's similar to the size of a school bus. There's an old oak tree planted on the right side of the house.

So I'm obviously on a farm, but where? I could be anywhere.

Somehow, I have to get Dad alone so I can let him know I'm here. So he can tell me how he ended up here, apparently in the middle of nowhere.

Dad leads the five men and women inside the farm house and into a large kitchen, where an older, pot-bellied man is stirring something on a stove. The stove is old-fashioned, with spiral burners that are kind of like the ones I saw in movies from the 1980s and 1990s.

I wonder if Dad has been going back in time to get this stuff for them, or if these people bought them from a genuine artifact reseller.

"Well don't just stand there. Take your seats," the old man tells the people who followed Dad inside. His accent seems to be southern, but it has an unfamiliar cadence to it. Everyone sits around a large, square, wooden table. Glass bowls and spoons are set at each seat, along with glasses already filled with water. One at a time, each person takes their bowl and the man serves them what appears to be oatmeal.

Dad grabs a spoon and bowl, too, and after having his filled, he leaves the kitchen and walks across the hall to a dining room. It has another long, rectangular table and white painted walls that are lined with rows of TeleNet screens. Some of the screens are in sleep mode, and some have operators in front of them, sorting through I don't know what. Images flash by so fast I can't make anything out.

"Good morning, Nate," a man sitting at the head of the table says. His voice sounds vaguely familiar, but I can't place it.

"Morning," Dad murmurs. He sits in an empty seat at the opposite end of the table from the man who spoke and digs into his breakfast, not bothering to talk to any of the other people. There are fifteen men and women total, plus a young boy who looks so pale that he's obviously sick. That excludes Dad and the three people working at the TeleNet stations. Everyone else is eating plates of eggs, sausage, and toast slathered in jelly. The scent of the food is heavenly. I used to get stuff like this most every morning with Aunt Grace. Now it's only an occasional treat, and it doesn't taste anywhere as good as hers.

But then I finally notice the man who spoke to Dad sitting at the head of the table and nearly fall over when I realize I recognize him. It's Jode Lincoln, the Purist who ordered the murder of all those people three days ago. My fingers curl into my palms. What I wouldn't give to strangle him.

Then a sick feeling makes my stomach churn. My father is here with a terrorist. How in the hell is that possible?

"How are the new recruits doing?" Jode asks, directing the question to Dad.

"They're hanging in there. I think they'll all work out," Dad says.

"I really hope they do, for your sake. That last crew you brought in was unacceptable."

"It won't happen again," Dad replies.

"It better not," Jode says, in between bites of scrambled eggs. "Not if you want that pretty daughter of yours in New Denver to stay perfectly safe."

Dad flinches but doesn't say anything.

And like a slap to the face, it hits me: I know why Dad is here with these people. Jode Lincoln is using me to blackmail him.

I feel dizzy. I step just outside of the doorway and cringe when one of the wooden planks makes a creaking sound.

"Did you hear that?" the woman next to Dad asks. "Sounds like someone's in the hallway."

Chaos immediately erupts. The food is forgotten as everyone jumps up from the table.

"Get the comm-sets," Lincoln shouts to the woman on his left. She rushes to a cabinet behind her, yanks open the top drawer, and takes out a tan briefcase. She sets it in front of Lincoln, where he snaps open the top and starts tossing comm-sets to the people around the table, including Dad. "Get to it," he growls. "It might not be a false alarm this time." To the woman, he orders her to take the young boy to their "safe spot," wherever that is.

While the people in the room are occupied with putting on the comm-sets correctly, I take the opportunity to dive under the table, right next to Dad's legs. Because no matter where I go outside, someone will be able to see me, and I have the feeling these people will shoot me no matter what I say to explain myself.

Everyone pulls stunners out of their pockets, except for Dad. While all the people who were eating at the table rush out to search the house, the ones at the TeleNet stations look uneasily back at Jode Lincoln.

"Keep working!" he barks at them. Then, while striding across the room, he says to Dad, "Guard this room with your life."

"I need a weapon to do that," Dad says.

"You had your chance with that, and you blew it. Figure out some way to keep this area secure."

Footsteps thud throughout the house while the others search. I wait until I hear the majority of them grow fainter before tapping Dad's right foot. To his credit, he stays perfectly still, then he peeks over the side, comm-sets in place. He should be able to see my outline in white, but the Jewill masks my words. So I press the stone to lower my cloak, and when I do Dad nearly falls off his chair.

"Activate it again and move to the center of the table," he whispers. "The others will take their search outside soon."

I give him a thumbs-up and press the button before gingerly making my way between the legs of the table to reach its center. There, I wait for an eternity before Dad waves for me to come out.

Dad tells one of the techs. "I think I see something in the yard. I'll be back in a few minutes."

"That's not what Jode told you to do!" the man says in a fearful voice.

Dad ignores him and exits the room, heading to a staircase to our left. We quickly ascend the steps and turn right down a long hallway. Dad goes into the last door on the left, waiting until he's sure I've followed him. The room isn't that big, but it's filled with bunk beds. Somehow they managed to squeeze three in a room the size of a large closet. Once the door is locked, I lower my cloak.

Dad hugs me tight for a few seconds before pulling back. "Dear God, how did you find me?"

"The same way I'm sure you found Vika. Can you shift just by thinking of a person, instead of a place?"

"Yes, but I had no idea you could do that as well."

"I didn't know either, until recently. All of these abilities are still new to me, and apparently we are the only two people who can do that. We're like unicorns." I try to smile, but I'm sure it looks more like a wince. "So . . . where are we?"

"We're on a farm several miles outside of Draperville, Georgia. Completely off the grid." Dad rubs his right hand over his head.

Being this close to him in person reveals the extent of his injuries. Scar tissue covers most of the left side of his body, and some of the right side. Still, his features are the same. His eyes are the same. I wish I could see him smile, but instead he's wearing a grim expression.

"You need to leave now," he hisses. "If Lincoln finds you he'll never let you go. He's been threatening to hurt you if I don't do everything he says."

Dad's probably right, but I didn't come here just to be sent away. "Not until you give me some answers."

Dad eyes flick to the window. "Sweetheart, it isn't safe here."

"I know. Let's make this quick. One, how did you survive the shuttle explosion?"

Dad looks like he wants to argue with me, but he just sighs. "I planted the bombs. They were in my shoes, and I set the timer shortly after the pilot took off. Once I overpowered my escort, I took off the Inhibitor they'd put on me, shifted out of the shuttle, and then shifted back with a body I'd stolen from the morgue. Perks of bending both space and time," he says, smiling weakly. "But I timed the drop-off of the body too close to the blast and was caught in it mid-shift. My recovery was hell."

I cover my mouth with both hands, shocked. "You killed two innocent people to escape," I say.

"Trust me, they weren't innocent. They had plenty of blood on their hands. I did what I had to do to survive."

I swallow a few times, trying to see it from his perspective. "Okay, I get it. But why did you come here? Why didn't you just try to get Mom again and bring her back to live with Aunt Grace and me?"

"I didn't because of your visit the night before I faked my death," he says. "You know exactly what I'm talking about. I was fully planning to take Adalyn to you, but what you told me changed everything."

Now feeling horrified, I whisper, "How?"

"From your visit, I learned several things. One, you did live with Grace for many years, but without me or your mom. Two, you were now living in this time with your mother, and I was no longer a part of your lives. That meant that if I brought Adalyn to the past, or even if I went there myself, that would change the timeline. And I refuse to do that. So I came back to Georgia to wait until after your seventeenth birthday, since you visited me right before that date, so I could reintroduce myself to you. It was the closest I could get to being home without actually going there."

"Why didn't you come, though?" I ask. "I just turned seventeen. From my point of view, I just went back and talked to you four days ago. But it's been eleven years for you."

"Because I mistakenly trusted Lincoln when he took me in. His crew found me stumbling around in the woods, half burned and barely alive. They took me in and help me to mend. I thought they were decent, hard-working people trying to survive in a world that didn't agree with how they chose to live. I understood that, even agreed with it. And when they discovered my unique situation, and that I hate the government as much as they do, they put me to work. At first it was just stealing supplies they needed and were usually denied. Food, drink, medicines, extra clothing. But after Lincoln's hackers learned of your existence, Lincoln started demanding that I do things I didn't want to do. Things I'm ashamed of." He looks away, tears welling in his eyes. "Any time I tried to leave, Jode would threaten to send one of his mercenaries to hurt you. I couldn't let him do that. I had no choice but to stay."

I dread finding out what he did that was so bad. So instead I ask, "You said they only threatened me. What about Vika?"

"They thought she was dead. They don't know that Halla cloned her. I found myself at their apartment one day when I particularly was longing to see Vika, since I had never had the opportunity to have a relationship with her."

Even from the bedroom, we can hear shouts from the lower part of the house, then footsteps pounding up the stairs.

"Go, Alora! You're out of time!"

"I can't leave without you, Dad. Please come with me."

Dad takes a big breath and straightens his back, as if he's steeling himself to do something. "I can't come with you because I'm a murderer. Those gunmen who shot up the museums? It wasn't different gunmen. It was me. I killed all those people at the same time. Using my Talents."

I reel back as if his words are a physical slap. Dad killed all those innocent people.

Someone begins to beat on the door. "Open up, Nate. What are you hiding in there?" Lincoln screams.

I'm repulsed by what he did. How can I accept that he did something so awful—even if it was to protect me? But there isn't time to mull it over. "Dad, we can work that out later. Just come with me now. Please."

"I can't, sweetheart. There's some things you can't undo. I can never forgive myself, but I can make sure you're safe."

Something—or someone—rams against the door. Again and again.

"Go, sweetheart," Dad says. "Just go."

Tears stream down my face. "What about you? They'll hurt you."

Dad cracks a hint of a smile. "Don't worry about me. I'll just shift outside and tell them I was out there the whole time."

With cracks showing in the door now, I touch Dad's hand one more time. "If you change your mind, you know where to find me."

Then I shift back to the Academy.

Later in the afternoon, after my last class with Professor March, Everly says, "I'm going to the gym to exercise. Want to come with?"

"No," I say slowly, glancing in Professor March's direction. "I need to talk to him for a few minutes. I might join you later."

She cocks her head to the side, eyes narrowing slightly. "Are you okay? You've been acting strange all day."

I've been trying to acting normal—like I haven't had my whole life turned upside down. But really, I want to scream for all the world to hear that my father is alive. And that he's been turned into an assassin, all because of me. The guilt is eating me alive. That's why I need to talk to someone who can maybe do something to help me. But I just say, "I didn't sleep much last night. But go ahead without me. I'll probably join you later."

After Everly departs, Professor March walks over to me and leans against a desk across from mine. "I don't have to read your mind to know something is wrong, Alora. What can I do to help?"

Like a dam bursting, I tell him everything. When I'm finished, I'm sobbing.

Professor March's face is ashen. He opens and closes his mouth a few times, as though deciding how to react. Finally, he says, "I'll do what I can, but I can't guarantee Nate's safety."

"Don't tell anyone at the DTA that he was with the Purists," I beg. "Can you give an anonymous tip or something? Just to make sure Jode Lincoln and his followers are captured?"

Professor March takes my hands and looks me straight in the eye. "I'll call my sister. We'll do what we can to protect Nate. I promise. And we'll just have to hope it's enough."

29

t's still pitch black outside when a piercing siren shatters the silence. Someone's triggered the new sensors that can detect anyone who is cloaked.

Nate's eyes fly open and he sits up, instantly alert. Years of training as a soldier, in his former life in the twentieth century as well as in this century, have sharpened his senses. He also learned long ago to never sleep too deeply. As if he could do that, anyway. When he sleeps, he always has nightmares.

His bunkmates are all alert as well. Everyone at the compound is required to sleep in their clothes, even with their shoes on, just in case they are attacked by the government. Jode Lincoln, their leader, puts them through drills at random. Daytime, nighttime. It doesn't matter.

Immediately, they retrieve their weapons from the wooden cases assigned to each of them, and don comm-sets stolen from the government. Not for the first time, Nate feels a surge of resentment as he slips on his lenses. Lincoln refuses to let him carry a weapon unless he's on a mission.

"What's happening?" a bunkmate asks.

Before anyone can answer, their door flies open. Lincoln strides inside, barking orders. "Everyone to your stations. We're under attack."

Nate's bunkmates march out, as if they're on autopilot.

"Are you going to let me have a gun now? I can't defend myself otherwise," Nate says, trying to keep his tone neutral. He learned years ago never to be confrontational with Lincoln.

"No. I have one." Lincoln peers outside the window, also wearing a comm-set. "Damn Space Benders are everywhere." Looking back at Nate, he says, "You're with me. Your job is to get me and my family to safety."

Nate breathes in, hard, through his nostrils. "And how am I supposed to do that without a weapon?"

"That's not my problem," Lincoln snaps. "If you don't help us and then report to your next assignment, I've left orders for my next-in-command to have your daughter terminated. Is that clear?"

It takes everything in Nate's power to stop himself from punching Lincoln repeatedly in his face. Clenching his fists, he says, "Yes, crystal clear."

"Follow me," Lincoln barks.

Before he leaves the room, Nate glances out the window. Four black-clad Space Benders are standing around a large white Department of Temporal Affairs transport shuttle that has just landed near the barn. Members of Lincoln's team that have already been captured, including the new recruits who were housed in the barn, are being herded into the shuttle, hands held high in the air.

For a moment, Nate thinks about shifting away, but Jode's threat to have Alora killed reverberates in his mind. He has no choice but to follow orders. How could he ever have thought Lincoln was a good person? Lincoln clearly took Nate in all those years ago and nursed him back to health for his own benefit, not Nate's. Lincoln knew he'd struck gold when he discovered that Nate was a Dual Talent on the run from the DTA.

Nate's senses take in everything as he follows Lincoln down the narrow hallway. Shouts coming from outside, voices issuing commands within the lower level of the house, tense voices yelling through his comm-set earpiece. Gunfire. A bitter scent fills his nostrils, making it hard for him to breathe. *Great,* he thinks. *Now they're using tear gas on us.* Would have been nice if Lincoln had thought to get gas masks for them to wear.

Nate and Lincoln make it to Lincoln's bedroom. Nate's been in here a few times. It's nothing fancy, just a standard double bed with a blue cover, white walls, and blue checkered curtains. Lincoln's features contort into disbelief as he checks in the closet and under the bed.

"Damn it, they're supposed to be here!" he shrieks. "I told her not to leave until I got here with you."

A hint of a smile touches Nate's lips. Lincoln's wife runs the whole show with him, though Jode is the official leader. But when it comes to their son, her protective instincts always take over. "Where would she have gone?" Nate asks.

"I have a small shuttle stashed about a mile from here. Just in case something like this ever happened." Lincoln runs his hands over his head. "She wasn't supposed to leave yet."

"I think we need to head there right now," Nate says in a tense voice. From what he's hearing through his comm-set, there are around ten Space Benders surrounding the premises, possibly more. Lincoln's men outnumber the agents, but the Space Benders have the advantage of having superior weapons and specialized training.

The same training that Nate once went through.

Hating himself for helping such a violent Purist, Nate says, "I'm going to shift outside, just below your window. I'll secure the immediate area while you climb down. Do you think you can handle that?" Nate already knows the answer, but he can't resist taking a jab at Lincoln.

Jode bristles at Nate's tone. "Of course I can, you simpleton. Why do you think I bothered drilling everyone all this time?"

Bowing his head slightly, Nate murmurs, "My apologies. I just want to make sure you're ready. Now may I ask again for a gun? I need something to distract the Space Benders."

Letting out a loud grunt, Lincoln goes over to his dresser and pulls a small pistol out of the bottom drawer. He hands the pistol to Lincoln. "Just go, already. I'm heading down now."

Nate checks to make sure the pistol is loaded, then quickly scopes out the immediate area through the window. Space Benders are stationed at all of Lincoln's personal shuttles, and one is standing between the two sheds on the property. "I'm going to shift to just behind the barn and see if I can draw their attention away. You get down to the ground and I'll meet you there in three minutes."

Lincoln gives a terse nod. Nate closes his eyes, visualizing the small clearing just behind the barn, picturing himself there. Instantly, cool night air kisses his cheeks. From this area, the gunfire sounds more distant. The temptation to flee is overwhelming, but he remembers Alora.

He can't let her down.

Pointing the pistol into the air, Nate yells and fires it twice. He starts running toward the woods and fires two more shots. Just as he crosses the treeline, he closes his eyes and pictures the large oak next the farm house. It's close to Lincoln's bedroom window—the closest place he can go to hide while waiting for him to climb down.

Nate appears behind the trunk and finds himself facing a Space Bender. The man's eyes widen, clearly surprised by the sudden appearance of one of Lincoln's men. Reflexes kicking in, Nate knees the man in the groin. He doubles over, allowing Nate time to grab him by the hair and slam his head against the tree. The man crumples to the ground, unconscious. Guilt tears through Nate, just like it does every time he hurts someone for Lincoln, especially when he's ordered to take innocent lives. At least this way, the man has a chance to recover.

Scanning the immediate area, Nate counts seven Space Benders still in front of the house. At least three of them must have taken the bait and gone to search the area near where he fired the gun. But then one of the Space Benders disappears and immediately reappears behind the house, close to where Lincoln should be any second.

"Are you on the ground yet, Jode?" Nate hisses into his mouthpiece.

"Yes, I'm next to the bushes."

"Be careful. You have company."

Before Nate can say anything else, he hears a muffled shot and the Space Bender close to Lincoln's location crumples to the ground. Nate flinches.

Crouching down, he closes his eyes again and visualizes Lincoln's face, then appears next to him.

"Can we go now?" Lincoln asks.

"Depends on what direction we need to go in. Most of the agents are concentrated near the front of the house, from what I can tell."

"The shuttle's in the woods on the far side of the cow pasture. I figured if we were ever ambushed, that would be the safest direction to go."

"What about the others?" Nate asks. "They're risking their lives for you. Don't you think we need to help them?"

Lincoln shrugs. "They knew what they were signing up for. They're loyal. If they're caught, they won't reveal anything. There's too much at risk."

A part of Nate agrees with Lincoln, but he still hates leaving them behind.

"Let's go, then. We need to catch up to my family and hope like hell they haven't left us."

Before they set out, Nate turns to Lincoln. "Do you realize that the government will send Time Benders back to investigate this? They'll follow us until they figure out where we are."

His eyes narrow. "I'm aware of that, Walker. That's why your job is to just get me and my family to the shuttle. They can follow us to an extent, but only after a certain amount of time passes. You know how they feel about their precious rules. But you, in the meantime, will shift directly to where I tell you to go and await further instructions."

Nate and Lincoln set out running across the moonless field, hoping nobody notices them.

Lincoln leads Nate down a narrow path for a half-mile, where a tiny black shuttle is parked. As they approach the shuttle, Jode slows down, looking around wildly. He activates the door to open the shuttle, enters, then reappears a few moments later, shaking with rage.

"They're not here! Damn Space Benders. They must have caught them."

Nate thinks to himself that he's not surprised. Lincoln's wife is tough, but their son is sick. It would have taken a miracle for her to sneak him past the Space Benders without being detected. "What do you want to do?" Nate asks.

Lincoln doesn't answer for a few moments, and the silence is heavy with the night sounds of the forest: owls hooting, crickets chirping, wind blowing gently. Then a few sporadic rounds of gunfire in the distance.

Lincoln balls his hands into fists and takes several deep breaths. "We can't do anything about them now. I need to get to the next enclave and regroup from there. You better be there when I arrive."

"Understood," Nate mutters. Before he can say anything else, a word flashes across his lenses: Ridgemont.

"You'd better be there when I arrive," Lincoln growls.

"Yes, sir," Nate says in a clipped voice, while thinking of Alora. He'd love nothing more than to shift to her right now, escape from this madman, but he knows he can't. Not if he wants to keep her alive.

So, as Lincoln pilots the shuttle away to the enclave in Ridgemont, Georgia, Nate closes his eyes and shifts there. Hopefully, by following Lincoln's orders, he can buy some more time and figure out a way to see his younger daughter again.

30

"Bridger, hurry up. Your grandmother is waiting for us outside the DTA building," Mom says over her shoulder as we exit the Maglev.

Mom and Shan are just ahead of me as we join the heavy crowd outside the station and start weaving our way through the thousands of people crowding the streets today. We're headed to downtown New Denver for the annual Unity Day celebrations. It's a huge national holiday that commemorates the end of the Second Civil War and the formation of the North American Federation. Basically, we honor the death and destruction by stuffing ourselves with too much food, partying at concerts, reliving the horrors of the war in Sim Games, and listening to politicians blather on about the greatness of our country.

I'd rather stay home, but Mom insisted. Lately, she's been on a huge we-need-family-time kick, especially since Shan was hurt in the shooting last month. I'm surprised that she's willing to risk letting him out in public, but apparently she thinks it's safer now. Two weeks ago, the news reported that the feds had apprehended a lot of the people responsible for the museum shootings. Even Lincoln's wife and sick child were taken into custody. They were discovered hiding out at a rural farm in Georgia thanks to an anonymous tip. The only ones to escape were the gunmen— the Space Benders—and their leader, Jode Lincoln.

Some people thought the festivities should have been cancelled this year, in light of all the unrest. But President Tremblay disagreed. He said we needed this celebration. We need the reminder that we're one nation— that we're all in this together. Which I find ironic, considering that he still refuses to repeal the Responsible Citizen Act. I'm beginning to think the president isn't too bright.

All the businesses and portable booths set up in the streets are flying the NAF's flag—the white rectangle with the colored triple rings. I cringe looking at them. Just add a ring of blue flame around the rings and you'd have the graffiti that the terrorists put up the day of the shooting. At least there are still hundreds of police and military officers on patrol.

Ahead of me, Shan flinches when someone bumps into him. Physically, he's fine. But mentally, not so much. He keeps looking back and forth, as if he expects someone to start shooting at him again. And it's not just today; he does that every time we're out in public. My fists clench and unclench. It's not fair. The feds may have captured those responsible, but no one can undo the damage they caused.

We finally arrive at the DTA building. We're going to attend a Unity Day luncheon here, then head to the grounds around the Civic Center a few blocks from here. That's where the majority of the celebrations will take place.

Grandma beams when she spots us entering the courtyard. "You're late," she says.

Mom gives her an exasperated look. "You know how the boys are. Never in a hurry to go anywhere unless it's something they want to do."

"I know what you mean," Grandma says, laughing.

I still can't get over the fact that they're getting along. Ever since the shooting, when Mom realized that Grandma was serious about wanting to be a part of our lives, they've been nothing but cordial to each other. We've even all had lunch together a few times. It's weird, but I like it. It's been too long since we've had a stable family.

I wish Dad could be here with us. But he promised that, as soon as he's finished with his plan to keep everyone safe from the Purists, we'll all be together again.

I hope that's soon. I'm tired of waiting. Tired of not seeing him. He hasn't been in contact since the night of the shooting.

After we get through the security scan, we take the elevator to the top floor of the DTA building. The entire top level is nothing but a banquet hall, complete with a huge kitchen in the wings where chefs prepare food on site. It's been a few years since we've been to the Unity Day banquet here, but it still looks the same. Black-and-white marble floor, tall pillars reaching up to the ceiling, round tables scattered around the room, and a white stage behind a long rectangular table that's set up for guests of honor.

While Mom and Grandma stop to talk to someone they know, I glance at Shan. "Let's check out the view."

"Sure," he says, rubbing the new scar on his cheek.

We make our way to the glass wall and stare down at the city around and below us. A few shuttles soar by overhead. Sunlight glints off skyscrapers. And we can just make out the heart of the city, where the Civic Center stands in a cluster of other government buildings. The people below us look like ants crawling on the ground, hunting for food and fun.

It looks so normal, and yet so wrong. I have this sick feeling in my gut, like something could happen.

But that's ridiculous. Ellis said he would come back and warn us before the bioweapon attack, and Dad is working to stop it as well. And the Purists responsible for the shooting have been caught. So we're safe, for now.

Then I hear Professor March's voice from behind us. "Well, I haven't talked to you two together in a long time."

Shan jumps, and his head jerks around. That bothers me so furing much. I hate that he reacts like that now.

"It's okay. I'm not going to bite," the professor says, his eyes shifting from Shan to me and back again. "I just wanted to talk to you for a bit." He leans a little closer to examine Shan's scar. "That looks better than the last time I saw it."

"When was that?" I ask. Professor March instructs Level 4 cadets, and Shan is Leven 1. So Professor March wouldn't have time to see Shan during the day. And he hasn't been on Warden Duty at the residence hall since before the shooting.

"I stopped by your mom's apartment once a week. I wanted to make sure Shan was doing okay."

That surprises me. Mom has never liked Professor March. Secretly, I think she was jealous of how close he and Dad were during their marriage. "And my mom actually let you in?"

Professor March grins. "She did. I was quite shocked, but I think she was grateful that I was with the two of you the day of the shooting. Your mom has mellowed out quite a bit over the past year, Bridger. That's a good thing."

A woman's voice interrupts us over the intercom system. "Ladies and gentlemen, please take your seats. We're about to begin."

I can see Mom over Professor March's shoulder, waving us over to the table where she and Grandma are already sitting. Shan mumbles a goodbye and walks past him, but Professor March places his hand on my shoulder.

"Are you staying out of trouble?" he asks quietly.

"Yeah. I just want to get good grades and get to Level 6 on time," I say.

"That's good. I know I've said it before, but let me know if I can help with anything."

I meet his eyes for a few seconds. I know Professor March is sincere now. I just wish I knew why Dad was so paranoid about him. His rationale was weak. Not how he used to be.

I join Mom, Grandma, and Shan at our table. Professor March strides to the front of the banquet hall and takes a seat at the Guest of Honor table, between his sister, Olivia March, and his mother, Rashida March. I remember his mother from when I was a kid. Dad didn't take us around the professor's mom too much because she was always busy with work, but the few times he did she was always kind.

General Anderson stands at the podium and says, "We have a special honor today. Not only are we celebrating Unity Day, but we're also celebrating the exemplary career of Brigadier General Rashida March, who has decided to retire from the Department of Temporal Affairs."

I'm surprised to hear that she's retiring. Professor March never said anything to me. Maybe he thought I had too many problems of my own to deal with. Still, I can't help but wonder why she's retiring now. I wonder if she could have been forced out—maybe because she's still advocating for creating more Dual Talents, while I know Anderson hates them.

Anderson goes on to state a long list of General March's accomplishments, but nothing about Project Firebird, which isn't really a surprise. I wonder what happened with that project after the day that Alora and I witnessed. From what Alora said, Anderson was leading the opposition, while General March was heading up the group that was adamantly for it. And now Anderson is the head of the entire military division. So maybe I can guess what happened to Firebird.

I wish I knew what Anderson wants with my dad. Why bother cloning *him*, out of all the deceased Time Benders out there? What made him so special?

I hear a loud sigh. Glancing to my left, I see that Grandma is sitting with her chin cupped in the palm of her hand. Her elbows are propped on the black tablecloth. "What a pompous ass," she mutters.

I smother a laugh. She's definitely right about that. But why does she hate Anderson so much? Her reaction to seeing him and Chancellor

Tyson in my room after my panic attack last month was so extreme. Does she know something about him that I don't?

I wonder if she would answer me if I ask her.

An hour into the banquet, I'm ready to slam my head against a wall. We've been subjected to speeches by General Anderson, Iliana Lopez—the head of the DTA's civilian division and Mom's boss—and Chancellor Tyson. It took *forever* before they even let General March say her words of thanks. But at least we got to eat during all that yapping. We were served real roast chicken with potatoes smothered in a creamy sauce and asparagus spears. Dessert was a choice of apple crumb pie or caramel cake; Shan and I took one of each. I haven't had anything that good since I stayed with Alora's Aunt Grace last year. And, well, Shan just likes to eat.

Thinking of Alora makes my stomach sink. I haven't talked to her since our fight last month. I have no idea if she wound up trying to contact her father. If she did, then it seems that nothing came of it. I haven't heard anything about him on the DataNet feed—and I'm sure I would have, if she'd found him.

The truth is that I'm not even mad at her. I never really was. Well, the way she reacted to what I said irritated me, but it wasn't that big of a deal. No, the reason I've stayed away is because of my father and his threat to turn her in.

I suppress a sigh. I still don't agree with Dad on that. I love him and would do anything for him, willingly, but forcing my hand like this isn't like him. But what can I do? I don't want Alora to get in trouble. So severing ties with her was all I could do.

My DataLink chimes. It's Elijah.

"Can I talk to him?" I ask Mom.

She seems unsure at first, then says, "Fine. Take it out to the hallway. But make it quick. It sounds like they're about to make the closing remarks, and I want to beat the crowd out of here."

"It's about time you replied, man," Elijah says. "How much longer are you gonna be stuck at that banquet?"

"Not too much longer. Why?"

"See if you can come out with Zed and me for a while. We haven't had a chance to go out together in weeks."

He's right about that. Since the shooting, Mom and Grandma won't let us go anywhere without one of them chaperoning us. It sucks, but what can I do? Even Dad asked me to lie low until he can implement his plan.

I peek back into the banquet hall. Anderson is blabbing at the podium again. That man must really love the sound of his own voice. I finish talking to Elijah, then take my seat again and whisper to Mom, "Can I go celebrate with Elijah and Zed for a while?"

Mom shakes her head. "I don't think that's a good idea."

My stomach sinks. Normally I'd have a sarcastic response, but I know why she's so hesitant, and I can't really blame her.

So I'm surprised when Grandma speaks up. "Morgan, let the poor boy go for a while. He's been cooped up with us for weeks. And besides, most of the perps from the shooting last month were caught. He should be fine."

Mom seems uncertain, so I say, "I have my DataLink, so you'll know where I am at all times."

She huffs out a sigh. "Oh, all right. But if you see anything suspicious, get to an officer immediately to report it."

"Thank you," I say, jumping up again. I notice Shan watching me. "Do you want to come, too?" I ask him.

He quickly shakes his head. "No, I'd rather stay here," he says.

That doesn't surprise me, either. It makes me sad, though.

Elijah said that he and Zed would wait for me in the courtyard in front of the DTA building. Once I'm outside, Zed slides his left arm around my shoulders. "Dude, I can't believe Morgan set you free. I could cry."

"Knock it off, Zed," Elijah says. "We haven't been able to go out, either, until today."

"But at least we've been together most weekends. Poor, poor Bridger has suffered alone."

I find myself grinning. It's good to get out with them today. It's not the same just hanging out at the Academy. This is real freedom. I've missed it.

As soon as we get to the square where the main Unity Day activities take place, Elijah says, "Hey, I think I see Tara over there." He points to a small clearing between the trees planted around the exterior of the square, towards the area next to a stage that boasts a band playing a song that was popular just before the Second Civil War broke out. Ironic, because the song talks about what you need to sacrifice to have peace. Apparently, nobody listened to it carefully.

We have to push through way too many people to get close to the stage. I'm starting to wonder how Elijah even saw Tara through this mess when we reach the clearing.

But then I understand. He didn't see Tara. He already knew she was there.

Because she's not alone. Tara is there with another girl with bright pink hair, sitting on a bench on the outskirts of the crowd.

And Alora is with them.

31

I don't know what to say. As soon as Zed and Elijah walk up with Bridger trailing behind them, I realize I've been set up.

My head swivels from Everly to Tara. "Seriously? You two had to do this?"

"You need to get over whatever little spat you two had," Tara says to me. "I can see you've been miserable, and when I'm with the boys, it's obvious Bridger isn't happy either. You two need to talk."

Everly holds up both hands. "Hey, I'm going along with what Tara said. I don't know anything about him," she says with a glance at Bridger, "But I do know that you're not acting the same as you used to. You're more . . . sullen."

My first thought is to tell them that they're ridiculous, but that would be a complete lie. I've carried around a heaviness for the past month, and it all started with the fight with Bridger, and immediately after finding my father—only to discover that he had been forced to kill all those people to protect me. Which is why I told Professor March, who in turned informed his sister at the DTA. From there, she delivered the information as a tip from an anonymous source. I got some satisfaction, at least, from learning that most everyone at that farm house had been arrested.

And that didn't include Dad. He got away.

But it's been still been hard to get through each day, and I'm not sure I would have made it without my mom, Tara, and Everly. The girls have been my lifeline. Even though they don't know what I learned about my Dad, they both noticed that I was sinking into an abyss afterward, and they tried to cheer me up. Soon, we were spending time together at school every evening before curfew.

I lace my fingers together in my lap and stare at them. What should I do? Get up and go find Mom? She's shopping at the vendor booths with Everly's mom. They became fast friends just as Everly and I did. It's through my mom that I learned that Everly and her mother applied to come to the US to get away from Everly's abusive father. No matter where they went in England, he always followed, ignoring the restraining orders they had against him. They were only able to escape him by getting approval from the NAF to come here, where he couldn't follow. The NAF would never agree to let a freaking psychopath like him in the country.

Elijah pushes Bridger forward. "What are you waiting for, man? Go talk to her. We'll give you some privacy."

Zed gives us a wolfish grin. "Yeah, I'm sure you two could use a little of what I saw the last time you were together."

Heat blooms in my cheeks while Bridger glares at him. "Will you shut up?" he says.

Zed clutches his chest, still grinning. "Oh, the heartache I'm experiencing. Your words slay me, Creed."

My lips twitch. God, I didn't realize how much I've missed being around Elijah and Zed until now. So I decide to give in. "Oh, fine. I'll talk to you," I say to Bridger.

Tara and Everly scramble to stand. I shake my head at them. "You two owe me."

"Oh no, I think you'll owe us. Right, Ev?" Tara says.

"Absolutely. Now to figure out how she can repay us."

"You can leave now," Bridger says, still scowling.

Tara loops her arm through Elijah's. "I want to dance. And don't even think about telling me no."

Elijah gets a pained look on his face. "You know I have no rhythm."

"I do, and I don't care," she answers as she pulls him away. Over her shoulder, she calls out, "We'll be back soon. Ev, get Zed out of there."

Zed turns to Everly and holds out his arm to her. "Care to join me, beautiful?"

She raises her eyebrows. "I'm just gonna tell you up front. I'm not into boys, so don't even think about hitting on me."

Zed doesn't miss a beat. "Well, that's unfortunate for me, but whatever. We can get something to eat. I haven't been invited to any feasts—unlike Bridger here."

Everly looks like she's not sure what to think about Zed, but she says, "You know, you're really odd. But I think we'll get along." Her eyes cut to me. "I hope we do, anyway."

After they're gone, Bridger sits on the bench next to me, careful not to touch me. We watch the crowd all around us. There don't seem to be as many Purists in the audience as there are Gen Mods. I had such a hard time identifying Gen Mods at first, but it's become easier over time. Almost every Gen Mod looks, well, perfect. Perfect skin, unless they have a scar like my mom's. Perfect hair. Perfectly proportioned bodies. Many are Talents, but they're impossible to tell unless they're wearing a uniform.

Bridger looks at me, his eyes wary. "I thought you hated me."

I lean back a little, surprised. "I don't hate you. Well, I did a little bit, then, but I had the right." I force myself to look him in the eye. "You dismissed everything I said the last time we were together. Why wouldn't you listen to me?"

"You know why," he says, looking around nervously. "This was a bad idea. What if my dad is spying on us again? He'll make good on his threat to turn you in."

"I don't think he will. I mean, if he wanted to, he would have done it already. How long has it been since you talked to last talked to him?" I ask.

"Over a month," Bridger replies.

"You know what I think? I think he's been too busy going on what-ever missions Anderson has been assigning to him. Try to relax. At least for today."

Bridger flashes a grin at me, displaying his dimples. "I'll try. So what's been going on with you? Did you ever go in search of your father?"

Here it is, the moment of truth. Answer honestly and risk rejection, or lie? But I don't want to lie anymore. Carefully, I say, "I did find him."

A tiny crease forms between Bridger's eyes, and nothing else. "Okay. And how did that go?"

My mouth goes dry. "Things weren't that great."

I tell him about the Purist compound run by Jode Lincoln, where Dad was practically being held prisoner. How they were threatening to hurt me to control him, how he wouldn't leave with me because he thought he was a monster.

"What did he do that made him think he was that bad?" Bridger asks.

If there was a time to stretch the truth, this would be it. But I don't want any more secrets between us. Still, I can't look directly at Bridger as I say, "Dad was the gunman at the museum massacres. They forced him to shift back in time over and over again, until he shot up all the museums that Jode Lincoln had chosen."

Bridger's eyes seem to bulge out and his face flushes. "He *what*? He was the person who hurt my brother?"

Oh God, I didn't think of how that information would affect Bridger. Now he will hate my father forever.

Bridger starts to say something, but the deafening sound of an explosion cuts him off. Fire and smoke shoot up into the sky to our right. Screams pierce the air like knives, and people begin running, trying to flee the area. Then another blast goes off to our left. And thirty seconds later, another goes off directly across from us.

I jump to my feet, but Bridger grabs my hand.

"Wait a second," he says, his eyes searching the crowd. My instinct is to get away as fast as I can. What if another explosion goes off closer to us? But I also understand what he's doing—we need to find our friends.

Elijah and Tara run at us through the throng of people trying to flee. When they reach us, Tara asks, "Did you see what happened?"

"No. Did you?" I ask.

"No," Elijah replies.

"Have you seen Zed and Everly?" Bridger asks.

Elijah and Tara shake their heads. Bridger suggests splitting up to find them, but I don't want any part of that. "We need to stay together, no matter what," I say.

They agree and we slip into the surge of people still running past us. My mom and Everly's find us first—she must have been tracking my DataLink. Mom throws her arms around me, and I feel her shaking. "Oh, sweetheart, I'm so happy you're okay."

"Where's Everly?" her mother asks in a frantic voice.

"She went with our friend Zed," I say. "We're looking for them now."

"I'll track her," she says, lifting her wrist to check her DataLink. "I thought she'd be with you."

I look at the ground. Everly was supposed to stay with me. I hope she's okay. She *has* to be okay.

I glance at Mom, but she's not focusing on me anymore. Her eyebrows shoot up when she sees Elijah and Tara. And when her eyes land on Bridger, standing off to the side, she looks stunned.

"It's you," she whispers, her face turning even paler. "Both of you remember?"

My heart skips a beat. Of all the places for her to learn the truth about Bridger and me, it had to be here. But I can't worry about that now. "Mom, we need to find Everly and Zed. We can talk later."

"Right. This isn't over," she replies, her eyes slitting at Bridger.

Everly's mother points behind in front of us. "I see her! Over there."

We all set off, dodging people who are still trying to run away. We call out Everly's name.

She turns around, her arms clutched against her chest. I gasp and her mother screams. She's covered with soot and blood.

Her mom races to her and yells, "Are you hurt?"

As we catch up, we hear Everly's response. "It's not my blood. It's not mine." She's sobbing, shaking. "He was right there . . . I left him in line because I needed to use the restroom, but I didn't get that far when I heard the explosion. I tried . . . I went back and tried to save him and I couldn't. I couldn't save him, Mom."

She turns to look behind her, and lets out a wail again.

Bridger's face loses all color. Elijah shakes his head slowly in disbelief. Police officers are screaming at everyone to clear the area. What's left of a nearby food booth is in flames, and injured people are scattered all around the blast perimeter. A few are writhing and moaning in pain. Most aren't moving. There's so much blood everywhere. And something else. As we advance, I realize what it is.

Parts of bodies.

My stomach lurches and I get a flashback of seeing Dad's body when he died in 1994, when his consciousness was uploaded by the team of Time Benders who recorded everything.

And then we see Zed.

Or what's left of him.

32

'm sitting on the edge of Zed's bed in our quarters. The room is barren now, devoid of his personality since both of his fathers cleared out his belongings yesterday. I glance down at the shimmery red shirt I'm wearing with a pair of black pants. It's an antique from the 1970s, with long, loose sleeves. The collar is the worst. It's long and pointed. I've always hated it, but it was one of Zed's favorites. He said it was his lucky shirt. If only he'd had it on at the Unity Day celebration.

I'm just happy that his fathers said I could have it.

My DataLink chimes. I think about ignoring it, but I'm sure it's Mom.

"Where are you?" she asks, her face twisted in worry. Her dark hair is pulled back from her face, and she's wearing a red dress. In the background I can see other people standing, all wearing red, too. She's already at the memorial ceremony at the Academy's ballroom in the main building. Red is the color for today, since it was Zed's favorite. My thoughts drift back to Vika's memorial ceremony. Everybody wore blue on that day. It feels like forever since that happened.

"I'm still in my room," I say. "I'll be there in a few minutes. Is Shan already there?"

"He is." She pauses for a second. "Do you need me to come over there? It'll just take me a few minutes."

"No, Mom, I'm fine. I'm leaving right now."

After I disconnect the comm, I look down at the shirt again. Red for Zed. Red for all the blood that covered him and the others who were blown up by those damn Purists. Most of the Purists who orchestrated the mass shootings last month had already been arrested. But more popped up, placing bombs in several cities during their Unity Day celebrations. It's like a saying about the villains from some ancient movies Dad used to love. You cut off one head, and two more appear to take its place. The ache in my chest begins to expand, threatening to devour me. My breathing grows labored.

I stagger out of Zed's room and into mine. Calmer, I need Calmer. Once I grab a vial from my dresser and inject it, I feel less panicky. But the emptiness is still there. I wonder if it will ever entirely go away.

I wish Elijah was here, but he didn't come to school today. He's been having an even harder time with Zed's death than I am.

I barely take two steps past the guard posted outside the residence hall before my DataLink chimes. I check it, thinking it's Mom again. But it's a text that instructs me to go to the back side of Phoenix Hall. I don't recognize the sender. I think about ignoring it, but curiosity gets to me. I head to my right, where the Rockies sit on the horizon, then circle around the building. Someone is standing at the rear corner, motioning for me to hurry.

It's Ellis.

He's still dressed exactly the way he was before—shabby clothes and cloth around his face.

I storm over to him and grab him by his jacket. His eyes go wide before he does a slick maneuver that easily pushes me away. I'm surprised. He's stronger than he looks.

"What's wrong with you?" he asks. "I told you I would come back right before the bioweapon attack to warn you. It's going to happen in two days, so you need to be ready to leave tomorrow, when I come for you. Your top priority is to prepare your mom, brother, and Alora to evacuate."

"You knew about the Unity Day bombings, didn't you?" I say, poking him in the chest. "Why didn't you tell me? One of my best friends died, and if you had said something, I could've saved him!"

He has enough sense to look away. "Look, I'm sorry. But my mission is to preserve the timeline up until the bioweapon attack. That's the only way I'll be able to stop it."

I throw my hands up. "How could saving Zed's life change the bioweapon attack?"

"I know how much it hurts. Believe me, I've lost everybody that I love. *Everybody.*" Ellis inhales sharply and looks away for a moment. "But sometimes sacrifices have to be made. If I had warned you, then that could've changed the plans for the bioweapon. Its location, the date it's detonated—any change would prevent me from stopping it. I need things to go exactly the way they already have in *my* past. I can only change things at the time of detonation."

Anger consumes me. "So what you're telling me is that it's just fine for you to come here and prevent the bioweapon attack in order to save everyone *you* love, but I can't do the same? And what about all the other people who died in the bombing? Who died in the shootings last month? They're not important? And what if you can't prevent the bioweapon from being detonated? Don't you think we should be warning people instead of trying to get a few of us to hide?"

"You're talking about a small number of people, Bridger. I'm talking about billions. Don't you get it? I'm trying to prevent what amounts to genocide. The only way I can do that is to take out the person responsible for the bioweapon."

It's as if someone poured ice over my head. My body chills to the core. "You know, I do get it," I say between gritted teeth. "But you shouldn't discount the people who just died. They didn't deserve it."

Ellis shakes his head, looking sad. "Nobody ever does. Now, can you please be ready tomorrow?"

"I'll try," I snarl before walking away. Over my shoulder, I call out, "Today I have to say goodbye to someone who doesn't mean a damn thing to you."

The last memorial ceremony I attended was Vika's. It was here at the Academy, too, and I only made it through because I had Zed and Elijah. And now I'm here for Zed's memorial ceremony. It isn't right. This shouldn't be happening.

I keep playing over and over in my mind the last time I saw Zed. I was a furing idiot for snapping at him. He was just joking. That was Zed: always joking about something. Sometimes it irritated me, how he never seemed to take things seriously. But to be honest, that's part of why we were friends. He had a way of making things a little brighter.

The world is a much bleaker place without him in it.

I look to my right, where Elijah and Tara sit beside me. Elijah is in a black suit with a red shirt, and Tara wears a floor-length red dress. The chairs lining the walls of the ballroom are mostly empty right now while the mourners mingle. I catch snatches of conversations. Some people are reminiscing about Zed. He was well-known on campus. But a lot are still gossiping about the bombing. How the government said we would be safe after they raided Jode Lincoln's compound and took most of the inhabitants into custody. But clearly we weren't.

Yesterday, President Tremblay announced that they had identified Lincoln as one of the Unity Day bombers—and that he had been killed along with the blast's victims. He was the only one of the bombers who died. Investigators say it appears that Lincoln was going to place a bomb at the food booth where Zed and Everly were waiting in line to get their lunch. But a military officer stationed in the crowd recognized Lincoln and tried to arrest him. But the officer's gun went off, killing Lincoln. And apparently the bomb was connected to Jode—when he died, it triggered the explosion. Zed was caught up in the blast simply because he was at the wrong place at the wrong time.

The feds also learned that while Lincoln had been living on his farm, he'd been stirring up a lot of Purists online. And when the Responsible Citizen Act was passed, it sent him into a frenzy of hate because he and his wife couldn't afford cancer treatments for their ten-year-old son, just like he said before the museum shootings. Lincoln talked a lot about bringing down the government. But it was all done through secret virtual chat rooms and people that he recruited to train at his farm, including hackers. That's how Lincoln was able to cover his tracks for so long, until the raid on his farm, when his wife and son and most of his recruits were taken into custody. Apparently Lincoln and the one other person who managed to escape were among the terrorists who planted bombs at the Unity Day ceremony. Fortunately, the others bombers were captured and confessed everything.

They said only one of the bombers was still on the run. Hopefully they can find him soon. Supposedly, he was shot in the shoulder before he shifted.

I'm shaken out of my thoughts when Elijah says, "This is so messed up." He's staring straight ahead, his face a stone mask. But his eyes are glassy. Tara is holding his hand, trying to make him feel better.

I focus on holding my own hands still because they've started shaking. I should have taken a double dose of Calmer. Because right now I want to hit something. Hurt somebody the same way I'm hurting.

Ellis is at the top of my list. I should have decked him outside.

Pressure is building in my head. I absently rub my temples, thinking a migraine is coming on. Then I hear Tara suck air in through her teeth.

"Who's Ellis and what did he do to piss you off?" she asks.

I turn to glare at her. "Don't ever read my mind again without my permission."

She holds up her palms to me. "I'm sorry, but you looked like you were about to wild out over there."

"Next time ask," I snarl. "That's what normal people do."

"Would you two stop it?" Elijah asks, his eyes now brimming with tears. "Now is not the time to bring him up. We can deal with Ellis later."

"You're right. I'm sorry," Tara says to Elijah.

None of us say anything for a while. It's too hard. If Zed were here, he'd be cracking jokes or doing something to make us smile. I'm going to miss that about him.

Tara sits up and waves at Alora, who we can see pushing her way through the crowd. She's in a knee-length red and gray dress with her hair slung over one shoulder in a braid.

She's beautiful.

I look away, thinking how Zed would have noticed me staring and made a smart remark. I'd give anything to hear that now.

"Hey, I didn't think you would be here," Tara says once Alora reaches us.

Glancing over her shoulder, Alora says, "I didn't either. It took a lot of convincing to get my Mom to let me come today. She really doesn't want me to come to school at all this week."

Her eyes seek out mine. I know what she isn't saying. Her mom doesn't want her around me now that she knows Alora and I remember each other. Just like my dad doesn't want me around Alora.

In the aftermath of the bombing, Adalyn pulled me to the side and told me that she wouldn't turn us in. But she wanted us to stay apart—she was afraid that being seen together would raise too many suspicions. She's right. And then there's my dad and his threat to have Alora's memories erased again.

Why can't everyone leave us alone? Let us live our lives the way we want?

"Where is your mom now?" Tara asks.

"She was cornered by Professor March. I figured that would be a good time to slip away."

"What about Everly?" I ask.

"She's not coming. Her mom is thinking about transferring somewhere else. Somewhere safer."

"That's ridiculous," Tara says. "They've caught the people responsible."

Elijah starts breathing hard, and he stands abruptly. "I've got to get out of here. I can't do this."

He doesn't wait for us, and we rush after him. He heads to the double doors that lead to the lobby of the main building. We catch up to him leaning his forehead against the glass wall facing the campus. Tears stream down his face.

I don't know what else to do other than hug him. Behind him, Tara and Alora both have tears sliding down their cheeks. The only reason I'm numb is because of the Calmer. Otherwise I'd be a sniveling mess right now.

We stand there for I don't know how long. When Elijah finally pulls away from me, he wipes his face and says, "Can you imagine what Zed would say? He'd be laughing and calling us a bunch of babies."

"Or worse," I add.

"I wish I'd known him better," Alora whispers, coming to my side. "I didn't know him long, but he was my friend, too." Her eyes seek out Elijah and Tara. "Just like you're my friends. I don't want to lose any of you."

I think about Ellis again. How he claimed everything had to happen in a certain order so he can stop the bioweapon detonation. I get what he's trying to do. And yet, how could he let so many people die the other day? Fifty-seven people lost their lives.

And I remember what Dad said to me the last time I saw him. That General Anderson has been manipulating events because he claims they had to happen to maintain the timeline. What if the DTA has been doing other things like that? Going back and making minor changes to suit their needs, using Anderson's excuse as justification?

I'm sick of the DTA lying to us. Lying about what happened to me and Alora, taking our memories. Lying about the existence of Dual Talents. Lying about not cloning people anymore.

Surely if they can get away with those things, then we can too.

"Let's go back," I say to Alora. "We still have the Chronobands. It's only been a few days. How much could we alter the timeline by saving Zed—and maybe a few others?"

Alora doesn't say anything right away.

But Tara does. "Are you serious? Bridger, you could completely destroy the timeline by doing that. The rules are in place for a reason."

I look to Elijah for support, but he slowly shakes his head. "She's right, man. You know I'd give anything to get Zed back. But we can't change what's already happened."

I back away. "No, I don't believe that. Ellis is planning to change the timeline. If he's going to save everybody, then why can't we save Zed?"

Alora has been quiet, but now she speaks up. "I don't see how going back a few days could hurt. I mean, we shouldn't only be able to travel to the past to record history or save artifacts. We should be able to change things if they're really recent."

Hearing her say that makes me feel more alive than I have in days. "Then let's go. Now."

Elijah's mouth drops open. "Bridger, you can't do that. And you can't miss the memorial ceremony."

I grab Alora's hand and head toward the rear exit. "This ceremony won't exist soon."

I want to break into a run across the grassy area that's between the main building and the rest of the buildings on campus, but I force myself to walk. I keep looking over my shoulder, but nobody is following us.

"Do you have your Chronoband in your room?" I ask.

"It's at home, but I can get it."

"Okay. Get that and the comm-set, and change into your uniform."

As soon as we enter my quarters, Alora shifts. I race to my room and dress as fast as possible. Right after I finish, Alora reappears next to my bed. Her face is flushed.

"Since we're shifting from here, we need to go back to at least an hour before the bombs go off to give us time to get downtown."

"You mean to give *you* time?" Alora asks.

I take her by the hands. "I know you want to just pop over and do this yourself, but we need to stick together on this one. It's too dangerous for us to be alone."

"Then let's do this," she says, punching in the destination date on her Chronoband.

I barely have time to do the same before the door to my quarters slides open. Professor March enters, followed by Elijah and Tara.

"You told him?" I ask, feeling my face warm.

Elijah can't even meet my eyes. "I'm sorry, man, but you can't do this."

"Why?" I ask. "We can save them. Don't you want that?"

"We didn't want you and Alora to get in trouble. So I thought we should bring Professor March to convince you," Tara says.

The professor steps past them, hands on his hips. "And it's a good thing they did. You two need to think about what you're doing. You might as well throw your lives away if you do this."

Alora's brows are creased and she looks from Professor March to me.

"I don't care anymore," I say to her. "Let's do it."

"No, Bridger, please!" Professor March pleads. "If you do this, I won't be able to help you this time."

Even though Dad doesn't trust Professor March anymore, I know now that the professor cares about me. But now he's starting to sound like a hypocrite.

"Yeah, sure. It was okay for you to take part in interfering with events just because Anderson ordered you to. Breaking the law is fine if the order comes from a big shot at the DTA."

The professor's brow knits. "You know that was different. Anderson knew those events had to take place. What you're going to do will have unknown consequences."

"Okay, fine, I get that. You did what you had to do because of orders. But I've been talking to a Time Bender from our future who says he's going to stop a bioweapon attack that's supposed to happen two days from now. I think Dad is working to help stop it, too. So if they can do that, why can't I save Zed?"

The look on Professor March's face is almost comically shocked. "What do you mean? Leithan is dead, Bridger."

"No he's not," I say. "General Anderson had him cloned."

"That's not possible," the professor says, taking a step back.

I glance at Elijah. "Show him the Sim that Ellis gave me. It's in my portacase."

"Bridger, what do you want to do?" Alora asks again, glancing toward the door.

Professor March shakes his head. "Bridger, Alora, don't do this. We need to talk instead. Tell me about Leithan. About the Time Bender from the future. Everything."

I'm done talking. I'm done having others deciding my fate.

"Now, Alora. Shift!"

33

ALORA
MARCH 30, 2147

As soon as we emerge from the Void, we take off running. It's weird, thinking that Zed is still alive on this date. I just hope we can reach him in enough time to save him.

It takes us nearly forty minutes to get to the New Denver terminal. We hadn't taken into account that the transport shuttles to and from the Academy only run at certain times, so Bridger and I had to wait twenty minutes in the shuttle at the Academy's transport lot, with our cloaks on so no one knew we were in the shuttle. To make it worse, only one other cadet even boarded the shuttle. Most everyone else had already gone to New Denver earlier in the day for the celebrations.

I was about ready to scream. I mean, I could have shifted straight to New Denver and found Zed already, but Bridger did have a point about sticking together.

As soon as the shuttle touches down in New Denver, Bridger jumps out of his seat and pushes past the lone cadet. I almost laugh at his expression. He had no clue that he wasn't alone.

"If we somehow get separated, meet me at the fountain on the southern side of the square, where the celebrations took place," Bridger says.

"Okay, but don't you think that's too close to where the first bomb exploded?" I ask. The targeted booth—a Purist attraction selling antique jewelry retrieved from the past—was on the right side of the large square, the fountain on the left.

Bridger shakes his head. "It's far enough away from the blast radius. We'll be fine."

The next few minutes are a blur of pushing through I don't know how many citizens. Their clothes blend together into an endless swirl of color. Somehow I tune out all of their chatter and hear only the sound of my breathing and my feet pounding on the pavement.

Bridger checks his DataLink. "Hurry! It's about to happen!"

I try to run harder, make myself move faster, but it's impossible when you're constantly having to dodge people.

That's why we're a block away from the square when the first explosion hits.

I recoil in horror. We're too late. But still, we keep running.

When we reach the square, Bridger slows to a stop, his mouth parting in surprise.

Everywhere, we see white outlines of people through our comm-sets, indicating cloaked Time Benders. Near the booth that just exploded, several are hunched over some bodies, the outlines of their hands hovering over the foreheads of the dying.

"Bridger, go! We can make it!" I scream.

We take off again, and barely get three steps away before the second blast hits—the one directly across from the first. That means we have thirty seconds to get to Zed. He was killed in the third blast, when the officer shot and killed Jode Lincoln.

But it's even harder to move now that everyone around us is screaming, shoving, and trying to get away.

"We're not gonna make it," I say, tears filling my eyes. It's not fair. We're so close.

Bridger ignores me and keeps pushing his way through. It's only when the third explosion happens that he stops. We stand helpless, staring at the smoky ruins just ahead of us. Cloaked Time Benders are already appearing, uploading the consciousnesses of more dying Talents. But again, only certain ones.

Why are they doing that?

I can't help but notice that there is no cloaked Time Bender around the area where I know Zed's body lies. I let out a choked sob. This is so beyond cruel, having to watch his death again.

Bridger says, in a strained voice, "We can go back again. Let's go somewhere clear and shift back thirty minutes."

"I don't think so," says a voice from behind us, just as two powerful hands grab my arms.

34

BRIDGER
APRIL 4, 2147

The holding cell I'm in at the DTA building is small. Much smaller than the one I was in last year at The Black Hole. Back when I thought I was going to be Nulled, thanks to General Anderson and his manipulations.

I wonder if Grandma knows what I've done. It doesn't really matter if she does or not. I broke the law, and now I'll suffer the consequences.

I'm sitting at a table in the room, and I'm shackled with an Inhibitor. There isn't anything else in here. And I've been in here for over an hour. I don't know what they're waiting for. Whatever it is, I wish they'd just do it.

So, when the door to the cell finally opens, I feel a slight sense of relief. That is, until I see who it is. The puppet master himself, along with my dad. I'm shocked to see Dad with Anderson. I thought nobody at the DTA was supposed to know that Dad had been cloned.

The last time General Anderson visited me in a cell, he played up the bad-tempered act so I'd completely trust Professor March when he came in afterwards to talk to me. This time, he appears to be much calmer. Dad, though, looks as if he's been in a fight recently. His hair is messed up, and his right eye is bruised.

"Hello, son," Dad says calmly, as if everything's perfectly normal.

"What happened to you?" I ask.

Dad snorts. "Oh, nothing much. Just had a little trouble. Everything's fine."

A worried look briefly crosses the general's face, but then he composes himself and asks, "How are you, Bridger? Are you comfortable?"

I stare at him incredulously. I broke the law, and he wants to know if I'm comfortable?

"What's going to happen to me?" I ask, looking from Dad to General Anderson. "Am I going to be Nulled for real this time?"

"You're not going to be Nulled, son," the general says. "I told you once before, I always take care of my own."

I cringe, but keep my mouth shut, still wondering what the hell he means by that. In the meantime, maybe I can get some answers out of him. Namely, why did he clone my dad in the first place? What did he gain by doing that? That's the one thing I could never get Dad to answer.

Before I say anything else, my eyes drift up to one of the cameras in the room.

"Don't worry about those," General Anderson says, following my gaze. "I had them turned off."

That really unsettles me. "Why would you do that?"

General Anderson exchanges an amused look with Dad, but doesn't answer. He shakes his head and pinches the bridge of his nose. "Bridger, I've done so much for you, and yet you keep messing everything up. It's like you're deliberately trying to sabotage yourself. How could you even fathom going back and trying to save your friend's life? He's dead. He's never coming back."

"That's funny, because you didn't think twice about having Vika and Dad cloned last year. And there's the fact that I saw a lot of cloaked Time Benders uploading the consciousnesses of Talents killed in the bombing, But nobody did that for Zed. Why?"

I'm not sure what I expect to hear, but it's not a chuckle from Dad. "Now we're getting to the good stuff."

That's a punch to my gut. Why would he mock my grief at Zed's death? This isn't like Dad at all.

"To answer your question, the Talents we chose to upload at the Unity Day bombing are valuable to us. We simply have to clone their bodies and reanimate them when we need them," Dad says, now grinning.

The general glares at him. "Enough of that, Leithan." Turning his attention back to me, he says, "Bridger, you know a lot of things you shouldn't know. I had your memories erased for a reason. There are some things you can't know just yet. You're not ready. All I ask is that you trust me and your father right now. We're going to take care of you and Shan."

The door to the cell opens again. This time Grandma enters, looking livid. "Why wasn't I told before now that my grandson is being held?"

General Anderson waves a dismissive hand at her. "It wasn't necessary at the time. But now you know."

Her face turns pale when she notices Dad. For a moment, I think that Grandma might faint. She leans to the side for a second, then squares her feet on the ground. "Leithan?" she asks tentatively.

"I wasn't expecting a family reunion so soon," Dad says. "Hello, Mama. I've missed you." He opens his arms wide, like he expects a hug.

Grandma regains her composure lightning fast. Glaring at the general, she asks, "You cloned him? What stabilizer is he using?"

"Clonitin 28."

"And how is it working?"

"Like a charm," Dad says. He comes over to stand next to Grandma. "It's *me*, Mama. Same memories, almost same body—just a newer model."

Grandma seems unsure of what to do. "I never thought I'd see you again."

Her arms twitch, as if she wants to reach out and hug him, but she remains still. Then, looking directly at General Anderson, she asks, "Why did you do this?"

"That's not necessary for you to know, Judith," General Anderson says.

"Oh, come on," Dad says. "This is getting ridiculous."

The general doubles down, saying, "I will decide when or if I will share that information. Now is not the time."

"Dad's right," I say. "This is ridiculous! I'm sick of everyone saying we can't know the truth. Just tell us what's going on!" I'm yelling so hard my voice is strained.

"Don't," the general warns Dad.

But Dad ignores him and focuses on me. "The answer is simple. You already know that my mother chose to use a sperm donor in order to have me. What you don't know is that she was matched with the general. He offered to be a part of my life, but *she* refused. So, in a nutshell, General Anderson is your grandfather. That's why he cloned me. That's why he did all that investigating when I died, why he covered everything up. All because we're family." He lets out a crazed-sounding laugh. "Now, are you finally satisfied?"

The rest of the world seems to shrink away. I can't believe it. All of that elaborate scheming. All of it was because the general wanted to protect my father. His son.

I look up at Grandma, hoping she will deny everything. She doesn't. She's too busy glaring daggers in the general's direction. At least he has the sense to not say anything.

"May I have a few minutes alone with my grandson, *sir*?"

"Denied," he replies.

"And may I ask why?"

"Certainly. You're about to be transported."

Grandma places her hands on her hips. "I'm not going anywhere, and I won't allow you to take Bridger, either."

"Try and stop me, Judith," General Anderson sneers. "I outrank you, remember? You will go where I say to go."

I'm practically seeing red now, so I can imagine how Grandma feels.

Dad breaks the tension by clasping his hands together so loudly that the sound reverberates around the room. "Okay, this is getting awkward. I thought our family reunion would be a little less hostile."

"Where are Mom and Shan?" I ask.

"They're on the way now," General Anderson answers. "Or rather, your brother is. I'm not sure what Leithan decided to do with Morgan. I left that up to him."

"What did you say?" I stand up, ready to hurt the general. I refuse to think of him as my grandfather.

Dad laughs. Actually. Furing. Laughs. For the first time in my life, I want to punch him.

"She's fine, son. I went to retrieve Shan, and she didn't want him to go. I didn't listen to her."

"You better not have hurt her!" I shout.

"Are you kidding? She hurt me. Look at this." Dad points to his injured eye. "It's gonna be swollen for days."

I begin to pace. All I can think about is getting away, finding out what happened to them. "I'm not going anywhere with you."

"You don't have a choice," the general says. "In fact, the transport is already here. We really should be going."

"You never said where you want to take us," Grandma says.

Dad and General Anderson exchange a look that I don't like. I stop pacing. This must be the part where they admit that the Purists are planning to detonate the bioweapon.

"You're going to an underground military base thirty miles north of here," Dad says.

"Why?"

"Because it's time for The Cleansing," Dad says. He's grinning, as if this is the best news he's ever shared.

But my stomach sinks. Ellis never said who detonated the bomb, but I figured it would be Purists. But the way Dad said those words leave me with a sick feeling. A cold uncertainty forms in my chest, slowly spreading out to numb me. This can't be right. Dad is supposed to save innocent people, not kill them. I can only stare at him, blinking, wondering if I heard him correctly. But I know I did.

"What's that supposed to mean?" Grandma asks in a sharp voice.

"That's none of your concern now," General Anderson says. He makes like he's going to leave the room, but Dad rushes ahead and blocks the door. "What are you doing?" the general asks.

"They have to know the truth," Dad replies, still smiling.

Anderson looks back at Grandma and me before telling Dad, in a more forceful voice, "Now is *not* the time."

Dad ignores him and charges on, talking to Grandma and me. "This society is sick. Full of Purists who are nothing but a burden. And now we've introduced Dual Talents, who are increasing in number and will one day overthrow us if we don't stop them. Not to mention regular Talents who support those abominations, and thus are dangerous."

"How could you call Dual Talents abominations?" I ask. "They're people just like us. They're just more evolved."

"Bridger, you have to be smarter than that. You've studied history. You've even *traveled* through history. You know what happens when a group of people become stronger than others. They eventually destroy those who are weaker. Dual Talents, like it or not, are stronger than us. They have an edge over us, and they *will* destroy us one day. That's why we're stopping them now," Dad says.

"Leithan, don't tell them anything else," General Anderson commands, his face turning bright red.

But Grandma goads Dad to keep talking. "How exactly are you planning to do that?"

"We have supporters who've helped us develop a bioweapon. It's a bomb loaded with a virus that will target specific individuals. Since we already have access to every citizen's genetic material, our scientists have programmed the virus to only infect targeted people. We need to take them out before they hurt us," Dad says. "And what makes it even better is that, thanks to Jode Lincoln, the Purists will be blamed. Two problems solved with one shot."

Grandma is too horrified to speak.

I am too. Did Ellis know that my father and Anderson were responsible for the bioweapon? Somehow, I manage to ask, "Where will this bomb be set off?"

"At the banquet the DTA is having tomorrow in honor of the latest Sim Game that's about to be released. President Tremblay is flying in tonight so he can attend. He wanted to be here in person to see the effects of The Cleansing, since he's one hundred percent behind it," Dad says proudly.

Grandma stares at Dad in horror, then looks at General Anderson in disgust. "You two are monsters."

35

The restraints holding me to this table are cutting into my wrists. I tug at them anyway. I've got to get out of here, somehow. But I can't, not with this Inhibitor around my neck, courtesy of General Anderson. I remember how he seemed to take great pleasure in snapping the thin metal band in place, telling me that soon I'd be one less problem he'd have to deal with. He's fast replacing Palmer as my least favorite person ever.

After Bridger and I were captured at the Unity Day bombing, we were forced to shift back to the present, where we were transported to the DTA building and separated. I don't know where they took him. Maybe he's in a medical room like I am, waiting to have his memories erased again.

Soon I won't remember how much this room looks like the one Dad was in when he was resurrected.

My stomach sinks as the door slides open and a young woman in a navy-blue uniform enters. Something about her looks familiar, but that doesn't matter. She must be the person who's been assigned to wipe my memories. It's useless, but I try to shift anyway. Nothing.

The woman activates the lock on the door before coming over to me.

"Please don't do this," I say. "Don't turn me into a Null."

A hint of a smile touches her lips. "I'm not here to do that."

I try to flinch away, terrified of what will come next, but instead the woman shocks me by undoing the restraints.

I sit up, rubbing my wrists. "Why did you do that?"

"Because my brother, Telfair, asked me to. And when he asks for a favor, I know it's serious."

Suddenly it dawns on me who she's talking about. "Professor March is your brother, right?"

"Yes. I'm Captain Olivia March."

"Thank you," I say as I slide off the table. I feel a bit lightheaded after lying there for so long.

"No problem. Apparently, there are quite a few people out to eliminate Dual Talents. We need to help each other out whenever we can." She pauses, noticing my jaw dropping. "Yes, I'm also a Dual Talent, like Telfair. Now, moving on, I heard about what you and Bridger tried to do. You can't do that ever again. You have no idea what the consequences could be." This time she gives me a look that reminds me of Aunt Grace when she wasn't happy with me.

"Have you freed Bridger yet?" I ask.

"No. General Anderson is with him, and I think he's up to something. I checked and the cameras in their room have been shut off. I also know that Bridger is being transferred very soon. They're going to take him to a shuttle that's waiting on the roof."

"I need to get to him. Bridger says his father is going to do something to stop a bioweapon attack, but I'm not sure that he is."

"Wait, you're telling me that Leithan Creed is alive?" Captain March asks. "Telfair didn't say anything about that. He just said Bridger claimed that a bioweapon is supposed to be detonated soon."

"Okay, this is going to sound strange, but since you're a Mind Bender, I want you to do something for me."

"What, exactly?" she asks.

I steel myself for what I'm about to offer. "I want you to read my mind. You need to see what I've seen."

Her eyebrows shoot up in surprise, then she nods. "Okay. Just try to relax. It'll be a little uncomfortable for you."

That's the understatement of the year. Pressure builds deep in my head, throbbing against my skull. My fingers grip the table hard.

Finally, the pressure dissipates. Captain March takes a step back, covering her mouth with her left hand. "I had no idea. Tel left a lot of things out when we talked earlier."

"So, can you help me?" I ask, anxious to get moving.

"I wish I could, but I don't have enough proof to confront the general. What I *can* do is pretend I've been ordered to escort you up to a shuttle, as well. That way you and Bridger could try to steal it and get away from here."

"I can get there faster on my own," I say. I start to activate the cloak on my uniform, but Captain March grabs my arm first.

"Don't do that!" she cries. "The building is filled with sensors to detect cloaks. You'll set off an alarm the instant you use one."

Just great—now I feel like the most juvenile dunce in the world. I should have known that; we've talked about those sensors in class. After multiple Unknowns had been detected here over the years—Bridger and me included—techs developed a way to constantly monitor all buildings without having to run periodic scans.

Captain March takes a pair of cuffs out of her pocket. "Hold out your hands. This has to look authentic if it's going to work."

Reluctantly, I do as she asks. The cold metal bands click around my wrists. For a moment, I regret listening to her. What if this doesn't work, and we get caught? But then again, what choice do I have? Staying here and doing nothing isn't an option, and there aren't many people in the DTA that I know for certain I can trust. Not anymore.

The next few minutes stretch into eternity after we leave my room. Every time we pass someone, I lower my head, but still I can feel their eyes searching me.

Once we exit the elevator at the topmost level, we enter a small foyer with stairs leading up to a door. Captain March climbs the steps and peers through the small window in the door. "The shuttle is there, but I don't see anybody with it yet. It's starting to get dark."

She turns back to me and reaches into her pocket again, this time pulling out a small square key card. She swipes it across the cuffs and Inhibitor to remove them. Once they're off, she says, "Keep the key card. You'll need it for Bridger. Now, go. And good luck."

"Thank you, Captain," I say. "You don't know what this means to me."

"Hopefully we'll never have to do anything like this again. I hope this bioweapon attack can be stopped."

When she gets back into the elevator, I push my way through the door and run across the roof, trying to figure out a strategy. I'm not sure who will be with Bridger. Will it just be General Anderson, or will he have guards with him? And what if they have weapons?

But then I realize that, since I'm on the roof and not inside the building, I can use my cloak. At least I'll have the element of surprise.

I barely have time to press the button and when the door opens again. Bridger comes out first, looking extremely angry. He's being followed by an older woman, General Anderson, and Bridger's father. Mr. Creed looks the same as I remember from when I saw him in 2013.

General Anderson orders Bridger and the other woman to stop. Then he calls out, "Alora Mason, I know you're out here. I checked the surveillance feed and saw that Captain March just escorted you up here."

Blood rushes in my ears as my heart starts pounding. How could this happen? I stay quiet, hoping he's just bluffing.

"You might as well come out," he continues. "Or I'll be forced to send someone to capture your mother. And I promise it won't be a pleasant visit for her."

I hate that man so much. Picturing all the different ways I could hurt him, I lower my cloak and step forward.

Bridger shakes his head and shouts, "Get out of here, Alora! They're going to set off the bioweapon. The Purists aren't to blame! You have to get away!"

A trail of fear mixed with anger shoots through me. How could they do that to their own people? "Not without you," I reply.

Bridger's father steps forward. "How sweet. I remember what it was like to be young and in love. It sucked because the girl I really loved rejected me. You might know her, Alora."

It strikes me how messed up this whole situation is. Bridger's father is showing obvious signs of becoming unstable. He's wild-eyed and is wearing a maniacal grin, as if he's enjoying himself.

I swear, this could be the plotline of one of those soap operas Aunt Grace used to watch.

The older woman twists her head around to stare at Bridger's father. "My son would never act the way you are right now. You must be slipping."

I get a tiny surge of hope, hearing her say this. So this woman is Bridger's grandmother. Maybe she can help distract the general and Leithan so I can get Bridger on the shuttle. If I could only get her attention.

Bridger looks at his father, too. "Can Alora go with us? I won't resist or anything if you let her."

General Anderson's mouth curls into a cruel sneer. "There is no way I'm taking a Dual Talent with us. She's going back in a holding cell, and I'll deal with her later."

I focus on Bridger. If I can get the general and Bridger's father to try to capture me, Bridger and his grandmother can board the shuttle and lock the door. Then I can shift inside with them, and we can leave.

That could totally work. Or it could get me killed.

I steel myself. I have to do it. Locking my gaze on an area just next to the door to the roof, I close my eyes and shift.

When I reappear, I immediately shout, "Get to the shuttle, now!" All four heads swivel to face me.

Bridger falters for a moment, but his grandmother grabs him by the arm and tells him to go. General Anderson runs after them.

That's when I hear a deep voice from behind me. "Get behind me, Alora."

I glance over my shoulder and nearly sag in relief. It's my dad. I have no idea how he got away from Lincoln, but I'm thrilled. But he looks even worse than the last time I saw him. He's dressed all in black, and he's clutching his left arm against his chest. I wish desperately that I could hug him, tell him how much I still love him despite what Jode Lincoln forced him to do for so long.

But I can't right now.

After I scramble to get behind him, Dad raises his right hand at Mr. Creed and beckons for him make a move. "Come on, Creed. Let's see what you've got."

Mr. Creed's nostrils flare. "I promise, it's more than you can handle."

Dad yells for me to get to Bridger, then charges at Mr. Creed. I start to shift, but I'm glued to my spot. It's devastating to watch our fathers fighting each other, especially since I can see so much pain etched on Dad's face. Mr. Creed fires his weapon at Dad. Dad shifts behind him, tries to grab Mr. Creed around the neck, but he wrenches away and takes a swing at Dad's face.

"Alora, go!" Dad shouts, while trying to grab Mr. Creed's gun.

I finally snap out of my daze, just as Mr. Creed disentangles from Dad. He charges at me.

Dad yells for him to stop, but he doesn't listen. I close my eyes, concentrating on Bridger's face so I can shift directly to him. But before I can, Mr. Creed shoves me hard. I stagger, turning just as I hit the edge of the rooftop's edge. I lose my balance, and in an instant I tumble over the side.

The last thing I hear is my father crying out my name.

36

A scream tears out of my throat as I fall. This shouldn't be happening. This isn't how I should die.

The ground is fast approaching. I'm going to die unless I do something. Unless I can shift. I stare at the space directly below me, then close my eyes, picturing the pavement below in my mind. Picturing myself, standing there.

Please work. *Please.*

And then I feel solid ground beneath my feet. My knees immediately buckle, and I crumple to the ground, shaking. I did it. I'm alive.

If Professor Jackson was here, I'd kiss him right now for forcing me to practice this kind of maneuver. But hopefully I'll never have to do it again.

I look back up at the sky, which is now a swirling mixture of dark blue, purple, pink, and orange. The building is so very tall, like a finger pointing in accusation toward the heavens. I can't believe I survived falling from there.

But Bridger is still not free. In the distance, the shuttle is a speck against the sky. There's no way I'm going to try to shift in there. One, I've never attempted shifting into a moving vehicle. And two, I don't want to alert General Anderson and Mr. Creed to the fact that I can shift to a place just by visualizing a person. The fact that I have an almost-unheard-of Talent would really make them hate me even more.

No, I have to wait until they get to their destination, and then I'll go and free Bridger and his grandmother. I'll give them an hour, because I suspect they're not going too far away. Not if what Bridger said is true about them being responsible for the bioweapon.

His words echo like thunder in my brain. I don't understand why General Anderson and Mr. Creed would want to set off the bioweapon, or why the people who helped them—weapons experts, scientists who specialize in creating biological-based weapons, other DTA personnel—would do it. How could all of them think that people like me are such a threat? It doesn't make sense. I can understand that coming from Bridger's father. He's a clone now. No matter what kind of drugs are developed to stabilize them, it seems like they never work for long, and from his behavior on the roof, he's obviously started losing his sanity. I think of Halla Fairbanks, and all she has to do to keep Vika from going completely crazy.

And Bridger said his father was working alone, only completing solo assignments. So who's even monitoring him to see that he's taking his meds when he needs to?

But it's harder to explain General Anderson's behavior. I remember from my trip to 2126 that he spoke out with such hatred against Project Firebird. His prejudice against Dual Talents was obvious. But even knowing that, how could he justify killing innocent people? He's acting like a psychopath.

I need to warn as many people as possible. Elijah. Tara. Everly. Professor March and his sister. Mom.

Hopefully they'll believe me.

Suddenly, Dad appears a few feet in front of me. "Oh, thank God you're alive," he says. "I tried to shift to you, but I couldn't at first. I was too angry at Creed. I couldn't connect to you."

I rush over to him and throw my arms around him. He winces slightly, favoring his left arm again.

"Are you okay?" I ask, pulling back and gingerly reaching out to touch his arm.

"I'll be fine," he says.

"What happened to you since I last saw you? I know that the feds raided Lincoln's farm and that both of you got away."

Dad lowers his gaze. "What else do you know?"

"I know that Lincoln died in the Unity Day bombings." I pause for a moment, thinking of Zed. "One of my friends was killed in the blast when he was shot."

Dad turns almost ghost white. "Oh my God, I'm so sorry, sweetheart. I wish I could have put a stop to everything Lincoln was doing years ago. It's just . . ." he trails off. I know he's remembering Lincoln's threats to have me killed if he didn't comply.

"I also heard that one of the bombers got away. Was that you?" I ask in a soft voice.

Dad's eyes glisten now. "I didn't have a choice about helping with the bombing. I feel like such a coward. The only thing I'm grateful for at this point is that I was able to shift away without setting my explosives off. I saw Lincoln get shot and killed. When I was shot, I was afraid that if I died my bomb would go off as well, and the blast would take out even more people. So I immediately shifted away."

"Where did you go?" I ask gently.

"Home."

He doesn't have to explain. I know he went to Willow Creek. "You didn't go back to Aunt Grace's time, did you?"

"Oh, no. Although, God knows, I'd love to see my sister again. But I would never put her in danger. I just went to the museum they made of her house in this time. I got rid of the explosives, found a doc to patch me up, then holed up for a few days to try to heal. Good thing I came back when I did. You had no business being up there by yourself."

We both look up at the sky, where the shuttle is flying north, and growing harder to see by the second. "Do you know where they're going?" Dad asks.

"No, but I know I can get to Bridger. But I think we need to give them a few hours before we shift to them, to make sure they aren't still in the air when we shift."

"I'm going with you."

For the first time in days, I feel happy. I've missed having my dad in my life. "Okay," I say. "But first we need to get Mom, and warn the others about evacuating the city."

37

"He's waking up," a familiar voice says. It sounds like Shan. I open my eyes and find myself lying on a bed in a dim room. Shan is sitting next to me, and Grandma is standing at the foot of the bed. They're both wearing Inhibitors around their necks, like I am.

I swear, I've never seen Grandma look so angry in my life. And I'm angry, too. At Dad, at Anderson—even at her.

"How are you feeling?" she asks, her face softening a bit.

"I'd probably feel a bit better if I hadn't just found out that the psycho leading the DTA is my biological grandfather. Why didn't you tell us?"

"Wait, what?" Shan asks, his mouth dropping open in shock. "Anderson is our—"

"Grandfather," I finish.

We both look expectantly at Grandma and she lets out a loud huff. "There was nothing to tell. He was assigned to me as a sperm donor. I had Leithan. I had the option to involve Anderson in Leithan's life, but I declined. End of story." I want to ask even more questions, but Grandma holds up her hand. "I said end of story. I will not talk about that man anymore."

I push myself into a sitting position and take in my surroundings. The room is windowless, with steel-gray walls and floors, and recessed lights. It holds just two beds in addition to the one I'm sitting on, a desk, and several sturdy chairs. Nothing extra for comfort.

"To answer your question, I guess I'm okay," I say. That's a lie. My head is pounding. "Where are we?"

"You can't remember what happened?" Grandma asks.

As soon as she says those words, the memory returns in a rush: my dad pushed Alora over the side of the DTA building. I lean over, gasping for air. It's like someone just punched me. Alora couldn't have survived that fall.

She's dead.

Just like so many more people will be dead after tomorrow. Ellis was right all along.

Grandma sits next to me and begins rubbing my back. "Bridger, you have to compose yourself. Anderson had to give you two doses of Calmer already in the shuttle. You don't need any more right now."

"But why . . . why did Dad do that? He didn't have to push her over the side," I say in a quivering voice. I cover my face with my hands and then run them down my cheeks. "And the bioweapon. We have to figure out a way to stop it."

"Aren't you even worried about Mom?" Shan asks.

"What? Of course I am." I glance around the room, looking for her. "Is she here?"

"Are you serious? Dad hates Mom. When he came to get me, she tried to stop him and he hit her with a full-blast stun three times. I mean, at least she punched him first." Shan's breathing is heavier now, and his face is scrunched up like he's about to cry. "But I don't know if she's dead or alive, Bridger. I don't know."

Shan's words, along with the look of horror on his face, give me a punched-in-the-gut feeling. Mom can't be gone. She can't. I know we've clashed a lot over the years, but I can't imagine my life without her.

I thought my world ended when Dad died last year. I didn't think anything could feel any worse. But this, I can't deal with it. Alora dead. Mom hurt or possibly dead. So many people doomed to die tomorrow. All because of blind hatred and fear.

It's Dad's part in this that's really killing me. I feel so betrayed. He was my hero. I've wanted to be just like him, my whole life. And now he's becoming this . . . thing.

Like Grandma said, a monster.

Grandma draws Shan to the bed and wraps her arms around us both. For a moment, we just sit. Then she says, "Boys, I want you to know that thing Anderson resurrected isn't your father. He may have his memories, and he may have a replica of Leithan's body, but he is *not* Leithan. Your father would never have agreed to murder so many innocent people."

"How do you know that for sure, Grandma?" Shan asks. He leans back and wipes tears from his eyes. "Dad worked with General Anderson for years. We don't know what Dad learned from him. I mean, on the way over here, Dad told me I could start calling the general Grandpa."

I almost puke, hearing Shan say that. The general's confession today was sick. We may share genes with him, but he'll never be family.

Grandma's features settle into a gritty determination. "It means nothing. They are nothing to us."

I still want to know where we are, but before I can ask the outlines of two people appear, wavering near the foot of the bed.

And then Alora and Nate Walker materialize.

38

Bridger, Shan, and their grandmother stare at me and Dad as if we're ghosts. I get it, since the last time they saw me, I was sailing over the side of the DTA building. I try to smile and give a little wave, but Bridger leaps out of bed and practically tackles me with a hug.

He holds me tight, as if he's afraid I'll disappear again if he lets go.

"Hey, I can't breathe," I say with a laugh.

He lets me go reluctantly. "How are you even alive?"

"Do you remember how I used to gripe about those lessons with Professor Jackson? Well, I'll never complain again." I explain how I managed to shift to safety mid-air, and how we had to wait several hours to make sure that they would have reached their destination before we could shift to them. So in the meantime, Dad and I convinced Mom to warn Professor March, Chancellor Tyson, and our friends to get out of town.

I notice how Bridger keeps shooting dark looks at my dad. Judith doesn't seem too happy that he's here, either. Then I remember—they know he was working for Jode Lincoln.

"I know what you're thinking, but please listen to me." I glance over at Dad. He's standing perfectly still, staring at the floor. "Dad didn't want to hurt anybody, but he didn't have a choice."

"What's that supposed to mean?" Bridger asks

"Lincoln forced Dad to do all those awful things because of me. He threatened to have me killed if Dad didn't follow every single one of his orders. No matter how terrible they were."

"I guess, under those circumstances, I can understand," Judith finally says once I'm finished speaking. "But that still doesn't mean I have to forget. You shot Shan, and you almost shot Bridger. You even took innocent lives. Your actions had grave consequences."

Dad makes eye contact with Judith. "I know, and I'm deeply sorry for what I did. It's something I'll have to live with for the rest of my life. But I'll do whatever it takes to make up for my mistakes."

"I'm going to hold you to that," Judith replies. Then she inclines her head toward the door. "Now, we need to figure out a way to escape. There's a guard posted just outside. Do you think you could steal his weapon and force him to open the door? It has a biometric scanner, so only one of the military personnel from this station can do it."

"Do you know where we are?" Bridger asks her.

"I think so. Or at least I have a general idea. Before the Second Civil War, the government was already building secret underground bases around the country in case war ever broke out. I'm sure we're in one—I just don't know *which* one. After Anderson knocked you out on the shuttle, I wilded out on him and his clone sedated me."

"It doesn't matter where we are," I say as I cross to the door and try and peek outside. The window is narrow, but I can just make out a guard to the left side of the door. If I can shift to his immediate right, I might be able to yank the gun off his shoulder before he knows anything. Maybe.

I turn around and ask, "Are there sensors in here to detect cloaks?"

"Probably. This is an old base, but I imagine Thomas had it fitted with them, to be on the safe side," their grandmother says.

"Just great," I mutter.

Shan joins me at the door. "I can get you guys out."

"What? No, you need to stay here," Bridger says.

"You don't understand. When Dad brought me here earlier today, he gave me a tour of the place to try to cheer me up. I have a good memory. I'm usually the first one to find my way out of buildings when we take time trips," he says, puffing out his chest a little.

"So, all those Sim Games have helped you, huh?" Bridger asks. He sounds like he's impressed with Shan.

Shan shrugs. "I guess. But anyway, I remember the way to the shuttle bay. So that means I'm going with you."

"Sounds like we don't have a choice." Bridger's grandmother stands on the other side of me and Dad and clasps her hands. "All right, kids, we have to go save some lives. Let's get started." Peering out the door, she whispers, "Alora, he's looking away. Shift now."

I take several deep breaths to steady myself, close my eyes, and concentrate on reappearing just in front of the door. When I open my eyes

I'm there, and I grab the soldier's gun. He's so surprised that he lets it slip right through his fingers. Backing away from him, I point the weapon at him. "Open the door," I say in a low voice.

He's a young soldier, maybe in his early twenties, and he looks scared. He hesitates for a moment, then places his palm on the reader. Once the door clicks open, I shove him inside.

Judith takes the gun from me and points it at the soldier. "Don't move," she commands. "I'm General Judith Creed. We are being held here against our will. You will do exactly what I tell you or I won't hesitate to put a hole through your heart. Do you understand?"

The soldier's eyes grow wide and he nods.

"Good. I can tell you're a smart boy. The first thing I want you to do is get undressed."

"Excuse me?" the soldier says.

Bridger hisses, "What are you doing?"

"We need to be accompanied by a guard when we travel the hallway, and he certainly can't be trusted. That means you get the job."

I'm sure my face is flame-red. "I'll just be over here," I say, retreating to a corner. Behind me, I hear Dad snickering. *Thanks for the support,* I think.

Several minutes later, Judith says, "Alora, you can stop being so damn modest and get over here now. We're ready to go."

I find the soldier in his underwear, tied up on the bed. They've ripped one of the sheets into strips to hold his arms and legs in place, and gagged him with another sheet.

I feel sorry for him as we leave. He's just following orders.

Dad's standing at the door with Bridger, who's now dressed in the soldier's fatigues and carrying his rifle. "Once we're out there," Dad says, "we'll have to move quickly. But do not run unless we're caught. Is that clear?"

Once we agree, Judith opens the door. Bridger goes out first and waits for us with the rifle clenched tightly in his hands. Shan directs us to head to our right. We go down several tunnels, all a dark, metallic gray with dim lighting. We make several turns—enough that I begin to doubt Shan really knows where we're going—and finally get to three sets of elevators.

"Take the middle one," Shan says. "That's the only one that goes to the top level, where the shuttles are parked."

But as soon as the elevator door opens and we take three steps, an alarm booms throughout the cavernous area we're now in—a shuttle hangar. Ahead of us, three rows of parked shuttles stretch across the space.

"Run!" Bridger yells.

Around the perimeter of the shuttle hangar, two soldiers stand along a catwalk, eyes trained on us through the scopes of their rifles. One of them fires a few shots at us. Adrenaline spikes through me and I run faster. In the distance, I hear someone else yell, "Hold your fire. They are capture only. I repeat, capture only."

We finally reach the nearest shuttle and scramble to get aboard. Judith immediately starts it and closes the door. I glance up through the cockpit window. The overhead blast door in the top of the shuttle hangar is also sliding shut. It's about halfway closed.

"How are we going to make that?" I ask in a frantic voice.

"I didn't become a Brigadier General just by looking pretty," Judith says with a smirk. Then she yells, "Everybody strap in. This should be interesting."

Dad buckles himself into the co-pilot seat while I stagger to the seat next to Bridger. Shan sits across from us, looking way too pale. Bridger's hand wraps around mine. "We'll be okay," he says. "Grandma is used to this kind of stuff."

The shuttle lifts off at a faster rate than normal, and heads straight for still-closing blast door. Over the intercom, we hear someone ordering us to turn around. Judith silences it.

I hold my breath as we approach the exit. It's three quarters of the way closed. Bridger's grip tightens on mine.

And then we're through, soaring into the cloudy night sky.

"Well, we're safe now," Shan says. "What's next?"

"We have to save everybody else," I reply.

And then Judith interrupts. "I need a little help up here. I've been shot."

39

e abandon the shuttle a little after seven-thirty in the morning. Alora's father had to take over flying after Grandma told us that she'd been shot in the leg by the perimeter guards. Alora and Shan made a tourniquet and led her to one of the passenger seats, where she passed out after instructing us to stay on course to New Denver.

Once Grandma woke up and realized we were being followed by two shuttles from the military base, she insisted that we land immediately.

That's where we are now, on the edge of a field ten miles north of the Academy.

Our problem right now is that she refuses to come with us, and she's decided that Shan needs to stay with her as well. "We'll slow you down," she says after I beg them to come with us again. I hate the idea of separating.

Shan scowls at her. "I can keep up with them."

"But I could use the company, Shan. You wouldn't want your poor grandmother to stay out here all alone, would you?"

Heaving a sigh, Shan says, "Fine, I'll stay."

"But you need to get to a med center," I say to her.

Grandma laughs. "The soldiers who are following us will be here soon." When she sees the alarmed expression on my face, she laughs again. "Don't worry. They're not going to hurt us. That idiot back who shot me is probably being punished as we speak. They'll get me to a med center and I'll be fine, and I won't let them hurt Shan. You, Nate, and Alora, on the other hand, need to get to the DTA building and find that bioweapon. Do whatever it takes."

I lean down to kiss Grandma on the forehead. "Are you sure you want to do this? We can carry you."

Alora says, "I can shift to a med center right now and have somebody out here in a few minutes."

"Absolutely not. I want all three of you to stay together. Is that clear?"

"Yes, ma'am," I reply. Alora does the same.

"Nate, take care of my grandson. Please. You owe me."

He offers a genuine smile. "I will."

We start to leave, but Grandma calls out, "One more thing. You do whatever is necessary to stop that bioweapon from going off. Do you understand? *Whatever* it takes. Don't let sentiment cloud your judgment."

I know what she's talking about, but I'm not sure I'm ready to go there. I realize the cloned version of Dad isn't stable. But he's been brainwashed by General Anderson. Maybe that means that there's hope—that there's some good left in him. Some way to make him see reason.

On the walk over, Alora comms her mother to make sure she left the city. She said she did, as well as Everly and Tara's families. But Elijah's parents refused. Adalyn begged Alora to shift to her now, and Alora had to end the call in tears.

"I hate doing this to her," she says, swiping at her eyes. "I'm all she has left."

Nate wraps his uninjured arm around her shoulders. "I promise, you'll see her again soon. Who knows? Maybe I can convince her to give me another chance. Or maybe not. But no matter what, we'll still be a family. Always remember that."

Damn, that nearly makes me tear up. I still feel a little bit of resentment toward her father, but at least I understand why he did what he did.

My dad is the one doing something unforgivable.

My DataLink chimes. It's Professor March. When I accept his comm, he lets out a loud sigh. "Good God, Bridger, I've been trying to track you for hours. You just came back into my viewing area. What are you doing north of the Academy?"

I give him the brief version of our ordeal.

He runs his hands over his head. "Anderson is certifiably insane. I'm on the way to the banquet now. I'll meet you there. You might need help getting past security."

I shake my head. "Professor, you should get out of the city. You're a Dual Talent. If we fail, you'll die."

"I don't care. Alora and her father are with you, and there will be other Dual Talents at the banquet. I can't abandon you or them. I have a feeling it's going to take all of us to make things right."

A half hour later, we reach the Academy first and take a shuttle to New Denver. By the time we get to the downtown area, it's ten minutes after ten in the morning. The banquet will take place at twelve o'clock sharp. Our objective is to get inside the building and find the bioweapon before it starts. The fewer people there, the better it will be for us.

Upon arrival at the DTA building, we discover that it's crawling with high-level security assigned to protect the president. The few guests to arrive this early are submitting to being scanned and searched.

We discuss our options and Alora comms Professor March. "New plan. We can't get inside from down here. We're more than likely on the wanted list for the feds."

"Then what are you going to do?" he asks.

Nate interrupts. "I'm going to shift to the rooftop and secure it. Alora and Bridger are will steal a Pod and pilot it to the roof. We'll enter that way, so keep an eye out for our signal."

"Is there anything I can do in the meantime?" March asks.

"I know President Tremblay will be the guest of honor. See if you can locate Anderson and my father," I say. "We need to find them if we want to locate the bioweapon."

Nate fixes me with an intense look. "You take care of my girl, Bridger. Understood?"

"Yes sir," I respond.

But Alora isn't having any of it. "Oh, come on. I can take care of myself."

Nate gives her a kiss on the forehead and shifts from view. With him gone, Alora and I don't waste any time. We take off running back the way we came. We passed a white Pod a block before we reached the DTA building. I just hope it'll still be there.

Alora and I don't get very far before someone to my left shouts my name. Emerging from a nearby alley is Ellis.

I split off and run in his direction. Sighing heavily, Alora sighs follows me.

When I get to Ellis, he hisses, "What are you doing here? You were supposed to be in the bunker by now. Away from the blast zone. *Safe.*"

"You said *you* were going to take me to a safe place. You never mentioned that I'd be forced there by General Anderson and an insane version of my father. And there's another thing you never explained. I still don't know why you want to save me, Alora, and the rest of my family. What makes us so special?"

Ellis pauses for a moment. "There's no point in hiding anymore, I guess." He then removes the gray cloth covering his face. I almost fall to my knees. Even though his face is thinner, and his hair is a little darker, he looks very similar to my dad. I take a closer look. Ellis has a faint scar trailing through the stubble on his cheek. I gasp. "Shan?"

His face lights up. "For a second there I didn't think you would recognize me."

I'm speechless. I glance from him to Alora, not sure what to say.

Alora's brow furrows. "Why are you calling yourself Ellis? And why bother hiding your identity?"

"I didn't want to change things. Besides, if I'd told Bridger earlier who I was, and that The General and The Clone were the ones responsible for destroying the country, he would never have believed me. And as for going by Ellis, my name is really Leithan Shan, so L. S. became Ellis. I thought it was appropriate to take on a new identity since I'd lost everyone I'd ever loved—everyone who made me who I was."

"What am supposed to call you now?" I finally manage to ask.

"Just stick with Ellis. I've been going by that for so long, it would be weird hearing someone calling me Shan."

"All right," I reply. It's hard to believe that this man, the same one I've been so angry with, is my little brother. The same one who used to be such a mama's boy, all grown up and taking charge. Trying to save the world. I reach over to hug him. "Even though I wanted to kick your ass the other day, I'm proud of you," I say. Then I wrinkle my nose. "But you need a bath."

He looks pained. "Bridger, that's a luxury in the time I'm stuck in. Having a decent meal every day is a luxury. It's hell there. That's why I want to prevent it from ever happening. And that brings me back to my original plan." He points at Alora and me. "You two shouldn't be here."

"Why are you so insistent on that?" I ask. "If you're successful, we'll be fine."

"That's the thing," Ellis says. "In my timeline, all of you died in the blast. I figured that if you went to the bunker this time, that would change everything."

"Maybe we need to change the strategy," Alora says. "What went wrong?"

"I don't know the exact details. After you guys split from me and Grandma, we were found and taken back to the bunker and locked up again. What I know is that The Clone was the key. I was told later by the base commander that the bioweapon was synced to a device that monitored his heartbeat. That way, if he had died prematurely, it would have detonated right away. From the comms that came back to the bunker, we learned that Bridger was threatening to kill him if he didn't deactivate the weapon."

My jaw drops. How could it be possible that, in his past, I was even considering killing my dad? "Are you serious?"

"Yeah. That's the last thing we heard before the blast. Anyone within a half-mile radius died immediately. The Clone, Anderson, both of you, Alora's father, Professor March, and thousands of other people. Then all Talents, and most of the Gen Mods, started dying within the following days and weeks as the virus infected them."

"Holy. Fure," I say, running my hands over my head. It's not every day you learn how you're supposed to die. "So, Grandma survived with you?"

Now Ellis's shoulders sag. "Only for the first six months. She insisted on going out on a scouting mission and was killed in one of the European Coalition's bomb raids."

"I thought the war was worldwide," Alora says.

"It was, eventually. As the virus spread across the globe, more and more countries started turning on each other. Sending in bombs to try to wipe out infected populations. Nowhere was safe after a while."

We're all silent as the implications sink in.

Finally, Alora asks, "What makes you think we can change anything this time?"

Ellis gives us a half-smile. "You have me to help."

Fifteen minutes later, I maneuver our stolen Pod onto the DTA's roof and park it between two much larger shuttles. We step outside and see Nate leaning against the doorway leading inside.

"It's about time you got here," he says while inclining his head to a small pile of stunners and guns near his feet. "Help yourselves. The previous owners are out cold for the time being."

While we stuff weapons into our pockets, Nate notices the new addition to our crew and asks, "Who is this, and why is he here?"

"This is Ellis. Well, Shan, but from the year 2155," I say.

Nate gives Ellis a closer inspection. "I bet you have one hell of a story."

Alora checks her DataLink. "Hey, it's almost eleven o'clock. Remember, the banquet starts at noon."

As we descend the stairs and make our way to the banquet hall on the top floor, I give him the short version of Ellis's role in getting us here. When I'm finished, Nate looks at him with admiration. "That's a brave thing, coming back here to try to change things. Have you thought about what will happen to you, though?"

This startles me. What *will* happen to Ellis if we succeed?

He shrugs. "Doesn't matter. What does matter is that the bioweapon must not detonate."

I shake my head. "It does matter. If we change things, you won't be *you* anymore. You could cease to exist."

Ellis stops walking and fixes me with an almost desperate stare. "You can't think like that. The entire world's future is at stake. And besides, if we're successful, I'll still live. Right now, my younger version is on the way back to the bunker."

When we reach the stairway leading into the lobby of the banquet hall, we find Professor March waiting for us, wearing his black dress uniform.

"Where have you been? The president just arrived with his entourage. We have to get in there now and stop this thing."

Nate moves next to the stairway door and motions for us to follow him. He peers through the small rectangular window and says, "Okay, two Space Benders are posted by the main entrance to the banquet hall. March, how many more are inside? And do you know the locations of Creed and Anderson?"

Professor March answers, "Six more guards posted around the room as of now. Three on each side. But I was told more will be posted soon. General Anderson is at the table on stage with the President Tremblay. As for Leithan, I haven't seen him."

"How many guests are in there?" Nate asks.

"Forty or fifty. But more are on the way. We need to do this quickly."

No joke. Once we stun the people inside, they'll only be immobilized for around ten minutes. That means if it takes longer than that to find the bioweapon, we'll have to deal with all of them coming after us.

Nate turns to look at us. "Alora, I want you to stay in the lobby and guard the doors."

"Oh no you don't. You're not going to make me sit this out. It's going to take all of us to shut down the security and find that bioweapon."

"That's true," Nate says. "But I do need someone to guard the door. They're going to call for back up."

"And the backup will simply shift inside. You know they will be Space Benders. I can handle this," she says.

I understand why Nate wants to keep Alora away from where the main confrontation will take place, but I agree with her. We're massively outnumbered. It's going to take all of us to get through this mess. "Stay close to me," I say to her. "That way we can watch each other's backs."

"That'll work," she says, eyeing her father.

He ignores both of us. "I'll shift directly into the banquet hall and start taking out the security detail near the guest of honor table. The rest of you come on through the door and work your way up. Concentrate on taking out security before civilians."

"Okay, let's do this," Professor March says as Nate hands him a stunner and pistol.

Before Nate can shift, Alora leans over and enfolds him in a hug. "Please be safe, Daddy."

They cling to each other, as if they don't want to part. Nate gives her one final squeeze and whispers, "I love you, sweetheart."

Alora steps away so he can shift. He looks at us one more time. "Remember, use stunners first. Resort to your guns only if you have no other choice. We don't want to kill innocent people."

Then he shifts. Alora tries to put on a brave look, but her eyes flick to the door leading to the lobby, and I know she's worried for herself and her father.

It suddenly hits me—she'll be going in there fighting alongside her father, while Ellis and I will be going in there to fight *against* ours. I never thought I'd be here. I thought I would do anything for my father.

I should have known a clone of my father would never work out. It doesn't seem fair, though, that whatever meds Nate is taking to keep himself stable seem to work, but drugs have failed my father.

Ellis catches my eye. "Stay safe, brother."

"I'll see you on the other side," I reply.

Professor March flings open the door and runs into the lobby, firing his stunner. He takes out both guards stationed outside the banquet hall. Screams filter out from the room as I hear Nate begin firing, too. We follow behind, aiming our stunners at anybody inside who moves too quickly, even the guests who arrived early just to mingle. You can't be too careful—anyone could have hidden weapons.

I rush to nearest column, my eyes searching the people trying to get to the exit. I fire at whoever is close to me, trying to find the security guards. They should be in dark gray uniforms like the guards posted in the lobby, identifying them as military Space Benders.

Queasiness settles in my stomach as I keep stunning one person after another. Innocent bystanders. I knew I had to do this, but it's harder than I thought. And where are the furing guards?

Normally we would be no match for anyone in the military. The main thing we have going for us is that we're attacking without warning.

I glance behind me. Alora is just across the hall, crouching behind the column closest to me. She fires a shot and takes out one of the security guards, then hits three guests in rapid succession.

I'm impressed.

I turn around to find one of the space-bending guards standing in front of me. I brace myself for the electric surge of her stunner. But before she can fire at me, Ellis takes her down.

"Eyes on targets, Bridger," he says as he pauses at my column.

Before I can thank him, Ellis takes off, trying to make his way to Nate's location. He stops to crouch by a column in the midsection of the banquet hall.

I wish he could have stayed with me a little longer.

By now, there aren't many people moving around the room anymore. Most of the guests are immobilized on the floor. Some have managed to escape. I fire a few more shots to take down some of the last guests. It doesn't feel right—they're both older men and look completely harmless.

But I've learned the hard way that you can't trust who you think you can.

One of the security guards is still active. He's hiding next to a covered table near the wall. Since he's closest to me I keep trying to take him out, but I can't get a clear shot. Professor March advances on the other side, hoping to sneak up from behind. But before he can make it, a new Space Bender appears and stuns him. Then two more Space Benders appear.

Air rushes out of my lungs. No, this can't be happening. I was hoping we could get to Anderson before more Space Benders arrived. With Professor March immobilized and backup arriving to stop us, our odds of finding the bioweapon in time have dramatically decreased.

Suddenly a voice booms through the hall. "Tell them to leave, Tremblay," Nate yells. With most everyone around us being stunned, the hall is mostly silent, and Nate's voice echoes eerily. I peer around the column. At the same time, Alora gasps.

Nate is standing by the guest of honor table now, with his good arm curled around President Tremblay's throat, and his stunner pointed at his head. I don't see General Anderson anywhere.

"Tell them to leave now, and I don't want any more Space Benders to shift in here. Do you understand?"

The president, a short man with light skin and blond hair, lifts his DataLink and gives the order for all military personnel to stand down. The Space Benders who just arrived shift away.

My heart begins to race. This could still go our way. I start to stand.

Suddenly, a slow clapping sound comes from the direction of the banquet hall's kitchen. I peek out from behind the column, toward the right side of the room as Dad pushes through the double doors, carrying a large black case with a handle. He's dressed in his black DTA uniform and smiling.

He stops when he reaches the center of the room. The center of all our attention.

"I have to admit, you're tenacious. I wasn't quite ready to bring out the big surprise." He sets the black case on the floor and calls out, "Bridger, you're not even supposed to be here. Especially not with that girl." He makes a tsking sound. "And to think, you always were my favorite. But I guess that's all changed. If only my other son were here. Oh, that's right, he escaped from the bunker, too. At least he and my mother had enough sense to let my guards capture them."

I exchange a glance with Alora. Dad has completely wilded out. This man is no longer anything like the father I knew. Now I understand why Ellis refers to him as The Clone.

Ellis steps out from behind his column, and Dad says, "Well, look who we have here. From your handsome looks, I'd have to say you're Shan. Right? An older version of my Shan, back from the future. Care to give your father a hug?" he asks, spreading his arms wide.

Ellis draws his pistol from his jacket pocket and aims it at Dad. "The Shan you knew no longer exists. He died a long time ago, just like my father did. And I'm here to make sure you don't unleash hell on Earth today."

Dad laughs and wags his finger back and forth at Ellis. "That's not going to happen. It's only designed to take out certain undesirable people. Then our country will be free of those who are trying to destroy it."

"I'm from your future, so I know what's really going to happen. You're going to kill just about every single Talent and a huge segment of the Gen Mod population in this country, all within six months. And then it begins to spread globally, which leads to all-out war. I can't let you do that."

"Aren't you worried about contaminating your timeline?" Dad asks, completely unfazed by what Ellis just told him. "You know that's against the law. Just ask your brother. He tried to do it and failed miserably. Why don't you join me, Bridger? Both you and Shan. It's time for another Creed family reunion!"

My skin crawls, but I find myself itching to move, or maybe to say something.

Alora shakes her head at me, telling me not to go. But I can't hide back here. Somehow, Ellis and I both have to stop Dad. He's our responsibility.

Holding up both of my hands, I step out from behind my column.

Dad chuckles. "And there's my no-longer-favorite child. Well, to be honest, neither one of you are really my favorites right now. No offense, Shan, but you're too much like your mother for my liking."

Ellis flinches. And in that moment, it hits me just how far gone Dad really is. A part of me, even now, had hope that we could bring him back. When Dad talked to me the night fourteen-year-old Shan was shot, he seemed reasonable. This man is far from that. He's becoming unstable at an incredible rate.

"Did your Clonitin stop working?" I ask. "Or has Anderson brainwashed you that much?"

Dad's eyes grow cold. "You have no idea what you're talking about. Now, I'm going to give you five minutes to get out of here. There are plenty of shuttles on the roof. Take one and get back to the underground base. That's your only chance to survive."

"I can't do that," I say.

Immediately, Dad springs toward Ellis, and they struggle for a few moments. I watch in horror as Dad tries to get the gun from him. Finally, Ellis drops the weapon, but Dad fumbles and gives Ellis time to knock it clear. I lunge for the gun and grab it, only to find that Dad has a pistol of his own out now.

Movement behind him catches my attention. In the chaos, Alora must have shifted. She snatches the gun from Dad's hands and shifts again, appearing next to me.

"I'll admit, Alora, I'm impressed. Your mother would never have had the nerve to do something like that." Dad takes a step back, spreading his arms wide. "Go ahead, shoot," he yells in my direction. "Kill your own father. But let me warn you, the instant my heart stops beating, the bioweapon goes boom. So what's it going to be? Detonation now? Or will you go back to the bunker, where you should be, and let the detonation take place as planned?"

I glance at Ellis. He swallows a few times, looking nervous. This his eyes flick to the case with the bioweapon, still in the center of the room. Suddenly I understand what he wants to do.

As Ellis dives toward the bioweapon, time seems to slow.

Ellis's arms extend toward the case.

Someone yells for him to stop.

Dad extracts a second pistol from his jacket.

The sounds are deafening as he fires it two times.

Ellis's fingers almost touch the case, but the bullets rip into his body before he can reach it. First his back, then his head.

By the time his body comes to a rest, Ellis's eyes are fixed in my direction.

But I know he can no longer see me.

40

I stare in horror at Ellis's body. He's gone. He never got the chance to go back to his own time, to see if he could return to a better world.

The look on Bridger's face breaks my heart—his features are contorted in anguish. He lunges toward Leithan. At the same time, Leithan fires a wild shot in Bridger's direction as he backs away, scrambling to return to where he left the bioweapon case.

My pulse spikes. I'm afraid that the shot could hit Bridger, but he easily dodges it and I breathe a sigh of relief.

But at the same time, Dad appears right next to the case. He leans down and wraps his arms around the bioweapon, wincing as he uses his injured arm to pull it close to him.

And then he looks up. His eyes search for mine. So blue, just like mine. Just like Aunt Grace's. Just like Vika's.

I know what he's going to do.

"No!" My voice sounds odd. Not like my own.

Dad whispers, "I love you. Always."

"Please!" I cry out. "Don't leave me!"

Then he closes his eyes for the final time and shifts out of the room.

I drop to my knees and scream.

41

White hot rage spreads through my body. This is not my father. I thought, somehow, I could save him. But he just murdered his own son. He just shot at me.

I'm numb as I fire shot after shot straight into that monster. He staggers back, his eyes going wide as he looks down at the hole where his heart should be.

"How could you, son?" he asks softly.

"You're not my father," I say.

He falls to the floor with a dull thud and takes several choking breaths before his chest stops moving.

I'm left with the dead clone I hoped would be my father again, but never could.

We saved the country and the world.

And yet I feel like I've died.

42

Just after I kill the cloned version of my father, President Tremblay gives the order for Space Benders to arrive again. Alora, Professor March, and I are immediately taken into custody. Medical personnel arrive to take away Ellis and my cloned father's bodies.

But a strange thing happened while nobody was looking.

Ellis's body vanished.

I choke back a sob. I wanted to say goodbye to him. Now I can't even do that.

Shan is still alive, I remind myself. Ellis got his wish. He saved us. Now all I want to do is hug my brother and never let him out of my sight. To step up and help guide him into adulthood. That's the best way I can honor Ellis's memory. His sacrifice.

When investigators inquire about him, I share the year that Ellis was really from. That he was in fact my younger brother. They don't believe me, but they still send Time Benders back to investigate the time that he initially approached me on the camping trip with Grandma and Shan.

And when they return with their report, we're officially cleared.

I'm still numb. Vaguely, I make out excited chatter from the investigators. Some speculate that Ellis's Chronoband automatically returned his body to the year he was from. Others argue that he ceased to exist because we changed his timeline. No matter what, he's still gone.

Captain Olivia March arrives next, and Professor March greets her. "I was wondering when you would get here."

"Normally I would have been here to help with the investigation, but since *you* were involved, I wasn't allowed to do anything." She glances at me. "Bridger, your grandmother is on the way."

"What about my mom?" Alora asks.

"She will be here shortly. But in the meantime, I'm going to escort you and Bridger downstairs to take your statements. You too, Telfair," she says, giving her brother an exasperated look. "I had no idea you were going to pull a stunt this wild."

"It was this or have everyone die. What would you have chosen? And besides, you pulled your own stunt by helping Alora escape yesterday."

She gives him a rueful smile. "Touché."

Professor March pats me on the shoulder. "How are you holding up?"

I consider lying, but what's the point? We all just went through a traumatic experience. "I'm not so great right now, professor. But I'll live."

"I'm here for you. That's never changed, and it never will."

I look up at him, blinking back more tears. "I know. Thank you."

As we're about to leave the banquet hall, I'm happy to be able to see General Anderson's face when he and President Tremblay are officially arrested. The investigation took a while to complete, but it clearly showed that they were guilty. I thought, because I didn't see him in the banquet hall during the fight, that he had escaped. Turns out Nate had stunned him first, and he was lying on the floor behind the cloth-covered table.

"How could you betray me?" Anderson bellows in my direction as he's handcuffed and hauled away. Then he looks at Alora, his face contorted with rage. "If I'd know you would have been here today, I would have left you to die in the past!"

Tremblay doesn't say anything, instead keeping his head down.

I want to let out a string of curses at both of them, but I keep quiet. I have nothing left to say at this point. Seeing him and Tremblay get what they deserve is good enough for me.

Still, nothing will ever make up for the fact that I've had to lose my father—twice now. That is so furing messed up. Imagine that, having to deal with your father dying, being brought back from the dead, then taken away again. And Alora is going through the same thing.

We're going to need lots of Calmer.

As Captain March escorts us out of the banquet hall, I take Alora's hand. She looks at me, but doesn't really seem to see me. I know exactly how she's feeling. It's not fair. We both searched so long for answers about our fathers. We both thought they were dead and gone, only to find them again.

What a cruel joke that we lost them again at the same time.

"Did you find out where your father shifted to with the bioweapon?" I ask.

"One of the investigators told me there was a huge, unexplained explosion above the surface of the planet."

I freeze. "Do you think it was him? I mean, could he really have shifted there?"

She thinks for a moment. "Yeah, I think he could have. His abilities were stronger than mine."

Alora and I are placed in separate holding cells to be questioned. I'm only in mine for a few minutes when Grandma cruises into the room in a shiny silver motor chair. I should have known a minor gunshot wound wouldn't keep her away.

I feel a surge of panic when I realize my brother isn't with her. "Where is Shan?"

"I took him to the hospital. He wanted to be with your mom while I came here to see you." She looks down at her lap for a moment, where her hands are folded together in a white-knuckled grip. "I don't think he could handle knowing the truth about Ellis. It might be too much for him to find out that the older version of himself was murdered by that clone of Leithan. He's already been through so much."

"So you don't think it's a good idea to tell him?"

"I'm going to talk it over with Morgan to make sure we're in agreement, but I think it would be best that we keep this from him."

We emerge from the DTA building late in the afternoon, after spending hours being questioned. On top of being cleared of wrongdoing in the banquet hall attack, we're not in trouble anymore for trying to save Zed. We've been officially pardoned because we successfully stopped the detonation of the bioweapon. Pardoning us was the least they could do.

Still, it doesn't make it any easier. None of this will bring my father back, or Alora's father, or Zed.

We meet up with Alora and Adalyn in the courtyard.

"What are we going to do now?" Alora ask, grasping both my hands.

"I don't know," I say. I look away from her, toward the street. It's weird—all around us, people are going about their days as if nothing major happened. I know a lot of people know an attack was thwarted—they just don't know what could have happened. I meet Grandma's eyes. "I think we need to see my mom and brother right now."

Grandma inclines her head in agreement.

"I have an idea," Adalyn says. "Why don't we all go visit her?"

I consider it for a moment. Before, Adalyn was determined to keep Alora away from me. I know for a fact my mom has said some nasty things about her in the past, and I'm sure Alora must know that. Normally I'd refuse to bring Alora into that environment. But under the circumstances, I'm willing to make an exception.

"I think she would like that."

We take a Pod to the hospital, courtesy of Grandma. Once we get to Mom's room, I immediately rush over to Shan and hug him. He awkwardly pats my back, slightly weirded out. "I'm okay, Bridger. Really. I'm sorry about what you went through today. From what I hear, you and Alora are heroes."

"That's right. I'm proud of you," Mom says. I hug her next and quickly pull back when she winces. "Are you going to be okay?" I ask in a rush.

"I'll be fine. The docs say I only need to stay one more night for observation, then I can go back home to torture you two again."

I look from Alora, to her mom, then to Grandma, to Shan, and back to Mom. "I think I'd like that more than anything in this world right now," I say.

Adalyn clears her throat. "I hope you don't mind us being here. I'm sorry you were hurt. If there's anything I can do for you, I'll be happy to help."

For a moment, I think letting Adalyn and Alora come here was a big mistake. Mom stares at them, her eyes giving none of her emotions away. Finally, she says, "Thank you. I appreciate it." Then her expression softens as she glances from Alora to me. "Maybe we should all get together some time. I think we have a lot to talk about."

"I'd love that," Adalyn says, offering a smile.

With those words, the tension evaporates. Shan begs us to give details about what happened at the DTA building. While Alora and I share a censored version, my mood begins to shift.

It's strange. Maybe it's because a medic gave me a dose of Calmer before we left, but I'm feeling better now. My emotions were so raw just a few hours ago. I'm still hurt. I still can't stop thinking about how Nate and Ellis sacrificed themselves. I can't get the sight of Dad's body out of my mind. And I know Alora is hurting, too. Even now, I can't help but notice the sadness in her voice, the dark shadows under her eyes.

But I know we'll be okay. We have our families and each other.

It's time to put the ghosts of our past to rest, and look forward to our future.

EPILOGUE

Sweltering heat and humidity surround my body the instant I emerge from the Void, greeting me like an old friend. It's almost unbearable—like stepping into a sauna—especially since Bridger and I just shifted from a much cooler temperature. I'm glad we both put on shorts and T-shirts retrieved from this era just before we traveled through time.

For us, it's December 17, 2149. It's been almost two weeks since I graduated from the Academy, and over two years since our fathers died. For Aunt Grace, it will have been almost a year since she last saw me. I could have chosen any date to see her again, but I wanted this to be special. In this time, it's her birthday.

I can't wait to see her.

We're standing at the edge of the tree line behind my former home, the old plantation house that she and her late husband turned into a bed-and-breakfast inn. Memories of my childhood surface. Aunt Grace having a tea party with me in the backyard when I was little, her reading bedtime stories to me and tucking me in each night. Me helping her prep the meals she served to guests who stayed with us.

I glance behind me. The path leading to the river is still there—the one that I used to run on daily.

I'm overcome with a sense of nostalgia, standing here looking at the place I lived for ten years. This still feels like home, and yet that life seems so far away. I've come to love living in my own time. I have my mom, Bridger and his family, and our friends. But I also long for Aunt Grace. When I lived here, I never felt like I fit in. But Aunt Grace always made me feel better. God, how I miss her.

Bridger's hand tightens around mine. "Are you ready?"

I straighten my spine, steeling myself for what I've wanted to do ever since Dad sacrificed himself to save our future. "Yeah, let's go."

As we cross the yard. I soak up everything. The smell of freshly cut grass. The sweet scent of the roses blooming in Aunt Grace's garden. Overhead, the sun is rising in the eastern sky. I chose to arrive at ten o'clock in the morning in case Aunt Grace had plans to go to the annual Fourth of July Jamboree that takes place in Willow Creek each year. Most of the years I lived with her, she wouldn't go, but on the final year—the year that I officially died—she insisted we both attend.

Aunt Grace's old truck is parked near the back porch, along with an unfamiliar vehicle. Hopefully, business is still good and she doesn't have to worry about money like she did for so many years.

"So how do you want to do this?" Bridger asks when we reach the back porch.

I think for a moment before replying, "Let's go around front and ring the doorbell. I don't want to march inside and have her freak out in front of any guests that may be around."

As we circle the house, we pass by the old oak tree that's near the front of the house. That was the one I had planned to climb down when Aunt Grace accidentally locked me in the attic. That was on the day I was trying to find out answers about my dad. It was also the day that Bridger first entered my life.

When we're on the front porch, Bridger squeezes my hand again. "You've got this."

I nod and ring the doorbell.

What feels like an eternity passes before the door swings open. Aunt Grace is standing in front of me, dressed in khaki shorts and a dark green T-shirt. Her pleasant smile morphs into a jaw drop, then she squeals and rushes forward, pulling me into a crushing embrace.

"Sweetie, I've missed you so much!" she says.

By the time she lets me go, I'm in tears. Bridger touches my shoulder, and Aunt Grace looks back and forth at us with a confused expression.

"Bridger? I thought I'd never see you again. Why are you here?"

His eyes search out mine, his face turning red. I can't say anything just yet, so Bridger nods. "Well, we're sort of . . . together."

"Like *dating* together?"

"Yes, ma'am," he says.

Aunt Grace covers her mouth with both of her hands and takes a step back. "Wow, that's fantastic. I'm really happy for y'all." She cocks her head to the side, now frowning slightly. "How old are you two now?"

I somehow find my voice. It's barely a whisper. "I'm nineteen and Bridger is twenty, but our birthdays are coming up soon."

"My word, this is so surreal," she says. "I wasn't sure I'd see you again. You or Nate." Now her eyes lock on mine again, then she looks over my shoulder—I can tell she's searching for Dad. "I thought Nate would . . ."

And my tears start flowing again.

"He's not coming back, is he sweetie?" Aunt Grace asks in a gentle voice.

"No," I whisper.

For a moment, I think that Aunt Grace might faint. She blinks a few times and seems to sway slightly.

"Are you okay?" Bridger asks, stepping forward to take her by the arm.

Aunt Grace holds up her hands to stop him. "I'll be fine." She looks over her shoulder, tears glistening in her eyes, then motions for us to enter. "Come inside. I need to sit down."

"What about your guests?" I ask, since I'm technically dead in this time.

"They're all from out of state, and most aren't even here right now," she says. "Everyone's getting ready for the Jamboree downtown." She glances up at the ceiling. "One couple's still upstairs, but at breakfast they said they were going to stay in most of the morning."

Once Bridger and I are seated on the couch in the front parlor, she takes one of the chairs across from us. Her hands clutch the armrests as she says, "Okay, I'm ready. Tell me everything."

It's like a huge pressure is released from my chest as Bridger and I relate what's happened to us over the past two years, starting with the events that led to his father and my dad dying on the same day. We end by sharing what's going on in our lives now: I'm about to start my first job as an artifact retrieval tech based out of New Denver, and Bridger is stationed at a military base just outside of Chicago.

"So, you're living with your mom?" Aunt Grace asks hopefully.

"No, ma'am. She transferred to the History Alive Network's main office in New York. She didn't want to go, but they offered her a raise that she couldn't refuse. I'm still staying at her apartment, and one of my friends is moving in with me next week."

I smile now, thinking of how Everly talked her mom into moving back to the North American Federation last year, once things finally began to settle down between Gen Mods and Purists. We were thrilled to graduate together.

After President Tremblay was arrested for colluding with General Anderson and others to detonate the bioweapon, they were all Nulled. His VP became president and she worked hard to improve relations throughout the federation. The Responsible Citizen Act was repealed, and biological weapons were banned. She even decided to publicly admit to the existence of Dual Talents. While some people reacted with the same prejudice as Anderson and his conspirators, most people welcomed them. After all, the Dual Talents that existed were already their friends and neighbors; people had just never known the extent of their abilities.

"How are things with you two?" Aunt Grace asks, raising her eyebrows. "You're in different cities. Is the long-distance thing working out?"

Bridger shrugs. "My family still lives in New Denver, so I fly down once a month to visit. Alora shifts to visit me whenever she wants."

Aunt Grace looks at me in amazement. "I still can't get over that. So, you're allowed to go anywhere you want just by thinking about it?"

"I'm not supposed to. We're only supposed to bend space while on the job, but I do it anyway," I say. "A few days ago, I went down to Mexico City to visit some friends who are assigned to the artifact retrieval division there. I had supper with them and was back in time to go to sleep."

Bridger gives me a side-eyed look. "I didn't know you visited Elijah and Tara."

"Sorry, I forgot to invite you. I was too busy planning this trip with your grandmother," I say.

Bridger and I both look down at the shiny Chronobands fastened to our wrists. Two days ago, Bridger's grandmother came by to visit me at my apartment. I was happy to see her, but still surprised to see her on her own. I usually only see her when Bridger and I visit her apartment, or when we go out to dinner with our families.

I was shocked when I found out why she stopped by.

Apparently, shortly after she took General Anderson's place as head of the DTA's military division, and after Bridger and I officially started dating, she decided to look more into my background. She was especially curious about how Aunt Grace's house ended up as a perfectly preserved museum in our era. Her investigation revealed that Grace willed the house to the state under the condition that it never be sold—it could only be passed to a direct descendant.

Which means that, in my time, I'm now the legal owner of the house, which I plan to leave as a museum.

When I asked General Creed the exact date that Aunt Grace set this up, she stunned me by saying that it was completed on July 7, 2015. General Creed traveled back in time to determine my aunt's motivation, and witnessed Bridger and me visiting with Aunt Grace today. From there they were able to figure out the date that we would depart from in our time. General Creed confessed that she was angry at first, then realized that we had Chronobands, which we would never have access to on our own, since the DTA confiscated the ones that Ellis gave to us.

Recognizing that our visit was a part of the timeline now, she knew that she would have to be the one to give us the Chronobands.

"You can't argue with history," she had said with a shrug as she handed me the Chronobands.

"Is this the only time you'll let me visit my aunt?" I had asked.

"I don't know yet," she had replied. "I'd prefer not to see this happen again, but I've learned that in this profession, you can never say never."

Aunt Grace suddenly stands, running her right hand along her forehead. "You know what? I think we should go on a picnic to celebrate. Let me get something together and I'll be right back," she says.

"No, we'll help," Bridger says.

After Bridger and I help her pack sandwiches, several pieces of pound cake, chocolate chip cookies, and lemonade, we head toward the dock at the river.

We spend the next hour laughing, talking, and eating. And oh man, the food is so delicious. So much better than what we have access to in our time. Aunt Grace fills us in on what's has happened in Willow Creek over the past few years. Of course, nothing much has changed.

"What about Mr. Palmer?" I ask, feeling slightly sick to my stomach.

"He's dead," Aunt Grace says in a flat voice. "I've been keeping an eye out for him, and I found out that he died in a car accident back in January."

Relief floods through me. I'd never wish something like that to happen anyone under normal circumstances, but Palmer was evil. At least I don't have to worry about him ever bothering Aunt Grace again, or hurting any other girls.

My DataLink chimes, alerting me that our time is up. When Bridger's grandmother helped set up this trip, even flying Bridger and me to

Georgia on a private shuttle so he could shift directly on the property, she said she was only giving us four hours to visit. She said we didn't need to contaminate the timeline any more than we had to.

Remembering that, I quickly share what happens to the house in the future. Aunt Grace's eyes grow wide. "I've never quite been sure what I should do with the place once I'm gone," she says. "At least I know it'll be taken care of, and you'll get it again one day."

I find myself growing teary-eyed again. Four hours isn't nearly enough time. I could stay with Aunt Grace for days.

But I know that's not possible.

"Don't forget the drawing," Bridger reminds me.

"What drawing?" Aunt Grace asks.

I pull a folded piece of paper out of my shorts pocket. Bridger's grandmother forbade us from bringing anything that could contaminate the timeline from our time to this year. But I thought something simple wouldn't hurt.

It's a drawing of me with Vika. I'd caught her up on the situation with Vika while we were eating our lunch.

Aunt Grace's hands shake as she looks at the drawing. "So this is Nate's other daughter. I'm glad she's okay now," she says.

"Alora, we've got to go," Bridger says gently.

And once again, I find myself hugging Aunt Grace and crying.

"Do you think you can come back again?" she asks.

"I don't know. I promise I'll try," I say in a quivering voice.

Aunt Grace pulls away from me and places both of her hands on my shoulders. Her eyes lock on mine. "I want you to do that. But don't do anything that can jeopardize your future. I know now that you're safe. You're going to even end up with the house, which makes me happy. No matter what, my heart's at peace knowing that you're still alive and well." She lets go of me, and takes a few more steps back on the dock. "Now, you two need to go. I don't want you to get in trouble because of me," she says.

"I love you," I say.

"I love you, too, sweetie. Always and forever."

I take Bridger's hand and this time I give it a squeeze. "Ready?" I ask him.

"Yes," he replies. "See you later, Grace."

"Look after my girl. I'll haunt you if you don't," she says, trying to smile.

We check our Chronobands and close our eyes. As I picture the return date and enter the Void, I push back the sadness I'm feeling. I'm going home, where I belong with my family and friends. But I'll find a way to see Aunt Grace again. If General Creed doesn't let me use a Chronoband, I can always free shift.

Even though I never felt like I fit in while I lived with Aunt Grace, that time is a part of me. I can't pretend that those years never happened, and visiting her today has made me fully realize that. In order for me to move on, I'll have to embrace both parts of my life. I will always be a product of two different eras. Two different eras that have shaped me into the person I am today.

I can't wait to see what the future holds for me.

The End

ACKNOWLEDGMENTS

I've often heard that writing your second book for publication can be a difficult task. Fortunately, I had a wonderful group of people offering encouragement that kept me going. To my editor, Rachel Stark, you are a superstar! Thank you for pushing me to make this book even better. I'm so proud of what we've accomplished together! Huge thanks to Adrienne Szpyrka for guiding me through the early days of drafting this book. And thank you to everyone at Sky Pony Press for believing in this book.

Many thanks to my fantastic agent, Suzie Townsend, and to Sara Stricker for the support. I love working with you and the rest of the team at New Leaf. (I miss you, Jackie!)

To the following ladies, thank you for the friendship: Christina Ferko, Melissa Blanco, Robin Lucas, and Jessica Wilde. You guys are the best!

Finally, much love to my family.

ABOUT THE AUTHOR

Photo credit: Memory Lane Photography

Melissa E. Hurst is a YA science fiction and fantasy writer, which means she considers watching *Star Trek* and *Firefly* research. She dreams of traveling around the world and maybe finding Atlantis one day. You can usually find her with a book in one hand and a Dr. Pepper in the other. Or consuming lots of chocolate. Melissa lives in the southern United States with her husband and three kids.

Visit her online at Melissa-Hurst.com.